W9-BSV-192

Days of Infamy

Days of Infamy

Newt Gingrich,
William R. Forstchen,
and Albert S. Hanser,
contributing editor

THORNDIKE PRESS
A part of Gale, Cengage Learning

Detroit • New York • San Francisco • New Haven, Conn • Waterville, Maine • London

Thorndike Press, a part of Gale, Cengage Learning.

Thorndike Press® Large Print Basic.
The text of this Large Print edition is unabridged.
Other aspects of the book may vary from the original edition.
Set in 16 pt. Plantin.
Printed on permanent paper.

LIBRARY OF CONGRESS CATALOGING-IN-PUBLICATION DATA

Gingrich, Newt.
Days of infamy / by Newt Gingrich, William R. Forstchen ; and Albert S. Hanser, contributing editor.
p. cm. — (Thorndike Press large print basic)
ISBN-13: 978-1-4104-0813-6 (hardcover : alk. paper)
ISBN-10: 1-4104-0813-2 (hardcover : alk. paper)
1. World War, 1939–1945 — Pacific Area — Fiction. 2. World War, 1939–1945 — Campaigns — Fiction. 3. Large type books.
I. Forstchen, William R. II. Hanser, Albert S. III. Title.
PS3557.I4945D39 2008b
813'.54—dc22 2008017508

Published in 2008 by arrangement with St. Martin's Press, LLC.

Printed in the United States of America
1 2 3 4 5 6 7 12 11 10 09 08

For the men of the United States Navy who, in the dark days of 1941 and early 1942, held the Japanese and Nazi Empires at bay, while back home, an aroused America prepared itself to go forth to save the world. Those chosen few, frightfully outnumbered, facing opponents with vastly superior technologies, nevertheless did show the world that, as one Japanese admiral exclaimed, "The Americans have Bushido."

"Now, who will stand on either hand and keep the bridge with me?"

— "Horatius," Thomas Babington,
Lord Macaulay

ACKNOWLEDGMENTS

This is our fifth book together with St. Martin's Press, and whenever it has come to acknowledgments, we always find that to be a daunting task. Literally dozens have helped us along the way, from Tom LeGore and General Bob Scales with our Civil War series, up to our current efforts now focusing on the early days of World War II.

A beginning point of thanks should be with the team at St. Martin's Press: our editor from the start, Pete Wolverton, our publisher, Thomas Dunne, and Pete's valuable assistants, with a special mention for Elizabeth Byrne.

On "our side of the fence," we have so many to thank. Our agent Kathy Lubbers, advisors such as Randy Evans, Stefan Passantino, Duane Ward, Liz Wood, our photo researcher Batchimeg Sambalaibat, and Rick Tyler. Captains Cuddington and Weisbrook who helped keep a watchful eye on various technical points, and "W. E. B. Griffin" III & IV., who have proven to be great and loyal friends . . . our standard running joke between us is "Gee, wish I had thought of that!"

Callista Gingrich has always been an inspiration, especially when I (Newt) have been locked away doing research, or during the long hours of writing and debating out ideas related to this book, and for Bill she has always been the most steadfast of friends, regardless of what hour he might call. Our technical editor, Steve Hanser and his wonderful wife Krys, as always, were there when most needed.

A special thanks to Sean Hannity and "Ollie" North for the interest they took in our book and to Duane Ward for organzing the special programming they dedicated to the launch of this series. We wish to thank as well the staff of professionals and volunteers at the National Memorial Park for the *Arizona,* at Pearl Harbor, along with the team that has worked so diligently to restore the pride of our fleet the USS *Missouri* and the museum built up around it, anchored now where the ill-fated *Oklahoma* came to rest at the bottom of the harbor. We also must mention the remarkable new facility on Ford's Island, The Museum of Pacific Aviation. The special tour they gave us, pointing out evidence of the attack that was still clearly visible, was unforgettable. We recommend, as well, that if you ever visit our fiftieth state, do take the time to visit the "Punch Bowl," sometimes referred to as the Arlington of the Pacific, where over 23,000 men and women who gave the last full measure of devotion during that war, rest in honored peace.

When the book *Pearl Harbor* was launched early in May 2007 we both went on a cross-country tour that finished up literally at Pearl Harbor in Hawaii. It was a profoundly moving experience, for beyond the hurried routine of racing to book signings and events, we both had the opportunity to stop more than once, and hear the story of someone "who was there," or remembered where they were and what they were doing when the news of what was happening at Oahu swept across our country. Some were children on the island on that dark day in 1941, others already in the military, and those moments were special to us and we cherished them. It was emotionally searing as we spent the last days of the tour looking out across that narrow harbor, slick with the oil still leaking from the *Arizona,* a wounded veteran still hemorrhaging after sixty-six years.

Sixty-six years, two thirds of a century have passed, and yet still the memory resonates in our culture, and we pray it always shall, a reason in part that we undertook the writing of these books, to present some of the great "what if's" of that war but also as a reminder that history does indeed repeat itself, and the price of freedom is indeed eternal vigilance.

And finally an acknowledgment to our daughters, Kathy, Jackie, and Meghan, who helped keep us on task, encouraged us along the way, and always showed their love for their fathers hard at work on this story.

Chapter One

The White House
December 7, 1941
19:45 hrs E.S.T.

President Franklin Delano Roosevelt looked up from the text of his speech as General George Marshall stood at the doorway, a flimsy sheet of telex printout clutched in his hand.

The President turned back to Missy LeHand, his secretary, pointing out where he had just crossed out a line for the address he was preparing for the nation, now scheduled for noon tomorrow before a joint session of Congress.

"Here, put this in the first sentence," and he pointed to his margin notes, " 'a date which will live in infamy.' "

She nodded in agreement.

He now focused his attention on his Army chief of staff.

"What do you have for us?"

"This just came in, Mr. President," and Marshall stepped into the room, unfolding the telex sheet and handing it to him. "It reports that a third strike wave of at least seventy Japanese aircraft is attacking Pearl Harbor. The line went dead approximately ten minutes ago."

The President scanned the few brief lines: "Oil tank farms struck. Fires out of control. Harbor channel blocked. Preparing to face invasion. . . ." The message stopped in mid-sentence.

The President crumpled the report up, ready to angrily toss it on the floor by the side of his wheelchair, but then thought again. It was a document now, a moment of history, and he instead tossed it onto his desk, to be filed away for later. Attack the United States, would they? On our own soil? Without a declaration of war?

He thought about this dastardly sneak attack. What could this ever be compared to? Even when the British attacked and burned Washington and this very building to the ground, we knew we'd survive. Could this onslaught be but the beginning? Hitler was at the gates of Moscow. Might the Japanese turn on the Soviets as well, together those two dark powers finish off Stalin and then fling their entire fury at England and then us?

It was sobering to be the President presiding over the crisis of Western civilization and its death struggle with the forces of modern evil in both Europe and Asia. Our civilization must not lose this war, or it would be, indeed, as Winston Churchill said, "a thousand years of darkness."

No, never think about the possibility of defeat, he thought to himself. If I allow that thought ever to take hold, it could permeate down across the entire nation. If ever America, if ever the entire free world, needed leadership that showed not just righteous anger, but also a firm, calm resolve that inevitable victory would come, it was now. Being an optimist was a trait he had acquired at Warm Springs, Georgia, when everyone else thought he should relax and accept that polio had crippled him and ended his political life. If he had given in eighteen years earlier, he would not be in the White House looking at General Marshall and dictating his most important speech to Congress.

No, he thought to himself, these Japanese will not turn me to thoughts of defeat, and neither will Herr Hitler. They have given us the possibility of bringing to bear the full force of our great people and the full resources of our great nation and now, after three years of quiet sustained effort, our preparedness program will show its results.

That strength had to be aroused through words. Words often meant more than ships and planes and tanks. It was words that aroused a people and focused a nation. He thought of his good friend across the Atlantic with fondness for his inspiring courage and language.

Though some of the more effete and cynical still privately shook their heads about Winston Churchill's posturing and rhetoric, there would never be a denial that the strength of his words and his pugnacious defiance were worth as much as an entire army in the field and had braced England in the darkest days of its long history.

I must do the same. I must be the war President. I must lead. If I show weakness now, even for a moment, then surely darkness will triumph. In fact I must become the President of inevitable victory transcending the war.

He stirred from his thoughts and looked back at Marshall, who stood silent by the doorway into his office.

"Anything else?" the President asked, fixing Marshall with his gaze.

"Not much, sir. Most cable links to Hawaii are down. Apparently the terminus on Oahu was damaged. Our Army radio monitoring at the Presidio in San Francisco reports that it can still pick up a civilian station that is frantically calling for volunteers to donate blood, and for anyone with medical training to report to the nearest military base. World War One veterans with combat experience are to report, too. The Lightning Division and national guard units are mobilizing and preparing to repel any landing attempts, but it is still too early to tell what's really happening.

"Other than that, sir, we are in the dark."

"Have you talked to Admiral Stark?"

"Yes, sir. I must say he is still in shock. It is his fleet that has taken the brunt of the immediate punishment. The only good news is this: Our two carriers still based at Pearl Harbor were out to sea and for the moment are assumed to be safe."

"Where are they now?"

"Halsey with *Enterprise* is believed to be somewhere southwest of Oahu. *Lexington* unfortunately is not in mutual support range; it is more than seven hundred miles to the northwest of *Enterprise.* They could hardly have been assigned farther apart. It was just random chance, sir, call it good luck or bad, with Halsey inbound after dropping planes off at Wake Island and Newton on *Lexington* outbound to Midway on the same mission. I just thank God they were not in the harbor this morning, which has usually been the typical routine."

Roosevelt, a sailor and former undersecretary of the Navy, could picture the scenario and already had the potential answer. Along with *Enterprise* and *Lexington* being out at sea, a month back *Saratoga* had secretly transited back to the West Coast, for a refit in Bremerton, Washington, and was just preparing to head back out to Oahu.

As Marshall had just voiced, thank God the timing of all this regarding the aircraft carriers had worked out as it did, otherwise they would be burned-out hulks resting in the mud and flames of Pearl Harbor, along with the battleships.

"Do we even have a remote idea as to the size of the Japanese fleet that hit us?" Roosevelt asked.

Marshall shook his head.

"Apparently no one has yet organized a proper search. It could be four of their carriers; Admiral Stark thinks maybe five or six. There is no clear indication. We don't even know what direction they came from."

The President grunted at the lack of intelligence and analysis. "Surely we must do better than that," he said to General Marshall, "and quickly."

One of the first priorities would be to get *Yorktown* and *Hornet* transferred out to the Pacific. Together, five carriers could be a potent match-up with the Japanese — if *Enterprise* and *Lexington* survived the next few days.

That was a very big if.

He considered the distances, the obvious aggressiveness of the Japanese attack force. If he could step inside the mind of their admiral in command, whoever he was, chances were he would not be satisfied with the destruction inflicted so far. The third strike was proving that. A more timid soul would have made the surprise attacks of the morning and then pulled out. This opponent was in it for the kill.

"The Japs could move between our two carriers out there and finish each off in turn."

"If their continued aggressiveness is any indication." Marshall hesitated. "I am not a naval officer, sir, but yes, that would be my assessment."

"I want those carriers to hit back, and hit them hard," the President replied sharply. "If whoever launched this attack wishes to seek out our carriers, I expect ours not to turn tail and run, but to fight," and he slapped the sides of his wheelchair. "To fight them, by God, and show them from the start that we intend to punch back."

"I know Admiral Halsey, sir," Marshall said quietly. "I think that is a foregone conclusion."

The President nodded. He reached into his breast pocket, opened his cigarette case, inserted one into its holder, and lit it. Never in the history of American arms, in the history of the United States Navy, had such a defeat been dealt. Perhaps in the war against the Barbary pirates, when America's only ship of the line, *Philadelphia,* had been lost, but not eight capital ships in one morning. And it was on his watch.

Now two carriers and what was left of the shattered fleet in Pearl, along with a couple of small task groups led by cruisers luckily out to sea as well this morning, were the only tools left to try and balance the ledger of this grim and terrible day. Later, thanks to the massive building program he and Carl Vinson had pushed through Congress during peacetime, there would be more than enough ships and planes. Last year he had called for fifty thousand planes to be built, more aircraft than existed in all the air forces of all the other nations now in this war. The factories to build them were still under construction, but soon the strength of America, would start to pour warplanes forth from those factories. Already tens of thousands of young men were in training to fly those planes yet to be built.

Come autumn of next year, a new fleet carrier would be sliding down the ways each month. Battleships, cruisers, destroyers, and submarines by the hundreds were under construction even now. But those forces were more than a year off. In the meantime, what can the Japanese, who have been preparing for years for this moment, do to us? Perhaps sweep the entire Pacific from the China coast to San Francisco and so entrench themselves that it could take a decade or more to push them back, if ever.

But it's a year or more before we can even begin to replace our losses, until then we have to fight with what we have. This evening it all rests on two understrength carrier groups, their crews, and the as-yet-untested young men flying antiquated planes.

"Please ask Admiral Stark to see me at once. I expect our boys to fight back, starting now, today. If we lose our carriers but deal it back to them" — he hesitated only for the briefest instant — "back to those bastards, then that is a risk we must be willing to take."

Aboard the Imperial Japanese Navy carrier Akagi
150 miles north of Oahu
December 7, 1941
18:00 hrs local time

"So what is the final tally of our losses?" Admiral Yamamoto asked, looking at Commander Genda.

Genda looked down at his notepad.

"All six carriers of the fleet have filed their reports. We lost twenty-nine planes in the first two strikes and another thirty-five damaged, twenty of them requiring extensive repairs and half of those to be broken down for spare parts, then jettisoned. The third strike was far more costly. Of the seventy-seven planes engaged, twenty-seven were lost, another twenty-one damaged, of which seven have been listed as no longer combat effective and should be salvaged for parts. That is a total of at least eighty-six aircraft that are no longer combat effective. Our strike capability has therefore been reduced to a total of just under three hundred aircraft."

Yamamoto, saying nothing, sipped his cup

of tea, then sat back, lit another cigarette with his American Zippo lighter, a gift from long ago, and exhaled.

"Expected. Remember when we war-gamed this in the fall we anticipated upward of a hundred fifty aircraft lost just in the first two strikes. We are still far ahead of the ledger of what we deemed acceptable."

He could see the glum faces, especially those of the leftover staff of Admiral Nagumo, whom he had replaced at the last minute. His third strike had more than doubled the total losses incurred so far, and they were not happy about it.

"And the report on the results of the third strike?"

"Photo recon planes are just returning now," Genda announced. "Developed film will be delivered shortly, but debriefing of pilots indicates a near-fatal blow to their base. Tens of thousands of barrels of oil are burning. There is a report that a cruiser, perhaps a heavy cruiser, has grounded in their main channel. Their submarines still in port have either been destroyed or damaged. Extensive damage to repair shops, several large cranes destroyed, their headquarters totally destroyed, and most important their large three-hundred-meter drydock totally eliminated. It is estimated that a score or two score of combat-ready aircraft still exist on the island compared to over three hundred, twelve hours ago."

As Genda spoke he nodded toward his closest friend, Lieutenant Commander Fuchida, still in his flight coveralls. They had been comrades for years, the perfect team, Genda the intellectual architect of the Navy's air fleet, and Fuchida the practitioner, the one who took the ideas, practiced and perfected them, and turned them into reality. After he was tasked by Admiral Yamamoto at the start of the year, he had conceived the battle plan to strike Pearl Harbor. Fuchida was the one who developed the training routines for the strike force, drilled them relentlessly for months, to a razor-sharp perfection, and then led them into battle this morning.

Genda could not help but smile inwardly at a romantic analogy that flashed to mind. If Yamamoto was their shogun, then he was the old loyal daimyo, the advisor who suggested the plan . . . and it was Fuchida, the bravest of their samurai, who would then train the warriors and lead the charge.

In spite of Yamamoto's orders to stand down and rest, Fuchida had been unable to sleep for long and begged to attend this briefing, which the admiral with fatherly goodwill had agreed to. Fuchida was most certainly the hero of the day. Having guided the first two strikes and then personally delivering the fatal blow to the drydock in the third strike, he had limped back to *Akagi,* his plane shot to ribbons, crash landed, and barely escaped with his life.

Admiral Yamamoto nodded good-naturedly at the two sitting across from him. Actual commendations and decorations within the Imperial Navy were rare; it was just assumed that all men would do their utmost duty, without regard for self, so why offer medals and rewards? It was a policy that he personally wanted to change, for though it was a most cynical comment, Napoleon had once said that it is with such "baubles" that men are led. He might not be able to offer medals to these two heroes, but when he returned to Tokyo, he already had decided, he would personally present Genda and Fuchida to the Emperor for the praise they so well deserved.

Yamamoto silently contemplated the tip of his glowing cigarette, flicking the ashes, taking another deep drag.

"But their carriers are still out there."

No one spoke.

Nagumo's overly cautious staff had whis-

pered that very thing throughout the long afternoon, expecting at any minute a counterstrike . . . but none had come.

"They are not north of the islands, of that I am now utterly certain. If they had been, they would have struck us this afternoon," and he nodded toward the open porthole. Twilight was beginning to settle on the tropical sea, which had flattened out significantly throughout the day.

No, there would be no American strike now. It meant that his gambler's hunch of earlier in the day had been right. The

American carriers were somewhere south or west of the islands, out of range, but they were out there . . . and now he wanted to sink them, to make this victory complete.

He was still shaken by the diplomatic news that had been filtering in all day. Radio stations on the American West Coast had been monitored: bitter commentary that the attack had been unprovoked, without warning, a "Jap sneak attack." That news had horrified him.

The Foreign Ministry had totally failed in their mission. When he had agreed to undertake the planning of this war, back early in the year, he had absolutely insisted, before the Emperor himself, that with his knowledge of Americans, their proper sense of diplomatic and military protocol must be followed. That a formal declaration of war must be delivered before the first bomb fell. Some thought him insane, loudly proclaiming that it was folly, that it would double, triple the losses, but he had always replied that the life of fifty, a hundred pilots, when placed in the balance of fighting an opponent who could not claim "a stab in the back," as Americans put it, would be worth the price. If their sense of correct behavior had been observed, their anger, though significant, would not be aroused to fever pitch. Just as an opponent in cards, knowing he was beaten fairly in a poker match, would withdraw as a gentleman, but if ever he suspected a sleight of hand, a bitter rivalry and hatred that could burn for years would be the result. Yamamoto now faced just such an opponent. The Foreign Ministry had left him with a terrible task. He could not just achieve victory here, he must achieve a crushing victory. It would have been far easier if their carriers had indeed been in harbor, but they were not. The Americans would now turn to those three carriers, *Enterprise, Lexington,* and *Saratoga,* and most likely within the month, *Yorktown* and *Hornet,* as the means of trying to gain revenge.

No, he had to give an even more crippling blow, a far more crippling blow, and in so doing hammer the Americans into so resigned a mood that only negotiation made sense, in spite of what he expected would be their towering rage.

Perhaps, he thought shrewdly, that rage can be turned to our advantage. An opponent in cards, when losing, tends to become reckless in his desire to win back what he has already lost. I must play to that and must take the risks as well.

Yamamoto stubbed out his cigarette and

leaned over, looking at the charts spread out on the table. He traced his finger around the waters south and west of Oahu.

"I am convinced that their three carriers, *Enterprise, Lexington,* and *Saratoga,* are somewhere out here," and then he drew a vague outline across nearly a million square miles of ocean, the vast triangle from Oahu northwest to Midway, over 1,100 miles away, and then down to Wake, which stood sentinel over the approaches into the Japanese-held waters of the Marshalls.

"Tomorrow we shall hunt for them there."

There was an uncomfortable stirring, and he looked over at Nagumo's chief of staff, whom he had retained, at least temporarily, for this mission.

"You object?"

"Sir, though I expressed concerns about your third strike on Pearl Harbor, I now bow to your wisdom. But this?"

"Go on."

"As Commander Genda already pointed out, we are down to less than three hundred aircraft. Their three carriers, which we know carry more planes than our carriers, might be able to marshal three hundred in reply. They might very well be anticipating even now our moving toward them and be ready, aided by what aircraft survived on Oahu to provide scouting reports. We could be at a serious disadvantage tomorrow. They can surmise where we are; we might not be able to do the same."

He paused.

"We don't know where they are; they can guess where we are."

"Not a single American scout plane followed us back from three strikes," Fuchida said softly, voice hoarse from exhaustion, the hours of flying, and the smoke inhaled after crash landing. "On the island of Oahu they have, at best, a score of planes for scouting or any other purpose. We have annihilated their land-based aviation for the moment."

Admiral Yamamoto nodded for him to continue.

"I suspect they still do not know where we are, and their own radio broadcasts indicate panic on the island."

"If we present them with a challenge they cannot refuse," Genda interjected, "I would venture that by dawn their carriers might very well be in range of Oahu to provide support and to seek us out. In fact we might be able to force them into placing their carriers close to the island and revealing their position."

"Go on," Yamamoto said with the slightest trace of a smile, already anticipating what his trusted lieutenant was going to offer. The two of them were so often in synch with each other's thinking.

"You mentioned an idea earlier today, sir," Genda replied, his voice now edged with excitement as he pointed at the charts. "During the night, send our two fast battleships *Hiei* and *Kirishima* down along the east coast of the island. They can be in position before midnight. Bombard their bases on the east coast, swing around Diamond Head, and then attack their fortifications and then finally Pearl Harbor itself. The firing mission would take three or four hours at most, but render yet more damage and panic. It would seem to indicate, as well, a traditional move prior to an amphibious assault come dawn.

"I have read the reports on their Admiral Halsey. He is highly aggressive, bombastic, and pride alone will drive him forward into our net. He will launch in reply and thereby reveal his position not in a strike against our carriers but against the battleships as they withdraw from Oahu after bombarding Pearl Harbor. Once his position is revealed by that strike we then counterstrike, catching their carriers as they are still recovering their planes from the attempt on our battleships."

He smiled.

"We hit them turning their planes around on deck and below in their hangar, planes that are being loaded with gas and bombs; if but one of our bombs strikes them at that moment," he paused for effect, "that carrier is destroyed."

They had run simulations and war games based on such a scenario. What would happen if a strike could be launched against an enemy carrier while its deck and hangar bay were fully loaded with aircraft, fueling up and arming? The calculation was always the same: utterly catastrophic. It had been, as well, the argument of the battleship admirals against deploying carriers into the front line of action — they were simply too vulnerable if caught by surprise, while a battleship could withstand relentless pounding and continue to fight.

Well, that would be put to the test come morning, he thought.

There was murmuring from several in the room. It was one thing to be battleship sailors and talk about the glory of a ship-to-ship action at sea, but to risk such precious assets in a shore bombardment, when an enemy fleet might be farther out to sea, boxing them in? To use battleships as bait? It was a very unsettling and unnerving concept. Only an airman could have proposed it.

Yamamoto smiled in reply. It was, of course, exactly what he had been thinking most of the afternoon. Such a bold and open challenge, a nighttime bombardment by two battleships, which could indeed inflict yet more punishing damage . . . such an act could not go unchallenged. The American carriers would have to reveal themselves. And to risk a battleship, even two, if by so doing he could bag the three American carriers . . . that was a risk well worth taking.

"To place two of His Majesty's battleships at such risk?" Nagumo's chief of staff replied, the shock evident in his voice.

Yamamoto looked over at him. The response, of course, was expected. So many in the navy were still emotionally linked to battleships. The ships were so big, so expensive and precious, that though admirals of all fleets talked about the moment of encounter, all actually shied from it, frightened of the risk even to one ship. The British and Germans had demonstrated that clearly at Jutland, when both at different stages of that battle back in 1916 threw away a chance for a stunning victory, out of a fear of potential loss.

It was not how Nelson, or most definitely for that matter, the legendary Togo, would view this moment. Nor how he himself would view it. At Tsushima, Togo had annihilated the entire Russian Imperial fleet by taking risks and being daring. Victory, not caution, was the goal of Togo, and it would be the goal of Yamamoto.

If disaster should unfold, if in fact all three American carriers did launch together and both battleships were lost, but in turn he could sink those three carriers and render yet more damage to the American bases on Oahu, the exchange would be worth it.

He stubbed out his cigarette.

"A task group then. Our two fastest battleships, escorted by our two lightest carriers, *Soryu* and *Hiryu,* which will remain farther out to sea in direct support of the battleships, are to attack the island throughout the night. The cruiser *Tone* will go as well, with her scout plane pilots trained in night observation and in marking targets with flares."

No one spoke. They had repeatedly wargamed night battles at sea, and the use of well-trained pilots, launched by catapults from two cruisers specifically designed to carry six seaplanes each, *Tone* and *Chikuma.* But never had it been actually tried for real, and in addition, against land targets off a hostile enemy coast. It would be a risky operation.

"The two escorting carriers will remain concealed farther out to sea, but ready to provide effective air cover for the battleships while the rest of our carriers will race to the west of the island during the night and be in position at dawn a hundred fifty miles to the northwest of the island, ready to react. If their carriers are to the south, *Hiryu* and *Soryu* will have the honor of the first strike. If to the west, our main task force will deliver the killing blow. When they move against our battleships it will reveal their positions first, as long as we evade any search planes from either their carriers or Oahu. If we can achieve that, we will sink all three without danger to ourselves. It will be a victory as significant as that we have already achieved.

"Regardless of outcome, the entire task force will then move to reunite by midday, farther to the west of Oahu."

"And the ships still in Pearl Harbor?" Rear Admiral Kusaka, Nagumo's chief of staff, asked. "They still pose a threat."

"Try to raise contact with our submarines

to move to block the channel," Yamamoto replied disdainfully. "They have done precious little so far. Perhaps during the night and tomorrow morning they can prove their worth and tackle any ships that try and sortie."

"Our oil supplies?" Kusaka asked.

Yamamoto looked over at his chief of staff. Rear Admiral Kusaka had originally been Admiral Nagumo's man. Yamamoto had kept him on after replacing Nagumo and taking direct command of the attack on Pearl Harbor. There were times in these last few days he regretted that decision, wishing he had made a clean sweep of it, replacing these older men of caution with men of audacity like Genda. But on the other side of the issue, perhaps he did need a man like Kusaka at times. His concerns about oil still available were well justified. In one sense, after all, it was one of the reasons for this war in the first place, to be able to seize the Dutch oil fields in the East Indies. On a strategic level it was Japan's greatest worry, and on this tactical level, of day-to-day operations, it was a key point of concern as well.

They had on board one day's supply for high-speed battle maneuvers, three to four days at standard speed. Night refueling was a very risky operation. No. He had to move now. He would order the fleet oilers up to a rendezvous. Once topped off, his fleet would have enough fuel to make it to where additional oilers, civilian tankers pressed into service, waited to rendezvous in the Marshalls. The tankers with the fleet would then run to the Marshalls to take on fuel and join other tankers he had sent there for this very contingency. It could get tight, especially if enemy subs or surviving aircraft located the oilers, but he was always the gambler, and it seemed worth the risk to him even if the battleship traditionalists could not understand it.

He looked at his staff.

"Signal the battleships at once, and the carriers *Soryu* and *Hiryu,* with their appropriate escorts. Mission signal is clear and simple. Proceed to the east coast of Oahu, bombard their Kaneohe airbase, then Fort Bellows," and as he spoke he traced the positions on the map, "but reserve most of their shells for positions along the south coast and then general area bombardment of Hickam and Pearl Harbor. If that does not bring out Halsey, I do not know what will."

He scanned his staff with an icy gaze.

"To your duty, gentlemen. It will be a long night."

Chapter Two

Kailua, east shore of Oahu
December 7, 1941
22:50 hrs local time

Commander James Watson sat back in the chair, closed his eyes, and tried not to think about what was coming next. His wife and mother-in-law were whispering in the next room, debating if they should treat his wounded arm or not.

Don't think about it, think about something else, anything else, anything but today and the war.

And yet his mind would not cooperate. He had been in the Navy for over twenty-five years, nearly all that time without ever hearing a shot fired in anger, his job as a cryptanalyst, a code breaker, almost clerk-like. Random chance seemed to have placed him aboard the ill-fated *Panay,* the American gunboat sunk by the Japanese in China. One could almost say he was one of the first casualties of this war, even though that wounding was nearly four years ago, back in 1937, a wound that had cost him his left hand. Retired out as disabled, he thought his life would be one of peace, teaching higher math at the University here in Oahu, until called back to service eleven months ago, lured back into the world of code breaking in the basement of CinCPac, Commander in Chief, Pacific, where he and his comrades had labored away tracking and trying to break the secrets of Japanese military signals. If war came again, he believed, he would experience it in the monastic basement office where never a shot would be heard.

Some dream, he thought, flinching as another wave of pain shot up his arm. He and his CO, Captain Collingwood, had suspected an attack might be coming toward Pearl, in fact he had actually written an urgent "eyes only" memo up to the top of the command chain, warning that a Japanese fleet might be in range of the Hawaiian Islands on the morning of December 7. And of course no one had listened.

Incredible, he thought, wounded yet again, in nearly the same spot, the stump of my left hand, hit when *Arizona* blew up. Damn, if I had not been hit while on the

Panay four years ago, chances are I'd have lost the hand today. Is Fate trying to tell me something?

Another thought flashed through: the last Japanese strike plane departing the target area after their third attack — an attack which had devastated the oil tank farms, shattered the main dry dock, and truly rendered Pearl Harbor ineffective as a base for months to come — the way that plane was flown: audacity, courage. He wondered. Could it possibly be his old friend Fuchida at the controls? Strange he should think of him now, at this moment. They had only met once, at the Japanese Naval Academy ten years ago, when he had paid a courtesy call there and given a brief talk. Their correspondence had stopped as the crisis between their two nations deepened. He found himself wondering if Fuchida was out there, even now, planning another attack. So strange. I'd kill him if given the chance, and yet I still do think of him as a friend. It made him think of the poem by Thomas Hardy, about killing an enemy soldier but if you met him in a pub you'd buy him a drink or "help [him] to half a crown."

He heard a sigh, his mother-in-law sitting down beside him. He opened his eyes.

"You really do need stitches, James," she

whispered. "I can do it, but we think you should go to hospital instead."

His mother-in-law, Nana, spoke in Japanese, peering thoughtfully at the wound, the bandage Margaret had put on it soaked clean through, and now peeled back.

"It will be OK, Nan," James replied. Given that her name was so similar to the American endearment for a beloved grandmother, he just simply called her Nan.

He looked down at the stump of his left arm, the hand lost in the *Panay* incident of 1937, and now, this morning, damn it, wounded there yet again, whether by a fragment from the exploding *Arizona,* Japanese strafing, or just random debris crashing down around him, he would never know. But he did know that it hurt, it hurt badly.

The side of the stump was slashed open nearly to the bone, and as Margaret had gingerly removed the leather straps of his mechanical "claw" he thought he would pass out from the firelike agony that was nearly as bad as the pain of the original wound had been four years ago.

Margaret, sitting at the kitchen table by his side, held his right hand tightly.

"She's right. I can drive you over to Fort Bellows infirmary right now."

He shook his head. They did not know

the chaos that undoubtedly reigned there; he did. And second, he did not want either of them anywhere near a military base right now. Random shots echoed from nearby Fort Bellows and an occasional thump from more distant Kaneohe. Everyone was on edge, panic stricken, and frankly he feared that the mere sight of his mother-in-law, or even his wife, who had mostly Japanese features, might set some hothead off. He remembered the nisei lined up, with hands over their heads, as he drove past a police station in Honolulu when coming home this afternoon. There was no telling how things might get on this island regarding Japanese civilians during a terror-filled night. And beyond that, there was no telling what the Japanese navy might do next.

"Stitch it up here," he said softly, forcing a smile. "Come on, Nan, you've dealt with worse."

As a child she had worked in the pineapple fields of the Dole plantation, carting water to the workers, and helping to stitch up more than one wound from machetes and the sharp prickly leaves of the plant that had provided a financial empire for some, and drudgery of the worst kind for the thousands of immigrants imported into the island to do the backbreaking labor. Nana had come over as a young woman in 1898, the same year the island was incorporated as a territory, and there met a Portuguese fisherman, with whom she had three children, with Margaret being the youngest. Tragically, two had died in the great flu epidemic of 1918, so Margaret, her Americanized name, held a special place in Nan's heart.

When first they had met during his posting to Pearl in 1920, the year Nan's husband died, lost in a storm, there had been an instant bond between Nan and him, as if he were a lost son, and in some ways a protective husband and father. Since he had never known his own mother, who died giving him life, Nan filled a deep role in his heart as well.

In some ways the marriage to Margaret, and his closeness to Nan, had changed his career as well. Languages had always come easily for him, and though the Japanese he learned was colloquial, nevertheless it made him one of the very few officers in the United States Navy who had a mastery of the language of what up until earlier this day was seen as a potential enemy but not truly a serious threat and now was a real enemy and a most serious threat indeed.

With the suggestion that she handle the

surgery to his injured arm, Nan visibly trembled but then nodded, becoming her old stoic self. She went into her bedroom and came back out a minute later with her sewing kit. Margaret helped her, bringing a small pot of water to boil, dumping in a couple of large needles her mother had chosen and a long length of thread.

As he watched them, he suddenly regretted his own bravado, feeling a bit lightheaded. Memories of the *Panay* hit him. He remembered lying in the mud, a chief petty officer tying a tourniquet around his lower arm. He remembered the raging infection that hit within a day, the amputation of his hand while he was still awake, and the doctor fearing to use a general anesthetic because of the pneumonia that had hit him due to his aspirating the fetid waters of the Yangtze River.

Now that his mother-in-law actually had something to do, she was all business, watching the water boil, telling her daughter to wash her hands and then pour more iodine into the wound.

The sting of the iodine as Margaret gingerly pushed back the fold of puffy flesh made his head swim, and at the sight of his pain Margaret struggled to stifle her tears.

"No crying now," Nan announced. "Be

brave like him."

Brave like him? He was all but ready to collapse in panic as his mother-in-law doused her own hands in iodine, fished the needle out of the boiling water with a spatula, did the same with the thread, expertly threaded the sewing needle, then turned to face him.

"Maybe you look away," she said in English, sitting down by his side. First she pried the wound open, looking at it carefully. The cut went clear to the stump of bone, blood rapidly oozing out as she spread it open.

"Don't see anything in there, looks like what hit you slashed across," she said in Japanese.

She gently closed the wound then held a needle aloft. Margaret grasped his good hand and he focused on her eyes.

Surprisingly the first puncture of the needle really didn't hurt all that much more, but after the third or fourth stitch, as she tightened the thread, pulling the open folds of the wound in together, he had to fight down the urge to scream. Even if he wanted to pull away he couldn't; the old woman with a powerful left hand was holding his arm in place, even as she stitched with her right hand.

Another eight to ten stitches went in. She even started to hum softly, and that did bring tears to his eyes. It was a traditional Japanese lullaby, one she used to hum to their lost child David when he was a boy, and also when he was sick and dying from leukemia nearly a decade ago.

From the corner of his eye he saw her draw the needle up one more time, bring it down, tie it off, bite the end of the thread off, and then smile.

"Good job," she announced proudly, and he looked down at her handiwork and, in spite of the pain, nodded. The stitches were well placed, even, close together.

The old woman wiped the bloody needle on her dress sleeve, dropped it back into her sewing kit, and then bandaged the wound.

"You go to bed," she ordered.

He fumbled in his breast pocket. It was empty, but for once Margaret did not object and reached around behind him for the half-finished pack of Lucky Strikes. She put one to his lips and even flicked his Zippo lighter.

"Thanks."

"Don't make it a habit," Margaret said, trying to force a smile. Leaning up, she kissed him on the forehead. "I plan to keep you around for a long time yet. The enemy can't kill you but those damn cigarettes will."

Funny the way she chose the word enemy. She was half Japanese. She couldn't bring herself to use the word Jap, but there was a bitter snap to how she said "enemy."

"I really should go back to the base."

"Not tonight you won't," Margaret replied forcefully, and her mother looked over her shoulder and nodded agreement.

"There is nothing more you can do tonight. Besides, you said your building was destroyed, and what will they need with a cryptographer anyhow?"

He looked at her a bit startled. In the eleven months since he had been called back to duty, not once had he used that word. He had even lectured his wife and mother-in-law on the fact that he could never discuss with them anything about his job other than that it had something to do with math.

"What secrets does a wife not know?" she said with a soft smile. "Remember I do your laundry, and you do have a habit of talking in your sleep at times."

She leaned over and kissed him again.

"Don't worry, dear. I'm not a gossip or a boaster the way some of these navy wives are. Your secret is good with me."

A flash illuminated the room. For a split second civilian thinking still held sway: it was a lightning bolt. Then more flashes, strobelike, one on another spaced fractions of a second apart. His mother-in-law stood by the kitchen sink, the light cascading in from the open window, covered by a curtain.

All three remained frozen in place, James unable to react.

Surely it couldn't be?

There was still silence, though out in the street below he heard screaming, panicked voices. A gunshot echoed.

A burst of blue glowing light ignited, holding steady, redoubling a second later, and then redoubling again. He thought he heard, as well, the distant sound of a plane engine, drawing closer.

He came to his feet, and going to the kitchen sink pulled the curtain back, ignoring the blackout order.

And he saw it, hovering over the airbase at Kaneohe, illumination flares floating in the sky.

The drone of the engine grew louder, and he pulled open the side door from the kitchen that led out to the open lanai and looked up.

Nothing for a moment. Another gunshot

from the street, followed by several more.

"The Japs are coming! The Japs!" It was his neighbor, Ed Simpson, shouting wildly, pointing his pump shotgun to the sky and then firing again.

And now, out to sea, more flashes, several dozen and concurrent. At last came the distant sound of thunder from the first salvo of star shells.

"James?"

Margaret was by his side, clutching his left arm, forgetting about his wound and the pain it caused, his mother-in-law standing fearfully behind him, peering out from around his shoulder.

He counted the seconds, ten, fifteen . . . and then the impacts on the naval airfield, where a dozen fires still raged from the earlier attacks.

Seconds later the shock wave could be felt in the soles of his feet, and then finally the distant rumble of the explosions of five-, six-, and fourteen-inch shells.

He turned and looked to his right. Fort Bellows was but a half mile distant, upslope. There was a single flash of light in reply, a couple of seconds later the concussion of the lone eight-inch coastal gun washing over them, causing Margaret and her mother to jump.

More flashes out to sea. He had them sighted now, standing out in stark relief against the nearly full moon rising behind them. It was hard to judge, but it was apparent the ships out there were moving southward. If they were hitting Kaneohe, Bellows would be next, most likely within a few minutes, and their small town of Kailua was smack in the middle between the two.

"We're getting out of here now!" he shouted. "Margaret, get the keys for the car."

"James?"

"Now. We're getting out of here now!"

He turned to go back into the house. Wincing, he struggled to get his soiled, bloodstained uniform jacket back on.

Then Margaret was by his side, helping him to get the jacket up over his shoulder, taking the time to button it up. Though long ago he had mastered getting dressed and properly buttoned with one hand, Margaret had always insisted upon helping when she was around, and frankly even at this moment, it was still endearing.

A thought hit him about the panic that was breaking out. He opened up the drawer of the nightstand by his side of the bed and pulled out a heavy Smith & Wesson .38 revolver, snapped it open to check if it was loaded, closed it, and stuck it into his belt, the weight of it making him feel a bit ridiculous, like some desperado. For safety he had always kept the cylinder under the hammer empty; more than one idiot had accidentally shot himself carrying a gun with a cartridge under the hammer. He pulled out a box of shells and stuffed them into his pocket.

Margaret, watching him, said nothing. She hated guns, objected to his keeping a loaded pistol in their bedroom, but she didn't object now.

"Where's Mother?" she asked.

He looked around. She had disappeared.

"Damn it, Mother!"

He headed for her bedroom and found her there. She was on her knees, a tattered cardboard box pulled out from under her bed. Weeping, she was carefully sorting through aged, yellowed photographs, setting some aside.

"We don't have time now, Mother," he said, trying to be gentle.

She looked up at him, crying.

"These are all I have," she said in Japanese, and a lump came to his throat when he saw that most of the photos she was drawing out of the box were of her and David, one a framed picture of him on his baptism day, his grandmother proudly holding him.

Nothing had ever been said between Margaret and him about it, but there was only one small photograph of David on display in their house, on Margaret's vanity, her favorite picture of the two of them on his first day at kindergarten, her little boy about to face the world . . . and David was clutching her, arms around her shoulders, crying in front of the school, and she in tears, trying to smile bravely as he had taken the image. He did not know that his mother-in-law, had, in fact, saved all the other photographs across the years. On the day David died, in a blind fit of anguish, he had taken the photographs down from the walls, swept them off tables and mantle tops, and thrown them out. She had obviously recovered every one of them.

If he had lived, David would be eighteen now. Eighteen and ever so proud of his father, he might have gone into the Navy, and perhaps at this moment be down in that hellhole at Kaneohe, or dead back at Pearl Harbor.

"Take that one," he finally said, pointing to the baptism photograph, struggling to hold back his own tears as he reached out with his one hand and got her to her feet.

Clutching the one photograph, she headed for the door, Margaret running to hurry her along, and he could not help but notice that Margaret was cradling her favorite photograph of David as well.

They went out the front door and Margaret paused to fumble with the keys. Though one rarely locked one's home in this neighborhood, she now planned to.

"To hell with that," he shouted, moving the two of them along to the car.

And then, in that instant, it hit, the shock wave of two fourteen-inch shells racing overhead. He had heard such big guns fired before, hundreds of times while aboard the *Maryland* or *Oklahoma,* but never like this, never on the receiving end. He had heard it described as sounding like a freight train roaring down a mountainside. He had never heard anything like it in real life. A split second later the two shells impacted two hundred fifty yards away, and three hundred yards short of one of the coastal gun positions at Bellows.

It took just under a second for the shock wave to hit them — and when it did strike, it was with hurricane force, palm fronds flapping, several breaking off from the trees around their house to come clattering down, one smashing a window, followed by a heavy thundering patter of debris, shrapnel, clods of dirt, and broken bits of trees rained down around them.

He instinctively put his arms around Margaret and Nan, forcing them down, until the storm had passed.

"Up! Move it!"

He started to open the driver's-side door, but Margaret shoved him aside.

"I'm driving," she cried. Gone was the usually loving deference of his bride, who still carried a touch of her mother's traditions. She was now thoroughly American. She had a wounded husband who even with his claw on had to take it a bit slow around some of the curves while trying to shift gears — and she was in charge.

His mother-in-law was already in the backseat. He went around the '37 Plymouth and slid in on the passenger side even as the engine roared to life and Margaret slammed it into gear.

Tires squealing, she went down the steep driveway, nearly hitting the Johnstons' Studebaker, which was careering down the street.

"Damn Japs, damn all you Japs!"

It was Ed Simpson, now down on the street, vaguely waving his shotgun toward them.

Margaret, in yet another uncharacteristic gesture, gave Ed the finger, hit the gas, and they were off.

"Where to?" she asked, anger in her voice.

He didn't know how to respond. Was the bombardment the prelude to a night landing? War games had theorized that if the Japs did attack and attempt a landing, a diversionary force might come into Kaneohe Bay, which could serve as a sheltered anchorage and secure the windward side of the island. In a protracted fight for the island, the airbases at Kaneohe and Bellows could be used by their bombers and fighters.

This could very well be the softening-up blow for that invasion. Get away from here, then. But where?

"Your cousin Janice," he finally said. Margaret nodded in agreement, taking the next corner fast and hard, weaving around a car backing out of a driveway with headlights off, dodging around people standing in the street. Ahead he saw traffic, cars, the taillights of dozens of cars, their drivers and families all filled with the same thought. Head up Pali Highway and get the hell away from here.

And now he heard it again, but this wasn't a single salvo, it was a continual roar —

dozens of shells screeching in, searching out Bellows, which was illuminated by star shells. Several of the fourteen-inch shells were short, one of them impacting into a storefront, a hair salon that Margaret frequented, just a block ahead. The explosion flipped a car high into the air, end over end, buildings to either side collapsing, and a geyser of water erupting up from a broken water main.

Margaret, now cursing loudly against the "damn Japs," wove around the wreckage like an expert, her mother sobbing at the sight of the broken bodies that had been torn apart by the blast.

Margaret ran the red light at the intersection, nearly getting hit by an old Model A as she skidded on to State Highway 61, where traffic was growing heavier by the second as more and more, in panic, started to flee, ignoring the orders of martial law. A lone cop, flanked by a portly national guardsman, holding an '03, stood impotent at an intersection, just watching the traffic race by.

And then everything slammed to a crawl, the twisting two-lane road ahead bumper to bumper.

More flashes of light, the air continually rent by the howl of incoming shells, impacting around Fort Bellows and the coastal gun positions up on the mountain slope. Several of the fort's guns were firing back, and cynically he knew that given the antiquity of the weapons and the ill-trained crews manning them, their reply fire was most likely splashing down miles wide of any target.

Crawling along at not much more than ten miles an hour, they started to gain up the side of the mountain, and he could see the ocean off to their left. Flashes continually rippled up and down along the horizon. Two heavy ships, undoubtedly battleships, were firing. Smaller, more rapid firing from closer in — those were destroyers — but then every couple of minutes, with almost stately precision, two giant eruptions of light, each turret lighting off a few seconds after the next, the gun blasts so brilliant, even from five or more miles out, as to cast shadows on the mountains, followed fifteen seconds or so later by geysering impacts of fourteen-inch shells, the concussion, even at this distance, numbing.

"The hell with this," Margaret snapped, and downshifting the car she swung out over the double yellow line, and hit the gas.

Her mother squealed in terror; he said nothing. When she hit one of these moods, which was exceedingly rare, he knew better than to protest — and besides, dozens of others, in front and behind her, were doing the same. Hardly any traffic was coming over the pass heading east, and if it was, it was being run off the road by the thousands now trying to flee into the center of the island.

They slowed for a moment, edging around the shoulder to get past where a head-on collision had occurred, most likely just moments before, one of the cars burning.

Strange how in little more than eighteen hours he had already become inured to the anguish created by war. Someone was inside the burning car, thankfully not moving. A woman clutching a child was beside the funeral pyre, screaming, being restrained by two teenage boys.

They reached the top of the pass, slowing for a moment due to the bumper-to-bumper traffic . . . and ironically the sea behind them was now dark. The bombardment had stopped.

A number of cars were pulled over by the side of the highway, people out, staring back at the place from where they had just fled.

At the top of the pass, working under the glare of several sets of truck headlights, some national guardsmen were setting up a couple of antiquated seventy-five-millimeter guns, relics of the last war. He shook his head. At dawn, if an invasion was on, this would be one of the first places they'd shell, or they'd send in a few bombers. They should be deploying on the back slope of the mountain, under concealment, not out in the open as they were now doing. My God, he wondered, are we really such amateurs? He wanted to stop, to shout some advice, but knew his suggestion would be ignored.

Margaret slowed in the traffic and finally came to a stop in the confusion.

"Is it over?" she asked. "Should we go back?"

He shook his head.

"No. Janice's place will be safer."

She shifted back into gear, went up over the shoulder on the eastbound side to get around yet another accident, this one fortunately not fatal and burning, and started down out of the pass.

She said nothing. He looked over at her, her so-attractive black hair, dark eyes and complexion, more oriental than occidental. And he felt fear. If this indeed is the first move of an invasion, what will happen to her?

He had been at Shanghai, had talked with his friend Cecil about Nanking. A beautiful woman like Margaret? He knew what would happen if this island paradise became a battlefield.

Or on the other side, might the rage be so intense tomorrow, invasion or not, that someone might decide to start stringing up Japanese civilians? It still happened with Negroes in the South; why not Japanese on Oahu after this day, or when the invasion started, if it started?

After coasting for several miles down the Pali Highway, traffic having thinned out somewhat, they turned off into a small development on the northern edge of Honolulu. Janice lived alone; her husband, God save him, was an Army major with MacArthur in the Philippines.

As they turned into her driveway he could see a flutter of curtains. A moment later the door cracked open and she came running out, falling into the arms of Margaret's mother, her aunt. Both spoke hurriedly in Japanese.

Janice had on her Red Cross uniform.

Margaret got out of the car and the two embraced and for a moment she didn't notice that James had slid over and was now in the driver's seat, the car's engine still running.

She looked back.

"James, what are you doing?"

"I have to go back to the base. If it's an invasion that's where I have to be."

"Damn it, James," she sighed, anger in her eyes, as if arguing with a recalcitrant child, "this is ridiculous. You're wounded, you've done enough."

"I have to do my duty," was all he could say in reply, wondering if the words sounded pompous, but knowing no other way of expressing it.

She leaned over, drawing closer to him, so close that he could smell her perfume, and it lowered his guard.

"What about us?" she whispered. "I might

be OK, but what about Mom and Janice? You heard what Ed Simpson was shouting. We need you here."

He felt his throat tighten. She was right, of course. Invasion or not, he should be thinking of his family now. They needed his protection, be it from the Japanese or some angry lynch mob that might go wild during the night.

And at that instant there were more flashes of light. It was impossible to see from which direction they were coming, or where they were hitting, but a deep rumbling echoed around them as the first shells impacted into Honolulu, as the attacking fleet rounded Diamond Head.

He thought of his comrades, Collingwood, the crew from the decrypt center. What the hell could they do now? Their building had been destroyed in the third strike. What can we do?

But he knew he had to go back, even if just to be with them. Annapolis, twenty years of active duty, were ingrained too deeply into his soul to turn his back on that duty now. He had to be with them, even if the gesture was useless, even if it meant leaving all he had left in this world.

He drew the .38 out from his belt, handed it to Margaret and clumsily fished out the box of shells and gave them to her as well.

"I'm leaving this here with you," he said, hesitating, "just in case."

"In case of what?"

He didn't reply at first.

"I wish to hell you had let me train you with this," he said.

She held the gun nervously and Janice came over, took the pistol, gripping it properly.

"I'll give her a quick run-through," Janice said. "I used to go shooting with Tom all the time. This is a double action, isn't it?"

"First cylinder's empty. Load it up," James said.

"Any news?" she asked, and he briefly told her about the bombardment on the east side of the island.

"I was getting set to go down to the fire station, where they're setting up a blood bank center," she said. "I'll get Nana and Margaret settled in first though, and show her how to use the gun."

"Thanks, Janice."

He hesitated.

"Maybe you should stay here as well," James finally said, "just in case things," again a pause, "turn ugly."

"It's only a couple of blocks to the fire station," she replied casually. "Besides this neighborhood is mostly folks like . . ."

Her voice trailed off, and her gaze was lowered for a moment.

Like us, he thought, Japanese or half Japanese.

"Promise me this, though," he replied. "If this is the start of an invasion, I want you to get the hell out. Get Margaret and Nan, get up into the mountains and wait it out."

He paused.

"Remember what I told you about Nanking. You got one pistol between the three of you, I expect you to know how to use it."

Damn, this was starting to feel like a bad movie, he thought. What am I supposed to do next, tell her to save the last three bullets for themselves?

"Got ya," Janice said airily.

She stepped back from the car window, casually flipping the gun open and taking an extra shell out of the box. She slipped it into the cylinder, snapping it shut and testing the feel of the gun. Her husband, career army, had obviously taught her well. James tried to reassure himself that they'd be safe.

Margaret came back alongside him, reached in, and touched his face.

"I'm sorry," he whispered. "You know I love you."

She hesitated, and he could sense that she

was tempted to try a coup, to simply pull the car door open and drag him out. And as he gazed back at her, only inches away, he silently appealed for her not to do it. He was weak, exhausted, in pain, and just might succumb, and then forever after hold himself in contempt.

The hesitation lingered, and then she leaned in closer, putting a hand behind his neck, drawing him in, kissing him passionately.

"I understand," she whispered, pulling back, her voice near to breaking.

He started to reach up to grasp the steering wheel and inwardly cursed. He no longer had his claw on. Fumbling, he braced the steering wheel with his legs, using his right hand to shift into reverse.

She stepped back from the car, tears streaming down her face.

"But if you get yourself killed, I'll never forgive you," she said.

It was an old line, she had said it a hundred times or more when early in the mornings, in what seemed like an eternity ago, he'd get up before dawn to take his Aeronca Chief out for a dawn flight, before the winds kicked up. But now it was real, it was deadly and real as more flashes snapped across the sky, the echo of incoming shells rattling the heavens, bursting with thunderclaps down along Waikiki Beach.

He backed out into the road, awkwardly turning the steering wheel and shifting into first, not looking back.

Damn it hurt, his left arm throbbing, as he used it to brace the wheel as he shifted into second.

Far down the highway, beyond Honolulu, he could see Pearl Harbor, where he was now heading. Though the bombarding fleet had not yet hit it, there was no need for gunnery fire directions tonight, for the fires ignited by the three air strikes still burned brightly, consuming what was left of eight battleships, oil tank farms, hangars, workshops, and the bodies of more than two thousand men.

225 miles southwest of Oahu
December 7, 1941
23:50 hrs local time

"God damn it!"

Admiral Halsey angrily rose from his chair, gaze fixed on the loudspeaker, as if it were an offending messenger and somehow he could take his rage out on it.

He turned to his signals officer.

"Broadcast that through the entire ship."

"Sir?"

"Are you deaf? You heard me. I want that broadcast through the entire ship now."

"Sir." It was Captain George Murray, who was in direct command of *Enterprise*. "The crew is exhausted. They need to get some sleep."

He hesitated for only the briefest instant, weighing the option.

"I want them to hear this. I want them to hear what they are fighting. Switch it on!"

He stalked out of the CIC and up to the bridge, the blackout switch automatically turning off the light in the corridor as he pulled the door to the bridge open, the glassed-in bridge illuminated only by red lighting.

"Admiral on the bridge."

No one turned, though all stiffened even as they stayed focused on their duty.

He looked over at the senior officer on the bridge, a young lieutenant, only a few years out of Annapolis.

"No change, sir," he reported stiffly, "heading 355, at ten knots. Course change to heading 040 degrees to commence in" — he paused and looked at the chronometer, illuminated by a dull red light — "in ten minutes, sir."

"Carry on."

He walked out onto the open bridge, again

the ritual of announcing his presence, no one daring to look back at him, observers posted at each corner, scanning with night binoculars, watching both their escorting destroyers, one of them silhouetted by the moon, which was now coasting higher in the southern sky.

Damn, a good night for a hunting sub.

It made his stomach knot up. Take but one torpedo now, on this the first day of the war. Take me out of this fight before we can even start. The thought was enough to make him sick.

He knew the crews of his escorts were on full alert, double watch posted, but they were moonlit on a sea that was flattening out. One of those bastards could be out there right now, setting up for a shot.

The loudspeaker out on the open bridge crackled.

"All hands, all hands." It was Captain Murray. "By order of the admiral. This is a broadcast from a civilian station in Honolulu."

The loudspeaker crackled again, signal lost for a moment, wavering, and then came in clear.

"Three more explosions. I can see them. The Royal Hawaiian Hotel is burning." The signal wavered for a moment. "A Jap ship is lying in close to the shore at Waikiki. I can see the flashes of its guns." A long pause. "I've just been handed this. Do not leave your homes. The island is under martial law. Only military personnel or those authorized civilians reporting to bases, hospitals, or emergency centers will be allowed onto roads. I repeat . . . stay in your homes. Turn off all lights, turn off gas lines. Do not use your phones. . . ."

No one on the bridge spoke, Halsey stood silent, looking out to sea, to the northeast, as if somehow he could actually see the flashes of battle.

"Oh my God, this is close, I think right over my head." A rumbling sound overwhelmed the announcer's voice, followed several seconds later by an explosion that overloaded the broadcast signal.

"That was damn close," the announcer gasped, barely audible. "They're bombarding downtown Honolulu now. I'm not sure how much longer we'll be on the air."

A moment later he could feel *Enterprise* beginning to heel over slightly as it turned forty-five degrees to starboard, zigzagging. He looked back into the bridge. It was exactly two minutes past midnight.

A minute later they trimmed out onto their new heading. His helmsman was good

— not the slightest deviation, no need to correct by even a degree or two. In the moonlight he could see the one escort on the exact same heading.

"I can see explosions. I think they're hitting Hickam," the radio crackled, signal wavering for a moment. "I've just received this. There is a desperate need for all negative type blood, especially AB negative, and positive as well. Please report to your nearest fire station where blood banks are being established. If stopped by military patrols, have them escort you to the nearest fire station. . . . There's more explosions, they're pouring it in now. My God it's horrible, just horrible."

Damn, he wished now someone would get the damn station to shut up. The Japs would, of course, be listening as well, helping them to adjust fire.

He went back in to the bridge, picked up a phone linking him back to the CIC.

"Turn that off, put me on."

"This is Halsey," he said, voice cold, even-pitched, his voice echoing through the ship.

"You just heard it. The damn Japs are bombarding Honolulu. Our civilians are now targets. Some of you men have families there, all of us have friends there. Now you know what we are fighting. At dawn we

launch and we'll send those bastards to hell.
"That is all."

He slammed the phone back down into its cradle.

No one on the bridge spoke. He stalked over to his chair and settled in.

At first light he'd launch, with only sixty-four planes on board. Instinct told him that the bombarding force might very well be a lure to bring him into range and reveal his position. But there was no way in hell he was going to back off now. If anything, he just might get in the first punch and catch them by surprise.

Go in harm's way!

That had been drilled into him nearly forty years ago back at the Academy. John Paul Jones's words were engraved on the soul of every midshipman. He had trained for this moment across all the years since. He knew the odds. There had to be at least four Jap carriers out there, maybe five or six, and if he launched first against the bombarding fleet, he could expect a full counterblow.

After the first two attacks, there had been an attempt to set a rendezvous with *Lexington,* but both ships were now holding to complete radio silence after the third attack and what was assumed to be the destruction of CinCPac on Oahu. Without radio contact from the island to coordinate their movements without their having to reply, neither he nor his counterpart on *Lexington,* Admiral Newton, was willing to risk disclosing their location by maintaining radio contact. He and *Lexington* would have to go it alone. To try and coordinate could very well bring in every Jap sub and surface ship within a hundred miles. Anyway, American doctrine had been for carriers to fight in units of one and avoid offering the enemy a bunched-up target. Being on his own felt comfortable and was exactly what they had practiced in peacetime.

If this was *Enterprise*'s last day, they would take as many Japs as possible with them.

IJN battleship Hiei
Five miles south-southeast of the main channel into Pearl Harbor
December 8, 1941
00:31 hrs local time

"Commence firing on Pearl Harbor," Captain Nishida Maseo, commander of the Imperial Japanese Navy battleship *Hiei,* announced.

Around him was a flurry of action. His gunnery control officer turned and picked up the telephone linking to the fire control

center, where their elite crew, who had so long anticipated this moment, was standing ready. The bombardments of the last hour and a half, hammering the air and army bases at Kaneohe and Fort Bellows, with several salvos into Fort Shafter and Honolulu, had been but a preliminary. They had saved the bulk of their precious fourteen-inch shells for this moment, this moment when the real bombardment, the unleashing of hell would truly begin.

With their sister ship *Kirishima* following a mile astern, firing three hundred shells as well, they would lay down the equivalent destructive load of a six-hundred-plane air strike in the next two hours. Let Yamamoto talk of his carrier-based planes. Now was the moment to prove that it was battleships after all that would ultimately prove who was still the queen of battle upon the seas. The additional weight of the five- and six-inch secondary batteries on both ships, and the guns of their escorting destroyers and cruiser, would add yet even more chaos.

He could feel the vibration, the four massive turrets, each packing two guns of fourteen-inch caliber, rotating, imagine in the fire control room the final coordinates being fed in, observations from the scout plane circling above Pearl, even now dropping illumination flares over the still flaming dockyards, oil tanks, submarine pens, workshops, and hulks of the now impotent American battleships. If the Americans thought they had faced the fury of Japan before, they were mistaken. In a few more minutes they would know what true fury was.

Each salvo would be eight shells, each loaded with half a ton of high explosives, each shell capable of shattering anything within a hundred meters of impact. A hundred of them, capable of completely obliterating a square kilometer of ground and anything resting upon it.

The massive turrets, illuminated by the beams of moonlight, were visible from the armored bridge. To stand in the open now would shatter the eardrums of any man not well protected.

A klaxon sounded, the signal that the huge

batteries, the massive fourteen-inches guns raised, were poised, waiting for the moment when stabilizing gyroscopes indicated that the guns were laying true and level.

The first turret lit off, its minute adjustments in angle and declination decided by the fire control team decks below in the armored citadel where the guns were controlled, though individual turret commanders could direct fire as well if need be.

The recoil of the fourteen-inchers actually staggered the ship. Those ill prepared and not braced for the blow were knocked off their feet by the massive recoil. Number two turret followed suit several seconds later, and then number three and four aft fired. Tons of shells winged upward, climbing to well over twenty thousand feet, reaching apogee, and then started to shriek down on the island. A mile astern the *Kirishima* exploded with a similar salvo. Sixteen massive blows were about to impact the wreckage-strewn Pearl Harbor and Hickam.

Pearl Harbor
December 8, 1941
00:32 hrs local time

He finally left his car in a side parking lot, beyond the main gate into the naval base. Traffic into the base was a mad tangle, stalled by a head-on collision between a Dodge convertible and an Army truck that apparently had come barreling out of a side street and plowed into the Dodge. Corpsmen were working on the driver of the Dodge as James stepped around him, the poor man a bloody mess, the driver of the army truck standing there woodenly, bleeding from a bad scalp wound and a broken nose.

As he looked around, he wasn't sure where exactly to go now that he was here. His headquarters was gone. He was not, in a sense, a fighting man. There were more than enough sailors, marines, and even some infantry swarming about in confusion, toting Springfields and BARs. A team trotted past carrying a heavy .50-caliber water-cooled machine gun.

He felt out of place now, wondering if he was just getting in the way. He couldn't even pitch in to help with the wreckage, or lift a stretcher; hell, he felt so light-headed he wondered if he should be on a stretcher himself.

Everything was illuminated by a lurid dim light, the flaming oil tank farms burning close enough that he could feel the radiant heat. Out in the harbor, *Arizona,* or what was left of it, was still awash in flames, thick coils of oily smoke from all the fires casting a heavy pall over the entire harbor and base, choking, dulling the illuminating fires so that there was a Dantesque feel to the entire scene, as if he had stepped into the first circle of hell.

He'd try for what was left of the office of CinCPac. Maybe someone there could give directions, point him to where Collingwood and the rest of the team were trying to set up operations, if such a thing was possible.

A brilliant, nearly blinding blue light ignited almost straight overhead just as he reached the main gate, which was still intact. All around him paused, looked up, pointing. A panicked sailor shouted, shouldering his Springfield and squeezing off a round at the parachute flare that hung several thousand feet above the base. A second flare burst into radiant brilliance, and there was the distant drone of a plane engine.

"We got incoming!" someone screamed.

A mad jostle started, men beginning to run, without direction, some diving to ground, others going beneath cars. A .30-caliber machine gun, emplaced in a circular sand bag pit by the gatehouse, pointed straight up and started to shoot blindly, tracers arcing up, and seconds later, dozens of guns were firing in panic.

He just stood there, watching, and then he heard it, that damn freight train rumble. He had driven from one bombardment straight into another.

The first two shells detonated somewhere over on Ford's Island, brilliant flashes of light. Several seconds later, two more. He could see dimly through the smoke a high geyser lifting up near the overturned *Oklahoma,* which was illuminated by the dozens of arc welders who were frantically cutting holes into the bottom of the ship, still trying to rescue comrades trapped within.

The salvo was shifting closer. He went to ground, not sure where the next four hit, and then seconds later more winged overhead, shrieking loud, mind-numbing, close, damn close, a series of explosions washing over him. One shell hit close enough that he felt the blast, the air being sucked out of his lungs, the concussion tearing through the ground, bouncing him. A split second later he heard the lashing roar of shrapnel, tearing into treetops, carving into buildings, windows that had survived the air raids now shattering in showers of glass.

Battleship veteran that he was, he knew he had a couple of minutes before the next salvo hit. He started to stand up, and then a higher pitched roar, lighter eight-, six-, and five-inch shells began to rain down, minor when compared to the massive fourteens, but deadly nevertheless to anyone out in the open and less than a hundred yards away.

He started to run toward the still-burning ruins of headquarters, others running alongside him. He looked up, and to his utter amazement he caught a glimpse of *Oklahoma,* sharply illuminated by a parachute flare directly overhead. The men atop her were either insane or the bravest he had ever seen. They had barely paused in their work, arc welding lights still glowing hot blue, sailors atop her returning to their mission of mercy, to save men still trapped within.

"Watson. Commander Watson!"

He slowed. It was a woman's voice. He caught a glimpse of her, Collingwood's administrative assistant from the decrypt center waving to him.

He went over.

"Dianne? Miss St. Clair? My God, woman, what the hell are you doing here?"

Somehow she still managed to look beautiful, in spite of her disheveled look, dress and blouse blood splattered, both nylons with runs, face mud smeared, but amazingly, her lovely blond hair still combed.

"Captain Collingwood sent me back here, to see if I could round up anyone from the team that might report in."

"Incoming!"

He grabbed Dianne by the shoulder and pulled her down to the ground by his side. More shells burst across Ford Island, one appearing to hit *Oklahoma,* then several more, these falling short, crashing into the sprawl of workshops back toward ten-ten dry dock, or what was left of it after the torpedo strikes against it in the third-wave attack. The continual higher-pitched shrieks of the five-, six-, and eight-inchers now were scattering down around the base. Overhead, another flare popped. Guns from all across the harbor were firing upward, more than a few panicked men most likely thinking the bombardment was coming from airplanes overhead.

The hurricane roar from shells washed over them. He tried to collect his wits, still on the ground, breathing hard, his left arm throbbing as he protectively held it over young Miss St. Clair, who in the strange, hellish blue light forced what she must have assumed was a brave smile, though the terror in her eyes was obvious.

"Incoming!"

She pressed in against his side, a shuddering sob escaping her. He turned his head to look up, wondering for a second if he could actually see the passage of the three-quarter-ton monsters. More detonations ignited within the flaming sea of oil from the ruptured oil tanks, vast sheets of burning oil soaring hundreds of feet into the air, spreading out, raining down. There were distant screams. He dreaded to think who was screaming — most likely firefighters now engulfed in the inferno.

He forced himself to concentrate. It was all random chance now . . . Either I lie here terrified, or I get up, accept the chance, and do something, anything.

He took a deep breath, pressed against the ground with his one good hand, and stood up.

"Come on, Dianne, where's Collingwood?"

She came to her feet, shaking, leaning against his side for support.

"He's set up shop at the radio repair shack, down by the east channel," she stuttered. "Do you know where it is?"

"No."

He was lying, but he just didn't feel right leaving her out here in this chaos, random or not. The Japs most likely did have a map of the base, and just might try and toss a few shells into what was left of CinCPac headquarters. Not that the radio repair shack would be any safer; it was less than a hundred yards north of the east channel, the main tieoff basin for several dozen destroyers and light cruisers.

"Come on, Dianne, I need you to guide me there," he said, figuring that it'd give her something to focus on, which it did.

She tried to run, but was still wearing a rather ridiculous set of heels. He was tempted to tell her to take the damn things off, but the road they turned onto was carpeted with broken glass, burning vehicles, and smack in the middle of the road the wreckage of what appeared to be a Japanese plane, still smoldering, the blackened, skeletal pilot still inside. Dead were simply dragged over to the side of the road, their faces covered with a shirt, a blanket, or a scrap of cloth.

Another brace of shells howled in. He didn't push her to the ground; shards of broken glass were everywhere. Already he was learning to judge the sound. The first new salvo thundered into Ford's Island, impacting into the channel, the second salvo again high, hitting into the north end of the base and the inferno of the oil tank farm.

They turned a corner: a building, burning

fiercely, white hot, screams from within, a volunteer fire crew using, of all things, a couple of garden hoses, out of which only a trickle of water was emerging — absurd looking, and yet so damn valiant. A lone figure emerged, the fire crew spraying him with a desolate trickle of water, steam rising from him, cradled in his arms like a child, a badly burned sailor, sobbing with pain.

Dianne slowed.

"Come on, keep moving," James shouted, and she nodded, moving in close to his side like a frightened child.

The rain of five-, six-, and eight-inch shells was clearly unpredictable, winging in without warning or pattern. He could see the east channel, a half-sunk light cruiser, down by the bow, a shot impacting amidships. Gun crews continued to fire straight up from nearly every ship still in port, and there was now a steady rain of exploded fragments and spent .30- and .50-caliber bullets smacking back down, a deadly rain of debris. Their own antiaircraft fire was one more danger as it fell back to earth, the shells often with faulty fuses that failed to air burst, but would detonate when they finally hit the ground.

They turned left back on to a main street that led straight down toward the channel.

It was ablaze with light, burning ships, flashes of gunfire, and then, terrifyingly, two fourteen-inchers impacting to the south of the channel, what looked to be an entire building soaring skyward, steel beams, wooden frames, more shattering glass, the concussion washing over them.

He spotted their destination. The blackout had been forgotten, and the door was open. Dianne had stopped momentarily to gaze, awestruck at the twin impacts. He grabbed her by the shoulder and pushed her into the shack.

It was a long narrow building, tucked in between two small warehouses. They were most likely made of nothing more than a few steel beams and wood, like the building that had just been blown to hell on the other side of the channel, but somehow their high bulk gave him at least a false sense of security.

The room was brightly lit, packed with several dozen men and a few women, most of them the crew from the basement of CinCPac, the others naval radio technicians. The walls and work benches were lined with radios of nearly every description, heavy bulky units pulled from destroyers, cruisers, and battleships and brought ashore for repairs. There were bins filled with every tube imaginable, the smell of solder heavy in the air. A seaman second class was seated just inside the door, bent over his work, panel off a unit, voltmeter probe in hand, carefully working away inside the radio as if nothing unusual were going on outside and winged death might not crash in upon him at any second.

"Watson!"

It was his commanding officer, the man who had recruited him out of retirement and back into the service in the cryptanalysis branch of Naval Intelligence, Captain Collingwood, pushing through the crush, coming up, hand extended. "You OK, man?"

James nodded and Collingwood looked down at his arm. The bandage had soaked through in spite of his mother-in-law's handiwork as a seamstress.

"You should have stayed home."

"Couldn't," was all he could say, and then they all braced for a second, looking up, the sound of more incoming thundering overhead, seconds later the concussion slapping through their feet.

James looked around at the confusion. Gone was the quiet, almost monastic atmosphere of their sanctuary basement in the now destroyed wreckage of the offices of

CinCPac.

"Some of the boys here know some civilian ham operators and had them drag their gear down," and Collingwood nodded toward three elderly men, and one young man, a nisei, standing around a massive unit the size of a small icebox, dials lit up. One of the three, with headphones on, looked up.

"The antenna. Go outside and check the damn antenna!"

A couple of young seamen technicians sprinted out of the room, and seconds later he could hear a clambering on the roof. My God, those boys were up there while all hell was coming down around them. Their courage gave him heart.

"Coffee, sir?"

It was one of the secretaries, Miss Lacey. If ever there was an actual boss to the decrypt center it was she. Dianne might be Collingwood's personal assistant, but it was Miss Lacey, with her schoolmarm looks, steel-rimmed glasses, and gray hair tied back in a bun who, more than one whispered, knew more about codebreaking than all of them put together. But tonight, here in the middle of hell, she was tending a coffee pot, offering James a mug, which he accepted with his right hand. He took a gulp and somehow it braced him.

"Dianne, give me a hand," said Lacey, and the two went off.

"What in hell is the picture?" James asked.

A momentary pause. This one was going to be close.

"Down!"

Everyone ducked. A second later the fourteen-incher detonated against one of the warehouses flanking the shack. Every window on the north side of the building blew in, showering the room with shards of glass. Someone started to scream. One of the civilians staggered up, the side of his face and left arm lacerated with shards.

Dianne and Lacey were immediately on him, leading him to one side of the room and sitting him down.

Coming out from under the bench, James and Collingwood stood up, both looking at each other with wary smiles, trying to conceal their fear.

"There's going to be a helluva fight out there," Collingwood said, pulling James to one side. "An hour before the bombardment started over on the windward side, tugs managed to drag some of the wreckage clear of the main channel. A tight squeeze, but Admiral Draemel was able to sortie aboard the destroyer *Ward,* before things snagged up again."

Draemel. The name was familiar somehow.

"Commandant of the Academy back in the thirties. Good man, tough," Collingwood continued. "He tried to get out aboard the light cruiser *Detroit,* but it then snagged on the wreckage in the channel, so he transferred his flag to the *Ward,* which was on the far side of the wreckage. Those are the guys who nailed that Jap sub before the bombing started."

"What sub?"

Collingwood was about to reply when a sharp, high-pitched whine whipped overhead: a five- or six-incher. They instinctively ducked; the shell passed on.

"Tell you later. So anyhow, word is he's out there, but we don't have any radio contact yet. There's a total of half a dozen or so destroyers, a few destroyer escorts, and the cruiser *Minneapolis,* which was off the coast when the first raid hit, and already had four destroyers with her."

"And they're facing battleships?" James asked, incredulous. "And the rest of the fleet is still bottled up here?"

Collingwood nodded, saying nothing.

"Got it!"

It was one of the remaining civilians,

gingerly working a dial, adjusting it slowly.

"Put it on loudspeaker," Collingwood shouted, and a second later came a thin wavery voice that with a minor adjustment came in stronger: Japanese. James listened, head cocked.

"It's in the clear," he said. "It's fire control orders from one of the planes."

All turned to look at him as he translated out loud.

"Dolphin one, no more targets, go to secondary." He paused. "Dolphin two, south six hundred meters."

He looked over at Collingwood, who had a fair mastery of Japanese as well and nodded in agreement.

OK, which was Dolphin one and two? Had that fire control adjustment just placed them in the crosshairs?

Long seconds passed and then they heard it, more incoming, a bracket of explosions igniting in and to either side of the channel, one shell bursting little more than a hundred yards away, more shattering glass showering the room.

"God damn," Collingwood hissed.

"Dolphin two, Dolphin two, on target, fire for effect."

James went over to the operator and tapped him on the shoulder, motioning for him to stand up, and took his headphones.

He scanned the face of the radio, not sure of the dial arrangement.

"Switch me to transmit."

The civilian leaned over and threw a switch. James picked up the heavy, stand-mounted microphone.

"Dolphin two, correction, correction," he said in Japanese, trying as best as possible to mimic the voice and accent of the observer orbiting above them. "Return fire to first target, eight hundred meters north."

As he spoke, he wondered who he was calling death down on. Target one was most likely the burning oil tank farm. Some poor souls might die, but the last salvo had wrought terrible havoc along the channel, impacting ships that could not escape the harbor.

There was a pause of a few seconds.

"Dolphin two, ignore that last. It is an American trick. Maintain fire."

"Dolphin two, ignore that last transmit, he is the American!"

Only Collingwood and a few others in the room knew what James was saying, but there were chuckles as it was obvious the two were arguing.

"Dolphin two, switching to frequency seven. American bastards."

"You're the American bastard," James snapped. He could hear the carrier wave snap off.

"Tell the Emperor he can kiss my ass, you sons of bitches," he shouted in English, and there were loud chuckles even as everyone ducked yet again. The salvo had stopped for a brief moment in the confusion, but had now resumed.

James took the headphones off, looked back at Collingwood, and shrugged.

"Nice try."

"It's the *Ward.* She's transmitting in the clear."

All turned to one of the operators on another radio, and Collingwood called for him to put it on loudspeaker.

"Repeat. Plan Alpha, initiate now!"

"That's Admiral Draemel," one of the seamen announced. "I can recognize that old man's voice anywhere. He is one crazy son of a bitch and a damn good fighter. Hit 'em back, damn it, hit 'em back!"

"Repeat. Plan Alpha. God be with all of you, now let's get the bastards!"

All stood silent. Plan Alpha? James wondered. Whatever it was, he sensed it was desperation and he felt a deep sense of desperation as well. With a proper communications hookup here on the island, at this very moment they could be helping to coordinate, staying in contact with the task groups *Lexington* and *Enterprise,* and the distant group of the heavy cruiser *Indianapolis* five hundred miles to the south off Johnston Island. Such coordination could help organize something of a response. He could see that was indeed where he might be able to help bring order out of chaos over the next day, and to try and monitor the Japanese broadcasts and maybe glean some tidbit of information upon which a battle might very well depend.

But at this moment there was nothing he could do but stand there, silent, listening, unable to help.

"Damn," he sighed, "I wish I was out there with them rather than here, taking this shit."

Another salvo came screaming in. Obviously James's subterfuge of the moment had not changed anything. All ducked back under the benches. Dianne was again by his side, and as the thundering roar of the incoming increased, he knew it would be close, damn close, and he pulled her in protectively.

Aboard the Hiei
December 8, 1941
01:10 hrs local time

Captain Nagita actually smiled at the obscene interchange between one of his spotters and the American who had momentarily interrupted their fire control, even though his final insult was directed against the Emperor, which triggered cries of outrage in the radio room from those who understood English. Clumsy — the man's accent was obviously foreign, colloquial Japanese, not the precise, highly trained phraseology that all observers were drilled in as a precaution against just such a measure. But still it had delayed one salvo.

So far, they had fired off one hundred forty rounds of high explosive shells, nearly half of their entire allotment, the firing mission to leave sixty high explosive shells in reserve. Their full reserve of one hundred sixty-five armor-piercing rounds for any ship-to-ship action was, as yet, untouched.

He had ordered that each magazine hoist have armor-piercing shells ready to shift over immediately if any enemy ships did attempt to sortie, but so far, according to the spotters, it appeared as if the main channel was still blocked, and the two submarines that had supposedly gained position at the entryway into Pearl Harbor had not reported in.

The klaxon sounded again. Seconds later, each of his four turrets lit off in sequence with their massive loads, the ship actually heeling over, its thirty-six-thousand-ton bulk shoved nearly half a meter to port by the concussive blows.

The infirmary already was reporting nearly a score of injuries, including one man dead in number two turret. He had not stepped clear of the terrifying recoil of the gun breech, and the life was crushed out of him in but a fraction of a second. Though the crew was well drilled, this was their first taste of actual combat.

The lighter five- and six-inch guns continued to bark away, firing randomly into the general area of Pearl Harbor. Their random fire was intentional, designed to sow confusion and fear, shells striking without warning between the heavier impacts of the main batteries.

He looked up at the bulkhead chronometer. A little more than four hours to the beginning of nautical twilight; an hour and twenty minutes left to this mission.

Yamamoto might be cavalier about risking battleships, but then again he always was heretical in his views. Five miles off the enemy coast Nagita felt naked. The fires lighting the shore from Waikiki over to Pearl Harbor were a glowing beacon that could silhouette any ship even twenty miles out. He had always felt that the number of escorts assigned to the entire task force was far too small: only nine destroyers, two heavy cruisers and one light one, and now his commander had split the fleet, Yamamoto giving him but two destroyers and the cruiser *Tone* as protection against submarines or the prospect that the Americans might have been able to slip something out of the harbor, or for that matter bring something up from farther out to sea.

Regardless of what Yamamoto wanted, he'd stay on station here for only one more hour, then find reason to pull out and put a good hundred nautical miles between this prize of the Imperial Japanese fleet and any enemy shoreline.

They had reduced their rate of fire to a salvo every four minutes to conserve ammunition and also to give the guns time to cool. A sustained rate of fire much beyond that, justified in a battleship-to-battleship fight, but not here, would cause excessive wear on the precious gun barrels.

He could feel the rumble of the turrets slowly shifting as the ship made a steady ten knots, running due west. In seven more minutes they would come about and trace back, fire lifting to hit Hickam again, and then back over to Fort Shafter, which to everyone's amazement was continuing to fire back defiantly, but with absolutely no result other than a single near miss on a destroyer more than half an hour ago.

"Enemy ships to port!"

Startled, he turned away from gazing at the distant shore, cursing inwardly, night vision dulled by the glaring fires.

The warning had come via an observer aloft in the fire control tower, rung down and announced from the phone by a young ensign, obviously rattled by the news.

Nagita fixed him with a cool gaze.

"I want a bearing, and repeat the order calmly or you will be ordered off this bridge!"

The ensign gulped, nodded, spoke into the phone, and then looked back up.

"Sir. Enemy ships to port, bearing 170 degrees, range estimated nine thousand meters!"

"Fire star shells from our secondary batteries to port!" Nagita announced fiercely, his attention now turned away from the bombardment. "Order all main batteries to shift to armor piercing!"

Aboard the Ward
01:15 hrs local time
Rear Admiral Draemel was silent out on the open bridge, night binoculars raised, trained straight ahead.

The silhouettes of the Jap battleships stood out clear against the blazing skyline of Oahu. Each bursting salvo on the all but defenseless base and city was a nightmare to watch.

How he had managed to slip out unnoticed was still a mystery to him. He had tried to sortie with every available ship that could turn screws, but after getting but three destroyers out to rendezvous with *Minneapolis,* his cruiser, *Detroit,* hung up on the wreckage in the main channel, blocking it off.

Ward had come in to pick him up. He was a bit surprised the young commander had risked this until he was piped aboard and recognized him as one of his cadets from the Academy, the young man grinning as he welcomed him. Together they had set off at flank speed to rendezvous with *Minneapolis,* which had remained twenty miles out to sea. He had planned to transfer his flag over to *Minneapolis,* but there was no time now. He'd use *Ward* for his flagship in this fight.

What an agonizing wait it had become

once the Japanese bombardment started. Turn and go in for a straight-on encounter off of Diamond Head, or wait out here? The bastards were not just going to bombard the east coast, he reasoned, but then again, they just might. Several scenarios postulated an initial landing there to gain a land-based airfield so the carriers could offload and then put farther out to sea. The bombardment over there could be the opening move for an invasion.

No, to bombard Pearl at night would be too much of a temptation. Let them come in, let them sink their teeth into it, and maybe, just maybe, he could slip in and deliver his punch. Try to meet them head on, their guard will be up and they'll start clobbering us at twenty thousand yards. Let them focus on the other target, though it would be devastating to sit back while they clobbered Pearl, and then slip in for the kill.

So for the last hour and a half that was exactly what he had been doing, slipping in at just under twelve knots, trying to keep the wakes of his ships down at slower speed. At high speed, the wake boiling up astern of a destroyer could easily be spotted by a scout plane. In tropical waters, it would actually glow from the phosphorescence of the plankton stirred up. What was equally nerve-racking was the moon, now high in the southern sky. How could they not have been seen by now? Spotters aloft on the battleships were most likely half blinded by the flash of the big guns, and naturally, nearly all attention was focused on their target.

But still, by God, they should have a scout plane out to sea, and at least one destroyer!

The tension was overwhelming. He'd kill for a cigarette, but they were under strict light security.

He stood silent, listening to the litany of his spotters.

"Range, nine thousand two hundred yards, closing . . . range nine thousand yards, closing . . ."

They were now within easy gunnery range, the popgun turrets forward, a single four-incher ever so slowly adjusting, lowering barrels an inch at a time.

"Range . . . eight thousand, eight hundred yards, closing . . ."

He looked quickly to port and starboard. Damn if it was not like Nelson's battle line closing in at Trafalgar, or a cavalry charge of old, the nine destroyers and destroyer escorts in line abreast, four hundred yards separating each vessel, while *Minneapolis* approached from two miles astern, ready to come about and open with all guns once they were spotted, staying farther back due to her higher silhouette. He felt a knot in his stomach looking at the moonlight glinting off the churning wake astern. He could actually see the outline of the heavy cruiser.

For God's sake, can't they see us?

"We are well within torpedo range, sir."

It was the captain of the *Ward,* a damn good lad. It had taken guts doing what he did this morning, actually firing off the first shot of the war, nailing a Jap sub at the entry to the harbor a full hour before the bombs began to fall. Though he would not curse the name of a dead comrade, nevertheless, Kimmel should have been on that in minutes and had the base on full alert, rather than still berthed and sleeping.

Not now, don't think of it now.

"Wait," was all he said. "I want it close, real close."

He raised his heavy Zeiss night binoculars, not government issued; he had paid for them himself, and at this moment they were worth every dime. He trained them straight ahead. The Jap battleship stood out clear against the flame-bright shoreline. It was hard yet to identify it precisely, but a young ensign, inside the glassed-off bridge, had the reference books out and was claiming it was either the *Hiei* or her sister ship *Kirishima.* Eight fourteen-inch guns, sixteen six-inch guns, eight five-inch guns, thirty-six thousand tons displacement — one ship that outweighed his entire attacking force. The secondary batteries on that one battleship were capable of matching every gun he had.

"Range eight thousand six hundred yards, closing . . ."

Flashes of light winked from the battleship . . . from its port side.

He held his breath, waiting.

"Range eight thousand four hundred . . ."

A burst of light high above, several hundred yards directly ahead, bright shimmering blue of a magnesium parachute flare. A dozen more bursting within a second, illuminating the sea with a harsh, lurid light.

"Flank speed!" Draemel roared. "Signal all ships. Flank speed and engage!"

Within seconds he felt the surge hit. My God, he had not been on a destroyer in years. It took a stately battleship or heavy cruiser long minutes to build up momentum; this was like a race car. The stern actually sank down as the twin engines accelerated up, even on this old World War I veteran, the engineering officer below having waited for this instant, hands most likely clutched to the steam valves, ready to spin them full open.

He braced against the splinter shield.

To either flank he could see the other destroyers accelerating as well.

"Range, eight thousand two hundred and closing!" The voice of the young seaman calling out the chant had raised half an octave.

More flashes from the battleship. Seconds later the first shells arched overhead, kicking up geysers far astern.

"Forward battery fire at will, fire at will!" the *Ward*'s captain shouted, and a few seconds later the single forward turret opened fire and began pumping out a round every eight to ten seconds, the other destroyers firing as well, while two miles astern, *Minneapolis* began to turn to port, its forward turrets lighting off, sending eight-inch shells screaming overhead in reply. As her turret astern was exposed, three more shells were on their way.

Someone hit on the first salvo, a flash on the deck of the Jap battleship.

"That's the stuff!" Draemel cried, slamming his clenched fist on the railing.

"Now charge, damn it, charge!"

It was the most un-Navylike of orders but it fit the moment.

Hiei
01:27 hrs
"All batteries engage to port. Signal engine room, full speed ahead, turn to heading . . ." he paused for a brief instant.

Damn Yamamoto. He had been warned of this. They were in the classic trap. On the lee of an enemy shore with no room to turn and evade, a clear target outlined by the fires ashore, and now an unknown number of enemy ships coming in on them from the open sea.

Turn in toward them?

No . . . run straight ahead. All our guns can bear while only their forward guns can fire in reply.

"Flank speed, bearing 260 degrees!" he ordered.

The heavy fourteen-inch turrets ponderously shifted, swinging about fore and aft, shifting to port, barrels depressing as the range finders aloft called down to the fire control center with the range and bearing of the rapidly closing targets, ordering ammunition loads switched to armor piercing.

It took a very long two minutes, a very long two minutes, but at last number one turret fired back.

Ward
01:29 hrs
The flash from the guns of their secondary batteries was blinding, burning out his night vision as he was focused on the ship.

"Range . . . seven thousand one hundred yards . . ."

The geyser of water blew two hundred yards forward of the destroyer to his port side, the column of water soaring a hundred feet into the air, seconds later the charging destroyer, pitching and rocking, slashing through the wake of the blast and the cascades of sea water showering down.

More flares were erupting above them. Suddenly a blinding spotlight clicked on, and then another, from the Japanese cruiser to the west of the battleship, the spotlight sweeping back and forth.

The flashes from his own single four-incher were blinding as well, so that he let his binoculars drop.

Eight bursts of light, as brilliant as the sun, fired in sequences of two, each sequence spaced a couple of seconds after the next from the battleship straight ahead, joined a few seconds later by the second battleship, which had been running a mile astern of his target. Their heavy guns were opening up at last.

My God, here it comes.

And it came, the fourteen-inch shells raining down, one striking directly between *Ward* and the destroyer to port, and then in a second his portside companion was gone, just simply gone, caught amidships, three quarters of a ton of armor-piercing slicing through the hull just above the water line.

The destroyer escort to his starboard side had taken a similar hit, but luck had held for her. The armor-piercing shells were designed for a plunging strike into an enemy cruiser or battleship, designed to slice through eight, ten inches of armor and then to keep on punching down before finally detonating. For the starboard-side destroyer escort, it had simply gone through the paper-thin superstructure of the bridge, killing four men, turning the ship's captain into a pulplike spray, and then punched through the starboard side to strike the sea a quarter mile away before exploding.

But for the ship to port, the shell had angled into the engine room, hitting a steam turbine which was encased with high-grade steel, and blown, the explosion breaking the back of the ship, tearing off the entire aft end, the flash bursting into the aft magazine for the five-inchers, igniting half a dozen tons of powder.

Another shell burst in the ocean seventy-five yards off the portside bow of *Ward.* Not a killing blow, though the overpressure underwater ruptured plates, and shrapnel eviscerated the crew of the forward antiaircraft gun, which had started to open up as well, silencing their brave but futile efforts.

"Range six thousand, five hundred yards!"

He looked over at the captain of the *Ward.* The lad stood not saying a word. Draemel smiled inwardly. Best damn tradition of Annapolis on display here. His boys were doing OK, and he was proud of them — but how many of these kids would die in the next few minutes, how many were already dead? He had heard some unsettling rumors. Suppose after all this their torpedoes weren't effective, suppose they just bounced off the armor siding of that thirty-six-thousand-ton monster straight ahead? If so, he hoped everyone on the damn ordnance board responsible fried in hell. He was pitting well over two thousand young men on this gamble. It had better be worth it.

He could not let his fears show now. There was only one order left to give, when to turn and launch torpedoes, and he prayed to God his nerve would hold long enough to do that — and that he lived long enough to do it right. He had seen the destruction in Pearl. It was payback time, and he wanted in on that first strike back.

There was a momentary eye contact between him and the young captain, illuminated by the flash of the Japanese guns. Both forced a smile, said nothing, but the look expressed a thousand words about fears, courage, the realization of what had to be done, and the realization of the price that job would require.

They were well within torpedo range now, almost suicidally close. But the farther out with his torpedoes, the slower the speed for the weapon once launched. At this range, to reach their target, speed would have to be set at under thirty knots. Hell, this old destroyer moved faster than that. He wanted them in damn close for a high-speed launch at maximum torpedo speed of forty-five knots. It was rumored the Japs could fire theirs from ten thousand yards or more away, but no, he wanted to be right on top of the sons of bitches and spit in their eye before he'd cut loose, to make sure they put her on the bottom of the sea.

Hiei
01:34 hrs

They were up to flank speed at last, running full out at over twenty-two knots, burning more fuel in a minute than they would cruising for a half hour at ten knots.

Another four miles and they would clear the west coast of the island and could turn northward and away.

Damn Yamamoto! He should have assigned all the destroyers with me, I'd have then had a protective screen to portside to intercept this unexpected attack, Nagita thought bitterly.

"Their range is four thousand meters!"

They must have launched by now, he thought. It would be suicide to come any closer. Already two of the attacking ships were gone.

He spared a quick glance to the charts. They had five miles of sea room to starboard. Should he turn in but then have no maneuver room, or race straight on?

He hesitated.

Ward
01:36 hrs

"Range four thousand, six hundred yards!"

Another salvo, another destroyer hit, bow shearing off, the ship for a second looking as if it would actually dig in bow first and upend over.

"Sir?"

It was the captain of the *Ward,* trying to

sound calm, in spite of the hurricane of noise.

"One mile out," Draemel shouted, voice nearly drowned out by the bark of the lone four-inch gun forward. "I want it so close we can't miss! We're almost under their big guns, they're shooting flat trajectory, their heavy rounds passing over us now," and even as he spoke the bridge was rattled by the howl of a fourteen-inch shell shrieking past them, so close the concussive blast of the passing bolt was actually felt. It was followed a few seconds later by a strike from a six-inch shell, hitting the smokestack astern, blowing it apart. He could hear screaming from down on the deck.

"Aye, aye sir. One mile it is."

Hiei
01:38 hrs
"Turn to bearing 300!" Nagita shouted.

The Americans were insane. They were closing straight in! He could not help but be filled with a certain awe. Four of their ships were definitely hit, what appeared to be a cruiser farther out engulfed in flames. *Kirishima,* apparently not the target of this mad charge, was concentrating her fire on the larger target. *Tone* was racing out on a bearing of 220 degrees, angling across the western flank of their attack, her guns engaging the American cruiser as well. Idiots! It was the destroyers now that were the real threat. The cruiser could have waited.

Ward
01:40 hrs

"Range two thousand nine hundred yards! . . . she's turning sir, turning away!"

He didn't need his binoculars to see it . . . the battleship's silhouette was shifting, turning in toward land, running obliquely away.

He ran a quick calculation: running speed of torpedoes, target angling away at forty-five degrees now from their attack, it would lengthen the run. Give it two more minutes.

He hoped the torpedo officer aboard this ship was trained well and knew his settings. They were only going to get one shot to launch from starboard.

"In two minutes we turn hard to port, and launch. Radio that order, in the clear, to the other ships."

Pearl Harbor
01:41 hrs

James and the others in the radio shack stood silent. The bombardment had lifted once the insane charge of the destroyers had started. There had even been a scattering of cheers both in the shack and from outside along the docks.

But they had been able to hear every word of command, broadcast in the clear: the distress calls from destroyers crippled and falling out of the attack, and also the sudden silences, which spoke volumes.

"This is *Ward.* All ships, on my mark, prepare to turn in sixty seconds to bearing 280 degrees, and then launch torpedoes. Mark!"

"Fifty seconds . . ."

And then the radio just went silent.

Ward
01:42 hrs

He was still alive — at least he thought he was. The six-inch shell had slashed into the forward turret, a torrent of splinters and shrapnel washing up over the bridge, piercing the tissue-thin skin of the so-called splinter shield, glass of the bridge shattering behind him.

His left side was numb. He felt nothing, he tried to reach around with his right hand to feel it, but couldn't find anything to grab hold of. In the flashes of light he caught a glimpse of a petty officer, staring at him in shock, and then he looked down in amazement.

His left arm was gone just below the shoulder, blood pouring out in a pulsing stream. The *Ward*'s young CO was on the deck by his side, at least what was left of his decapitated body.

He felt *Ward* begin to heel over hard. They were turning, preparing to launch. The petty officer was by his side, saying something about sick bay. He snarled at the man to stand fast and remain at his post.

The battleship was visible before him, now impossibly big, flashes of light, guns of every caliber firing, a torrent of shells slashing into the *Ward,* which was beginning to lose way even as it turned.

Damn it, God, give me a few more seconds, just a few more seconds!

"Torpedoes away!"

He turned and saw the splashes as the eight torpedoes, launched by pneumatic bursts of high pressure air, hit the water, one after the other. Looking back to port, it was hard to see, but it seemed that at least one other destroyer was still in the fight, turning, launching as well . . .

"OK, you bastards, now it's your turn to get some," he gasped.

Hiei

01:44:30 hrs

"Sir — torpedo wakes inbound!"

He held his breath, scanning the waters. Searchlights swept back and forth, one stopped, focused on a white, bubbling wake coming straight amidships.

Closer, it was racing in . . . too late to order evasive maneuvers. They were going to take this one!

He stepped back and away from the railing. The flash could roast a man alive. He prepared to shield his face with his arm.

Something hit, he could feel it . . . but nothing, no explosion.

By all the gods! He almost wanted to laugh . . . It was a dud.

And then a cry that more torpedoes were coming in.

Ward

01:45 hrs

Ward was dying. The engine room was reporting flood. He could barely hear it, he could barely hear anything now as he stood braced against the shattered splinter shield, hanging on with his one hand.

The petty officer, ignoring his protests, was bracing him up.

"I'm taking you to the doc now, sir!"

"Another minute," Draemel gasped. "They should have hit by now!"

"Goddamn torpedoes," someone was screaming, "Goddamn torpedoes! Duds, we're firing Goddamn duds!"

He felt an infinite weariness. My God in heaven, after all this, please God no. Don't let these men die in vain.

And then, as if in answer to his final prayer, it happened. A brilliant flash, so close he could feel the concussion as it raced through the water after hitting the Jap battleship amidships, and then, five seconds later, a second flash, far astern. Something told him that had to be one of his, one from the *Ward,* one from this crew.

"You did it, boys," he gasped, "by God you did it! Proud of you!"

The world was darker now. He could barely see the flash; everything was drifting out of focus.

"Proud of you, sir." It was the petty officer, laying him down on the blood-soaked deck. "You did it."

But Draemel no longer heard him as he drifted off, some memory floating for a moment, strange, not here. The grandkids, God, I'll miss them growing up. . . .

He was already gone when seconds later a direct hit from one of the *Hiei*'s six-inchers burst in the forward magazine, delivering the death blow to a gallant ship and all but twenty of her hands.

Hiei
01:47 hrs
"I want a damage report now!" Nagita shouted, looking back at his wide-eyed staff.

Phones in the bridge were ringing, but he didn't need to be told that they were losing headway and the ship was no longer answering the helm.

His senior damage control officer was on one of the phones, talking rapidly, and yet still maintaining a sense of calm. Nagita knew he too had to regain control of himself.

The officer finally hung up the phone and turned back to face his admiral.

"One torpedo amidships, port side, detonating in a fuel bunker. Damage can be contained, but we'll lose most of the fuel. Transfer pumping has started.

"The second, though, sir. It struck portside astern. Possible damage to portside screw, and the rudder is not responding to the helm, sir. It's either gone or bent. We don't know yet."

Nagita took it in, saying nothing.

Yamamoto's foolishness, he thought bitterly, and now this. He looked to starboard. The enemy coast was little more than four miles away, shoreline bright with fires.

"The enemy?"

"All ships apparently destroyed, sir, or retiring."

He nodded.

"Foolhardy," he whispered, "but valiant. I never expected such courage from them. They could have launched from twice, three times the range but did not."

No one spoke.

"Signal our destroyers to prepare to take us into tow. We must clear these shores before dawn."

He walked back out onto the open bridge and leaned over the railing to look aft along the port side. Even in the dark, illuminated now by the burning hulks of two of the enemy destroyers, he could see where the water was darker and flattened out. They were hemorrhaging their precious oil and with each passing second slowing down, even as *Hiei* started into an uncontrolled turn to starboard, now listing as well. Back on the bridge he could hear his chief engineer taking control of the situation, ordering counterflooding to balance out the list, and to prepare a harnessed diver to go over the side to examine the rudder.

It was not yet two in the morning local time. In a little more than three and a half hours, the eastern horizon would begin to glow — and they would indeed be bait for the American carriers, if they were out there. He now wondered if that was Yamamoto's intent all along, a damaged battleship that the American aircraft carrier commanders could not resist attacking, and thus reveal themselves. If so, and he survived, he would take this to the Naval Board, the government, if need be even the Emperor. To toss aside a battleship for their flimsy carriers was criminal and must be punished.

Chapter Three

Enterprise
210 miles south-southwest of Oahu
December 8, 1941
1:55 hrs local time

The radio in the CIC had been silent for over ten minutes, no one speaking, many still looking at the loudspeaker as if somehow it would come back to life.

My God, Halsey thought, Draemel had guts. An inner voice whispered to him that the man was dead. It'd be like him to go out like that.

He inwardly raged at the silence. There had been one garbled transmission from one of the destroyers, unidentified, reporting two hits on the Jap battleship, but no follow-up as to extent of damage.

One of those monsters, bigger than anything the Navy now had afloat, could take three or four torpedoes and keep right on going . . . but then again, one crucial hit, like the legendary shot on the *Bismarck* . . . she just might be crippled!

He looked over at the plot board, illuminated by the dull red glare of the lighting in the CIC, a seaman first class standing with grease pen poised, ready to mark the latest position.

All they had were two Jap battleships. Where the hell were the carriers?

What was their admiral doing? Who was it? With this aggressiveness, it felt like Yamamoto.

They had to have at least four carriers out there, maybe six, perhaps even their entire known fleet of eight. If so, his sense of pride and honor would most likely mean that Yamamoto had sailed with them. He had read everything he could on the man. He'd been the topic of conversation more than once since word was revealed of his promotion. Several had met him, saying he was one helluva poker player, a master of the bluff, the audacious move, ready to gamble all on the throw of a card and yet with a razor-sharp mind, instantly calculating the odds. He was, as well, a man who seemed to be blessed with that rare gift, luck, the throw of the card usually going in his favor. If that was indeed him leading out there, from the front, in the tradition of Nelson,

Farragut, and John Paul Jones, it showed him to be a man of guts.

He could have pulled a raid and by now be hundreds of miles away. No, he was hanging on — and his desire? Perhaps an invasion itself, but something told Halsey that wasn't the case. CIC had been monitoring reports for over eighteen hours now. The Japanese were hitting everywhere at once, across nearly a sixth of the earth's surface. They had to be spread thin when it came to logistics, transports, troops, the nuts and bolts of staging an invasion and then holding an island like Oahu. Perhaps the gambler Yamamoto was going for that.

Perhaps.

That was a probable the more panicky would grasp on to. He was focused on the moment, and invasion or not, he knew with utter certainty what Yamamoto was really after this morning: him. The surviving American carriers, that was what he was throwing the dice for now.

In spite of the panicked radio broadcasts out of Honolulu, the reporter on the air giving a blow-by-blow account of the fight out at sea, as if reporting on a ball game — and not knowing a damn thing about what he was talking about — at least had given them one valuable clue: the bombardment had stopped, at least for the moment.

There were reports of Jap paratroopers landing in the Dole plantation, another of landing craft coming in at Kaneohe. He doubted both. The Japanese simply did not have the transport planes to reach Hawaii with paratroopers.

He looked at the chronometer: 02:05 local time.

Until someone dragged a dead Jap paratrooper or Imperial marine in front of him, the hell with those reports. What he did know for certain was that Draemel had gone down fighting and possibly crippled one of their battleships, which was most likely limping away from the coast at this very moment.

"I want air crews awakened at 03:30, and make sure they have a damn good breakfast," he announced.

He didn't add the grim thought that for many it would most likely be their last.

"Entire crew to stand to at 04:00. Search planes to launch at 05:15."

His air boss, Lieutenant Commander Wade McCloskey, stood silent, but he could read the man's thoughts. McCloskey had been temporarily promoted to CAG, Commander Air Group, replacing, at least for the moment, Commander Howard Young, who had flown on to Pearl yesterday morning, taking off at dawn to return to base. It was standard procedure, planes flying back in once in range of the island, giving the men some added air time, and a morale booster for those selected, since it meant they got back home hours ahead of their ship.

But yesterday's morale boost had flown straight into disaster. Young had taken off with eighteen planes from VB-6 and VS-6, all Dauntlesses, what could have now been part of his big punch. Most of them were dead, either dropped by the Japs or shot down by panicky sailors and soldiers on the ground.

The air units McCloskey now commanded were little more than half the normal strength for *Enterprise.* He had but nineteen Dauntlesses and eighteen Devastator torpedo bombers on board. Halsey thanked God he had not sent on the boys from VF-6, his fighter squadron, so he still had nineteen Grumman F4F-3 Wildcats, enough to provide a screen for an offensive strike while at the same time enough remained behind to cover this task force. It meant he had a total of fifty-six aircraft on board, just a little over half of what *Enterprise* was capable of handling . . . and here they were now in the middle of a war and he felt like a pugilist with one arm already tied behind his back.

McCloskey stood silent, waiting for any additional orders. Being pulled off the line and up onto the bridge obviously rankled the man, but he was damn near forty years old, Halsey thought when making the decision, a very old man indeed to be out there in a dogfight. McCloskey would have to run things from the bridge, and he was a man Halsey knew could be trusted to see it done right.

"Can I lead?" McCloskey ventured, looking him straight in the eye, but already sensing the answer.

Halsey shook his head.

"I'll need you here. Besides, when was the last time you slept? Those going up at dawn need to be fresh, and you'll be up the rest of the night getting the strike ready. Sorry, Commander, your place is here with me."

McCloskey nodded reluctantly.

"I know the boys aren't trained for night launch, but we can't wait for dawn. First search planes out at 05:15, fully loaded strike force prepared and on the deck as well."

"Yes sir," and the reply was wooden, without emotion. Both knew that given the experience of their pilots, more than one of them would most likely crash on takeoff in the predawn darkness.

"I want every plane available for launch at 05:45. Ten fighters to be held back as CAP, five of them in the air at all times, other five ready to launch immediately."

"Sir?"

"Didn't you understand me? At first twilight we start to launch our strike wave."

"Sir, without a report from the scout planes?" McCloskey asked.

Halsey pointed back to the plot board.

"They got a battleship out there that is hit, maybe crippled. By dawn it will have moved only forty, maybe fifty miles at most."

"That's still thousands of square miles of ocean to find him in, sir."

"That bastard will run due west to the Marshalls," and Halsey walked over to the plot board, stabbing at it with a stubby forefinger. "He'll be there, and the Japs will have fighters over her. If we can get in there by dawn, ahead of their own air support which they'll send in to cover the cripple, then maybe, just maybe we can track the incoming fighters sent to cover the battleship, do a reciprocal bearing, and find the carriers!

"We'll make full steam due north till it's time to turn into the wind. That puts us a hundred miles south of them. Our boys will be over her before dawn, ahead of the Japs, and we'll find those carriers and get in a first strike."

"And if they aren't there or get there ahead of us?" McCloskey asked cautiously. "Then what?"

"If that's the case," Halsey replied with a sarcastic smile, "on December ninth, I'll be beached, and someone with more sense will be in command."

He didn't add that chances were that finding the Japs first or not, they'd most likely be dead before nightfall. With less than forty strike planes, half of them antiquated Devastators, flying death traps, his boys would be lucky to take out one, at best two of their carriers, leaving at least one, maybe upward of three or four of their carriers to launch an overwhelming attack in reply.

Caution whispered to him. Turn about now, stay out to sea, try to link up with *Lexington* as he had first planned to do, until the third strike wave had hit Pearl and all communications via CinCPac had ceased.

But now? The Japs were most likely finished with Pearl. With a damaged battleship to sweat over, they'd head back to the Marshalls. Newton might be running south to try a hookup, or then again, north in an attempt to cut off the Japs if they were indeed north of the island. He wasn't going to gamble *Enterprise* on such guesses. But regardless, if he could get a solid first strike in now, *Lexington* could do a killing follow-up.

This was about pride now as well. The Navy, across a hundred and sixty-five years of her history, had never taken such a blow as it had this past day. If he turned tail and hid, sure there'd be defenders who would say he had made the wise, conservative choice. But in his mind the name of the *Enterprise* and his own would be forever besmirched as the ship and the admiral who turned and ran, rather than go in harm's way, perhaps even leaving *Lexington* to die alone.

Admiral Draemel had had the guts to do what he knew had to be done, knowing the odds. With such an example, could he do anything less?

He paused, looking at the plot board, drawing an arc from northwest of Oahu to its west.

"Four scout planes to go up, and that is it, the rest of VS-6 to stay with VB-6 as a strike force. Scout planes to first proceed toward where their battleship will be. Hell, if she is crippled, we'll find her soon enough, then fan out and try and pick up the bearings of any Japs coming in. Once they are well clear of our group, have a couple of the pilots radio into Pearl, see if they can raise someone and coordinate a search with whatever they have there. If need be they should draft some damn civilians and anything left that can still fly to search to the west and north of the island just in case the Japs do play cautious and pull back."

"What about the rest?" McCloskey asked, pointing out the other two hundred and seventy degrees of ocean surrounding them.

He emphatically shook his head.

"Searching that will take another dozen planes. We've only got thirty-seven strike aircraft, minus the search planes on board, and nineteen fighters. We conduct a full-out search and our remaining strike force is cut in half."

He shook his head. It was a damn tough balancing act. If *Enterprise* were at full strength he could afford to send out twenty planes as scouts and still have upward of sixty attack planes ready to go. Every additional plane sent out as a scout was one less bomb dropped on their carriers in what he assumed would be his one and only chance to take a swing at the bastards. It was all a gamble. He'd be leaving tens of thousands of square miles of ocean unsearched, and if he was wrong, if the entire Jap task force had circled with the battleships, they could very well be southwest or due west of him, and not northwest off Oahu as he now assumed and was betting his pile on.

Get there first over the battleship, then fan out and search, that would be his game now. It was the only card he felt he could play against whoever it was who was playing out his own on the other side.

"No. They have to be north of the island and are moving southwest, and will be somewhere in here by morning," and again he pointed to the plot board, the tens of thousands of square miles of ocean west of Oahu.

"All strike aircraft to be armed with torpedoes or armor piercing. Strict orders: They are to go for the carriers."

"That battleship if they can't find the carriers?" McCloskey asked.

"What can it do to us?" Halsey snapped. "If they've got a damaged battleship out there, that means at least one carrier or more close by providing air cover as they pull it out. That's what I want.

"Now get to work!"

He left McCloskey to work out the details,

climbed the ladder up to the next deck, and went into his cabin, closing the door. The blackout curtain over the porthole was drawn shut and he double-checked it before turning on the light over his bunk.

Without bothering even to take his shoes off he lay down and snapped the light off.

Damn all. If only I had a full complement of aircraft. I've got a strike force of less than forty bombers. Chances are half, two thirds would be lost, especially the aging albatrosses, the Devastators. The poor kids on those planes were doomed, and he wondered how many of them were sleeping soundly at this moment, and how many were lying awake in the dark as he now was, wondering what dawn would bring.

Five decks below the admiral, Lieutenant Dave Dellacroce stared into the darkness. The room was blacked out, the only sound the snoring of his roommate, Lieutenant Pat Gregory.

That son of a bitch can sleep through anything, he thought ruefully, almost angry at him for his composure, his eager excitement expressed over dinner, that in a few hours they'd be giving payback to the Japs.

Yet again Dave played back the story, constantly repeating in his head, of just how the hell he had got here. Born and raised in Lafayette, Indiana, he had, of course, gone to Purdue, planning on being an electrical engineer, and then one day he'd seen a poster on a bulletin board, a very seductive poster: he could learn to fly for free, at Uncle Sam's expense and wouldn't even have to join up.

It was a deal too good to pass up, and he, along with dozens of other guys, had shown up at the airport adjoining campus. Amelia Earhart had even been there to give them a little pep talk about the joys of flying. And she sure as hell was right.

He took the physical, passed, then signed a little bit of paperwork, kind of noticing the fine print that if he was accepted into the program, took the lessons, and got his license, in the event of a "national emergency" he was subject to mobilization. But what the hell, he would be with the Navy, an officer and a pilot. And besides, except for the squabbling in Spain and somewhere in Africa, and China, who could ever imagine a national emergency? And the skies called.

He soloed in only seven hours in a Piper J-3 Cub, a little beauty, damn near cracked her up five hours later when he buzzed his girlfriend's farmhouse and got a little too close. She was, in fact, a big reason he'd gotten into a plane to start with. He wanted to impress her since she was starting to talk about some guy going to Indiana University who wanted to be a doctor. In fact, she ditched him just a couple of weeks later anyhow.

Someone reported his nearly fatal buzz job, most likely her father, the old goat, and his instructor, a kindly old guy with a limp from the Great War, chewed him out a bit, then took him out and showed him how to do it safely, this time over another girl's house, Betty, who he was now engaged to. They'd even played dogfights, with his instructor blowing up a balloon, tossing it out the open window, and telling him to find it and hit it.

So he was just about to graduate from Purdue, class of 1940, had a hundred-plus hours flying with "the club" — and then the letter came in the mail, telling him there was indeed a "national emergency."

Actually it had all been rather exciting. The little sixty-five-horsepower Piper Cubs and Aeronca Chiefs were left behind for Stearmans, then up to hefty T-6s, and he had qualified in the spring for the Navy's F4F Wildcat. In June he had made his first carrier landing — damn, that was a sweat-soaked moment — and in November been assigned to *Enterprise,* just barely catching up with her before she sailed last week.

It had postponed yet again getting married to Betty. Though he missed her, longed for her, the thrill of being on the *Enterprise* was some compensation, and after this posting, there would be plenty of time.

Yesterday had changed all that in a matter of seconds. The game of just fooling around with life was over; now it was real. The other guys had spent the day cursing the Japs, and then clamoring for action, and word was in a few hours they were going to get some.

He had boasted along with the rest; after all, that's what carrier fighter pilots were supposed to do. But now? In the dark, he just stared at the ceiling, feeling the vibration of the ship as it ran through the night, course changing every fifteen minutes, some hammering a couple decks above, crews doing final work on a plane most likely, sound of a hoist nearby, bringing up bombs from the magazines buried deep below the waterline.

He wished now he had married Betty. Though he'd never admit it to any of the guys, when it came to women he had never gotten all that far, in fact not far at all. Betty was a devout Methodist and drew clear lines and kept to them. If I get out of this alive, I'm getting her over to Oahu any way I can and marry her the same day, he thought. But thinking about that was nearly as maddening as thinking about what was coming in a few short hours, and alternating back and forth between the two, he did not sleep a wink . . . not knowing that except for a very lucky few, all were lying awake, captivated by the fear or anticipation of what was to come.

Akagi
105 miles west-northwest of Oahu
02:45 hrs local time

It had been a tough operation, one rehearsed dozens of times, but never until now actually attempted under combat conditions: a nighttime refueling.

The last of the tankers had finally cast off from abeam of *Akagi.*

They had not been able to top off. Only two of the four carriers of his group were running with full loads of fuel; *Akagi* was seven hundred tons of oil short, *Kaga* nearly eight hundred tons, but it should be enough for one full day of fast combat operations with sufficient oil left to take them into the Marshalls, where the reserve civilian tankers were waiting.

That was not his concern at the moment, however. Yamamoto still was quietly seething over Nagita and the damage to *Hiei,* how he had allowed a night attack from seaward to strike his ship and cripple it. Rather than placing his destroyers landward, they should have been covering out to sea, anticipating that some of the American ships had managed to slip out of Pearl and past the submarines, which had failed so abysmally in keeping the port bottled up.

It was an aspect of the plan made by Nagumo that he had allowed to stay in place, the ridiculous waste of suicide midget subs, tying up the heavier fleet subs that had to carry them into position. Nagumo had allowed the rest of the subs to be scattered about, rather than concentrating all near the entryway into Oahu, keeping perhaps one or two as pickets farther out for rescue of downed pilots.

Every last fleet sub available should have been positioned off the main channel. They had, as an entire group, proven worse than useless so far. Repeated attempts to raise them had been futile; they were laying low and thus out of radio contact for a change in orders.

He would address that later. He had to

focus on the moment, knowing that exhaustion was taking hold. He had been up more than twenty-four hours now and needed to get at least a few hours' rest.

Yamamoto looked at the latest telegraph reports from *Hiei:* only able to use two of its four propeller shafts due to the explosion astern, which had also bent the rudder; barely able to make five knots, meaning it would be less than twenty nautical miles west of Oahu at dawn. If the Americans did indeed have any land-based aircraft left, that would be their target at first light.

Let them come, though he doubted there would be more than a handful left after the punishment delivered to their bases.

What he hoped for now, though he would never dare to say it even to Genda or any of his closest advisers, was that the crippled *Hiei* would indeed act as a lure — a lure for American carrier-based planes.

And the scout planes and fighters of *Hiryu* and *Soryu* would be waiting, circling high above, observing the inbound track of the enemy attackers and then sweeping out on a reciprocal bearing.

Of course he did not want to lose *Hiei,* but her damage might be heaven-sent to guide him in to his opponent's fleet. A trade of a battleship for their three elusive carriers would be worth it, even if many back in Tokyo would howl over the loss.

It was nearly three local time. Refueling done, his own task force would pick up speed to twenty knots, moving to be a hundred fifty nautical miles west of *Hiei* come dawn, deck loaded with every plane available for a massive strike while *Soryu* and *Hiryu,* a hundred miles farther south, would cover attacks from that direction. His main task force would cast their net westward, the second force to the south, and either they would find the Americans, or the Americans themselves would reveal their position when they went for *Hiei.*

He yawned, knowing he needed to sleep, even if only for an hour. Turning off the light, he lay down on top of his bunk, not bothering to take off his shoes.

Hiei
15 miles west-southwest of Oahu
04:45 hrs local time

Seething with frustration, Captain Nagita turned away from his anxious staff on the bridge, subduing a curse.

They were making little more than six knots. Leaving the enclosed bridge, he paced the port-side railing and looked aft. The list had been corrected by counterflooding, and from the port railing, pumps were shooting out a steady cascade of oily water, which was, of course, leaving a shimmering wake that stretched twenty miles astern, all the way back to where they had been hit nearly three hours ago. The waning moon to the southwest cast a wavery reflection off the oil slick.

The damaged bunker had been sealed off, but was now filled with seawater. They'd have to go all the way back to Yokohama and into dry dock to have the twenty-foot-wide hole blown into their side repaired. It would take weeks to get there — under tow, because the real damage to *Hiei* had not been the blow amidships. Two divers had gone over to examine the hit far astern, one losing his life when his safety line had tangled and then parted under the strain of trying to keep him in position, the exhausted surviving diver bobbing back up minutes later, reporting that it looked like the port-side propeller had a blade blown off, the others were bent, inboard portside the shaft was also bent, and the rudder was definitely twisted, thrown completely out of alignment. Full power to the starboard engine barely compensated for what would be a perpetual turn if not for the counteracting pull of the destroyers, which were laboring at full steam, thus eating up dozens of tons of yet more precious fuel, as they angled far to port, hauling a towline secured to the bow of the damaged battleship.

He knew what would happen come dawn. The Americans would be on them like carrion flies. He had considered ordering *Kirishima* to stay alongside, her antiaircraft batteries to lend fire support, but decided against it. To lose their sister ship while trying to save *Hiei* would be a crime unforgivable in the eyes of the Emperor. He had ordered her to make full steam to the rendezvous with their two escorting carriers, *Soryu* and *Hiryu,* which were lingering a hundred miles to their southwest, ready to provide protection for the crippled battleship.

He could only hope that somehow Yamamoto's mosquitoes, as he called them, flying off those two carriers, could somehow keep the American planes at bay until they were safely out of range.

And he knew that in less that thirty-five minutes, nautical twilight would begin to brighten the eastern horizon behind them, and in an hour and a half they would stand out clear, unless the gods, by some divine favor, sent a fog or a storm to conceal them, but in answer to that, the stars overhead twinkled uncaringly through a high scattering of tropical clouds that covered only half the sky.

Enterprise
135 miles south-southwest of Oahu
December 8, 1941
05:20 hrs local time

"Launch the scout planes," Halsey ordered quietly. He was leaning against the railing, sipping his third cup of coffee since awakening a half hour ago.

Enterprise turned from her race to the north, into the northeast trade winds. Off the starboard quarter the horizon was beginning to show the faint deep purple glow of a tropical dawn, while to the west the moon was starting to arc back down toward the horizon.

The boys had minimal experience with night launches at sea, with the flight path illuminated only by dull red lights set to either side of the flight line. Red-colored flashlights were used by crews guiding planes into position.

The first of the four scout bombers, with a thousand-pound armor-piercing bomb strapped beneath it, was revved to full power, bursts of flame snapping from its exhaust pipes as the heavy fourteen-cylinder radial engine was pushed to maximum power. The launch chief stood to one side, waving a red-hooded flashlight over his head in tighter and tighter circles.

The aft elevator crew was hard at work, bringing up every available plane. First came the nine Grumman Wildcats that would provide escort. They needed the least run-out space on the carrier deck, and once the four scout planes were cleared, they would be spotted just forward of amidships. Behind them would come the fifteen Dauntless dive bombers, each burdened with a single half-ton armor-piercing bomb, and then behind them the eighteen Devastator torpedo bombers, each carrying a one-ton torpedo.

It was tough work at night. His crew had trained to some extent at night ops, but never for the preparing of a full launch in the predawn twilight. As fast as he trained a crew, men were reassigned to other ships as the Navy struggled to meet its explosive growth demands, the thinking being to leaven crews with men of experience. And night launches were dangerous. Already one man was dead, a nineteen-year-old who backed into the whirling prop of a Devastator, decapitating him, and though Halsey hated to put the statistic so grimly, the accident had taken that plane out of the lineup until its props could be replaced, slowing down the launch prep.

The launch chief motioned with his flashlight for the boys securing the chocks to the first Dauntless to pull clear, and then a few seconds later dropped down low, pointing his flashlight forward.

The pilot released his brakes, and the heavily laden plane, fuel tanks topped off, a half ton of explosives under its belly, began to roll forward into the wind, thirty-three knots of it delivered from the whirling turbines below deck, driving the thirty-thousand-ton carrier forward at flank speed, ten knots more from the early morning trade winds, coming straight down the length of deck as *Enterprise* ran on a heading of 60 degrees.

With stick full forward, the tail of the Dauntless rose up after but a hundred feet of rollout, the pilot giving her nearly full right rudder to counteract the torque of the engine. It swerved slightly. Halsey held his breath. If the kid flying the plane should lose his orientation and skid over the side, it could trigger a conflagration that would stop the entire launch and ignite a flare of light that any Jap spotter or sub could see from twenty miles away, or worse yet the bomb slung beneath would detonate, taking *Enterprise* out of this action on the second day of the war.

The young pilot corrected, started to ease back on his stick, a little less rudder as airspeed built up, wind slamming against the vertical stabilizer, which was now able to provide more bite and counterforce to the torque. He lifted off a good seventy-five feet short of the bow.

Even before his roll-out was finished, the second scout plane started forward. Thirty seconds later the third was up, and then the fourth.

Halsey was able to relax for a moment, while down on the deck a mad scramble now ensued as the deck crews for each of the forty-two planes preparing for launch spotted them into position, engines roaring. In the darkness another man died, though none of his comrades knew of his fate until a half hour later, when someone noticed that the red-headed kid, nicknamed Red of course, seaman second class and a new transfer onto the *Enterprise* only three weeks before, was missing. By that time he was already dead, blown off the aft end of the deck by the prop wash of a Devastator as it revved up to full power for a magneto check. Unable to swim, and without a life

jacket, his fate had been mercifully swift, unlike the fate so many of his comrades would face this day.

Akagi
165 miles west-northwest of Oahu
05:25 hrs local time

Bleary-eyed, Fuchida could not keep away, even though he had been specifically ordered by Yamamoto himself to stand down from operations this day. He had slipped out onto the main deck, out of sight of his admiral, to watch as the first of the scout planes was launched.

From each of the four carriers in the task

group, five planes were going aloft, spreading outward like fingers or the tentacles of a squid, in an arc from north around to southwest, each plane to run out two hundred fifty miles, turn ninety degrees to port for fifteen minutes, then do a reverse track back in, the process to continue throughout the day until the enemy carriers had been spotted.

A visit to the pilot ready room, though, had revealed to him what had transpired while he had sweated through his nightmares, haunted by his friend Matsuo, drenched in flames, slumped in front of him as the rescue crew had dragged him screaming and protesting out of the wrecked Kate.

He finally heard that *Hiei* was crippled, slowly heading away from Oahu. *Soryu* and *Hiryu,* detached and with but two escorting destroyers, soon to be joined by the battleship *Kirishima,* were deployed to the southwest of Oahu, ready to provide air cover for the cripple, while the rest of the task force was here, northwest of Oahu, searching westward for the Americans.

It was a risky plan. If *Hiei* had not been crippled, the entire task force was to have rejoined by midday, all six carriers in mutual support of each other. As it was now, their planes could overlap each other above *Hiei*, but if the three missing American carriers were together, and struck either group, the risk could be grave. It all depended upon who found whom first.

The five scout planes took off, banking out to the north to northwest, disappearing into the night, while the aft elevator team was already at work, bringing up the dozen Zeroes that would provide combat air patrol over the fleet. Down on the hangar deck, the Kates and Vals that could still fly after yesterday's hard fighting were even now loading up with ordnance for when the Americans were found.

Inwardly he prayed they were not found today. Yamamoto's orders had been strict. The hero of the third strike on Pearl Harbor was to rest today. So, like his friend Genda, he would be stuck on the deck, watching as others flew off to glory.

It would be, he feared, a long, frustrating day ahead.

Pearl Harbor
05:55 hrs local time

"This is X-ray Delta. This is X-ray Delta. Hickam or Ford, do you read?"

James Watson came over to stand behind the civilian ham radio operator who carefully adjusted the dial, bringing the signal in more clearly on the small speaker.

"That's a carrier scout plane frequency," a petty officer announced. "It's gotta be *Enterprise.*"

The airwave they were on crackled and hissed, but there was no response. Watson looked over at Collingwood, the senior officer in the room.

"Hickam must have some radio on line by now," Collingwood whispered. "They can't be completely shut down."

"A lot of incoming was impacting around there," a young naval ensign, the left side of his face bandaged from a burn, replied, slurring his words a bit.

"This is X-ray Delta. This is X-ray Delta . . . Hickam or Ford, do you read?"

The voice was more insistent now, but still no response.

More eyes were turning to Collingwood.

"We might be the only radio station up and running," James whispered to him.

"What about a radio on any of our planes?" someone asked.

"What planes?" the ensign replied coldly. "I was over at Hickam just before the battleships hit us. They most likely blew what was left to hell."

"This is X-ray Delta. This is X-ray Delta . . ." A pause. "Damn it, does anyone read me over there?"

"Give me the mike," Collingwood said. The civilian operator motioned for him to sit down by his side and slid it over.

"X-ray Delta." Collingwood paused. "This is Pearl. Come in."

A pause.

"This is X-ray Delta, stay off the air, Pearl, I'm raising Hickam or Ford."

Collingwood sighed. What did he dare to say in the clear?

"This is all you got, X-ray Delta. Repeat, this is all you got."

"How the hell do I know you're not a Jap? Give proper code identification."

"Oh for Christ's sake," Collingwood muttered, mike still switched on.

James said nothing. Is this what they've reduced us to, he wondered? Were Hickam, Ford Island, Wheeler, Kaneohe, Ewa, and all the naval and army airbases off line now? If so, just how in hell do we coordinate any kind of response?

James leaned over Collingwood's shoulder and with his one hand pressed the transmit.

"X-ray Delta, this is Pearl. Name your favorite club and I'll tell you where it is."

He felt damn foolish but could think of no alternative.

"Screw you, you gotta be kidding."

"I'm not kidding, X-ray Delta."

Again a pause.

"Della's."

James stood back up and looked around the room, which was now illuminated by the early light of dawn, blackout curtains drawn back from the shattered window frames.

"All right, do any of you know where the hell that is? If not, we're screwed trying to coordinate with *Enterprise.*"

"Yeah, Della's," a petty officer growled, unlit cigar clenched between his teeth.

He went up to Collingwood's side and pressed the transmit key.

"Yeah, kid, it's on Wahela Street and supposedly off limits to all military personnel. You'll get a dose for sure if you go in there. How the hell do you know about it?"

Another pause.

"OK, Pearl, this is X-ray Delta inbound. What trade do you have for me?" and James felt he could detect a slight chuckle in the reply.

What any of them knew was sketchy. All command structure had broken down in this mad night of confusion. Rumors were still floating that the Japs were landing at Kaneohe.

There was a moment of silence from the

dozens pressed into the radio repair shack.

"Exactly what do we know?" Collingwood finally asked, looking around. "I don't want rumors, I want hard facts."

"That Jap battleship was definitely hit," the ensign replied. "We know that, and it was retiring westward."

"We got the shit kicked out of us," the petty officer snapped bitterly. "That's about it as far as any of us know."

Collingwood nodded to the petty officer. "You got his trust, tell him."

The petty officer pressed down on the transmit button.

"Listen, kid. We got hit hard by two Jap battleships during the night. We know one of them got clobbered in return and is limping off to the west of the island. You should be able to spot him. That's all I can tell you."

"Any fix on their flattops?"

The petty officer looked over at Collingwood and James.

Sure, they had pretty well figured the strike had come from the north, though no one, as far as he knew, had gotten that information out. In twelve hours, steaming at twenty knots, they could be anywhere inside a circle nearly five hundred nautical miles across, over two hundred thousand square miles of ocean to choose from.

Both shook their heads. If X-ray Delta was indeed flying from the *Enterprise,* Halsey's guess as to where to search was more likely a damn sight better than anything they could provide. It was frustrating beyond belief. There still must be a few dozen planes capable of flying this morning, and dozens of civilian planes tucked into the small private strips around the island. Someone had wandered in reporting that several of the surviving B-17s, now up at Wheeler, were getting set to try and hit the battleship.

"Repeat, any fix on their flattops?"

The petty officer pressed down on the send button.

"You got the same coordinates we do," the petty officer replied.

Another pause.

"Good reply," Collingwood whispered. "The Japs have got to be listening," and as if in response, a shrieking warble suddenly overrode the frequency. The Japs had listened long enough and were now attempting to jam.

"Right, Pearl." The reply was hard to pick up over the jamming, but still came through, which meant the search plane must be fairly close.

"Will relay. Over."

Collingwood sighed, leaned back in his chair.

"Sir, a suggestion."

It was the civilian operator, and James realized he didn't even know the man's name.

"It looks like nearly all communications are up the creek without a paddle. I own a radio repair shop in town and I'm president of the ham radio club which meets there. Get me some official-looking paperwork and a truck. I'll round some guys up with their radios, clean out the gear in my shop, and maybe we can get something running. I'm willing to bet everything has pretty well been knocked to hell if that kid can't raise anyone but us."

James said nothing. The man who was talking was obviously Japanese.

Collingwood looked up at James as if reading his mind. If this guy tried to get on any base unescorted now, he'd most likely be shot. How the hell he had even managed to get here was a mystery. He had just pulled in and offloaded his rig out of the back of a small Model A truck marked *Joe's Radio Repair, Free Delivery,* and toted in the gear they were now using.

The truck, riddled from a nearby hit, was sitting outside the door, all four tires flat, a puddle of rusty water underneath from the blown-out radiator.

"Hey, Dianne," James asked. "Can you dig me up some CinCPac stationery?"

The exhausted woman was half asleep under one of the repair tables. She looked out at him with bleary eyes.

"You gotta be kidding sir. The building is gone." She sighed.

"There must be paper strewn from one end of the base to the other," James replied.

"Find some," Collingwood ordered. "Commander Watson's on to something. Forge a signature, any signature, otherwise this guy and his friends won't get anywhere. Round up some guards for them, preferably some marines, to provide escort, and those of you standing around here doing nothing, go with our friend here. I want radios up and running at every base on this island by midmorning. We know *Enterprise* is out there, *Lexington* too. We've got to get communications running again. Now move."

James, glad for any kind of order, something to do, looked around the room, made eye contact with half a dozen radio techs, and motioned for them to follow. Joe, the cigar-chomping petty officer, and Dianne fell in with the group.

Akagi
06:00 hrs local time

Admiral Yamamoto looked at the transcript handed to him, the conversation monitored between an American scout plane and a radio on Pearl.

It spoke volumes to him. They had no idea where he was, otherwise there would have been some indication; the mere fact that the question was asked, rather than coordinates communicated, revealed that. Also, it meant that whatever damage the air strikes had rendered, the battleships had done their job well. All communications, and therefore coordination between land and their ships at sea, were either severed or tenuous at best.

And it told him, as well, that at least one of their carriers must be nearby.

The game was on.

Scout plane X-ray Delta
Twenty miles south of Oahu
06:00 hrs

"This is X-ray Delta. Got 'em! Oil slick ten miles off the coast south of the island, turning to heading 270 to follow!"

Lieutenant Nathan King gave a slight nudge of his stick to port, his Dauntless slipped into a ten-degree bank, and less than a minute later he saw it! Battleship, it had to be their crippled battleship, six, maybe eight miles ahead, oil slick leading straight to it. The ship appeared to be under tow.

God damn, it was a sitting duck!

"This is X-ray Delta! Jap battleship, estimated twenty miles southwest Oahu. Can't miss her, it's bleeding oil like crazy. Am closing."

"Sir, we going for it?"

King picked up his intercom mike, connected to his tail gunner.

"You got any better ideas? It's begging to be hit! We unload on her then circle till the strike group comes up."

"Sir, what about continuing to look for their flattops?"

King hesitated. The darn kid was right. The admiral had made it a point: They were out here for the carriers, the battleship could wait. But damn it, the flattops were most likely hundreds of miles off, in someone else's sector. The Japs would be insane to have them playing nursemaid to a crippled ship this close in to shore.

He was closing at two and a half miles a minute at ten thousand feet. Punch a bomb into this bastard, maybe finish her, and then just spot their planes coming in and relay the reciprocal bearing back to *Enterprise.* He'd lead the way for the strike against the carriers and have a battleship to his credit as well. Hell, that would make the admiral happy and a damn hero as well, with the first big kill of the war.

Half a dozen black puffs ignited in the air, far short, a mile ahead of him, first ranging shots of their heavy antiaircraft. He could even see their five-inchers winking.

Pull away, wait for the rest of the strike wave?

Hell, they might be getting vectored even now onto the carriers in another section.

"We're taking her," King announced, sliding his canopy shut, pulling down his goggles. Feeding in full throttle he started to climb, wanting to get up to fifteen thousand feet before rolling into a dive. It'd throw their gunners off as well.

"We got Japs! Four of them coming down. Break right! Break right!"

King pushed his stick hard over to starboard even as he nosed up. Looking back over his shoulder he saw them coming out of the southwest, the direction he was supposed to turn and search along, before finally heading back to *Enterprise.* How the hell did they get here ahead of us? We were told we'd be on it first!

Damn, were their carriers off that way?

He didn't even have time to make a call. Within a few seconds he was flying full out, skidding with opposite rudder and stick, nearly going into a stall, the low speed causing the first two Japanese fighters to overshoot and scream past while gunner's mate Gary Olson, in the aft seat, fired back with the single, pitiful .30 machine gun, the only protection the Dauntless had. What kind of fighters were these? They were not the old Jap 96 models they had been briefed on. What the hell are they?

"I'm jumped by four Jap fighters," he managed to get out, then dropped the mike.

There was no time to line up in a classic dive. He pushed over, heading in at a forty-five-degree bank for the *Hiei.* The enemy fighters circled back around for the kill.

Hiei
06:02 hrs

It was over before it had even really started. The lone American plane had barely got into range of his five-inch gunners when it detonated into flame, rolled over, and went down.

There was cheering on the bridge, but Captain Nagita said nothing.

Two things had been revealed. One was

patently obvious. The Americans knew where he was; they had monitored the scout plane report. It was no surprise; the oil slick from their bleeding wound would lead them in to him all day until finally someone broke through.

But it had revealed as well to the Americans that he was being protected by carrier planes and at least one of their carriers was in range.

The battle was now on.

Chapter Four

Enterprise
130 miles south of Oahu
December 8, 1941
06:03 hrs local time

"X-ray Delta, this is Phoenix. X-ray Delta, this is Phoenix, come in."

"He's gone," Halsey said quietly, the petty officer operating the radio looking back at his admiral and nodding in agreement. McCloskey, standing to one side, gave a nod of agreement as well.

They had broken radio silence long enough. He didn't want to risk another minute on the air and perhaps give the Japs a better chance at getting a bearing on him. With the appearance of his scout planes, they now knew he was out here. That was all he wanted to give away, and calling a plane that was most likely down was far too dangerous.

From outside he could hear the roar of

the last of his planes launching, the slow, lumbering Devastators. The fighter and dive bomber squadrons were now aloft. Groups formed up, circling at five thousand feet while their slower comrades took wing.

He looked back to his other radio operators. One radio was assigned to each of the four search planes. Operators shook their heads, protocol accepting that at such a crucial moment, the men didn't need to take their eyes off their instruments or speak.

He looked back to the plot board. If search plane X-ray Delta was off the chart — and even as he contemplated that, a seaman with a grease pencil put a question mark next to the symbol of the plane at its last reported position — then one whole leg of a return sweep would be lost.

His strike force, now airborne, was heading almost due north, toward the reported position of the crippled Jap battleship, his assumption being that by the time they reached it, the search would reveal their flattops, one of which definitely had to be shadowing the enemy cripple. The appearance of the enemy planes confirmed that . . . but where the hell were they?

And just as frustrating, he had listened in to the conversation between X-ray Delta and Pearl. My God, if all radio communications were down at every airbase on the island, how did they coordinate? He had hoped that by now someone over there would be doing their job right, and have the Jap carriers pinpointed to vector them in.

It was all a gamble now. Suppose the strike force reaches the battleship but then they can't find the carriers?

He turned to stare at the plot board. The two seamen manning the translucent Plexiglas display were talking softly into their mikes, using grease pens to trace the northern track of the forty-two planes. One of them reached up and erased the question mark next to X-ray Delta and crossed off thc symbol for thc planc. Λ fcw inchcs away, the symbol for the Japanese battleship stood out clear.

He looked at the clock. 06:05. It'd be 11:35 Washington time. One of the radio operators, monitoring a commercial station out of San Francisco, had announced earlier that the President would address the nation at noon East Coast time. Just about the time the strike force reached the enemy battleship. He stood silent, watching . . . waiting.

The White House
Washington, D.C.
December 8, 1941
11:30 hrs local time

The black limousine flanked by motorcycle police moved up Pennsylvania Avenue in a stately procession.

Americans lined the avenue watching their President as he rode to the Capitol for a historic joint session address to the Congress. They knew it would be broadcast on radio, but they were here in Washington and they wanted to share in this moment of history with their own eyes.

The crowds were quiet, solemn, respectful.

They were enraged that their country had been attacked.

They were infuriated that someone would cheat and launch an attack without warning.

They were shocked by the ferocity and rumors of the casualties and the damage.

They were not frightened.

They were deeply determined.

They were Americans — even if they had only been here a few years, they identified themselves as Americans. No matter where their relatives came from, they thought of themselves as Americans. The bad guys had

had their shot. Now it would be our turn.

They watched the President's car with deep respect.

He had carried them through the Great Depression and given them hope.

He had always been strong and optimistic and cheerful.

He was their leader and the leader of their nation.

They wished him well, and they were going to listen to him carefully.

Many of them prayed as he rode past. They wanted him and their country to be strong and courageous and determined and victorious.

FDR felt the warmth and the support that was evident in block after block of silent people watching his car. Occasionally someone would wave, but mostly they stood silently and prayerfully.

What a remarkable difference from inaugural parades, he thought to himself.

Inaugurations were happy political times, and the winners had come to town to celebrate. They were a time to smile and wave and express happiness at political victory.

This was totally different. He sensed that he was now going up to Capitol Hill not as a political leader but as the war leader of an aroused nation. Today was a day for history and not for politics.

He wanted to achieve three things in this address to the joint session.

First, he wanted to communicate to the American people the sense of rage they already felt and to bind them to a deep dedication to win no matter what the cost.

Second, he wanted to signal Prime Minister Churchill and all our allies that America was prepared to fight. This speech had to overcome any doubts or uncertainties created by the defeat at Pearl Harbor and the ongoing fight around Hawaii.

FDR knew it was important to turn defeat into opportunity, and confusion into the certainty of victory. This speech was an important building block toward that moment of shifting from defense to offense.

Third, he wanted to send a signal to Tokyo and also to Berlin: America is now in the war, and America is going to win. He wanted to shake their sense of certainty and begin to get them worrying about the full might and power of the American people.

Now it was up to him to deliver a speech that would resonate and echo around the world, so that everyone understood . . . and everyone would remember.

It was funny how the first job of a war

commander was words, and how those words then shaped and directed the war.

Even in a wheelchair I can still direct the words so others will know why they fight and what they must fight for. Now let's talk to the world, he thought as the car pulled up to the Capitol.

Hiei
06:15 hrs local time
He glanced at the handwritten transcript of the radio report of one of the Zeroes, now circling in a screen around his ship. A report that numerous American planes were reported from the southeast.

They were at full battle stations. There was nothing more he could do. The destroyers had cast off their towlines and sped up. No sense in having them as a target as well. Without the counteracting force of the destroyers' laboring engines, they were now in a wide banking turn to the north, running at twelve knots, the imbalance of the damaged rudder causing an unsettling vibration to run through the entire ship.

Akagi
06:16 hrs local time
"Are they certain?" Yamamoto asked, look-

ing over at his chief communications officer.

"Yes, sir. The outer ring of the air patrol over *Hiei* is reporting an American strike wave approaching from the southeast. It will be over *Hiei* in another fifteen minutes."

He took it in. "How many planes?"

"The Zero reported at least twenty."

Damn, only twenty. It could be a lead element of a bigger attack, or even one that was uncoordinated and had not grouped correctly, or it could be a strike from but one carrier. He had hoped that the three enemy carriers just might be grouped together, but there was no guarantee that such was indeed the case. They would be grouped together in the Japanese Navy, but the Americans seemed to do things differently.

He did not want to break radio silence with any more long-distance messages to *Soryu* and *Hiryu.* He could only hope that at this moment they were monitoring their own planes providing cover for *Hiei,* and would now surmise where the enemy had come from.

Twenty miles southeast of Hiei
06:20 hrs local time

Dave Dellacroce, sweat beading his forehead in spite of the cold at fifteen thousand feet, could see them. Two Japanese planes, painted white, circling above them, five miles or so off. Dawn was breaking up here, the glow of sunlight reflecting off their canopies. They had undoubtedly seen him as well, but neither side was closing to engage.

He banked slightly, following as starboard wingman in a section of three, and spared a quick glance back over his shoulder.

Where the hell were the Dauntlesses and Devastators? They had to go in together. But go in on what? The Jap fighters were already over the battleship; the hope of getting there first and then getting a vector on where they approached from was blown. And none of the other search planes had reported a damn thing other than empty sea.

His section leader, as ordered, was going into a three-hundred-sixty-degree circle, the Wildcats looking for the bombers that were supposed to be right behind them, but had somehow disappeared in the scattering of clouds over the last fifteen minutes.

He could see four Jap planes.

His radio crackled. It was the squadron leader.

"Anyone see the rest of our boys?"

No one replied.

Damn!

"OK. Keep your formations tight. Stick to me like glue. We're going in!"

What?

"Hey, ain't we supposed to wait?" someone called back.

"They're above us and building up. We're dead meat if we wait down here. Let's clear the way. The bomber boys must be right behind us."

A momentary pause. No one replied, and Dave as the most junior of pilots in the squadron knew he'd be nuts to say anything.

"We either fight now or get bounced from above. There's only four of 'em, target practice for us. Keep your formations tight and stay with me!"

Dave throttled up with the other Wildcats. Noses pointed high to gain precious altitude, fuel mixture nudged up, carb heat check for a few seconds and then shut off, trigger guard flipped back.

In spite of his fear, for the next few seconds he could feel the exhilarating surge of it. It was a helluva long way from cruising around a Midwest airfield in a sixty-five-horsepower trainer. At full throttle the twelve-hundred-horse Wildcat accelerated, leaping heavenward, vibrating, sending a corkscrew thrill down his spine.

They had been told by Intelligence that the Japs were still flying their old '96 models off of carriers, planes that would supposedly be dead meat against a Wildcat. But these fighters looked sleeker. Retractable landing gear; they weren't '96s.

What the hell were they? The new Zeroes that there had been rumors about? But they were supposedly not assigned to carriers yet. There wasn't time to think about it now. The four Jap planes were breaking into two sections of two, turning in to meet him.

He spared a quick glance down. A scattering of morning tropical clouds was drifting across the ocean. Through a hole in one he could see what appeared to be the oil slick from their battleship. Don't think about it now.

Where the hell were the bombers? He looked back over his shoulders to both sides. The Devastators must be below the cloud cover. The Dauntlesses, not in sight.

Range was closing fast, damn fast. Whatever they were, these Jap planes had power.

The first pass through was a head-on which for a brief instant terrified him, the Jap fighter opening up while boring straight in, the two of them playing chicken with each other. He thought he clipped off part of a wingtip, felt the shudder of a hit as well, both banking hard right in the final split second before a head-on impact.

He pulled back hard, stick in his gut, rudder full right, banking turn almost ninety degrees, plane ready to shudder into an accelerated stall, the pressure of the four-G turn narrowing his vision.

He looked straight up and back. Where the hell were the other guys of his section?

"Damn it, Dave, stick with me!" It had to be Gregory shouting.

As he came through a hundred eighty degrees of turn he saw a fiery trail spiraling downward. Was it Gregory? Where was the Jap?

For all in his squadron this was their first fight. Sure, they had practiced before against Army pilots in P-36s and 40s, but not now, not for real, and already, one — no, two — planes were flaming torches spinning down, both of them Wildcats.

All formations had broken up, no coordination with wingmen. He caught a glimpse of a Wildcat below him about a thousand feet or so, a white Zero cutting in behind him, twin contrails appearing off its wingtips, triggered by the wing vortexes in the warm humid tropical air.

He did a half roll coming out of his turn, pulled the stick back, dropping inverted and from three hundred yards astern of his unsuspecting target, which was closing in on the Wildcat it was pursuing.

Dave's four .30-caliber Browning machine guns opened up, forty rounds a second slashing out, calibrated to converge into a target at two hundred fifty yards, the convergence crisscrossing just ahead of his target, beginning to spread. Sixteen rounds slashed across the forward cowling of the Zero, severing an oil line, two more cutting into the fuel line, a red-hot tracer sparking the spray of gas into a flash of fire. A second later the Zero was trailing smoke, snap rolling to avoid his fire. He shot past the enemy plane, losing sight of him.

It had yet to even register whether he had done anything or not.

My God, it is all so fast. Damn fast. No time for bullshit heroics or witty comments back and forth like in the movies, where the enemy were all so clearly visible, and slow, and just sitting ducks. He lost sight of his target.

"Number seven! On your tail!"

It took a second to register: I'm number seven!

He caught a glimpse of tracers snapping over the top of his canopy, and he was still in a forty-five-degree dive, inverted.

Pull stick, and fly into it. Roll, he's got my wing. He pushed stick forward, instantly pulling two negative G's. Damn, I always puke with negative G's.

He was too frightened to vomit now. The tracers were dropping away. He pulled a sharp half roll, reversed stick, instantly back to two positive G's, looked aft. The Zero was gone. Another smoking trail of fire visible for a second, this one a white plane in flames, going down. My kill?

"He's still on you, seven!"

He strained to look aft. Caught a glimpse of the Zero following him, tightening his turn inside of him. Damn, they can outturn us! Everyone said our planes outturned theirs! Someone gave us the wrong info!

Reverse roll, he's got me. Try to outturn, he's got me. They were still at twelve thousand feet.

He slammed his stick forward, stomach feeling like it was up in his throat, and he began to vomit even as he nosed over into a power dive nearly straight down at eighty degrees.

Outrun him, go for a cloud below.

Damn! I'm supposed to be part of the squadron. Where the hell are they?

He fumbled for his mike.

"Diving! Can't outturn these bastards!"

His mission was to provide air cover and support for the attacking bombers. That was gone now. He was flying to save his life, tracers winking past him first to port, then starboard, as the Zero tried to line up on him, the heavier Wildcat beginning to pull away . . . and then they were into the clouds.

He had no idea what the bottom ceiling was as his plane shuddered slightly from the change in air density of the cloud and the turbulence within it.

Tropical, morning. Most likely less than a thousand-foot base above the ocean. He was redlining at over 320 miles per hour and down to three thousand.

He pulled back hard, G load building up again, four, then five, world going darker, blurry, vision narrowing, orientation lost inside the gray-shrouded world.

Blinding flash of sunlight — he was out of the cloud, blue ocean below, a moment of panic again: I'm going in — and then he leveled out, five hundred feet above the gently rolling Pacific.

And then a buffet, a flash of fire and smoke. He had come out of the cloud with a Jap battleship barely a mile off his starboard wing. Their gunners were opening up.

He pulled into a chandelle, climbing and

turning, caught a glimpse of another Wildcat popping out of the cloud, this one, amazingly, actually on the tail of a Zero, stitching it. Flaming wreckage tumbling out of the cloud behind the dueling planes; impossible to tell if was a Jap or one of his.

He felt like a complete and total idiot, for a few seconds imagining standing before McCloskey or even Halsey himself — if I get out of this alive, he thought — explaining not only why he had failed to escort the bombers but had gotten separated from his squadron as well.

The bombers? Where the hell were they? Where were the Jap flattops?

Flashes of tracers again. He looked aft. The bastard had chased him all the way down, popped out of the cloud behind him and was lining up for a kill, flying through his own antiaircraft fire from the battleship.

Dave pulled back on his stick, rolling out of the banking turn, and popped back up into the cloud . . . and for the moment out of the fight.

Eight miles south of Hiei
06:28 hrs local time

Lieutenant Commander Dan Struble, leading the combined squadron of fifteen Dauntless dive bombers, caught glimpses of the air battle raging eight miles or more off his starboard wing, listening in on the same frequency as the fighters, hearing the near panic, thin trails of smoke streaking down.

Now what?

He could see the Jap battleship. We can be over it in less than three minutes. Hold back? Where the hell were the flattops?

"This is B-17 Gloria Ann, anyone out there read me?"

Jesus Christ, what the hell was a 17 doing out here, he wondered.

He keyed his mike.

"Go ahead, Gloria Ann, this is Phoenix Three."

"Are you bombers?"

He hesitated. It could be a Jap.

"Can't say, Gloria Ann," he replied finally.

"Well damn it, whoever you are, there's three of us and we're taking out that Jap battleship. If you're nearby I'd appreciate some help. I'm coming in from Wheeler."

Do I support or not? They had flown little more than a hundred ten miles. Plenty of fuel left for an hour of searching before having to head back. But search where? The old man said he wanted their flattops. Well damn it, no one was telling him where they were, and his fighter escort was gone.

"You with me, Phoenix?" It was almost a

plea. He could actually see them, or at least the bursts of Japanese gunfire that was now shooting towards the northeast.

"Skipper, we got Japs at five o'clock high!"

His tail gunner's voice cracked with excitement. The kid was barely eighteen.

He looked aft. Couldn't see them.

"How many?"

"Three coming in, sir!"

A second later there was a flash of light. One of his bombers off his starboard side, flying in echelon astern, snap rolled over, wing trailing flame, a Jap cutting up through the formation. It was one of their new fighters he had heard rumor of. That decided it!

While he was looking aft another bastard had snuck up on them from below!

We're going to get cut apart up here if we hang around any longer.

"Come on, Phoenix, help us!" It was the B-17, and he could see that one of them was trailing smoke as they lumbered toward the battleship.

He keyed his mike.

"Phoenix three, follow me. Let's get the battleship!"

Halsey would most likely hang his hide out to dry, but then again, that would only happen if he was still alive an hour from now. There was no way in hell they were going to outfly these new damn Jap fighters, loaded down with half-ton bombs, without their own escorts covering them.

Enterprise
06:29 hrs local time
"God damn it," Halsey snapped, angry gaze fixed on the loudspeaker. It was getting hard to discern anything. Radio discipline was breaking down entirely, but it was clear enough that his fighters, flying ahead, had not cleared away any of their fighters, or for that matter picked up an inbound track, and his dive bombers were committing to the battleship.

"Damn all."

And he stalked out of the CIC, up a flight and from there out to the bridge.

The reserve Wildcats, five of them, were spotted on the deck, engines turning over slowly, waiting to launch if an incoming were picked up by the new radar unit, its antenna looking for all the world like a giant mattress spring turning atop the highest mast.

Hang Struble when he gets back?

No, God damn it. If they're getting bounced by fighters without any cover from our fighters, there's nothing they can do now but unload on the nearest target and get the hell out.

The Japs had gotten there first, which meant that either they launched in total darkness or were a damn sight closer to that battleship than he was. Losing X-ray Delta, he had no search going on to his northwest and west-northwest, and his gut instinct now told him they were somewhere over there.

"Sir."

It was the captain of *Enterprise.*

He nodded.

"Sir, we're picking up the broadcast from the mainland. The President is about to speak."

"Pipe it through the ship," Halsey said coldly, hoping that their commander-in-chief would say something, anything, to boost morale and the fighting spirit of his crew.

Hiei
06:29 hrs local time

The three B-17s, flying in a V formation, were coming straight in, at a suicidal three thousand feet. Two Zeroes were on their tails, hammering them hard, flying as well into the wall of antiaircraft going up. The fifty 25mm guns mounted on the starboard side of the battleship were sending up a fusillade of fire. Its five- and six-inchers, barrels depressed, were firing as well.

One of the 17s suddenly rolled over, its entire portside wing shearing off from a direct hit, part of the wing spinning back in the plane's slipstream, smashing into the trailing Zero, destroying it as well.

Hiei couldn't turn or maneuver.

"Enemy bombers to port. Dive bombers!"

Nagita raised his glasses, spotting them within seconds. At least two planes were on fire, and he felt a momentary flash of anger. Too much attention had been focused on the approaching 17s. On the two surviving enemy heavy bombers, bomb bay doors were opened, and a second later each plane unloaded ten five-hundred-pound general-purpose high explosives. No armor piercing could be found in the shambles of Wheeler.

All Captain Nagita could do was stand and watch, hoping the two bombers had dropped short. The second one, trailing smoke from a flaming outboard engine, banked up sharply and away.

Eight seconds later the first bomb hit the ocean a quarter mile to starboard, just forward of the bow, and at half-second intervals the other nineteen bombs walked in toward *Hiei,* each hit sending a tower of foaming water two hundred feet into the air, concussion racing through the ocean, rattling the thirty-six-thousand-ton mass of the ship.

The drop from the one bomber walked across the bow of the ship, missing by less than fifty yards.

Someone pulled him down flat, his damage control officer, and then it hit, the eighth bomb from the lead 17 impacting into the starboard side of number one turret, the blast not penetrating through, but nevertheless tearing across the deck, wiping out three of the twenty-five-millimeter mounts, annihilating their crews, splinters howling across the width of the ship and halfway back to the stern, shattering a window of the bridge, decapitating the assistant helmsman. A fragment of bomb casing penetrated the wall aft, killing two more men in the corridor.

Nagita picked himself back up, and looked over the railing. Smoke was still swirling around number one turret. Though the bomb had not penetrated, it was obvious the blast had dismounted the gun from its bearings. It could have been worse.

"They're diving!"

He looked up.

The American dive bombers, at least ten of them, were beginning to wing over.

Honolulu
06:30 hrs local time

It had not taken James long to find a scattering of paper outside the wreckage of CinCPac. In fact the ground was carpeted with paper, shattered filing cabinets, and what he suspected was even part of one of their ultrasecret IBM calculating machines used for decrypting.

Dianne had finally spotted a blank sheet bearing the letterhead of the Office of Personnel, CinCPac.

Dianne had a pen in her purse, which somehow she had managed to hang on to throughout all this insanity, and he quickly forged an authorization that the bearer of this note was temporarily drafted to assist with the repair and deployment of radios, by direct order of Admiral Kimmel, authorizing the bearer to commandeer whatever personnel and equipment needed, dated it yesterday, and with a flourish made an indecipherable signature, since he could not, at this moment, possibly remember the man's name.

He hung on to the note and with its power in less than ten minutes had a Navy deuce and a half, with a driver and three armed marines, who seemed to be glad to be dragged away from standing around, guarding the still burning ruins of CinCPac. He loaded his team into the back of the truck and headed for Joe's radio shop. James rode up front, ready to stick the note in the face of any Shore Patrol or cop who tried to stop them, and stuck Joe in the back, out of sight, since the appearance of someone Japanese might trigger an undesirable reaction.

With the truck backed up to the front door of the shop, Joe busily directed the team as it stripped out shortwave radios, ham radios, and bins full of radio tubes and tools, loading them onto the truck.

James stood silent, watching, the thought crossing his mind that at this moment, this man was loading out thousands of dollars worth of equipment, and there was no damn inventory. It'd be a snowball's chance in hell that he'd ever get compensated.

Joe was on the phone, which amazingly was still working, at least in this part of town, making calls, and within minutes several cars pulled up, Joe introducing them as friends who knew radios.

"Hey, everyone come over here," one of them cried, bursting into the doorway of the shop and pointing out to his polished black Cadillac.

He ran back to his car, popping the doors

open. The car was still running, and mounted in the dashboard was what looked to be a very expensive radio with shortwave frequencies.

"It's the President. He's going to speak!"

Everyone fell silent, work for that moment forgotten. The crowd gathered round the open doors, with James standing to one side. Farther down the street he saw where a car had come to a dead stop in the middle of the road, the driver shouting for some men futilely training a couple of garden hoses on a burning house to come over.

"Mr. Speaker, the President of the United States . . ."

The sound of the applause wavered, distorted, the owner of the car gingerly working the tuning dial.

James's focus shifted. Dozens of plumes of smoke rose nearly straight up in the still morning air, flattening out several thousand feet above Honolulu. One could easily pick out where Pearl was, a solid black column of smoke darkening the western sky. A lone ambulance raced past, weaving around the car in the middle of the street, where a crowd was gathering, bell clattering. As it roared past he could see that the sides of the ambulance were flame scorched and had been pierced by shrapnel.

And as it receded all seemed strangely quiet: small crowds gathering around parked cars. Somewhere off in the distance, a loudspeaker was on. So strangely quiet and hushed. And then that voice, that voice familiar to the entire world could be heard, crackling on some radios, sharp and clear on others.

"Yesterday, December seventh, 1941, a date which will live in infamy . . ."

Infamy. He hadn't heard that word used in years. It had a Victorian era ring to it. He looked back at the oily black smoke twisting up into the morning sky over Pearl, heard the distant receding rattle of the ambulance, an air raid siren warbling in the distance, aware now that it had been shrieking thus ever since they had arrived at the radio shop.

"Always will we remember the character of the attack against us . . ."

He thought of the dead marine by his side, of watching as *Oklahoma* rolled over in its death throes, taking hundreds of young men with her, of his mother-in-law, sobbing as she salvaged but a single photo of her dead grandson before fleeing their home. He remembered the row of bodies, not even decently covered with a sheet or blanket, lined up outside the ruins of headquarters, while he and Dianne had picked around

between them, looking for a blank sheet of paper to forge a document.

"Our answer . . ."

How do we answer, he wondered. Damn, I hate the bastards, but how do we answer? With what?

A distant explosion rumbled over them. He looked back toward Pearl. Something had blown; a fireball was climbing heavenward. God, was there anything left there to blow up? Was the bombardment starting again?

He suddenly felt all so tired, beyond exhaustion. When did I sleep last? He'd been up the entire night before the attack, and his left arm was throbbing He looked down at the bandage, stained dark from congealed blood. Two days now without sleep?

He tried to focus on the President's words. Should I be at attention? It was the commander-in-chief speaking. Does he know what is really going on out here?

He looked at the group gathered around. All were silent. Joe's hands were clenched with anger barely suppressed. Dianne had started to cry, tears coursing down her

cheeks as she shuddered and held back a sob.

". . . a state of war exists between the United States and the Empire of Japan . . ."

No one spoke. Another explosion rumbled across the island: a cruiser hit during the night bombardment was torn apart as its forward magazine ignited.

". . . and win through to the inevitable victory, so help us God."

There was an eruption of applause on the radio, but around him all were silent, grim.

Several turned to look back to him. He was in command here.

Am I supposed to say something, he wondered. The fireball from the exploding cruiser was spreading out in a dark oily plume, its burnt offering mingling with the hundreds of other fires out of control.

"Let's get back to work," was all he could say. The President had said what needed to be said. Now it was time to get back to work.

What happened next he wasn't quite sure. For a moment he thought it was Margaret, and then to his shock and embarrassment a whispered voice.

"It's Dianne, I'm not Margaret."

Apparently he had collapsed and was now in the backseat of the Cadillac, jacket off, and she was gently moving his good hand away from her waist.

"He OK?"

It was Joe, looking in anxiously.

"Just exhaustion. The guy hasn't slept in days."

Joe was holding a cup of water. Dianne took it and held it to his lips, and he drained it.

"This might hurt," she said, and she lifted up his left arm, bringing the bandaged stump to her nose, loudly sniffing at it.

"What are you doing?" he whispered.

"I once thought about being a nurse, did a semester at school, but didn't have the stomach for it," she said. "Anyhow, I don't smell any infection, but I don't like the looks of it.

"Keep the bandage on, sir. Now why don't you grab forty winks."

"Can't."

She smiled and patted his cheek lightly.

"Just like my Jeremiah," she said softly.

"Who?"

"My boyfriend. Never sleeps."

"How would you know?" he ventured.

She gave him a playful pat.

"None of your business, sir."

"Where is he?"

"With the Air Corps. Flies P-36s, based at Bellows. I bet he got at least one of 'em yesterday."

He could hear the strain in her voice.

He didn't reply, remembering the message of yesterday, that a lone P-36 out of Bellows was going up against the entire third wave. Chances were, her Jeremiah was dead.

"I should get back to work," he whispered, and in spite of her protests he got out of the car, still lightheaded. The men loading up the truck looked at him appraisingly, no one saying anything. A war was on, and they had work to do rebuilding the radio grid, and that was his job now.

One mile south of Hiei
06:33 hrs local time

Commander Struble, of course, had no idea whatsoever of what the President was saying at that exact moment, nearly five thousand miles away. He was too busy trying to stay alive, skimming over the Pacific at less than thirty feet, slamming rudder hard left and then right, skidding, jinking his plane to throw off the antiaircraft gunners who were still hammering at him, geysers of water kicking up to either side of his plane.

"Did we hit it?" he shouted. "Damn it, did we hit it?"

"Johnson got her, sir. God damn, look at

it! He nailed her good!"

He spared a quick glance aft as he went into a left skid, caught a glimpse of a fireball erupting aft, black smoke soaring up from amidships.

"What about us?"

"Didn't see, sir," and he knew his tail gunner was lying. Damn it, he missed, he knew he missed by a good fifty yards or more. He had completely forgotten about the new electrical release switches that had just been installed, forgotten to tell his men to turn them on, and had released his bomb the old way, using the manual lever. At that speed, to divert attention for even a second with one hand off the throttle could throw aim off by fifty, a hundred yards or more.

"Damn it!"

He was half tempted to come about and at least strafe the son of a bitch with his two forward thirty-calibers.

Insane.

They were out of the range of the 25mm guns, though an occasional five- or six-inch burst nearby, aim off.

"How many with us?"

"I count seven, sir. I think Greenspan and Kelly bought it on the way down."

How was he going to face his squadron when they got back? At least two of them had made solid hits, and he'd missed. And then there was the admiral to face for disobeying orders and going for the battleship rather than turning aside and hunting out the carriers, which had to be out there.

"Keep a sharp watch for any fighters," he finally said. "Now let's go home."

He set a course bearing south-southeast, the expected rendezvous point with *Enterprise,* slowly climbing back up to three thousand feet once clear of the five-inchers. The dogfight between the Wildcats and Zeroes was over. He had no idea where that was now, or who had won.

Nor did he see the lone Zero, at over eighteen thousand feet, directly above them, the smoking engine of one of the surviving Dauntlesses leaving an unmistakable trail, while a dozen miles to the east, the five surviving Wildcats, also heading back, were being stalked back to their carrier as well.

And farther to the southwest, the Devastators, their commander having decided to steer far clear of the battleship, had his squadron spread out in a wide search formation, running more to the west, the plane farthest to the south almost stumbling on *Soryu,* which as the Devastator flew by but eight miles away was momentarily obscured by a low bank of clouds.

CHAPTER FIVE

Hiei
December 8, 1941
07:20 hrs local time

Captain Nagita braced himself against the explosion, a magazine of five-inch shells aft lighting off, killing all fifty men of the damage control team that had been trying to douse the raging fires below decks between number three and four turrets. The magazines for the aft fourteen-inchers had already been flooded, but the electrical supply for the pump into the smaller five-inch aft ammunition storage area had been severed.

They were listing ten degrees to starboard, dead in the water, six of the boilers blown out by the first of the two dive bomber hits. His escorting destroyers were circling back in to secure a new tow line.

He watched their efforts, saying nothing. It was all but a forlorn hope now, and in his mind he could not help but play out the scenarios of a different history. If only Yamamoto had withdrawn the way Nagumo most certainly would have, this pride of the Imperial Navy would be safe. If only Yamamoto had assigned to him two, even one more destroyer that he could have kept to seaward, the surprise attack by the Americans during the night would have been detected and destroyed before it even got within range. If only he had turned but five seconds later, the torpedo that hit astern would have passed harmlessly by. If only . . .

The only certainty he had now was that his ship was barely surviving and the Americans would be back.

Akagi
07:20 hrs

He had said nothing for the last fifty minutes, still absorbed in what the American president had said. "Infamy . . . dastardly . . . treachery, win through to absolute victory . . ."

Silently he damned the Foreign Minister and all who worked in that office. Every last one of them should be out here now, on the front lines. They had failed utterly. America would be aroused to fury, no longer seeing this as a war about economics, or even about imperialism aimed at China and the need for Japan to secure that anguished, wracked nation, bring order, and perhaps one day even be seen as a potential ally against communism. No, now they would see it as a moral crusade, the kind of war Americans would embrace without the political division that he had hoped would eventually bring them, as a divided nation, to the negotiating table.

His only hope, Japan's only hope now was to continue to inflict such hammer blows of damage that somehow he could break their will to pay the price for the absolute victory their Roosevelt had called for.

One thing, though, was certain at this moment. At least one of their carriers was due south of Oahu, a hundred twenty miles off. A Zero covering *Hiei* had trailed a damaged Wildcat back to what was reported to be *Enterprise.* Another report was just in from a second scout plane, trailing their dive bombers. The two reported different coordinates thirty miles apart, frustratingly typical, especially from pilots and spotters not specifically trained for the task. But still it was confirmation, and *Soryu* had ventured a very brief break in radio silence, informing him that they and *Hiryu* were preparing a full launch to lift off within a half hour.

Enterprise
07:25 hrs
"Sir?"

He turned back from the side of the bridge where he had been watching the first of the returning Wildcats, number seven. It was obvious the plane had been in a fight, scorch marks streaking back across the wings from the four machine guns, what looked to be a hole just behind the cockpit. The pilot bounced it hard, snagging the last line, nearly going over the safety barrier before being pulled up short.

There was no jaunty climbing out of the plane for this one. The crew chief was up by his side, helping him to stand up, the pilot turning his head aside, bending over to vomit the moment he was on the deck.

"Sir?"

Halsey looked back. It was McCloskey.

"Bad news. Radar is certain they picked up at least one plane trailing the Wildcats, another probable with the Dauntlesses. One of the pilots just radioed in that he thinks he saw it, the plane up high, having pulled a contrail for a moment."

Halsey took it in.

"And the Devastators?"

"They are heading back in now, sir. Nothing."

He nodded. He had taken the first swing and it had gone wide, into thin air. Sure, they were claiming a kill on the battleship, but the hell with that. There was plenty of time later to get it, if what was left on Pearl didn't finish it off first. No, he had swung wide, missed, and now the Japs had a fix on him.

"How long before the torpedo planes are in?"

"At least another forty-five minutes on this heading, sir."

Damn.

"All right. I want coffee and sandwiches all around for every kid down there manning the guns. Launch the remaining Wildcats. Bombers to be spotted on deck, refueled and loaded. With luck we might get them off again before the Japs find us."

"I think we should order the Devastators to jettison their torpedoes," McCloskey, standing to one side, offered.

"Why?"

"Increase their air speed. We still have fifty fish on board. Besides, one of them screws it on landing and that load detonates, we're history."

Each fish cost over ten thousand dollars. His senior flight officer was suggesting dumping nearly two hundred thousand dollars' worth of ordnance. The day before yesterday, a trick like that and he'd be back in Washington before a review board with some damn senator howling for his head over the "profligate waste of our military."

It'd buy maybe ten minutes in recovery time and make the landings safer. But they'd lose twenty to thirty minutes reloading them.

He nodded.

"Dump 'em. Every minute we spend on this bearing gives me a knot in my gut. I want us turned about and out at flank speed the moment the last plane is aboard. Have the squadron commanders for the fighters and dive bombers report to me directly as soon as they are aboard."

McCloskey looked at him, saying nothing.

"I'm not sure yet if it's an ass-chewing or a medal. It was my call to start with. The Japs beat us to the punch getting their planes there first. Just have them report here to the bridge."

He turned back to watch as one after another the Wildcats and Dauntlesses staggered in, five of the fighters, seven of the dive bombers, and finally the Devastators came into view, slowly lining up one after the other to land. The rest of the Dauntless search planes had already been recovered as well.

And then the word came at last. Radar was reporting a large inbound from the northwest, thirty-plus planes, range thirty miles out, speed at 180. They would be on them in ten minutes.

The last of the Devastators touched down, and even before the recovery crew unhooked it from the arresting cable, *Enterprise* started to heel over hard to starboard, engines pounding up to flank speed, her escorting screen of destroyers and cruiser moving in closer to provide a protective ring.

McCloskey handed him a helmet and he put it on. All hell was about to break loose.

The minutes dragged out, radar reports coming in every minute, and then first contact by the Wildcats, and within seconds that fight sounded like it was going horribly wrong.

What in hell is wrong with our planes and pilots, he wondered. Wildcat after Wildcat was getting splashed, pilots screaming the damn Jap planes were faster and could turn inside them.

He left tactical command to the captain of this ship, fire control to the gunnery commander, what was happening down on the deck to the air boss and his crews. At this moment he was merely a spectator.

He realized that he was about to come under fire for the first time in his life. Chances were, as well, that not a single man aboard this ship had ever faced it before. He suspected that most, like himself, were so well conditioned that they now functioned automatically no matter how frightened they were. That was what training had always been about, to so condition a man that he could do his duty, even when scared witless.

They were running on a southerly heading at flank speed and then, with a shouted command from the captain, who stood beside him, head craned back, binoculars pointed straight up, the order was passed for hard aport, and seconds later *Enterprise,* like a lumbering but still agile racehorse, started to turn, heeling over.

Jap dive bombers were winging up and over, coming down.

Every gun to port and starboard was pointed nearly vertically, a fusillade pouring straight up with a cacophonic roar. Twenty-millimeters, the old 1.1-inch guns, the thunderclap bark of five-inchers. The screen of destroyers was adding in their punch as well, tracers crisscrossing, heavier shells bursting, most behind the flight of dive

bombers.

"This one is gonna be close," someone cried.

He spared a quick glance down on the deck. Crews were working feverishly to turn around the Dauntlesses, Wildcats, and Devastators, their pilots still in the cockpits of most of the planes, frozen in place, looking heavenward.

"Four torpedo planes bearing 265 degrees!"

He turned away from the planes overhead, swinging about. Sure enough, they were coming in, damn low, a lone Wildcat in pursuit, splashing one even as he watched.

"Hard to starboard!"

Enterprise, jinking and weaving, leveled out, and gradually began to turn to the west.

He could see two dots detach, one of the dive bombers, even as it released, breaking up, flames engulfing it.

The two dots resolved into stubby cylinders, coming down. Men on the deck forward began to scramble, running.

It was going to be tight . . . damn, it was going to . . .

The first bomb detonated when it hit the water fifty yards off the port bow, where *Enterprise* would have been if it had continued on its course of just thirty seconds ago . . . but the second one came straight down, punching through the deck close to the stern, aft of the elevator. For a brief instant the impact was nothing more than a small shower of splinters as the bomb penetrated the teak deck, punching a hole little more than three feet in diameter. Less than a twentieth of a second later it blew in the hangar deck, striking a small electric-powered tractor used to move planes, tractor and its driver blown to oblivion, the blast then taking with it the shot-up Wildcat the driver had been pulling toward the machine shop for repairs, the blast wave washing back through the hangar deck.

As designed, the sides of the hangar deck were open to the sea, not just to provide a steady cooling breeze for the men laboring below, but also as open vents if an explosion should occur.

A three-inch pipe for pumping up av gas from one of the fuel tanks below was severed. In another tenth of a second the spray of pressurized gas ignited in a fireball, blast and flames washing into the aft machine shop, killing all within.

A fair amount of the blast blew straight up, expanding the entry hole, which could originally have been covered over with a few heavy sheets of plywood, into a gaping, flaming hole, twenty feet across, at that instant ending the ability of *Enterprise* to recover planes.

Some of the blast punched downward through the hangar deck into the galley deck below, killing and wounding a score of men. Within seconds the automatic sprinklers in the hangar deck were turned on, a fire crew, standing ready, turning a foam spray onto the flames, even though of those still alive half were wounded from the blast.

Up on the deck, men were down, sprawled flat, heads covered with their arms, or curled against any protection to be found, a stanchion, splinter shield, or, ironically, under the parked planes loaded with 100 octane gas, as debris soared to the heavens and then came raining down.

The successful dive bomber pulled out at nearly deck level, banked sharply, and raced out to sea.

The captain of the *Enterprise* watched the impact for only a few seconds and then swung his binoculars on to the incoming torpedo planes lining up for a quartering attack astern.

"Twenty degrees starboard!"

One was dropped by the trailing Wildcat. A second Kate blew apart as he passed near the bow of an escorting destroyer. The remaining two dropped their fish from a half mile out, the two planes splitting in opposite directions. At the same instant a cry went up that four more dive bombers were winging over.

Still he said nothing. It was no longer his job. He stood silent watching, with another call coming in that a second wave was approaching from west-northwest, fifteen miles out and closing fast, twenty-plus planes.

Leveling out from its turn to starboard, *Enterprise* was racing full out at nearly thirty-five knots. Reports were the Jap torpedoes could do forty-five to fifty knots. A stern chase. Halsey ran a quick calculation in his head, knowing the captain was doing the same: about two minutes; turn or run straight?

Antiaircraft fire was soaring upward, the smell of cordite from the guns forward whipping past the bridge. It was going to be tight. One of the dive bombers was hit, turning, wing shearing off, but the other three bore in. A second one ignited into flames. Two dropped, bombs coming down, misjudging, he could see they'd strike to port, but the Val wrapped in flames . . . My God, the man was coming straight in, not releasing, steepening his dive at his target, which, racing at flank speed, was trying to run out from under.

"Down!"

He needed no urging, was flat on the open bridge, the howl of the engine cut off a second later by a thunderclap, as dive bomber, pilot, and gunner, with a five-hundred-kilo armor-piercing bomb, crashed forward of the bridge, into the starboard gunnery deck. The armor-piercing bomb blew when it hit the heavy steel of an antiaircraft gun's breech. The Japanese plane burst apart, engine cutting through the deck, which projected out from the side of the carrier, and scraped down the side of the carrier, trailing flame, the exploding bomb slicing out a section of decking, tearing a gaping hole into the gunnery deck thirty feet across, but not penetrating into the vitals of the carrier. A fireball of flame erupted as shrapnel from the bomb tore open one of the Devastator bombers that had been spotted forward, instantly killing its crew, spilling out more than two hundred gallons of fuel, which instantly flashed, threatening to spread under the rest of *Enterprise*'s planes on deck. The heat was blown back by the thirty-knot wind slapping against the bridge, so Halsey had to shield his face.

The phone on the bridge rang. A young ensign, sticking his head out, shouted, "Captain, we got a report of torpedo running to starboard!"

Halsey went with the captain around to the starboard railing and looked out. It was a blood-chilling sight, the wake of a torpedo cutting through the water, running exactly parallel to them less than fifty yards off, slowly overtaking the carrier. A few seconds later another call, reporting a second torpedo, this one to port, on the same track.

Enterprise was boxed, unable to maneuver as two more dive bombers winged in. And somehow running straight ahead, unable to turn, saved them. The dive bomber pilots, side by side, coordinated their release well, and the bombs detonated where *Enterprise* would have been if she had started to turn in either direction.

From bow clear back to the bridge *Enterprise* seemed to be burning, listing now several degrees to port, plates below the waterline crushed in from the near misses.

Deck crews were valiantly struggling to save their planes, unable to move farther aft due to the bomb explosion in the recovery area, nor forward because of the fire raging along the deck forward of the bridge. Firefighters were turning their water hoses and foam sprayers on the planes, soaking them down, while other teams sprayed foam underneath to try and contain the spreading pool of av gas from the destroyed Devastator and the Val. A second Devastator burst into flames, crew trapped inside. He could hear their screams.

If the deck had been packed with the ship's full complement of nearly a hundred planes, rather than the thirty survivors of the first strike and patrol, there would have been no room to move aircraft, and a massive chain reaction would have ignited them all.

Thus momentarily saved, *Enterprise* staggered into a low-hanging mist, an early morning tropical shower, still engulfed in smoke and flames. The second wave, this one from *Hiryu,* was upon them, eight Kates, nine Vals, and seven escorting Zeroes. Through the clouds the strike leader in a Val saw one of the escorting cruisers, *Salt Lake City,* momentarily mistook it for a small carrier, half obscured by the smoke trailing astern from the *Enterprise,* and at the same instant heard an exuberant report from one of the surviving Vals from *Soryu* that the first enemy carrier was awash in flames and starting to roll over.

He went into his dive on the cruiser, followed by the rest of his group, and a minute later the cruiser was a flaming wreck, hit by three bombs and bracketed by three near misses. The group leader for the Kates, flying lower, at the last possible moment countermanded the order to hit the cruiser, but then was torn apart by antiaircraft fire from a destroyer, his group then splitting up, four heading for *Enterprise,* the other three for the burning cruiser. One of the surviving Wildcats died fending off the attack on *Enterprise;* a second pilot rammed a Kate when he ran out of ammunition. One of the torpedoes, however, took the cruiser amidships, breaking its back. Another Kate declared a hit on the *Enterprise* and proudly announced it was sinking. In reality he had missed, the torpedo striking wreckage falling off the ship astern.

And then it was over, the attack wave leaving, planes scattered out, a lone Wildcat of their combat air patrol reporting the Japs were retiring to the northwest, the same direction they had come from. There remained a total of four American fighters still alive over the carrier. There was no place for them to land, and McCloskey gave them the option of circling until the deck was cleared, when they could try a landing without arresting gear, or running instead for Pearl. There was a hesitation, and then their leader loyally said they'd hang on and circle. They had guts. It'd been practiced before, landing without arresting hook on, assuming a hit to the stern of the ship, but the entire deck would have to be clear to give them enough space for a rollout, with brakes locked, a temporary barrier set up at the bow as a final stop point, though hitting the wires strung there would smash the prop and take the plane out of action.

A brief tropical squall lashed the deck for a moment as they steamed through the low-hanging clouds. The cooling rain was a relief, and it helped a bit with the fire, and then the ship burst back out into sunshine. Halsey thought for a moment how such random things, that momentary squall, might one day be seen as a significant part of the battle, a hand of God that perhaps saved his ship.

Fire crews were out all along the deck, pouring water down into the hole aft, other crews foaming down the impact along the railing. A small dozer, driven by a crewman in an asbestos suit, was pushing the twisted, burning wreckage of the two Devastators over the side railing. Halsey caught a glimpse of a chaplain walking alongside the tractor, making the sign of the cross in blessing as one plane after another went over the rail, her dead, flame-blackened crew still strapped in, and disappeared into the sea.

"Stubbs. I want a report!"

He was overriding the captain, but the hell with protocol.

The chief engineering officer for *Enterprise,* Commander Stubbs, was out on the bridge, helmet off, wiping his brow. During the excitement of the attack he had nearly chewed through his unlit cigar, which hung now at a drunken angle from the corner of his mouth.

"Sir?"

"How bad?"

"We got fires down in the main galley, a severed gas line aft which has been secured. Aft machine shop is still burning. Reports of at least twenty hull ruptures, nearly all on the starboard side from bulkheads fifteen through thirty-five, from near misses. Watertight security is holding, though. Thank God no direct torpedo hits."

He forced a smile. "She'll hold, sir."

"Good man. Now how soon can I launch?"

"Sir?"

"You heard me, damn it. How soon can we launch?"

Stubbs went over to the railing of the bridge and looked at the fire still raging forward.

"Give me an hour, sir."

"Fine."

"But sir, what about recovery? We won't be able to land a full strike force for hours. Those birds up there now, the fighters, we can squeeze in, but the others?" and he shrugged his shoulders. "The entire arresting system was blown out, and it'll take hours to cover that hole once the fire is contained. And that covering is going to have to be reinforced to withstand the shock of touchdown from the heavier planes."

"I'll figure that out later," Halsey replied. "Just get us ready to launch as soon as possible. I think the Japs are close, real close. Maybe less than a hundred miles off. I want to hit those bastards before they get in a second blow. Now get to it, man!"

Akagi
08:00 hrs

The first after-battle reports were coming in, picked up from squadron leaders of *Soryu* and *Hiryu* returning to their ships.

One *Enterprise*-class ship, most likely the *Enterprise* itself, was reported as listing and sinking, deck awash in flames. Strangely, a second ship — the squadron leader insisted it was a carrier as well — was sinking. His report was countered though by an angry Zero pilot from *Soryu,* insisting the *Hiryu*'s men had hit a cruiser.

Frustratingly, his search to the west was proving fruitless. The first search planes were returning, and a second wave was preparing to go out. The task force of four carriers had yet to strike a single blow this day. All the action had been by the pilots of *Soryu* and *Hiryu.* They had most likely made a kill, but to be certain, they should go back for a second attack as soon as possible.

Enterprise
08:50 hrs
Halsey glared at the three squadron leaders who stood before him on the bridge. *Enterprise* had only eight of the original Dauntlesses left, augmented by the Dauntlesses used as search planes and five Wildcats to escort. The Devastators were still intact as a group except for the two lost when the Val had hit them.

"You got separated this morning, no coordination. Do that again and all three of you are beached and will be teaching student pilots somewhere in North Dakota. Do we understand each other?"

No one spoke.

"Form up here, within sight of this ship, then track northwest, together, as a single unit. They're less than a hundred miles out, I think at least two Jap carriers for certain, and I want them both."

He spared a quick glance back down to the deck. Steam and smoke were still billowing out from the hit astern.

They had slowed to ten knots, running southwest, away from their intended target, but going relative to the wind so that the fires still burning on the hangar deck aft were not fanned. Smoke was coiling out from either side, billowing straight up in a funereal shroud. Forward the last of the fire had been suppressed, though smoke and steam were still rising. Half a dozen miles astern all could see where *Salt Lake City* was still burning, broken in half, going down.

"I want payback," Halsey snarled.

"Sir." It was Struble. He nodded toward the torn-up deck astern.

"What about recovery?"

Halsey nodded, hating to say what he was about to order. It would mean his ship, as a truly effective combat force, was out of it, once these planes were launched.

"The target is most likely a hundred miles southwest of Oahu. After you hit it . . ."

He paused, looking aft toward the still torn-up deck.

"Unless you hear otherwise from me, you are to proceed on to Oahu and land there."

"Word is our planes that landed there yesterday got shot to hell," Struble replied, trying to sound calm.

Halsey nodded.

"Let's hope they have their shit in order today."

"At least they won't be able to track us back," Struble finally replied, and Halsey nodded in agreement.

No one spoke in reply.

"Now go sink some Japs."

The three saluted and scurried off the bridge. He watched them go, shaking his head. No one a week ago was talking about the Japs having the rumored Zeroes on their carriers, and now his planes were getting shredded by them. This was a forlorn gesture he was now ordering back into the fight against them. He wondered if any of them would still be alive an hour from now.

He looked over at Wade McCloskey and could see the pleading look in his eyes, and he was almost tempted to yield. Hell, once this flight lifted off, there'd be no job for him, but instinct told him to keep this man on board for now. There'd be use, damn good use for him later.

Down on the deck he could see pilots looking up at the bridge in anticipation of McCloskey giving the flag signal to begin launch. And in his heart he knew he was looking at men as doomed as those who went in with the Light Brigade or Pickett's Charge.

It was hard and cynical, but that was what was needed if *Enterprise* was going to even the score and take at least one Japanese carrier out of the fight.

Lieutenant Dellacroce saw the three group leaders come running out from the bridge onto the deck, heading for their planes. On a large chalkboard, secured to the side of the bridge, a navigation officer was writing out, in large letters, the up-to-date coordinates of *Enterprise,* their route to where it was believed a target might be, and the bearings from there to Oahu, or back to where *Enterprise* might be two hours hence. Hand shaking, Dellacroce tried to write down the update on his knee pad.

He stank of vomit. His crew chief, a guy who had him thoroughly intimidated when he had first come on board and landed way too hard, nearly cracking a strut according to the air boss, was now quiet, almost like an older brother. He had brought him a ham sandwich and a thermos of ice cold Coke. The Coke had settled his stomach a bit. He'd skipped the sandwich, and together they had waited, enduring the terror of watching the dive bombers winging in while he stayed in his plane, and the long hour since then as the strike was prepared, Devastators were reloaded with torpedoes, ammunition replaced, bombs slung under the few Dauntlesses left.

He was scared to death, literally shaking with fear. McCloskey leaned over the side of the flame-scorched bridge and set the flag in signaling launch.

His crew chief patted him on the shoulder. "You'll do good, kid. God be with you," and he was off the wing of the plane, coming around to the front, hands raised up, crossed, indicating for him to hold as three of the Wildcats forward started their run-ups. He now raised a hand, circling it, signaling for throttle, and Dave edged it in, not too fast — it could flood, stall the engine — vibration rattling him, noise deafening, not just heard but felt in every fiber of his being. It used to be such a damn thrill. Now it was frightening.

More power, full throttle. Oil temperature going up, final scan of instruments. The first plane was rolling out, the second one . . . Glance back to his crew chief, who was watching the air boss on deck commanding the launch. A nod. Signal to the crewmen to pull back the wheel chocks. Fist high overhead from crew chief, circling fast, who saluted then pointed to the launch master, the "Airedale" in a yellow shirt, passing command of Dave's plane over to him, the commander of the launch, who was making the same gesture. This was the man now in control of his fate. The yellow shirt suddenly crouched down and pointed forward.

Dave had been jamming down hard on both brakes. He released them, pushed stick

forward, fed in right rudder. The Wildcat lurched forward, tail raising up, and rolled out past the still smoldering deck where the two Devastators had burned. God, he could still hear those men screaming. His plane drifted, the beginnings of what could be a ground loop . . . Damn it, focus! He pushed in yet more right rudder, straightening out, edge of the deck coming up, stick felt light, center it, now just a touch of back pressure . . . and he was off.

He flew on straight, lifting his landing gear, notching up flaps, watching airspeed. At one hundred twenty true air speed he began to turn to port, watching the Wildcat ahead, slowly circling up now to wait for the rest of the group to form.

"Dear Jesus," he whispered, "don't let me screw this one up."

Chapter Six

Soryu
160 miles south-southwest of Oahu
December 8, 1941
09:41 hrs local time

The first set of his rearmed and refueled Zeroes was ready, the deck crew having worked wonders. It was the fastest time yet for recovery of a strike force, rearming and now launching for a follow-up attack. The bombers would soon be ready to go as well.

Rear Admiral Ozama looked over at his sister ship, *Hiryu,* half a dozen miles to port, obscured by a passing shower, and could not help but grin a bit with inner delight. It had been his men that got the *Enterprise,* though *Hiryu*'s men were insisting they had hit a second carrier, while his pilots reported it was definitely only a cruiser.

Already his crew were boasting of having taken out the famed *Enterprise.* This mission would be a follow-up coup. For surely

if *Enterprise* had been to the south, then Yamamoto had indeed guessed wrong. It would not be like the Americans to leave their carriers scattered about. Chances were that somewhere nearby *Lexington* or *Saratoga,* perhaps both, were still waiting to be hit. His losses of the previous two days had been heavy, over half his strike force shot down or so badly damaged as to no longer be flyable. But between *Soryu* and *Hiryu,* he could still send over thirty strike craft and an escort of fifteen fighters, while leaving ten fighters in reserve.

Soryu turned into the northeasterly wind and began to launch.

Seven miles southeast of Soryu
09:41 hrs local time

"Skipper, there it is!"

Lieutenant Commander Struble looked to where his wingman, Lieutenant Mark McCarthy, was excitedly pointing, broadcasting in the clear.

They had been flying at five thousand feet, punching in and out of the already towering cumulus clouds that promised a day of showers, the clouds he hoped were concealing their advance. Remarkably, he had managed to keep his entire force, the five Wildcats, seventeen Devastators, and eight Dauntlesses intact, not wandering off as they flew into zero visibility for a few tense minutes, and then punched back out into brilliant tropical sunlight.

Sure enough, McCarthy had seen them. Ten degrees off to port, about eight miles out, wakes of ships visible as they were turning about, to the northeast . . . Damn it, straight into the wind — they were launching!

He clicked into the general frequency all planes were set for.

"This is Struble. We got 'em. Jap carrier eight miles out, ten degrees to port. Attack formation. Let's make this one count, guys!"

He wagged his wings twice, then pulled

back on the stick. His climb rate with half a ton of bomb slung beneath was around eight hundred feet a minute. No time to circle around to get up to an optimum fifteen thousand, maybe up to ten thousand at best. The climb would slow the dive bombers while the Devastators would go into shallow dives, which would level out a hundred feet above the water, and come in at just about the same time he began to wing over. This time they were together and this time they were going to do it right.

"Jap! Two o'clock high!"

Sure enough, one was diving in, circling out slightly to get in behind the Devastators, which were flying in tight formation, dropping down.

"We're on the torpedo planes, stick to me!"

It was the fighter squadron leader.

Right call. The Devastators were flying coffins. If he could get up to dive altitude, they could punch through any fighter screen. The slow, lumbering torpedo planes were sitting ducks. God help them.

He flew into a cloud and for a moment the oncoming battle was lost to view.

Soryu

09:43 hrs

"Launch! launch!"

The first of the Zeroes was already clear of the deck. One after another the rest of the strike force was revving up, the deck chief breaking with any protocol of safety. As quickly as a plane ahead began to roll, he signed the chocks of the next plane in line to be pulled without waiting for the previous plane to clear.

Admiral Ozama held his breath, looked over at the captain of the ship, who had turned to face aft, binoculars raised.

"Prepare to turn hard to port!"

Ozama said nothing. If they started to turn now, the wind coming down the deck would shift, putting the planes taking off into a dangerous crosswind.

The Zeroes were off, the first of the Vals was rolling out.

"Hard aport!"

Enterprise

09:44 hrs

"Straight in, go straight in . . ." The radio loudspeaker in the CIC crackled, signal lost for a second.

"That's Lindsey, with the Devastators," McCloskey whispered.

"Got 'em! Look at the size of that bastard . . . Hey, they're launching!"

"Two Japs, coming in on our six. Where the hell are our fighters?"

"Shut the hell up. Start your runs!"

"Hit. God damn, going in . . ."

Halsey stood silent, listening, hearing the excitement, the fear, praying for those boys, who he knew would press in regardless of odds, and almost certainly die doing it.

Four miles southeast of Soryu
09:44 hrs

Lieutenant David Dellacroce banked his Wildcat into a turn so tight he feared for a second that it would snap into an accelerated stall, the stick in his hand, the rudder pedals beneath his feet shuddering with the vibration. He grunted, the four-G turn pressing him down, his vision narrowing. He rolled out onto the tail of a Zero that was pouring its load of 7.7mm bullets and 20mm shells into a Devastator. The frantic tail gunner of the torpedo bomber was only able to offer feeble resistance with his lone .30 machine gun, which now apparently had jammed as well. He could see the kid trying to chamber the jammed round free and then collapse back in his seat, canopy ripped apart by the fire from the Zero, a second later the Devastator nosing straight over, slamming into the sea.

But he was on the damn Zero, tearing a burst into its tail from less than a hundred yards out. Not more than a second's worth, the enemy pilot instantly reacting, pulling back hard on his stick, soaring straight up.

Dave knew enough not to chase. He had learned already the bastards could outturn him. It was slash and then run, hoping they didn't get on his tail.

Maybe it was a kill after all. Part of the Jap's starboard elevator sheared off, fragments of debris falling away from the enemy plane as it climbed into the sun, trailing smoke.

Again, it was all so damn fast. Quick glance to port and starboard.

The Devastators were leveling out. My God, anyone flying those crates had to be insane. Level flight at 120 knots, then keep level, low, get to within a mile, better yet half a mile before dropping.

The first bursts of antiaircraft were opening up, a spreading wall of black smoke. A Jap destroyer was racing in their direction, light 25mm guns firing, tracers streaming up.

How many left?

He wasn't sure.

A flash of fire. Port side — it was the group leader. The Zero behind him banked sharply away. The Devastator was pouring flame out from under the cowling.

Merciful God, the pilot inside must be burning alive, and yet still for another ten seconds or so he held straight and level. He dropped his torpedo. Futile — they were still four miles out.

The Devastator winged over to port and cartwheeled in, the ocean enveloping it — a mercy, ending the anguish of being burned alive. Yet another horror, he now realized, when it came to the torpedo bombers. For the fighters and dive bombers, up higher, you had altitude to bail out. These poor bastards, flying at fifty to a hundred feet, could only ride their fireballing planes in, and thus die with them.

Tracers snapped past his canopy.

God damn!

A Zero coming in from his left, at nearly ninety-degree deflection.

He didn't even have time to react. The Zero passed over him, clearing by not twenty feet, and for a split second he swore he could see the pilot, goggled, looking down. Was he saluting or giving him the finger?

Did Japs give the finger, he wondered.

He started to turn to starboard, try to cut in behind the Jap, who was banking hard to port, lining up on a Devastator.

The Jap fired a burst that all but tore off the wing of another torpedo bomber, and it too cartwheeled in before Dave could even fire a shot at the attacker, who pulled up sharply, rolling . . . He was gone.

Merciful Jesus, the Devastators were getting slaughtered, and yet still they pressed in. He caught a glimpse of one of his comrades rolling up into a high inverted turn, canopy blowing back, pilot tumbling out, parachute popping, a couple of seconds later the Wildcat nosing straight over and going in. But the parachute was on fire and the pilot as well, writhing in agony. He flew past him, caught a glimpse of his face, wreathed in flames.

"Oh God, oh God . . ." Dave screamed.

The parachute flared and then collapsed, trailing smoke. The pilot plunged into the sea.

We're getting slaughtered. We're all getting slaughtered! He was suddenly aware of the pistol in its holster under his arm. He wanted to unsnap the safety loop, have it ready. Not like that, Jesus, I don't want to die like that . . . Forgive me, I'll shoot myself if I start to burn.

They were into the heavy bursts of five- and six-inchers. Another Devastator flashed into a fireball, a direct hit, the torpedo blowing up, the blast taking out the next Devastator to starboard.

Five, maybe six left at most. Two miles out.

Dave turned in sharply, trying to run down their length, ready to somehow cover their asses as they streaked in across the final deadly forty-five seconds of their approach . . . flying wide-eyed into what was almost a certain death.

Five Devastators left, they were almost within range . . . Drop and get out now, he silently begged.

Two Zeroes swung in, he squeezed off a burst, seconds later an explosion . . . The Zero disintegrated, spinning onto its back, was that me that did it?

A thousand yards out. Lieutenant Dellacroce, terrified, hung on with the four Devastators, kicking rudder back and forth, skidding behind them, and trying to throw off any Japs closing in on their tails, even though they were now flying through a blizzard of flak.

Release!

Two of the planes dropped, one of the two suddenly sheering off to starboard, almost standing on its wing, then rolling over on its back and going in.

Dave and another Wildcat stuck with the last survivor, heading straight at the carrier. Turn away now and get ripped to shreds. It was straight in and over and pray the gunners on the other side were asleep.

But the Devastator he was following didn't climb up, flame pouring from under its cowling, and in that instant he knew.

My God, what a fate the pilot had just chosen. The kid in the back had not chosen it, though, but his fate was sealed as well. He bowed his head over, making the sign of the cross.

The strike angle was too shallow as the Devastator plowed across the stern of *Soryu,* fifty meters aft of the bridge, smashing into two Vals, tossing the first one into the air, the second spinning around. Both were gassed up and exploded in flame. A shudder slapped through the ship.

Dave zoomed over *Soryu,* skimming the stern, the fireball from the Vals scorching his plane, blinding him for a split second, then he was into the clear, diving back down low, now past the carrier and racing away to the east.

No one fired at him for several long seconds, giving him a quarter mile lead

before the first 25mm gun opened up on him. He skidded slightly, looking aft at the fireball from the crashed Devastator, still expanding. He caught a glimpse of one other Wildcat . . . but no Devastators.

The look aft nearly cost him his life: a slight nudge forward on the stick, a sudden sensing of a change in lift, ground effect, meaning he was within feet of the world below, the rolling ocean. Panicking, he yanked back on the stick, zooming up a hundred feet, leveling out.

"The dive bombers!"

It was Gregory, closing up on his tail.

He looked aft again, didn't see the dive

bombers, or any impacts from the Devastators.

Christ in heaven, they were all dead, and not one hit. He felt tears welling up, but then tracers snapped past his canopy, and no emotion other then terror now held sway as he dived back down to skim the waves, jinking and weaving to escape.

10,000 feet above Soryu

As he climbed up to attack position, heartsick, Struble watched the slaughter of the Devastators and the valiant attempt by the escorting Wildcats to hold the Zeroes back.

"Arm your electrical releases!" Struble ordered, and as he passed the order to the seven Dauntless dive bombers with him, he flipped up the toggle of the electrical release. This time he would do it right and nail the bastard below.

It was a new addition, according to the technicians who had installed it, a helluva lot easier than the old manual release lever. Once armed, you just pushed a button and the bomb was away, rather than having to reach over while in an 80-degree dive and pull a lever.

And as he flicked the switch, his plane surged up.

"God damn! Belay that order! Belay that order!"

"Son of a bitch, sir!" It was McCarthy. "I just lost my bomb!"

"I'll kill those bastards if we get back!" It was Mullins, his bomb gone too.

"Don't touch the damn switch!" Struble shouted again. "Count off. How many still have their bombs?"

Enterprise

Fuming with rage, Halsey said nothing, though he'd personally make sure that whatever dumb bastard had thought up this new improvement sat out the war somewhere up in Alaska.

"Got mine, skipper . . ."

"Still have mine. . . ."

Five had reported in. What was left of his strike force had nearly been halved by the most asinine of glitches.

As for the Devastators, they had heard the radio reports and then silence.

"All of us go in," Struble's voice crackled.

"And do what? Piss on them?"

"We all go in. Draw fire. Get ready . . ."

"Do it," Halsey snapped. "Damn it, do it!"

Above Soryu

"To starboard . . . now!"

Struble led the way, winging up and over, rolling his Dauntless onto its back and then pulling the stick in, the classic turn into a dive.

He was at near vertical, dive brakes spreading open on each wing, engine throttled back several hundred rpm. The Jap carrier was nine thousand feet below, still turning. Twenty seconds to release, it'll travel three hundred yards in that time . . . calculate where it will be then.

They had practiced this a hundred times, but always on towed targets. Now *Hiei* this morning, but damn it, after all the years of training my bomb is gone.

Line up anyhow . . . eight thousand feet . . . seven thousand . . .

Dellacroce caught a glimpse of them. Seven dive bombers coming down, nearly vertical. Fire in his direction had slackened, then ceased, all attention focused on the dive bombers.

He started to pull up, heading toward the base of the clouds. There was nothing he could do to help the dive bombers now, and he thanked God for that. To turn back into that kind of fire . . . he just thanked God he

was beyond range.

"Where the hell are their fighters?" It was Gregory.

"On the bombers."

"Now what?"

He didn't reply, suddenly mesmerized.

The first bomber pulled out of its dive, but apparently nothing fell away, the same with the second, this one in flames though, crashing astern of the carrier . . . but the third! Its bomb hit just aft of the bridge, a brilliant flash of light, fireball erupting heavenward, followed seconds later by another bomb hitting forward.

"Burn, you bastard!" Dave screamed.

Enterprise

"She's burning. Damn, the whole carrier is burning! Scratch one flattop!"

The radio signal crackled, distorted. Cheers were erupting in the CIC. A chief petty officer interrupted, shouting for the men to be silent.

"This is Struble. That's two hits confirmed . . ."

Halsey, arms folded, looked at the plot board, trying not to show any emotion. It was a strange mix within: exultation — they had finally hit back. Rage and frustration as well. If not for the damn electrical releases it could have been four or five hits.

One Jap carrier down . . . perhaps. Three, maybe four or more still out there. And they would be back and he was down to a combat air patrol of but two Wildcats, and a hangar deck emptied, where there had been nearly sixty planes before dawn.

"All Phoenix force, form on me." It was Struble. "We're heading to land."

Halsey said nothing.

"Repeat please?"

Halsey realized the rest of the pilots had not been briefed on his decision that the strike force should head for land rather than attempt a return to Enterprise.

"God damn it. I've got two birds crippled,

we'll never get them back home, and besides, you want the bastards to follow us back?"

Wisely, he didn't say a word about the damage to *Enterprise.*

There were murmurs of approval around Halsey, and he nodded in agreement. If he got out of this, and that pilot got out of it, he'd pin a medal on him.

Five miles north of Soryu

"Gregory, you got that?" Dave asked radioing over to his friend flying a few feet away. Something didn't seem to be right with him.

His plane was badly shot up and flying erratically.

"Sure do. Fine with me."

His voice was strained.

The question was, where the hell were the bombers anyhow? They were into the clouds, visibility damn near zero. He could barely make out Gregory by his side.

"You OK over there?"

"Hey Dave, I took one."

"What?"

"Shot. Shit, I'm gut shot."

"Just stick close on the wing, buddy," Dave replied, and now his voice was tight. He'd only known his wingman for three weeks, but what they had gone through in the last twenty minutes was a bond that could stretch across a lifetime.

"We're heading to land. Stay on my wing."

He looked at his compass, guessed that a heading around 70 degrees or so would take them in to Oahu.

"Just stick close."

Enterprise

"Latest damage control report," Halsey snapped.

Stubbs, who was in a corner of the CIC, phone pressed to his ear, ignoring all else that was going on, looked over at the admiral.

"Sir, fires on the hangar deck are contained."

"Once the fire is under control" — and he looked at the plot board, the estimated position of the Jap carriers, and drew a reciprocal bearing, directly away — "turn to 130 degrees. We are getting the hell out of here. Flank speed."

He paused. Do that for twelve hours and his destroyers would start running dry. This had been his biggest surprise operationally. The peacetime estimates of fuel use were totally wrong. The destroyers used far more fuel than expected when operating in wartime speeds. They would have to recalibrate everything to this new reality. By nightfall they could refuel the destroyers from *Enterprise* if they had to. The big carrier held more than enough fuel for an emergency transfer to the destroyers. Then they would have to find a tanker or get to Pearl. He'd have to leave them behind and pray that somehow, someone could get an oiler to a rendezvous, otherwise in another two days she'd be without escorts. He'd worry about that later.

"Sir?" It was one of the radio operators, looking over his shoulder, holding up a

sheet of note paper, and Halsey took it.

It was from the *Indianapolis*! She had been far south, down at Johnston Island doing gunnery practice, and had turned north to rendezvous and was now less than a hundred fifty miles off, momentarily breaking radio silence, looking for him.

How do I reply?

"One signal, short and quick," Halsey finally said. "Not more than ten seconds. We don't want them to get any fix, if possible. Check with navigation, estimate where we'll be in six hours, then tell them to head on to that bearing at twenty knots, nothing more."

He left the CIC and went back out onto the bridge.

Whoever he was fighting . . . he had just knocked down the first hornet's nest, and they would now be looking for *Enterprise* to finish her.

It tore into his guts to have to say it.

"We are getting the hell out of here while we still can."

Chapter Seven

Oahu
December 8, 1941
10:41 hrs local time

"Greg, get your landing lights on, wheels down, and stick close to me!" Dave announced.

He still had Gregory with him, but had no reply from him for the last twenty minutes. Another Wildcat, number eight, he couldn't remember the guy's name, had formed up with them as well. The four Dauntless dive bombers they were escorting were trailing half a mile back. He hoped that all the trigger-happy gunners on Oahu would recognize the distinctive stubby wings of the Wildcat and not open fire. The Dauntless could be, from a distance, mistaken for a Japanese Kate.

They ran parallel to the beach, a mile out. There was no need to get any navigational fix on Oahu. One could easily pick the island out from fifty miles away with the buildup of clouds above it, and the other clouds made up of black smoke.

He had tried to raise Hickam, Ford Island, even Wheeler, but no luck, though he had managed to talk with a B-17 radio operator who told him the ground stations were still out and advised that nearly everyone was taking ground fire and to try coming in with lights on.

He lined up, turning onto final while still out to sea, wagging his wings.

Something hit. He saw flashes of gunfire from down on the beach. From a thousand feet up he could see men running about, more flashes, and a few tracers going wide.

Damn idiots, if I make this in alive I'm going to go over there and kick someone's butt, he thought.

A glimpse of motion to starboard, a plane turning.

God no, not more Japs!

It turned: a Brewster Buffalo, flying slow, wagging its wings. Pilot guiding in alongside him, canopy back, a wave and then pointing forward.

Someone was thinking down there. The Buffalo, edging ahead, leading him in. An Army plane, more recognizable to all the trigger-happy fools on the ground.

He saw Hickam, a nice long runway. A moment of fear: a bulldozer out in the middle of the runway plowing dirt into a massive crater. He'd have to come in and touch down long, clearing the crater. The control tower was gone, only smoking wreckage. The trade winds were blowing, and smoke from the burning oil fields half obscured the main landing strip.

He throttled back, mixture rich, adjusted prop. He felt a bit of a shudder — one of the props must have been hit; he could feel the vibration.

Ease back a bit on the stick . . . throttle closed off.

Damn! A few more tracers, and then it stopped, the Buffalo still leading the way, just ahead, frantically wagging its wings as a signal to those on the ground that the incoming planes were friendlies.

He could barely make out the bulldozer, and someone atop it waving his arms as if to signal him to break off.

Dumb idiot, of course I can see you, he thought, but I gotta land somewhere!

He cleared the dozer, felt the ground effect take hold, the Wildcat floating. Pull the stick back, it was nearly in his gut . . . a lurch, bit of a bounce, another lurch . . . he was down.

He stuck his head out to see past the nose of his plane, caught a glimpse of a ground crewman, waving for him to taxi left. He followed the man's lead, turning off the runway, knowing that his comrades were coming in only seconds behind him.

The blessed Buffalo was soaring back up, turning over the harbor, disappearing into the smoke.

He was off the runway. There was nothing but wreckage, burned-out hulks of dozens of planes, some still smoldering. There was another bulldozer at work, simply plowing the once proud aircraft aside.

His ground crewman signaled for shut-down. He gave a brief throttle up, then cut it back and threw the magneto switch off. The propeller spun for a few more seconds and then came to a stop. The blade pointed nearly to the vertical . . . was twisted back at the leading edge, half a foot chopped away.

Someone was up on his wing.

"You from the *Enterprise,* sir?"

He looked at the young Army corporal.

He couldn't speak, just merely nodded.

"Let me help you out, sir."

He felt strong hands grasp him. He didn't protest, he wasn't even sure if he could actually stand up. Someone else was up on the wing, helping. He stepped out of the cockpit, legs wobbly, glad for the help, and climbed down.

The air was thick, acrid, stinking of burning oil, gas, that strange metallic smell of melted aluminum.

The first of the Dauntlesses was touching down. His two remaining Wildcats were parked to either flank of his own plane. Gregory was not moving. Someone was shouting for a medic. He should go over, but knew he just couldn't, not for a minute or two.

He just stood on the ground, knees trembling, breathing in the warm tropical air that stank of destruction. An ambulance, red cross on its side, pulled up. A couple of medics jumped out, and one ran over to Gregory's plane.

He couldn't move, barely realizing that one of the ground crew still had an arm around him.

This must be what hell looks like, feels like. The funeral pyre of planes lining the runway, the smoking wreckage of the control tower, the massive inferno of the burning oil fields, the battleships he had caught a glimpse of on his way in. Jesus, how different from but two weeks ago, when *Enterprise* had put to sea, its crew grumbling once clear of Pearl because the old man had announced they were not going out for just a few days of maneuvers, but were making a delivery run to Wake Island. And now coming back to this.

"Christ almighty, look at this!"

He half turned. More ground crew were coming, almost like orphans whose own planes had been taken away, and now at least a few others had come back for them to nurse. One of the men was pointing to a hole in the fuselage, just aft of the canopy, big enough to put one's fist through. In fact his entire plane seemed like a sieve. Part of his vertical stabilizer was blown clean off.

He still couldn't react, turning to watch as the last of the four Dauntlesses touched down, bounced hard, almost nosed over in recovery, slammed down hard with a jolt. One by one the four planes taxied over to line up beside the Wildcats. On the third plane, he could see the tail gunner slumped over, a horrifying sight. Nearly decapitated, the gunner must have been hit by a twenty-millimeter shell or a piece of flak. His blood had streamed out, caking the aft end of the plane. The pilot was wounded as well; ground crew were running up to help.

"You OK, sir?"

It was the corporal who was still holding on to him.

He nodded, not speaking.

A medic came up to him, practiced eyes scanning.

"Sir, why don't you come over here and sit down."

The medic put his arm around Dave's other side, and they walked the few dozen feet to the ambulance and he sat down on the tailgate . . . and then the shaking hit.

He felt nothing but shame. He was supposed to be going around now, slapping his comrades on the back. That's the way they always showed it in the movies. What comrades? I had a dozen this morning; there's three of us left — and as he watched them gingerly lifting Gregory out of his cockpit he wondered if it was down to two. Gregory wasn't moving.

"You hit, sir?"

He looked up at the medic, still not able to speak, afraid if he did so it would just be childlike gibberish, or worse yet, tears. He shook his head, but he could feel the corpsman running his hands over his body as someone helped to take off his Mae West, leather helmet, and goggles.

"Sir, we heard you got the bastards good!"

He looked up. It was a young army lieutenant, holding a clipboard.

He didn't react.

"Your name, sir?"

"Dellacroce, David."

The lieutenant wrote it down.

"How many of their planes did you get?"

How many?

Was it one on the first strike? Two on the second?

The kid stood there eager, waiting, pencil poised. Kid? Hell, he's most likely five years older than me, but still he somehow looks like a kid. He's not yet been "out there."

He didn't say anything, just stared at him.

"The guy's in shock," someone whispered. "Leave him alone for now."

"I've got an intelligence report to fill out."

Behind the intelligence officer the oil fields were burning. An explosion made him flinch; the others didn't seem to react.

"Sir, drink this."

The medic handed him a paper cup. He didn't ask what it was, he just upended it. The whiskey hit with a jolt, warming, easing.

He saw Struble approaching, walking slowly, as if drunk. He started to stand up, but Struble motioned for him not to move and then just extended his hand.

"You OK?"

He nodded.

"Goddamn bomb switches," Struble snapped angrily. "But still we left the bastard burning."

"I saw."

"The Devastators?"

He could only shake his head. "All gone."

No one spoke for a moment.

"Who did the suicide? I saw him hit. Damn, the whole aft end of the carrier was burning."

"I think it was Mina."

"God damn, I want to see that he gets the Medal of Honor for that one."

"As if it matters to him now," Dave said softly.

Struble looked at the intelligence officer.

"Where's the ready room? Where do we go?"

"We're using the mess hall. The ready room got blown away in the bombardment last night."

"I want these planes turned around." It was a chief petty officer walking past the ambulance. "Patch what you can, load up, they're going back up!"

"We're going back up?" Dave asked.

Struble said nothing. Just turned and walked away.

Dave bowed his head, sick with the thought that others would see the terror in his own eyes.

"Excuse us, sir."

He looked back up. It was the stretcher bearing Gregory's body, blood leaking through the wool blanket that covered him.

"Damnedest thing," the medic escorting the body said, looking at Dave. "He was dead in the cockpit. The kid must have hung on to bring his plane in, and once safely down, he died. The damnedest thing I've ever seen."

Dave stood to one side, again looking about at the landscape of total devastation. It was not how he had ever imagined war to be. It was supposed to be knights jousting in the skies. You salute an enemy as he wings over in flames, share a drink with him later if he survives. That was the stuff he had read about in the pulp fiction about the last war.

The last war . . . Nothing in there about the burning, the stench, the fear, the way blood dripped from Gregory's stretcher as they hoisted it up and slid it into the back of the meat wagon.

Greg's fiancée. He couldn't remember her name. Was it Carol, Carolyn, or Kathy? If I get out of this, I have to go see her, tell her.

"Sir, you want a ride?" It was one of the medics, beckoning to the back of the ambulance.

He shook his head, and the door was slammed shut, the ambulance roaring off across the runway.

The Dauntless pilots stood in a cluster, watching it go. His one surviving squad mate — he blanked on what his name was — was with them, all of them smoking.

He slowly walked over to join them, feeling wobbly. They looked at him appraisingly as he approached, and he wondered if they knew what was in his heart, the terror.

Struble extended his hand.

"Heard how you stayed with the Devastators, took down two Japs."

"I don't quite remember," was all he could say.

The intelligence officer was hovering to one side and made the ridiculous sound of clearing his throat and holding up his clip board.

"Ah, gentlemen, I have to file an intelligence report."

Struble looked over at him coldly.

"We bombed a Jap carrier, it definitely took one hit amidships, maybe two. One of the Devastator pilots rammed it. Think it was the *Soryu,* or maybe the *Hiryu.* Left it burning from one end to the other, it's a goner."

The lieutenant scribbled down some notes.

"Now, who dropped the bombs that hit" — and then he turned to Dave — "and how many of their planes did you shoot down?"

Struble stepped up to the lieutenant and shoved him back, nearly knocking him over.

"You just don't get it, do you?" Struble shouted. "*Enterprise* launched sixty planes this morning. We're what's left. Now get the hell away from us or so help me God you're dead. Leave us alone!"

Startled, the lieutenant stepped back, Struble eyeing him coldly.

Those standing around watching were

silent, some turning away so if need be they could claim they had not witnessed an officer striking another.

The lieutenant straightened himself.

"I'm sorry," he whispered, "I didn't know," and he walked away.

Struble turned back to look at Dave.

"Who flew that Devastator?" he asked softly.

"I think it was Mina," Dave said woodenly.

"Be like him," Struble replied.

"Kid in the back seat, it would have been Anderson. Good kid, flew with me several times," one of the other Dauntless pilots whispered, as he reached into his pocket and pulled out another cigarette, lighting it off the butt of the one he was just finishing.

He offered the pack to Dave, who without comment nodded and took a cigarette as Struble flicked open his Zippo and helped him light it, almost gently holding his hand so others would not see he was trembling.

It was his first cigarette. It went straight to his head. He liked it. If anything, it blocked out the other smells blanketing the field.

They slowly started to walk toward the mess hall, no one speaking.

Strange, he thought of a college lit class, a professor reading from *Henry V.* "We few, we happy few . . ."

Bullshit. Six out of sixty. We few, we sick, terrified few . . .

Akagi

"*Soryu* is severely damaged, but already had half its planes aloft when they were attacked, and *Hiryu*'s group has joined them. They have a good fix on the target and are closing."

Yamamoto nodded as Genda spoke.

Charts were spread out on the table, latest positions marked.

Soryu and *Hiryu* were a hundred and twenty miles to the south. The other three carriers of his group were within five miles, having steamed with him.

He had yet to pinpoint the *Saratoga*-class carriers. He was all but certain now they were not to the south, so they had to be to the west.

Launch a strike to support *Soryu* and *Hiryu*? By the time my planes get up there, what was left could already be sunk, two hundred fifty miles away. Then what if we do spot two more carriers to our west? I could be outnumbered more than two to one.

He said nothing, closing his eyes.

One of two things. Either there was one American carrier to the south — it had launched the first strike against *Hiei,* its torpedo squadron not participating, recovered its planes, and launched the second strike, which they had just faced — or there was indeed a second carrier, and the claim by the *Soryu* pilots of a kill was correct. Both of them might very well be sunk already. There was no definite report of actually seeing one go down, only the excited claims of pilots who saw the hits, and then the confusion about whether the second ship was even a carrier after all.

Too many variables, he thought. His instincts told him that at least one, maybe two of their ships were still to the west, otherwise the attack on *Soryu* would not have been a dozen or so planes, it would have been a hundred or more.

"Sir, we need to come about anyhow now to recover our combat air patrol and the returning search planes," Genda said quietly.

He remained silent, staring at the chart, drawing imaginary lines, sorting the complexities, and of course gambling out the odds.

At last he stirred.

"*Hiryu* and *Soryu* can finish off what is to the south. We keep our strike aircraft in reserve until we pinpoint their *Saratoga*-

class carriers, which I am convinced are west of us."

Genda nodded excitedly. Fuchida, who was standing in the corner of the room, looked at his admiral hopefully. Perhaps the ban on his flying today would be lifted.

"And *Hiei*?" his chief of staff asked.

"It is finished," Yamamoto said coldly.

"Are you abandoning one of his Majesty's most valuable ships?" Kusaka asked heatedly.

"Yes, I am," Yamamoto replied coldly. "It has served its purpose well. The Americans have a saying, that one cannot make an omelet without breaking an egg. *Hiei* revealed the presence of at least one of their carriers and destroyed numerous planes and shore facilities. If we are afraid to risk our battleships, and at times lose one, then why bother to have them in the first place? With such thinking we should leave them anchored in Tokyo Bay for the rest of the war."

Kusaka opened his mouth as if to reply, then just turned away.

"The rest of our planes?" Genda asked.

"Held in reserve. I want all remaining strike planes fully loaded, ready for launch. We turn about just long enough to recover our air patrols and search planes, send up the next wave of searchers and air cover, then come about again to the west.

"You are dismissed."

The group filed out, leaving him alone, his attention focused on the map.

Is that Halsey still to the south? Or is he somewhere to the west? Strange, in the battles of long ago, you knew your opposing general or admiral. You could even see him and seek him out for single combat.

So is this single combat now? Halsey and me? The aggressiveness of their response indicated Halsey, who bore the reputation that of all the American carrier commanders he was the most reckless and daring. It was obvious he had tried to place his first strike over *Hiei* by dawn, not to hit the battleship, but to track on the incoming defensive fighters. He had lost that gambit.

There was another problem emerging. The damn wind from the northeast. It meant coming about and running up to flank speed every time they had to recover and launch. It was eating up too much fuel, far more than he had calculated. To send out a strike wave now, against a target at extreme range, then maybe have to come about yet again if the *Saratoga* or *Lexington* was discovered closer in . . . Fuel would become tight indeed. This was a new reality that would have to be factored into all future thinking about fleet campaigns. It was the destroyers running low on fuel that defined everything. The big ships were fine, but the little ships got very empty very quickly.

He realized he was learning something new here, in this the first carrier-to-carrier battle in history. He who found the other first usually won — but the question was, how do you find him? There was far more random chance in this than perhaps in any other form of battle in history — and it appealed to his gambler instincts.

Enterprise

He was back up on the bridge, watching as the last of the temporary planking was laid down to cover the hole in the deck astern. Up forward, the smoldering fires had been contained.

The four destroyers and two cruisers escorting were ringed in close to provide covering fire, one more several miles ahead trying to spot for subs. They were running at thirty knots. If a Jap sub was out there, its only hope of getting in a shot would be from head on. The other three destroyers were now forty miles aft, picking up survivors from *Salt Lake City,* which had gone down minutes after being hit.

We're eating up fuel at a prodigious rate,

he realized. The tin cans will be dry by this time tomorrow if we keep it up. How could our peacetime calculations have been so wrong? Still, this is war. Move quickly or die. Keep the task force together or die. If we go slow we stay in range, and with only two flight-worthy fighters that would be suicidal. It is time to run.

From the corner of his eye he saw the signals officer stepping out on the bridge, and he knew by the man's face what was coming.

"Sir, radar reports forty-plus aircraft, inbound, sixty miles out, bearing 290 degrees. They'll be here in twenty minutes."

General quarters was again sounding, crews working on repairs dropping tools, running to their battle stations.

"Order the remaining planes to launch as well."

"Sir?" McCloskey asked.

"Launch now, damn it!"

"We're not into the wind, sir."

"Don't you think I know that!" and he pointed to the squall line of clouds on the horizon to the southeast.

"If I turn into the wind, we might lose that cover. Launch now!"

His air boss stood silent and then saluted, turning away. Leaning over the railing he pulled out of its socket the signal flag for "hold" and replaced it with "launch!"

Deck crews, sensing something was coming with the call to general quarters, leapt to their duties, and less than a minute later the engine of the lead Wildcat powered up. The second followed suit, engine stuttering, a balky cylinder not firing, exhaust black, but it had to go.

Halsey could see the hesitation on the part of the launch director on the deck. The man actually looked back up to the bridge. *Enterprise* was not turning into the wind . . . It was to be a crosswind takeoff, minus the extra lift provided by the trade winds blowing straight down the deck.

McCloskey signaled for a go. The launch director waved his hand over his head, signaling the pilot to throttle up to full power. There was a momentary glance from the pilot to the bridge. Was it anger? Halsey wondered. The man snapped off a salute, which Halsey returned.

At full throttle the Wildcat's twelve-hundred-horse engine was screaming, jets of blue flame flashing from its exhaust stacks. Wheel chocks were pulled, and it lumbered forward, tail beginning to rise, right rudder to compensate for torque, left aileron over to fight against the fifteen-knot crosswind.

Rimming the flight deck, antiaircraft guns were being cranked up, turning to face aft, gunnery chiefs patched into the CIC to get the latest radar read on altitude and range — though chances were there could be torpedo planes coming in low, under the radar.

The tension was electric, engine room pushing rpms to the max, *Enterprise* up to nearly thirty-three knots, helmsmen ready for the first order to maneuver once the attack started. The destroyer to port cut a magnificent wake of white foam as it sliced through the ocean at nearly forty miles an hour, five-inch guns pointed heavenward in anticipation of hell.

"Report from blue team one," the loudspeaker on the bridge crackled. "Forty-plus planes inbound, thirty miles out, bearing 290. Closing to engage."

"God damn!"

It was McCloskey. Halsey turned to look forward. The first Wildcat had lifted off and even now was banking around off the port quarter, having turned straight into the wind, but the second plane with the balky engine was skidding. On a land airbase it would have been called a ground loop, a pilot losing it in a crosswind takeoff or landing — once started, it was damn near impossible to get out of. The Wildcat weathervaned to port, turning into the wind. There was no room to compensate on a carrier deck, and it skidded off the landing deck, portside, fifty yards aft of the bow, wheel catching in a forty-millimeter gun mount, crushing the crew as it collapsed, wing tanks rupturing, spilling out two hundred gallons of 100 octane av gas over the gun crew as the plane upended, hung for several seconds inverted, the gas now spilling into the still howling radial engine, igniting in a fireball . . . The landing gear snapped off. The plane went over the side, as fire spread along the gun deck.

Enterprise was empty . . . It had shot its bolt.

All he could do now was stand back, wait, take the blow, and pray that his ship survived.

He did not have long to wait. The first report of a visual sighting came in, and seconds later he was jolted as the aft five-inch guns fired the first salvo of antiaircraft shells.

Off to port and aft the guns on the destroyers and cruisers opened up as well.

The fight was on.

As admiral in command, it was no longer

his place to give tactical orders. Again he was a bystander, watching. Glimpses of the Japanese dive bombers were visible through the fifty percent cover of cumulus clouds that dotted over the ocean. Almost directly astern he could make out approaching aircraft, one of them on fire, the torpedo planes bearing in.

It was going to be bad this time.

Five miles aft of Enterprise

Strike Leader Ugetsu, flying off of *Hiryu,* unbuckled his harness and half rose out of his seat, struggling to fix his binoculars on the American ship. It was hard work; the late morning air was turbulent, and the Kate surged, rose, and plummeted down in the moist tropical air.

Was this the same ship?

There was a fire on its port side forward. Damage from a previous hit? He could see a slick of fire trailing aft — perhaps a crash on takeoff?

They had spotted a vast oil slick, wreckage, and three American destroyers now sixty kilometers back to the northwest, near where the first attack had taken place. It must have been one of their carriers. This had to be the second one.

"Sir!"

His pilot was signaling to look down and banked the Kate slightly to port.

Excellent. The torpedo bombers were going in. There would be no escape for this American carrier.

He slipped back down in his seat, refastening his harness. Ahead and low, a black puff of smoke: the first of their antiaircraft guns opening up.

Nowhere near as bad as yesterday during the final strike at Pearl.

"Attack now!"

Akagi

The voice, sounding remote, crackled on the loudspeaker: "Attack now!"

All were tense, waiting. Was this the second American carrier? Should Yamamoto have sent in planes to support *Hiryu* and *Soryu*?

It was too late now to change that; the range was too great.

He stood expectant, waiting.

Enterprise

Heeling over, *Enterprise* turned hard to starboard, cutting a curving wake, the sky overhead and to the northwest black with bursting flak. The first wave of Japanese dive bombers, six attacking in pairs spaced five

to ten seconds apart, were coming in. The nearest bomb burst, a close one, rocked the ship less than fifty yards off the port bow. If they had continued on their course but a few more seconds it would have been a hit.

Halsey braced against the railing, feet spread wide, thrilling to the roar of the gunnery, the sharp crack of the five-inch guns, the staccato of the 1.1-inchers and light twenty-millimeters, tracers crisscrossing the sky.

Now aft, the wall of flak was increasing, the torpedo bombers well into range, spread out as they approached. One squadron was making a wide, sweeping turn to the west, to set them up for the classic anvil attack, simultaneous drops from two directions so that no matter which way they turned, something would hit.

It was going to be tight.

Their port side escort, the cruiser *Northampton,* was tucked in close, barely two hundred yards out, her captain expertly turning with them, even though in peacetime he'd have gotten his ass chewed for being this close in.

Enterprise straightened out from its starboard turn only for an instant. Then orders were shouted inside the bridge, and she started to cut to port, turning away from the torpedo strike to the west, but presenting a broadside to the torpedo planes coming in from the north. At nearly the same instant, the next wave of dive bombers was on them, then pulling out. The first bomb detonated two hundred yards forward of the bow; the next one walked in closer, a hundred yards, kicking up spray. A Val, trailing smoke, apparently came straight down at them, then went into a spin. A wing sheared off, and the plane crashed into the ocean nearly amidships.

He caught a quick glimpse of the pilot. It was obvious he had been trying to ram them, dying in flames . . . He felt an instant of pity for him, going out like a warrior.

"We're gonna get one!"

He looked up, tightened his grip. A shudder ran through *Enterprise* as the fourth bomb of the second wave struck square on the forward elevator, piercing the deck, blowing up below on the hangar deck. The elevator, dismounted from its hydraulic lifts, pitched up twenty feet, then slammed back down, tilted drunkenly.

We're out of action now, he thought. As if it mattered: he had no planes left to fight with, other than the few Wildcats still aloft and rapidly running out of fuel. They'd most likely have to ditch. The bridge loudspeaker crackled with their excited reports:

"I'm on him, got him . . . got him, you son of a bitch . . ."

"This is blue two, closing on torpedo bombers to the north . . . Come on, tighten it up!"

"Vince . . . He's on your six . . . He's on your six . . . !"

The loudspeaker crackled off for a moment, carrier wave lost, and he could see a plane, sky blue belly, a Wildcat, breaking up, a second one diving straight down, Zero on its tail.

He swung his binoculars aft, caught a glimpse of a Wildcat trying to intersect the torpedo bombers, Zeroes from above pouncing.

"Another!"

Men around him ducked. He instinctively followed suit. He felt a damn hard slap. A geyser of water erupted directly abeam the bridge. He stood back up, water cascading down around him, wiped his face, raised binoculars, scanning to port. Nearly every gunner on the port side had lowered their barrels, was now pouring it into the wave of Jap torpedo bombers. It was hard to see with the smoke — six, maybe seven, one of them on fire, going in.

They were pressing in faster, a lot faster than Devastators.

Enterprise started to turn again heeling back over. He kept the torpedo bombers in focus, four at least still boring in, one after another releasing, but still coming straight in after dropping, not exposing their bellies, skimming low, so low that gunners could no longer depress their barrels to hit them. At the last instant they pulled up, skimming right over the deck of *Enterprise*. Damn, they were good, one pilot actually saluting the bridge as he roared past, but the tail gunner, with a far different attitude, had his 7.7-millimeter machine gun depressed, aiming at the bridge, firing. Several shots flashed off the steel siding.

The torpedoes?

He could see two wakes, tracking in.

The blows from the two torpedoes striking starboard amidships, spaced a hundred feet apart, were stunning. It felt as if the 27,000 tons of *Enterprise* had been physically lifted half out of the water by the explosion of half a ton of high explosive in each one. In those first few milliseconds of detonation, the expanding blast actually pushed hundreds of tons of water back and away from the hull, creating a near vacuum. The detonation at nineteen feet below the water line ignited an upward rush, a column of water over two hundred feet high, a geyser weighing a thousand or more tons, until finally gravity brought it back down in a crushing shower that could knock a man flat. Some of the explosion blew in the bulkhead, rupturing through a fuel tank filled with fuel oil, designed that way to actually serve as an outer shield of armor. The blast was so intense, though, that the shockwave burst through the fuel oil, cracking open the main hull.

Less than half a second after detonation, the outward push of the explosion was finally overcome by the weight of water, which now slammed back inward, filling the

vacuum created. A tidal wall burst into the initial hole cut by the explosion itself, tearing aside steel plates as if they were sheets of paper, smashing in through the oil bunker and then into the bowels of the ship. Less than a second later the lives of forty men were snuffed out seven decks below Halsey, crushed by the thousands of tons of water that tore apart dividing bulkheads, watertight doors . . . thousands of tons of water in less than thirty seconds added its mass to that of the *Enterprise,* initiating a list that if unchecked could eventually cause the ship to roll over and turtle.

Halsey stood silent, watching the flight

deck relative to the horizon, saying nothing as with each passing minute the list increased.

Enterprise seemed to be dying.

CHAPTER EIGHT

The White House
December 8, 1941
18:30 hrs EST

This home of the President was steeped in history, FDR thought, and never did he feel the weight of it press down as heavily as it did at this moment.

As his Secret Service agent pushed the wheelchair toward the closed doors of the conference room in the basement of the White House, he allowed a moment of thought beyond the present crises.

Is this how Lincoln felt when word came of First Bull Run, the bloodbath at Antietam, or the futile charges at Fredericksburg? He remembered how Lincoln was moved to tears when reading the casualty reports after yet another failed battle lamenting, My God, what do I tell the people?

He knew already that his speech delivered little more than six hours ago had served to galvanize a nation and put the world on notice. Where forty-eight hours ago there had still been voices of doubt, of dissent, even of fear, now Americans were a people united with a single goal.

But to reach that goal? He had spoken of the enemy onslaught, but the new reports coming in all afternoon, each one darker than the next . . . Could the Japanese indeed push us so hard, then keep us off balance for so long that our national will, aroused at this moment, might waver?

Lincoln had faced that wavering during the dark winter of 1862 and the horrid debacles in the spring of 1864, when the North was bleeding out over two thousand casualties a day, and even then, as the national will faltered, he had held the course.

I must do the same. We can be as brave and as determined as Lincoln and his generation. Our losses, appalling as they are, are small compared to the Soviets and British. During the summer and autumn, and even now, the Soviets were enduring a hundred thousand casualties a week. If we have to pay the same price to defeat this enemy, we will do so. He could conceive of no other answer except Yes, if need be, we will pay that price, we must pay that price.

His friend Winston was indeed right: this was not just a war about imperialism, or economics, it was a back-to-the-wall stand of Western Christian civilization against the dark forces of totalitarianism. If we lose our will, if we turn aside now, the world will indeed be plunged into a thousand years of darkness.

The increased military presence around the White House was highly noticeable. Though he thought the reaction was extreme, there were rumors of saboteurs targeting the White House or the Capitol, and as in 1861, troops were now positioned nearby to repel any threats. Even the door to the conference room ahead was guarded by two well-armed Secret Service agents, one of them opening it at his approach.

As usual, he preferred to roll himself in rather than be pushed in and took over the wheels of his chair. Waiting for him, in what was already being called "the map room," were the secretaries of War and Navy and their military counterparts, Admiral Stark and General Marshall. All stood as he came in, and he motioned for them to be seated as he slipped into place at the head of the table.

He paused for a moment, putting a cigarette in its holder, lighting it up, and inhaling deeply.

"Two things," he began, without any preamble. "I want to know the situation now, as of this moment, and what your projections are for the next few days. Let me add, I have already spoken to Prime Minister Churchill once today. He is all full of enthusiasm, and I will talk with him again after this meeting. Our disaster seems to be his opportunity. I need to know the hard truth of the matter."

He scanned the room, and Secretary of the Navy Frank Knox stirred, clearing his throat.

FDR knew the real report would come from Admiral Stark, but a sense of protocol indicated the Secretary should speak first. Frank was by no means a heavyweight, though a good man and a solid manager. He was a Republican and had run against the Democrats in the 1936 election as Landon's vice presidential candidate. He had been brought into the cabinet in 1940 as an attempt to build bipartisan support for the impending war and had turned out to be, at least as an advocate to the Congress, the news media, and the American people, a good choice. Republican but an avowed anti-Nazi who was passionate about preparedness, he was, interestingly, a combat veteran, having fought alongside Cousin Teddy as a Rough Rider in Cuba, back in 1898.

The President nodded for him to begin.

"I'll leave the operational details to Admiral Stark," Knox said, "but, sir, it is grim, and getting worse by the minute. There is the distinct prospect that within a week there might not be a single major American warship afloat from the coast of China to Hawaii. Hawaii itself might very well be enduring an invasion. If not Oahu, the Japanese might venture to seize one of the smaller islands in the chain. We must assume that Wake and Midway islands will be attacked as well."

He stood for a moment, arms folded, looking over at the map of the Pacific Ocean on the north wall of the room. Numerous pins of red and some of blue were affixed to it. He then turned his attention to Admiral Stark, who sat patiently, and motioned for him to start.

Stark stood up, clearing his throat. He held a sheaf of telex printouts in his hand.

"Sir, these are the latest reports from our naval monitoring station at Mare Island and the Army station at the Presidio in San Francisco. They've been able to monitor some radio transmissions and have wired them here."

"Are the cable connections to Hawaii back on line yet?" the President asked.

"No, sir. There must have been a direct hit where the cables came ashore; either that" — he paused — "or they were sabotaged."

"Sabotaged?"

"Sir, that was our primary concern all along, and I think it should still be one. Tens of thousands living on Oahu are of direct Japanese descent. They even had their own Japanese-language newspaper on Oahu, which would print reports of the latest victories of their 'gallant army' in China. I think, sir, if you checked with Mr. Hoover, you would see that the FBI has dossiers on scores, perhaps hundreds who traveled back to Japan this year, some to volunteer for their army, others undoubtedly to get orders, and then came back to Oahu and even to California. It will require action on your part."

The President nodded, taking that in, not reacting though. The subject, now that war was declared, was a delicate one. In the last war there had been excesses against those of German descent that proved to be a national embarrassment by the time calmer heads had prevailed. Besides, it was not the top priority this evening.

"But at this moment, now, what is happening to our Navy?" he asked.

"These are the latest reports monitored in San Francisco," Stark said, holding up the flimsy sheets of paper, and he scanned through them.

"Kaneohe, Bellows, Pearl, and Hickam were bombarded for several hours by at least two Japanese battleships. The bombardment has exacerbated the damage already inflicted by the air strikes of yesterday.

"A battle was fought off the coast by the cruiser *Minneapolis* and a small flotilla of destroyers led by Admiral Draemel. It appears as if our losses were severe. *Minneapolis* is definitely gone, nearly all the destroyers as well, but we did cripple one Japanese battleship, either *Hiei* or *Kirishima.*

"An air strike, launched by Admiral Halsey at dawn, reinforced by several B-17s from the island that survived the attacks of yesterday, did further damage. The report, picked up from a ham radio operator claiming he was broadcasting reports handed to him by naval personnel, states that the Jap battleship is foundering thirty miles southwest of Oahu."

"Excellent," FDR muttered, but my God,

the price in return. A flotilla of destroyers and another cruiser lost? And yet, taking out a Japanese battleship would be greeted as something of a victory.

"Our carriers?" he asked.

Stark hesitated.

"No word at all from the *Lexington.* It is still operational somewhere between Midway and Hawaii. There was the intention for it to move to the southeast and *Enterprise* under Halsey to the northwest for a link-up. But both ships are now maintaining nearly complete radio silence, so there is no information there.

"*Enterprise* has only broken radio silence once today, for what we think is a rendezvous signal to a small group made up of the cruiser *Indianapolis* and its escorting destroyers. We've also monitored several Japanese reports, transmitted in the clear. They are claiming to have sunk *Enterprise* along with a second carrier in the same action, and our queries broadcast out of San Francisco have not been yet been answered."

"Merciful God," the President whispered. He lowered his head for a moment, then looked back up at Stark. "Do you think it's true?"

"Sir, regarding the *Enterprise* and its

group under the command of Admiral Halsey: They only had sixty planes on board when this started. They definitely did strike at the battleship. And we monitored plane-to-plane communications that a Japanese carrier was damaged, perhaps destroyed in a second strike, though our losses were severe. Few if any of our aircraft survived, and they are coming into Oahu, not back to their ship, which would indicate the loss of *Enterprise*. As to their claims of a second carrier being sunk, I think it doubtful. There was not enough time for *Enterprise* and *Lexington* to effect a rendezvous."

"Why go after a battleship if it was already damaged?" Secretary of War Stimson asked. "Couldn't your surface ships have finished it off?"

Roosevelt turned to face him. Interestingly, he was, like Knox, a Republican as well as a friend of his cousin Teddy, having served in his administration and been Secretary of War once before, under Taft. A bit ironic, Roosevelt thought yet again, that both of the top civilian military leaders were Republicans, the party that had leaned most toward isolationism.

But this evening, Republican or Democrat didn't matter. Their mission was to build an American front, regardless of parties. The old ideal that politics stopped at the border in times of crisis had to hold true, otherwise they would not win. Marshall had already voiced a fear of that to him, in the months before their entry into this conflict, the adage that "no Democracy can withstand a seven years' war." Politics as usual would finally take hold, sapping public support. It was a sobering concept, given that some analysis, what with the Nazi triumphs of this year, and the stunning onslaught of the Japanese, indicated it might take until 1950 to finally bring the Axis powers to their knees.

"I can't speak for Admiral Halsey," Stark replied, interrupting the President's thoughts, "but I suspect he launched toward their battleship in the hope of finding their carriers nearby, got pulled into a fight, and his pilots had to drop their ordnance on the closest available target.

"We do know for certain, from a broadcast picked up from an Army B-17 that had been shadowing the Japanese fleet, that a second strike, launched by Halsey, hit and perhaps sank a Japanese carrier, but only a handful of our planes survived and apparently have returned to Pearl Harbor rather than to the *Enterprise*."

FDR nodded and said, "Shrewd move.

Their scout planes could not follow our strike wave back."

"But the question still is out there. Is *Enterprise* gone? Returning to Pearl Harbor rather than their ship is an indicator of that reality," Stimson said.

"Or a shrewd move by Halsey to throw the Japanese off," Stark retorted, "and make them think the carrier has indeed been sunk when in reality it is merely damaged, perhaps unable to recover aircraft but still out there."

"Don't you think it is reckless that Admiral Halsey ventured one half-armed carrier against at least four or more of theirs?"

"To go in harm's way," FDR said softly with a smile, stepping figuratively between the two. "Remember I'm a former Navy man myself. That has always been the doctrine. From what I know of Halsey's reputation, he could not do otherwise and let them slip away unharmed."

Stark did not reply, and Roosevelt wondered if there was some subtext between Stark and Halsey.

"I think we have to assume *Enterprise* is out of the fight. Either crippled or sunk. If it is still afloat and seriously damaged, and now without planes, Halsey will not resume radio contact until he is certain he is well clear of their carriers."

"So that means only one other carrier left to face three, maybe four or even more of theirs," Stimson replied. "And then suppose this is the forerunner of an invasion of Oahu? It means the Navy cannot provide any air support."

The President extended a hand in a calming gesture.

"Admiral Halsey had to strike when he could, with what he had. I will not fault him for that. In this situation I want our commanders to be taking risks. And besides, Henry, look at the map. If the report on the Japanese fleet location is accurate, they are smack between Task Forces Eight and Twelve. The chances of effecting a rendezvous are slim."

"Nevertheless, he initiated an attack with a weakened and divided force."

No one spoke for a moment as the President snuffed out a cigarette and then lit another one.

"Gentlemen, I think it appropriate to set a precedent here at the start. I will never, repeat never, fault a commander for being aggressive. Timidity, especially at this moment in our nation's history, will indeed be the path to certain destruction. Do we understand each other?"

No one replied; there was simply a nodding of heads, and he could see the visible relief on Knox's face. He had suspected that Stimson was going to try and deflect some blame for the debacle of December 7 onto the Navy, by castigating Halsey's daring counterstrikes of this morning.

"The tradition of our Navy, in perhaps its finest hour, was during the War of 1812, when but a few frigates raised absolute Cain with the British Navy, much to their chagrin. The odds did not matter. That tradition must stand, and I expect to hear, as soon as possible, a clear report of the gallant action of Admiral Draemel and his men. The entire nation must hear of it and every sailor in uniform look to it as an example of the audacity that will eventually win this war for us."

He turned on his best charming smile, and the others nodded in agreement.

"Now, let us return to the current situation, gentlemen."

Admiral Stark nodded and returned to the map on the wall.

"We must function under the assumption that Admiral Halsey and his *Enterprise* task force are now out of the fight, as is the group accompanying *Minneapolis. Indianapolis* is far out of range, and I should add, the accounting of fuel resources that we had on December sixth" — he paused to look down at a note pad on the table — "prevents her from any rapid pursuit."

"What is the fuel situation at Pearl?" Stimson asked.

Stark shook his head. "The only reports we have so far, again via the civilian radio contacts, are that much, perhaps most of the entire oil reserve, four million barrels, is at this moment burning, either as a result of the third air strike or the nighttime bombardment. *Indianapolis* and its escorts cannot sustain a high-speed pursuit of more than twenty-four hours without running dry."

Again, no one spoke. For a nation that was used to swimming in oil, with vast reserves stockpiled where needed, the news was shocking.

"Then I think, gentlemen, to maximize this time together we should address four issues," the President interjected. "Let me cover the first two of them.

"First, should orders be sent now to *Lexington* to avoid all contact? And second, are the islands of the Hawaiian chain subject to further attack and perhaps occupation? If they are indeed to be attacked or invaded, we must address that now."

Stark cleared his throat again as all eyes turned to him.

"Sir, our radio communications are spotty at best. As I have already informed you, our only reliable source, until cable is reconnected to Hawaii, is via our monitoring out of San Francisco. We are not even sure if we can raise *Lexington,* and so far Admiral Newton has, except for a few very brief attempts via scout planes far removed from the location of their ship, maintained strict radio silence, as is proper."

"Do you think the Japanese have a fix on him?"

"I doubt it, sir. They did linger near Oahu this morning, perhaps in part to cover their damaged battleship. We know that two of their carriers were not west of Oahu, but actually to the southwest, those being the carriers that Halsey struck later in the morning. There are undoubtedly several more of their carriers somewhere out there as well, to either west or northwest. I doubt they would split their fleet out of mutual support range. Therefore, I think they will attempt to link their carriers back together and steam westward."

"Why not resume the attack on Oahu?" the President asked. "From the sounds of it, our defenses there are now on the ropes."

"Oil is for them just as deep a concern as it is now for us. We must assume they have reserve tankers awaiting them in the Marshalls for refueling. They most likely believe they have finished off our carriers to the south. If I were their commander, I would spread my carriers wide but still close enough to be within mutual support range, and do a western sweep, hoping to pick up whatever is left. They must assume we have three, perhaps even four carriers in the Pacific, when in reality we have only two, as *Saratoga* is still on the West Coast for refit."

"When will the Japanese break silence?" Marshall asked, in his first comment of the meeting. "And I must assume by what you are saying that this task force's mission was to attack, destroy our battleships and carriers, pull out, and not support a general invasion."

Stark nodded toward him as if thanking the head of the Army for his question.

"I will stake my reputation on the fact that this is not the preliminary for an invasion. The reports the British have so far indicate that a full-scale movement is developing against Singapore. The Japanese are occupying Guam. They are bombing General MacArthur in the Philippines. Their overall strategic goal will not be Hawaii but instead southward into the Dutch East Indies to get the oil they need so desperately from the fields in the Indies. After that they may switch their target to Hawaii or India or perhaps even Australia. First, they simply must get to the oil supplies before they run out of oil in Japan itself. Their stockpiles are very limited and will not sustain a long war. They must have oil. No, sir, I think Pearl Harbor was a spoiling raid. They are not fools. If they have war-gamed this out at all, they would know that to even have a remote hope of occupying Oahu they would have to commit three or more divisions of troops to counterbalance our infantry there, and the tens of thousands of naval and marine personnel that would resist along with thousands of reservists and even civilians. No, they can not take that island now.

"Even to grab one of the secondary islands, Molokai, for example, and try to develop a landing field there would require tremendous logistical support as a follow-up. I think you would concur that creating a usable airfield and then supporting it is a tremendous undertaking. Sir, I recall some reports, studies of what could be called the philosophy of their naval forces. It is all about rapid offensive strike, what won their war against Russia thirty-five years ago.

They lack, however, depth, the nuts-and-bolts things like logistical support, extra tankers, specially trained units for building bases and airfields, the stuff of a long-term war. They have built a superb navy, but it is a navy designed for a sharp, decisive strike for a short, decisive war. I, therefore, would be surprised if the Japanese would make such an attempt in their opening move against Hawaii, while at the same time committing to so many other fronts.

"Unless we are sadly mistaken in our analysis," Stark continued, "I would venture that their next step, after this spoiling raid to sink our battleships and carriers, would be Wake and Midway. They could use those islands as their logistical base, since both are within support distance from the Marshall Islands, and then challenge us for possession of the Hawaiian chain later. Also, by seizing those two islands, they snatch from us bases and airfields that have already been built and put them back into operation within a matter of days, rather than having to build new ones from scratch, which for them could take months."

Marshall nodded, and the President could sense his agreement with this well-thought-out review.

"As to the first part of your question,

Admiral Newton will break radio silence when he is certain that it no longer matters, that is, when the Japanese have a confirmed fix on his location. Until then he will stay under cover."

"What do you think he is doing?" FDR asked.

Stark paused for a moment.

"Going in harm's way, sir, the same as Halsey. He has a full complement on board, over one hundred aircraft. If he has monitored the attack by Halsey's aircraft, which has claimed a kill of at least one of their carriers, he will most likely steam east or southeastward through the night, and be ready to launch at dawn. The range might very well be close to a hundred miles or less, and if he strikes first, he will inflict grievous harm upon them."

"Should he not come about and hold back for now till a better assessment can be gained?" Stimson interjected. The President could sense the question was not a serious one. The Secretary was playing more the role of devil's advocate at this point.

Stark shook his head. "If he can surprise them first, he might strike a fatal blow to one, two, or more of their carriers, and frankly that would be payback and more. I hope he goes for them."

"Should we communicate this?" Marshall asked.

"No, sir. Within the confines of this room we know that Naval Intelligence has successfully broken some of the Japanese diplomatic codes this last year but with far less success for their military codes. In contrast, if an order comes from this office to seek out and engage, we must assume the Japanese will monitor it, and we must assume they have gained access to our codes as well, until it is absolutely proven differently. I think silence is best, and let Newton and his task force fight their battle as they see fit."

FDR slowly nodded in agreement.

"The positions of the Japanese fleet and this B-17 Army airplane which found them," FDR said, making it a point of nodding in acknowledgment to Stimson and Marshall. "Do you think their navigator is correct in his reports?"

"I believe so," Marshall interjected. "Remember, sir, the name Flying Fortress was first used not to describe its defensive firepower, but instead to imply it can serve literally as a flying fortress that can range hundreds of miles out to sea to protect our coastlines. The navigators trained over these last few years have been well drilled in the art of fixing a position out to sea and accurately reporting it."

The President could sense the touch of pride in Marshall's voice.

"It was good enough to guide in Admiral Halsey's second strike and perhaps sink one of their carriers. I believe the position is clear and indicates as well that the Japanese are now steaming toward the Marshall Islands."

"I concur," Stimson said.

The President summarized: "Then in essence, our agreement here is for us to do nothing for the moment regarding Hawaii. To sit back, wait, and let our commanders in the field fight their battles."

The other four in the room nodded.

"Mr. President, you said there were four issues to discuss and I think I can surmise what the others are," Stimson interjected.

"Go on."

"What was alluded to first. The question of sabotage on the island of Oahu. There are tens of thousands of Japanese on that island, and it could be fair to assume that a significant number, even an insignificant number of but a few hundred, could raise havoc. Losing the cable connection to the mainland could have been a lucky hit from their bombardment, but it could also have been just two or three agents and a suitcase full of explosives."

He paused to look over at Knox.

"Sir, months back we had every reason to believe that Japanese agents were monitoring our forces on the island and reporting in. They are most likely still doing it."

"What do you suggest?" FDR asked directly.

"Place under incarceration every Japanese resident on the island at least until this crisis of the moment is resolved."

The President said nothing, leaning back, closing his eyes.

"Is that practical? Hawaii has a very high proportion of citizens of Japanese descent. I doubt if the islands could function if we did this. Do you really believe the sabotage threat is that great?"

"We do," Stimson replied.

"Sir, I would be cautious," Marshall interjected, and FDR turned to him.

"Go on."

"The resources needed to round up tens of thousands on short notice would be daunting. Then where to put them on an island that small at such short notice, then feed and house them? And frankly, sir, given the passions of the moment out there, it could turn very ugly."

"How so?"

"Sir, as you know, we have had racial antagonisms that have flared into riots, lynchings, and mob behavior. We have to be very careful about getting people emotionally enraged against each other."

Franklin sighed, saying nothing. He could well imagine facing Eleanor if he made such a decision now.

"Security around facilities that have survived is undoubtedly in place," Marshall continued. "I think the suggestion, now, is locking the barn door after the horses have run. Whatever sabotage was planned has most likely been done. And if anything, it seems we overreacted to the threat of sabotage in the way we positioned our planes and ships prior to the attack. If any more attempts are made, then there will be more direct cause. But for the moment I suggest keeping the status quo. If there are enemy agents, let them play their hands, and we will get them then. But I am willing to bet, sir, that the vast majority of Japanese out there, who — remember — left Japan of their own free will years ago, are loyal to America. If we incarcerate them, and the Japanese then do invade, we'll have created a massive fifth column that might go over to their side rather than stay on our side. I think now is the moment to act with trust."

"I'll postpone this one for the moment," the President finally announced. "Once communications are back up and we can get a better picture of what really happened, I'll decide then."

Marshall smiled and nodded his head.

"And the fourth point, sir. What about MacArthur?" Knox now interjected, and Franklin could see that here was interservice rivalry playing out. Word had come in that most of MacArthur's air force had been annihilated in a Japanese air attack hours after Pearl Harbor had been hit. The disaster was inexcusable.

"Sir, frankly I think he should be dismissed now," Stark announced, "and Wainwright put in his place."

Franklin looked to Stimson and Marshall. He knew that in Marshall's case, in particular, there was no love lost between them.

The fact that MacArthur's air force was all but wiped out already, caught on the ground by a Japanese air strike long hours after Pearl Harbor was hit, was inexcusable. And yet, to change horses now? If there was one man who had any kind of feel for the troublesome Philippines, it was Douglas, like him or not. His father had been military governor there during the insurrection of forty years ago, and the Philippines had been young Douglas's first posting after he graduated from West Point.

His position was technically a unique one. Though still a member of the United States armed forces, he was, as well, "Field Marshal" of the Philippine Defense Force, the only "field marshal" in the history of the United States military. It was quipped by more than a few of his detractors that he took the position just so he could have more gold "spaghetti" on his hat.

He stood unique, a man who could display incredible genius, but also moments that were incredible lapses of judgment, such as his brutal handling of the "Bonus Squatters," so many of the men in that improvised encampment comrades from the last war, and now this.

But to change command now, at this moment? What message would it give? Furthermore, the Filipino government trusted him and looked to him for military leadership. Their confidence must have been severely shaken by Pearl Harbor and the loss of aircraft on the ground in the Philippines. Would relieving America's most senior general in the earliest days of the war simply collapse any possibility of cooperation between Americans and Filipinos?

Roosevelt shifted uncomfortably in his chair. Though the steel braces were off his legs, spasms of pain were streaking up his back. Constant pain was part of life for him; he had barely slept or lain down since yesterday afternoon.

"Given the current situation around Hawaii," he finally replied, "realistically, what does that mean for the Rainbow plans?"

Marshall sighed, looking over at Stark. Again, he could sense the interservice rivalry.

The new Rainbow plans, hammered out over the last few years as addendums to the old Plan Black, war with Germany, and Plan Orange, war with Japan, had been postulated upon a number of points, and a key one was an intact Pacific fleet on the first day of war with either potential enemy.

It had always been assumed, since the first Plan Orange evolved out of American occupation of the Philippines and the Japanese victory against Russia in 1905, that if conflict ever erupted between the two nations, it would most likely ignite along the coast of Asia.

It was, therefore, postulated that the Japanese would make a thrust to seize the Philippines, rich with resources and one of the finest harbors in the world, Manila, and then her battle fleet would lie in wait, as they had for the Russians prior to their great victory at Tsushima. An American relief force would sortie from Pearl, have to fight its way through the Japanese-controlled waters of the Marshalls and Marianas, and somewhere in the Philippine Sea meet and defeat the Japanese fleet, thereby ending the war with a clear naval victory. It was to be a fulfillment of the doctrine of the legendary turn-of-the-century naval theorist Alfred Mahan, that once an enemy's primary fleet had been destroyed, victory was a foregone conclusion.

It had been generally assumed that the Japanese counterplans envisioned the exact same scenario as well, except, of course, that they would assume they would win the great battleship-to-battleship encounter. Their assault on the Philippines would be the bait to draw us out.

MacArthur had been sent to the Philippines to create a viable defense force that could stand against a Japanese invasion, built around a backbone of ten to twenty thousand American troops and a modern air force that could resist and perhaps even throw back the first Japanese attack. Then even if the Japanese did seize some of the islands, this force would pin them down until the Navy, with all its might, steamed in to finish it with a climactic battle that would end the war with our victory.

The Navy all along had absolutely refused to forward-position any of their heavy ships in Philippine waters, claiming there was no proper logistical support and, as well, that it would leave them completely open to a successful first strike, in the same way the Japanese had launched their first move against the Russians at Port Arthur in 1904, crippling the Russian Pacific fleet by surprise on a Sunday morning.

No one, absolutely no one had ever taken seriously the prospect that there would not be a first blow on the Philippines, or even British-held Singapore, but Hawaii instead.

And now the bulk of our Pacific fleet rested in the mud of Pearl Harbor, one of our carriers might already be sunk, or at least knocked out of action, and the other was about to face a battle at desperate odds — and the first line of defense in the Philippines, the Army Air Force of B-17s, was only flaming wreckage.

The Orange and Rainbow plans had always had two wildly different assumptions. The Army plan postulated that a defensive force in the Philippines could hold out for at least 120 days or more, until such time as the Navy came to the rescue. The Navy plan had always said it would take two years to mobilize the fleet and fight across the Pacific to the Philippines. Because there was no joint planning system, the two services had simply built their plans on their own assumptions. Now it was obvious the Navy could not reach MacArthur in the time he was prepared to hold out. The Army plan had been unrealistic in the planning stages throughout the last ten years, and given the destruction at Pearl Harbor and the news of the near-total annihilation of MacArthur's air forces as well, it was impossible.

It seemed almost moot now, but only five days ago, someone had leaked to the press the entire Rainbow plan. *The Chicago Tribune* and other papers that were decidedly anti-intervention had without regard for national security splashed the entire plan across their front pages, giving to the Germans and Japanese secret information, the worst of it being the admission within the plan that it would take up to eighteen months to achieve full mobilization and offensive capability, especially if the U.S. was caught in a two-ocean war.

The absolutely reckless release of that as front-page news by the press had triggered a fire storm that had raged across the nation, until radio stations started to interrupt their regular broadcasts on Sunday with news of a place few had heard of before: Pearl Harbor.

It had been the major news item in the papers and on the radio until the bombs began to fall at Pearl. It was all moot because a major component of that plan, the battleships burning at Pearl Harbor, were out of the lineup; their purpose — either to buy time or, if possible, to relieve the Philippines — was now gone.

He looked from Marshall to Admiral Stark.

"Do we have the assets available to realistically bring relief to MacArthur?" Franklin finally asked.

Stark shifted his gaze back to Marshall.

"If MacArthur had responded properly and immediately dispersed his air force, he would still have a first line of defense that could have repelled any Japanese landing attempt. Then yes, I would say that once our Pacific Fleet was properly reinforced with a transfer of ships from the Atlantic, we might have tried to get some resources to him. It is impossible to implement the Rainbow plan in this setting. Given our immediate losses, we may have to wait for the preparedness plan to deliver the new ships in 1943 before we can risk a major battle around the Philippines. We are going to be reduced to skirmishing with the Japanese along the periphery until we bring into being a new fleet. Thank God for your foresight and Congressman Vinson's leadership in passing the legislation for that fleet during peacetime. If not for that, we would be talking today about 1945 or worse before we could be ready to fully take them on."

"But we don't have those assets today," Marshall shot back coldly. "So the President's question still goes unanswered. Can MacArthur be supported if the Japanese invade the Philippines? The answer is no, and the sooner we face it the better off we will be."

"We both know," Stark replied sharply, "that inspection reports indicate a less than adequate level of preparation and training. The general himself said they were woefully underfunded, supplies were short, and it would take at least another year even to have a remote hope of a proper national defense force for the islands."

"Then the answer is no," the President interjected decisively, seeing that the normally unflappable Marshall was beginning to bristle.

This was not the time for an interservice fight to explode. He needed them working together. The issue in the days to come might not even be the Philippines at all; it could very well be Hawaii itself, or even the prospect of a Japanese carrier raid striking the West Coast.

Marshall looked back at the President.

"If the *Lexington* can cripple the bulk of their carriers later today or tomorrow, and if there is an immediate transfer of all carriers in the Atlantic to the Pacific, with proper mobilization of a marine expeditionary force, backed up by infantry and heavy armor and artillery from the West Coast, yes, it could still be possible to reinforce MacArthur, but not to provide strategic relief. He is going to have to hold out for a year or more to have that happen."

"But that is not possible now," Stark interjected heatedly. "MacArthur had more than enough time to prepare not just to withstand a hundred and twenty days, but six months or a year if need be. He has not, and with the catastrophic failure to protect his aircraft he lost his first line of defense on the first day. Frankly, Mr. President, I think we will lose the Philippines and must consider them to be a writeoff. To try and venture a sortie with what resources we still have left would be to invite a debacle."

"My God," Secretary Stimson said. "No American military force of such size has surrendered since the end of the Civil War, and that was American to American. What will the nation say?"

"It is war," the President said coldly. "That is what it must face now. It is war. The Russians lost three quarters of a million men in the Ukraine in August and still they are fighting. The British tens of thousands at Dunkirk, Greece, Crete, and North Africa. Gentlemen, we are going to have setbacks, terrible heartbreaking setbacks, in the months, perhaps even years, to come."

He paused for a moment.

"Especially if Germany, as I suspect they will, declares war on us as well. We must see this through and" — he paused, scanning the room — "we must work together, without blame or recriminations for the past. I, too, must shoulder responsibility for what happened yesterday. It was not just the Army or the Navy that dropped the ball yesterday, it was all of us.

"Do I make myself clear?"

The four in the room stiffened.

"So let me conclude," and he made a point of looking at his wristwatch. "I am scheduled for a call shortly to Churchill and have to attend to that.

"There can be no directives to our remaining forces in the Pacific at this moment without a complete sense of security regarding those transmissions, so we must leave control of the battle in that region to those on the scene.

"Second, and it must stay in this room at this moment and go no further. If the Japanese attack the Philippines, which they almost assuredly will do in the days to come, our forces there will be expected to put up a valiant stand, but there is little if any hope that they will see relief. We have to look to blockade runners, submarines, long-distance aircraft transportation, and other devices to get moral support to General MacArthur and his forces, but the fact is that we will be engaged in morale-building operations of help, not in a serious effort of relief. However, the American people will require us to do everything possible to help our young men and women who are now trapped in the Philippines. We cannot simply abandon them. We must use every creative opportunity to sustain their morale and get them help even if it is limited in quantity. Both our duty and our national will require this effort.

"Third, and most important, remember

that Germany is the much more dangerous threat. Despite everything the Japanese have achieved in the last two days, they are a much weaker nation than Germany. The Prime Minister and I have agreed that we need a focus on Europe, and that defeating Germany has to be our first priority."

He paused. Not even here would he voice the deepest of concerns, triggered in part by a letter from the famed physicist Albert Einstein. The briefings on what that letter had triggered, a secret known only to a few, were terrifying when contemplated against the backdrop of a Germany that had conquered the rich resources of Russia and perhaps the Middle East as well.

"Despite the legitimate rage the American people are currently focusing on Japan, we must not allow our emotions to cloud our reasoned judgment. We will do what we have to to contain the Japanese while we focus on defeating Germany first.

"Take the risks we have to with Hawaii, but remember we are now in a global war, and we cannot allow the immediate and urgent to drive out the permanent and important. Make your plans and allocate your resources accordingly," Roosevelt concluded in a commander's tone. Clearly, he was now truly speaking as commander-in-chief. His subordinates nodded yes.

"We'll meet again tomorrow when the picture becomes clearer as to the fate of *Enterprise* and *Lexington.*"

He rolled his wheelchair back to the door and knocked once. A Secret Service agent stepped in and guided the President out of the room.

Marshall and Stark sat back down, gazing at each other.

"If we tell Douglas he is a writeoff," Marshall said, "it will be ugly. He doesn't trust any of us on a good day, and this is certainly not a good day."

"We don't tell him," Stimson replied sharply. "That issue is closed and, as the President said, stays here."

Clark Army Air Force Base
Luzon, Philippines
December 9, 1941
08:00 hrs local time

Douglas MacArthur walked alone through the flaming wreckage strewn across the field, .30-caliber ammunition still lighting off from a burning P-40, at the edge of the tarmac.

His escorting guards, armed with Thompsons, walked just behind him, weapons cocked and poised.

Fire crews raced past him, most not even noticing the presence of the general, snaking out hoses in futile efforts to save what was left — and there was damn little left.

Inwardly he was now allowing a moment of self-doubt to settle in.

Intelligence reports had indicated that it was all but impossible for the Japanese to launch a heavy strike from Formosa. The range was simply too great; only their heavier two-engine bombers or his own B-17s could have leapt the distance. But they had indeed done so, swarms of their planes striking just before dusk of the evening before, all but destroying his ability to repulse an invasion.

General Wainwright, his second in command, walking by his side, had the good sense not to say a word, as silent as MacArthur was as he took in the scene of devastation.

Beyond everything else, they were cut off. The cable links via Pearl Harbor and Hong Kong had been severed, and given the severity of the onslaught, they could not trust any radio communications.

If the extent of damage to Pearl Harbor, which the Japanese radios were openly boasting about, was true, he knew he was indeed cut off.

Though he would never admit it to anyone, his hope of survival now rested with the ability of the Navy to send relief, and from past experiences, he held little trust that they would place him at the head of their priorities this day.

He finally turned to Wainwright.

"Make sure the surviving aircraft are sent out to secondary fields now. Prepare, as planned, for a Japanese landing on Lingayen Bay within the week, perhaps as early as today. I'm going back to Manila."

Wainwright saluted, saying nothing as he turned and stalked away.

Once in his staff car, flanked ahead and behind by scout cars mounting machine guns, he started back to the city. Already, panicked civilians, particularly the wealthier ones, were loading up, heading out of the city, scattering out to the countryside to sit out the impending fight.

Plan Rainbow Five. Would Knox and Stimson, let alone the President, honor it? Or would they leave him and his men out here to die, forgotten, now that the Navy that was supposed to bring relief was at the bottom of Pearl Harbor?

He could sense the answer to that one. And he knew, as well, that the so-called fortress position of Bataan was that in name only. If forced back there, his forces would hold out less than two months. He had tried to warn them that he needed ten times the supplies provided so far, and at least another division, preferably two, of well-trained American troops to form the nucleus of a Philippines Defense Force. For what was obviously pending for these islands, the fault rested in Washington, not here.

Any hopes for relief were gone, especially in light of the civilian broadcasts monitored throughout the night, describing the bombardment of Hawaii and what must now be a carrier battle off their coast. The Navy would undoubtedly lose more ships rather than pull back and regroup. While he thought it unlikely, within the week the Japanese might very well attack Hawaii again, this time with a landing force, and then he and his valiant men would be completely forgotten.

He was on his own and he knew it.

Government Command Bunker
London
December 9, 1941
00:15 hrs local time

Winston Churchill looked at the clock. The call was scheduled for fifteen minutes from now.

The night had been quiet, a nuisance raid of a few bombers an hour earlier, nothing of course anywhere near the dark nights of the winter of 1940–41. But nevertheless, there would be some more deaths to read about in the morning, a row of homes in the East End collapsed, or perhaps another beloved memory of London before the war gone forever. Or should one say "wars" now? He, like Roosevelt, had made an official call for war against Japan.

New situation maps were going up in the planning room even as he sat alone in his tiny cubicle of an office. The Japanese had already hauled down the Union Jack over Hong Kong. That was of course a foregone conclusion and he pitied the small garrison stationed there, the chaps knowing their defense of the city would be merely a symbolic one and then God knew how many years of dark internment afterward.

It was Singapore that was the concern, what so many called the Gibraltar of the East.

He thought of his friend, his "personal agent," Cecil Stanford. His last report, cabled out the day before things had boiled over, was an update on the sighting of the Japanese transports, obviously moving with hostile intent, past French Indo-China, and without doubt heading either for Malaya or the Dutch East Indies. Cecil had reported his intent of heading to the north end of the Malay peninsula to "sniff things out," and he had not heard a word since. He hoped his friend was still alive up there. The Admiralty had reported their intent to stage a sortie by *Prince of Wales* and *Repulse* to intercept the Japanese transports and destroy them before they could offload. Gallant move, but it did cause some trepidation. Singapore, like so many other far-flung points to defend, had been far lower on the priority list for precious Spitfires and bombers, what with events in North Africa, the Middle East, and the bloodletting in the North Atlantic. He was assured that the battleship and battle cruiser would be beyond effective range of Japanese aircraft ranging out of Saigon, but nevertheless it was cause for concern. They were the only two heavy ships Britain had in the Pacific, doubly precious now that the American fleet had been destroyed.

Only four months ago he had been aboard *Prince of Wales,* crossing the Atlantic to meet with the American president off of Newfoundland. He had grown fond of the ship, the lads aboard who were obviously so proud that "their" Prime Minister, their former First Lord of the Admiralty, had crossed the Atlantic and back with them. More than one he had come to know on a first-name basis, and he could picture their cheerful eager faces. Those aboard that ship had become something personal to him, and he offered a quick prayer for their safety. Furthermore, Admiral Tom Phillips had been his planner for the seven months he was First Lord of the Admiralty before becoming Prime Minister. He had a personal affection for him. His thoughts had been going all day to Tom on that lonely bridge off Malaya.

The phone on his desk rang and he picked it up.

"Sir, we are connecting now to America," a crisp young female voice announced.

"I'm standing by."

He could hear the shifting in tones, a bit of crackling. This was a secured cable link, carefully guarded, a scrambling system installed at both ends so that if somehow the Germans did manage to tap into it, all they would hear would be garbled gibberish.

There was a click on the other end, a voice with a distinctly American accent spoke.

"Mr. Prime Minister, sir, I will connect you to the President."

A momentary pause.

"My naval friend?"

Who could not recognize that voice, Winston thought with a smile.

"Yes, my naval friend, and how are you tonight?"

It was a bit of a boyish code they had developed, given that the President had once been an assistant secretary of the Navy and he had twice served as First Lord of the Admiralty.

"I am well, sir, and you?"

"Your speech to the Congress today was riveting. It has galvanized the world to action against those perfidious foes we now face together in the Pacific."

There was a momentary pause, a soft laugh. Both were masters of flattery when flattery would advance what they wanted. He took pride, of course, in his own ability to say the right words when necessary. He had known that Franklin liked to deliver what he called fireside chats, which had a different tone than parliamentary speeches, but the President had certainly delivered a historic speech when it mattered. He sensed that "a date which will live in infamy" would equal his own "we shall fight them on the beaches."

"I studied your speeches," FDR replied

cheerfully, and Winston chuckled in reply.

"Mr. President, what is the latest word regarding your aircraft carriers? We have monitored reports from our radio facilities, and frankly we are filled with concern."

There was a pause.

Though the line was secured — they were both assured of that — nevertheless, both knew and understood caution.

"I must be frank and admit that at this moment, I know nothing more than you do. Radio silence is being maintained by all ships involved. All we know for certain is that our planes have crippled, perhaps sunk one of their battleships, and crippled, perhaps taken out a carrier as well."

"First blood then," Winston announced with enthusiasm. "Bravo for the American Navy."

"It is small retribution so far for what they did to us," and he could sense the determination in Franklin's voice.

"It is only the beginning, the first step. When this is finished, when this is done, you and I will meet in what is left of Tokyo to dictate the terms of surrender."

He paused but for an instant.

"As we shall also do in Berlin."

A pause now on the other side. He was at the core of the issue. He had prayed that perhaps, just perhaps, Franklin would simply take the plunge and add but two more words into his demand for a declaration of war: . . . "Germany." "Italy." He had not done so.

"In due time, Winston, in due time, but for the moment I have done all that I can do. Perhaps Herr Hitler will now do us a favor."

"I think that guttersnipe will do the job for you," Winston replied. "He'll think you've taken a knockdown punch and will now want to join in. Just like a jackal after a lion has made a kill. Mark my words."

Again a pause.

"We shall see, Winston, let us hope so."

"Is there anything at all England can do now to help you?"

"At this moment, no. The situation is still not clarified in those waters. I'll be certain you are kept posted as the reports come in."

"As I shall with you. I can say that two of my big friends are planning a visit against them."

Regardless of how secured the line was, he would not actually say the name of the two ships involved, but knew the man on the other end of the line would know.

"I wish them God speed, and my prayers are with them."

"Thank you. And I have a suggestion that might help our planning in this new situation. My schedule over the forthcoming holidays is not yet cast in stone. I think it is time that you and I, and our staffs, meet to plan out a joint response" — he paused for a brief moment — "to all the threats that will have clearly developed by then."

"I would be delighted for the visit," and Winston could read the slight note of hesitation. Of course Franklin would hesitate, especially if Germany did not declare war on America by then. Japan, no matter how perfidious the attack, must be the secondary concern of the moment. Hitler was literally at the gates of Moscow, and regardless of Stalin's assurances to the contrary, if that city should fall before Christmas, chances were the Soviet resistance would collapse, and by spring, England would again be standing alone — unless it could count America on its side.

"It is late here, sir, so I will sign off. So we are agreed upon a visit and some time to chat. I'll have my staff start immediate coordination with yours. Perhaps several days before Christmas would be good."

"Eleanor and I will be delighted to see you. Plan to stay at the White House with us."

"Good, then it is settled. God be with you and your men this day."

"And also with you and yours."

"Until later then, my naval friend," and he waited until the carrier signal went dead, signaling the connection had been closed down.

He sat back in his chair and puffed another cigar to life, pouring a little scotch into a lot of water and sipping it slowly.

Damn all. Franklin still would not commit to Germany. If Hitler did play it smart now, he'd make some sort of gesture to America, a promise, of course to be broken later, that he was withdrawing all U-boats from the western Atlantic. Do that and the America First crowd would cheer, saying they could now go after Japan hammer and tongs, and worry about the Nazis later.

Still, even to have America in half of the world war was a step in the right direction, and now he would have to calculate how to make maximum use of that development. He smiled as he closed his eyes and began to imagine various stratagems to be used in Washington over Christmas.

Chapter Nine

Hickam Army Air Force Base
December 8, 1941
13:45 hrs local time

"CQ, CQ, CQ. This is Kilowatt Two, George Easy Charlie, broadcasting out of Hickam Air Force Base, Hawaii."

James Watson was stretched out on the concrete floor, resting on a wool blanket, half dozing.

A crowd was gathered around Joe and the multiband rig he had just finished installing in the only hangar on the base that had survived the air strikes and naval bombardment.

"CQ, CQ, CQ . . ."

Joe began his call again, tweaking the dial slightly, on to a frequency the army operators told him was always monitored out of the naval base at Mare Island and the Presidio in San Francisco.

He sat back, looking up at the aerial rig

running up to a hole blown through the ceiling. Out on the roof some young sailors had cobbled together an antenna.

Farther down the table two more short-range radios were already up and running, one for guiding in air traffic, the other for general purpose monitoring of naval ship-to-shore transmissions. A noisy diesel generator outside was providing the power.

"CQ, CQ, CQ . . ."

He switched off to receive and waited. The carrier wave hissed and crackled. A momentary signal, garbled, not English . . . and then a clicking, a voice drifting in, dropping off, drifting back in again.

"Kilowatt Two, George Easy Charlie, we read you. This is a friend stateside. Who are you?"

James sat up, attention focused. Now the game would begin. Was it the Presidio or Mare Island monitoring station?

"Stateside friend, are you in San Francisco?" Joe asked.

"A question back, Kilowatt Two, are you who you say you are?"

As the senior rank present, with Collingwood passed out on the floor, dead asleep, James realized he had to step in yet again. He sat up wearily and went over to the desk, motioning for Joe to surrender the chair. This young man had done a remarkable job and yet the kid, born in Japan, did have an accent that, well, sounded Japanese. Joe did not resist as he stood up.

Several sailors slapped Joe on the back, thanking him. Interesting, James thought. When I brought him in here, holding up the fake orders from CinCPac giving him access to the base, he was met with barely concealed hostility. But after we worked together for a couple hours, that melted away. Joe is now "one of us."

He wondered if Margaret and her mother were OK. Already there were rumors circulating that all Japanese and those of Japanese descent on the island were to be rounded up and placed in isolation. My God, if they did that, he had announced loudly, he'd go to the damn camp with them.

So far it was only rumor, but what was not rumor was the report that two Japanese males had been shot to death down on the beach along the southwest coast where crowds had gathered to watch the smoke plumes from the Jap battleship that was out there, and still burning. Some damn national guardsman claimed he saw them with a radio in their car, leveled his BAR, and fired. The radio, pulled out of the wreckage, was nothing more than a standard civilian shortwave set, unable to transmit.

He could not think about any of that now. He sat down before the radio. Joe indicated the proper switch, and he threw it.

"Stateside friend, this is Commander James Watson, United States Naval Reserve speaking. I was stationed at," he hesitated, "CinCPac, until it was hit yesterday."

"Kilowatt Two, how do I know that for certain? The last voice sounded like a Jap to me."

He looked over at Joe, who said nothing, eyes suddenly impassive.

"By the way, Kilowatt Two, you know West Point always whips Annapolis at football."

He smiled. A tipoff. They were linked to the Presido, if indeed it was an American station and not a damn good clever Japanese trap.

"Give him your serial number," Dianne said, "name a few professors you had at the Academy and classmates. It'll take time, but they can run a check."

He should have thought of that. There was no way in hell he could say over the open air that he was a cryptologist, a code breaker. The Presidio was Army, but surely they'd have a land line open to Annapolis, to Washington.

"Stateside friend, it's Navy that can carry the ball." He paused, hoping they'd figure out the obvious, that they were talking to someone in the Navy. "Now, take this down," and he did as Dianne suggested, adding that they could check his pilot license number and the registration number of his small Aeronca Chief, the number being something that if he was a prisoner, the enemy would most likely not think to ask about.

"Get back to me, we're keeping this frequency open. And while you are at it, stateside friend, you damn well better prove to me who you are as well."

He clicked off and sat back. The carrier

wave was still on. More garbled transmissions drifting in and out, what sounded like jamming for a moment. Are the Japs on to us? He stood up, took a cigarette from Dianne, who had already lit it, and walked the few dozen feet out to the open hangar door.

A bulldozer was working back and forth across the huge concrete landing strip. The main runway was so wide that planes could easily maneuver around the cratering. A bunker loaded with munitions had survived, including some armor-piercing bombs and torpedoes. There was also an av-gas tank, buried underground, loaded with twenty thousand gallons, which had miraculously survived as well.

He watched a B-17, having made the short hop from Wheeler, come into the pattern, turning from base leg onto final approach, lining up. Damn good pilot, coming in a bit hot because it was a crosswind landing, touching down with two wheels, keeping his tail high for better control, plane rolling out for a thousand feet until finally letting the tail settle. A slight swerve, which he corrected, and then he rolled out to the north end of the runway.

The east side of the runway was being used as hard stands; a fuel truck and a couple of deuce-and-a-halves were waiting.

Dozens of Army Air Force personnel gathered round, ready to manhandle off the bomb load, each bomb or torpedo with canvas slings under it, and physically carry them to be hoisted up under the plane. No one could find any surviving trolley cars that were designed to move heavy ordnance around, pulled by a small tractor or truck. So every weapon, the torpedoes weighing nearly a ton, had to be manhandled into position, a damn dangerous job.

Two P-36s passed overhead, flying in slow circles, the only air cover available if another strike should come in.

"Kilowatt Two, Kilowatt Two . . ."

"They're back," Joe shouted, and James stubbed out his cigarette and went back to the radio.

"Kilowatt Two here."

"You check out OK. And your plane, it's a fifty-horse Chief, registration number 776 BX."

He chuckled.

"Stateside friend, wrong on that one. It is 777 BX, upgraded to sixty-five-horsepower."

A pause and then a different voice came on.

"Kilowatt Two, this is Colonel O'Brian,

United States Army, chief signals officer at the Presidio. You are the same Commander Watson with a hook?"

"The same. A souvenir from our former friends."

"When did you get the hook and which hand?"

"*Panay,* and it's the left hand." He almost wanted to add "damn it," but he didn't blame O'Brian; he was just being cautious.

He had a memory of this man, who held a position similar to his, monitoring Japanese transmissions. They had met at a joint Army–Navy meeting six months back, which was supposed to be for the sharing of information on Japanese codes and had turned, instead, into something of a protective turf battle on both sides. He remembered O'Brian, liked him, sitting in the back row, disgusted as the generals and admirals argued back and forth.

"O'Brian, you have red hair, do you not?" James asked . . . in Japanese.

"I'm bald headed, you bastard," O'Brian replied back in the same language.

"We're on the same wavelength then," James responded with a laugh.

"The same, Kilowatt Two. Kilowatt Two, it seems you are our only link."

That was perhaps giving away too much

to anyone listening in, but he realized it was undoubtedly the truth. It was reported it could be days before the cable transfer station was repaired. By either incredible skill on the Japaneses' part, or the worst damn luck for our side, a fourteen-inch shell had blown the cable access link where the heavy wires that supported civilian and military traffic back to the mainland came out of the ocean and were tied into the mainland, severing all the lines.

The pounding at both Hickam and Pearl had taken out their transmission centers as well. Wheeler had always relied on a land link to Hickam or the cable for linkage back to the States. Its base radios were short-range only.

Joe and his ham radio friends were now the link and the experts to keep it up until the cables could be repaired.

There was a pause on both sides. Now that he had the only stateside link, at least an official link, what to report? And for that matter, what to ask? Neither side had a common code source to refer to at this moment. That would be sorted out, but it could take hours, even days or weeks. Their coding systems had been destroyed when CinC-Pac was hit. And that made him realize just how badly they'd been hit. The delicate infrastructure of cable and radio links, updated coding systems, coordination on when to change codes, their own information here on the island about Japanese codes, all of that was lost in flaming wreckage. In one swift blow the Japanese had not only crippled the fleet and taken Pearl Harbor off the charts for months as a viable base, they had also wiped out their ability to monitor and even to communicate. Now that they had a link back to the states, what could they even do with it, other than talk in the most vague and general terms?

"How bad is it?" O'Brian asked.

"Bad. There were three air strikes yesterday, you undoubtedly know that. During the night we endured three hours of bombardment from at least two, repeat that, two Japanese battleships of the *Kirishima* class. One was crippled but still afloat reportedly twenty-five miles southwest of Oahu."

He looked out the hangar door. Several more planes had come in. It was obvious the Army and Navy were at least cooperating with this one, a strike was being prepped up, but against what, he didn't know, nor would he discuss it on the air.

He wasn't even sure if he should report yet on the fact that the *Enterprise* pilots were claiming they had crippled and most likely sunk at least one Japanese carrier.

Just what the hell else do I report? Would it be safe to give the last reported position of the Japanese fleet, in the clear? It had been radioed back by one of the valiant B-17 pilots who had found what was believed to be the main fleet, and not the two carriers struck earlier. The pilot reported four flattops, which added to the carriers the *Enterprise*'s boys had attacked meant they had six, perhaps five if the report of one being sunk was true. It would tip off the Japs, though chances were they knew they'd been spotted, but it might, just might be monitored by *Lexington* or any subs out there.

He went ahead.

"Here is the last reported position of the main Japanese carrier force. Four carriers confirmed, a second group of two, one crippled or sunk."

He looked over at a petty officer holding a note pad, who held up the sheet with the longitude and latitude listings, and read it off.

"Got that, Kilowatt Two. Good information. We'll see it gets passed along."

"I'm transferring the mike over to one of the base radio operators," James said. "This station is now permanently on line until ordered otherwise. Do you have any news for us before I sign off?"

A pause.

"Just let folks know the entire nation is mobilizing up. I've never seen anything like this. Recruiting stations are flooded. Help is on the way to you out there. And those Jap bastards have no idea what they've started, but by God we're going to finish it."

An idea that Dianne had come up with earlier was now laid before him as she slipped a piece of paper in front of him, the question already written out.

"Stateside. Do you have any bohunks around?"

"What was that?"

"You heard me, you stupid mick, I'm asking for a bohunk."

He didn't say more. If they were in the same room he would have actually given O'Brian a big wink, like in the movies. There was silence for long seconds, and he did not dare to repeat the question. It'd be too obvious then.

"Got you on that one, Kilowatt Two. We'll get it taken care of."

"On the same wavelength then, stateside," he said with a grin. "Thanks, stateside, I'm turning the mike over now."

He stood up stretching, a seaman first

class taking over his chair. He caught Joe's eye.

"Thanks."

"Glad to help, sir."

He hesitated but had to say something.

"My wife, she's nisei, half Japanese," he said. It sounded wooden, uncomfortable, the way he remembered more than one man saying, "Why, some of my best friends are colored," and then the inevitable "but . . ." afterwards.

Joe did not reply.

"I guess what I'm trying to say is this . . ." and his voice trailed off, not sure exactly what it was he was trying to say.

"I think there's going to be some tough times," Joe said quietly.

Those listening to the conversation drifted back a bit, obviously nervous, James bringing up the subject a reminder that it was an uncomfortable one.

"We're all supposed to be Americans, you as well," James finally said, knowing that sounded almost as lame as his comment about Margaret.

"I'd like to think so," Joe replied.

"I'll give you my address, phone number. You have any problem, you contact me at once. Once things calm down a bit, I'll see if I can snatch some more CinCPac letterhead and get a letter of commendation drawn up for you, also a voucher for your equipment."

Joe tried to force a smile.

"Thanks." He hesitated. "I owe this country a lot. If this equipment is payback, that's fine with me. If still over there, I'd most likely be drafted into their damn army and be in China or some godforsaken place fighting for that jerk of an emperor, and I've got two boys who'd get sucked into it too. I'm glad I could help."

No one spoke. A sergeant, listening in, stepped up, without saying anything gave a friendly slap to Joe's shoulder and walked off, others now nodding as well.

"Can you rig up another radio? I got some frequencies I'd like to see monitored."

"Sure, what are they?"

"Japanese."

"I'll get on it."

He nodded his thanks and walked out of the hangar. The northeasterly breeze was blowing the roiling clouds of smoke from the oil storage depot across the base. Flames continued to flicker from a bulldozed pile of what had once been P-36s and P-40s. Out in a cleared area, three B-17s, two PBYs, five Dauntless dive bombers, half a dozen P-40s and -36s, and three Wildcats were lined up — this time well spaced apart, with ground crews scurrying about, loading up munitions. A fuel truck was parked next to a B-17, hose connected up to a wing tank. From an old Ford truck, sailors were off loading five-gallon jerry cans of gas, hauling them over to a P-40 where an Army mechanic perched on a ladder was pouring the gas into the plane with a funnel.

"Sir, why don't you go home?"

It was Dianne.

He smiled and shook his head.

"Once we get a monitor back on their main naval frequencies, then I'll take a break. By the way, that was a great idea, using Hungarian. Unique language with no connections to Latin, Slavic, or Germanic-based roots. Not a chance in hell the Japs have someone who can speak it with their fleet."

She smiled.

"My older sister married a bohunk — I mean Hungarian — guy back in New York. They met at NYU. My folks threw a fit at first. He wasn't Princeton or Yale like they had hoped for, but at least he's Catholic, so they got used to it. Great guy; they got two kids now. So it just sort of came to me. He taught her how to say some rather dirty words and no one understood a word of it."

"Well, it was brilliant, and I think they got the message."

When she had cooked up the idea, he and Collingwood had first laughed it off. Where the hell were they going to find a native-speaking Hungarian in this chaos, until one of the sailors standing nearby overheard them and announced he had a buddy who was a cook who grew up there. That cook was now sitting in a corner of the hangar, obviously overwhelmed by all the brass wandering around, and by the way he was being treated with deference. Once someone stateside who could speak the language was dragged in and put on the radio on the other end, they'd at least have some semblance of coding that could throw the Japanese off for a little while. Hopefully, someone on board the carriers knew the language as well and could listen in.

She helped him light another cigarette. Without the hook it was difficult to get a match lit. He winced slightly when out of old habit he raised his left arm to take the cigarette out of his mouth, having mastered the art both with his rubberized hand and with the hook.

The damn thing was starting to hurt again, but the pain was different, deeper, and he wondered if it meant infection was beginning to set in.

He didn't have time for that now, and he went back into the hangar, warm in the afternoon sun, the air thick with the smell of burning oil, settled back down on the blanket spread out for him on the floor, and dozed off.

Mess hall now serving as ready room
Hickam Army Air Force Base
13:55 hrs local time

Lieutenant Dave Dellacroce found it difficult to swallow. He thought of the shot of whiskey that a medic had given him after landing this morning, wishing he had another, in fact the whole damn bottle. Instead all they had given him now was a warm bottle of Coke. He put it down, eyes fixed on the officer approaching them.

Along with thirteen other pilots he sat at a mess table while the briefing officer, an army colonel, came over to the corner where the pilots waited. Several were actually asleep, sprawled out on the floor or on tables. The call came for attention and their comrades roused them.

Dave caught Struble's eye. Both knew that in a few more seconds they'd find out if there was any chance left of living through this day or not.

"You men get something to eat?" the colonel asked, trying to sound friendly.

Several nodded; no one spoke. Dave felt he was crazy. Eat now? If he didn't puke it up immediately, it would definitely come up once he was into the air.

The colonel hesitated and then opened up his briefcase and pulled out what was nothing more than a hand-drawn map and put it on the table.

"Jesus Christ, not the carriers again," one of the Dauntless pilots whispered. "What about the battleship?"

"The Navy says they are moving a sub into position now to finish off the battleship. It's a sitting duck."

"And if the sub misses or gets nailed?" another pilot asked. "Hell, he could get away after dark."

"Not far, and they think they'll have enough of the channel cleared to start getting destroyers out again by nighttime as well. That battleship is dead meat. But the carriers aren't. One of your comrades located what we think is the main fleet."

"Stupid son of a bitch," someone whispered.

"We're dead meat," Brandon Welldon, the pilot of B-17 Gloria Ann, sighed.

The colonel looked at him, not responding, almost embarrassed.

"We bombed their battleship this morning with three bombers, the target moving at ten to twelve knots, unable to maneuver, and got one, maybe two hits, sir," Brandon said. "You're asking us to go after a well-protected carrier, doing thirty knots? Sir, frankly that is insanity, and when it is over this island won't have a single plane left."

There was a muttered chorus of agreement, and the colonel stiffened.

"Those are the orders, gentlemen. Wheels up at 14:30 hours. Good luck to you."

The colonel turned and walked away.

"Yeah, good luck to us," Welldon snapped, "bullshit. We'll see you in hell, sir."

The colonel pivoted on his heels and the other pilots were on their feet moving in by Welldon's side.

"What are you going to do about it, sir? Ground me? Go ahead, it'll mean I will live to see tomorrow."

"Twenty years in Leavenworth, how does that sound?" the colonel replied coolly.

"You ever see a plane go down in flames, sir?" and he placed cold sarcasm on the word "sir." "You ever see a man bail out, on fire, parachute burning when he tried to open it, sir?"

The colonel stood silent.

"You're talking insubordination in the face of the enemy," he finally announced, but his voice was shaking slightly and pitched low.

No one spoke, the tension about to explode.

"What the hell." It was Struble, the dive bomber pilot. "We're all dead men anyhow with this war, might as well get it over with."

The tension eased off ever so slightly. Welldon, shaking his head, snatched up the hastily drawn briefing map with the last reported coordinates of the Japanese carriers.

"Let's go," he sighed and started for the door, brushing against the colonel as he passed, forcing the man to step back slightly.

Dave, glad he had not had anything to eat, stood up, legs shaking, and moved with the group.

"Lieutenant."

It was the colonel.

Welldon barely slowed, looking back over his shoulder.

"I have seen men burn," the colonel replied. "I flew on the Western Front in 1918, and we didn't have parachutes then."

Welldon stopped, eyes fixed on the colonel, and he finally nodded.

"I wish I was going with you," the colonel said softly. "I can't. I'm sorry, but those are the orders."

"Yes, sir," was all Welldon could say.

The colonel made the gesture first, raising his right hand in a salute.

"God be with you," he said, voice husky.

Welldon and the others saluted in return and headed out the door to their planes.

Dave looked back as he left the room and saw the colonel leaning against the wall, head bowed. He was crying.

Who is he crying for, Dave found himself wondering. Himself, all of this, for us?

This was never how he imagined war would be.

U.S.S. Lexington
Five hundred miles west-northwest of Oahu
14:00 hrs local time
Rear Admiral Newton, commander of Task Force Twelve, looked at the transcript, scaned the information, then handed it to Captain Sherman, who was in direct command of *Lexington,* the old Lady Lex.

Newton still felt uncomfortable having left his natural command post in a cruiser. He knew that in a carrier fight he ought to be near the air component to have better dialogue about the proper tactics, but it still felt odd. He had been a surface warrior all his life, and here he was commanding-ship one of America's biggest and most powerful aircraft carriers. Still, he would do his duty and lead the task force against the Japanese to the best of his ability.

"This puts the Jap fleet three hundred and twenty miles east of us," Sherman said, looking up from the transcript of the radio message intercepted from Oahu and then over at the plot board.

He handed the paper back to Newton.

"Think it's valid?" Newton asked. "It could be a Jap ruse."

"Don't think so," Sherman replied. "I know Watson. We served together on *Saratoga* for a while, about ten years back. He was a year behind me at Annapolis. Good man. I remember hearing how he lost a hand when *Panay* was hit. Doubt that the Japs would know some of his details, and our radio operator who monitored it said it was definitely the Presidio broadcasting. This is the right stuff."

Newton went over to the plot board, measuring out the distances.

"If the Japs are steaming west, and we go up to flank speed; we might be able to get a strike in before dark."

He said it more as a question than a statement.

Sherman shook his head.

"Too many ifs, and besides, it will be dark in four hours. If we order a full strike now, the wind will require turning into the northeast for starters, angling us away from them. At least a two-hour flight out for the Devastators, two hours back — that's recovery after dark, and that is predicated upon everything going right.

"It won't work."

Newton nodded his head in agreement.

"So tomorrow morning then?"

"Yes, sir."

Newton traced a line out with his finger.

"We continue on this course at twenty knots, they continue on their course at the same speed, we could pass right through each other in less than twelve hours. The last thing I want is a surface engagement at night against the Japanese."

"Agreed, sir."

They had monitored Draemel's reports when his small task force had struck the Japanese battleships at night and been slaughtered. It was obvious the Japs had the edge in night combat, something that had been speculated about for years at war games and in reports from the few observers allowed to witness their fleet maneuvers. Beyond that, they had one hell of a tough battleship still in action with their fleet. Meet that at night and it could rip their more lightly armed task force to shreds.

"But, if we do this," and Sherman traced out a different line, "and they continue due west toward the Marshalls, if at dawn we're ready to launch, we just might get the first punch in, maybe even tear them apart."

Newton smiled at the thought.

"That's what I was thinking as well. We change course in fifteen minutes."

He sighed.

"I wish to hell Halsey had waited, just maneuvered. If we had been able to combine and caught them while together, it would have evened it out."

"You know Halsey," Sherman replied with a shrug of his shoulders. "Anyhow, I'd have done the same. It was his only shot. He had to take the risk and do it."

"Still . . ." and his voice trailed off for a moment. "Hell, I wonder if he's even alive anymore. I am afraid the Japs got him."

Akagi
14:05 hrs local time
A zero winged in low, wagging its wings as it passed at a right angle over the deck and then soared back up, part of their covering patrol, which orbited at five hundred meters above the water to keep an eye out for any torpedo bomber that might slip in out of the low tropical clouds, while a second flight of four orbited to the east, fifteen thousand feet up, ready to pounce on any raid that might come from Oahu, now nearly two hundred miles astern.

Fuchida watched the fighter with envy. Over forty Zeroes were maintaining watch over the carriers, burning a lot of fuel and engine time, but until well clear of any strikes from Oahu, they had to watch in all directions. The PBY and B-17 that had been tagging them were nowhere to be seen, but they had monitored the radio reports.

A strike from whatever the Americans had

left on Oahu had to be expected, even at this range. There was also the report from *Soryu* and *Hiryu* that after being attacked by naval planes, they had not returned back to their carrier but had flown on a heading back to Pearl. They would have been turned around by now and perhaps were already coming this way.

Scout planes, ranging westward, had yet to spot any additional carriers, and even Genda now wondered if perhaps there had been only two American carriers in the region after all, and both had been sunk by *Soryu* and *Hiryu.* Though, of course, logically, he wished for that to be true, in his heart part of him wished that it was not. Then when the admiral lifted the ban on his flying tomorrow, he could lead a strike to finish off what was left of the American fleet. Perhaps there was still one, maybe two more of their carriers out there to engage.

"You want to be up there, don't you?"

It was his friend Genda, joining him on the open bridge, and he smiled, nodding.

"I'd like to boast that if I had been flying cover over *Soryu,* it never would have been hit."

Genda shook his head.

"Such courage. I was in one of our planes. It was faster, I knew it would get me through. But their old Devastators? That was suicide to send them against our Zeroes."

"It troubles the admiral, too," Genda replied. "He says it shows they are enraged. We've been listening to their radio reports from the mainland. What they are saying is pure hatred of us now."

"How would we react," Fuchida said softly, "if it had been them surprising us and bombing our ships in Tokyo Harbor? Of course they are enraged. The only factors now are those that should concern us. Will their rage make them reckless? I think we saw that with their attack this morning. And second, how do we beat them so they give in and negotiate despite their anger? We must sink every ship of theirs in the Pacific, that is obvious now."

"I thought you'd find this interesting," Genda said, and handed Fuchida a couple of typewritten sheets of paper. "One of their radio stations on Oahu is back up and broadcasting. We monitored it."

Fuchida took the paper, scanning the transcript of the transmission, chuckling at first and then stopping.

"Did they get this right?"

"Yes. I remember you talking about him."

He read the line again.

"This is Commander James Watson . . ."

He felt his throat tighten. James Watson. It was how long ago? Nearly ten years ago they had met at Etajima, the Japanese naval academy, both of them there to give guest lectures, James on Japanese–American relations, he to pitch naval aviation to the cadets.

They had formed a bond the night they met, drinking Scottish whiskey together with their mutual friend Cecil Stanford. And where was Cecil?

A close bond had been there with both, even though he and James had actually been together less than a day. It was one of those things that just happened at times between men of nations that might one day be enemies, but who at that moment shared a mutual love for their professions, and respect for their counterparts.

He had even introduced James to flying, giving him a ride back to Tokyo after their speeches, triggering in James such a love of the experience that he had gone on to get his own plane.

The friendship had broken down after China. Cecil had bitterly confronted him while he was based at Nanking, denouncing what all in the Imperial Navy found equally disgusting, the medieval-like pillage and rape of that city. He shared that outrage but had to defend the honor of his nation to Cecil, who had stormed out of his office, severing all contact.

Cecil had told him about the tragedy James endured, the loss of his hand when the *Panay* was bombed. There had been a few terse notes between them after that, James making a point of sending a photo of himself with his new plane, a hook rather than his hand clearly visible.

And so their friendships had died as their respective countries, once such good allies, had drifted toward war. The two old friends, however — well, he still considered them to be friends — had often lingered in his thoughts. Now this, a radio intercept of James broadcasting vital information back to the mainland of the United States.

So he was at Pearl Harbor, most likely bending all his efforts now to fight back against Japan.

Damn all. Did he see me yesterday? Did I or one of my comrades kill friends of his? Most likely so.

He forced a smile as he read further: Watson using the registration number of his plane to help verify who he was.

I'm sorry about that, my friend, he thought, remembering how he had introduced him to flying, the bond it had created between the two.

Perhaps someday when this is all over, and hatreds burn away, just perhaps . . .

He handed the papers back to Genda and said nothing.

Enterprise
14:20 hrs local time

He was never much for literature — that was the stuff that the white-jacket officer types up on the bridge would talk about — but at this moment, it did remind him of *Dante's Inferno,* not the book, but a movie he had seen several years earlier starring Spencer Tracy where the guy wound up on a ship that was on fire and sinking, Tracy risking his life to close some steam valve, that on a real ship never would have been located where it was.

And yeah, it did look like that Dante guy's book as well.

Commander Stubbs, sloshing through knee-deep water, respirator strapped to his face, goggles on to protect his eyes, followed the fire hose aft.

He was six decks down, on the starboard main corridor. Flood control doors were open here to allow access to fire crews and repair teams. *Enterprise* still had a pro-

nounced list; he felt a bit like a drunk out for a walk, leaning against the tilt, looking for a moment at the water sloshing about on the deck, gauging the angle: at least ten degrees. The counterflooding was still not containing the intake of water cascading in, compounded by the water pumped in by the fire hoses, which was flooding down into the lower decks.

The water was warm, almost hot. He put his hand on a bulkhead and pulled it back. Fire must still be raging on the other side from a ruptured av-gas line.

The smoke was getting thicker. He saw a chain-gang crew working, men stripped down, shirts off. They should have helmets and shirts on, face protection for flash burns. If we do that, though, these kids would pass out in the heat. They were manhandling out a magazine stacked with forty-millimeter shells, passing each one up, shells going up the ladder for four decks to the hangar deck, where they were being heaved over the side.

Stubbs slowed for a minute, stepped into the line, helped move a couple of shells. Damn, the things were hot, almost blistering hot.

"Keep at it boys, that's the stuff!"

He patted a couple of them on the backs and pushed on. The chain gang snaked down the corridor for a dozen feet and then turned out to the starboard side to where the magazine locker was located, smoke pouring out of it.

A young ensign was leading the crew inside the locker. A fire crew was playing a stream of water on him and the racks of shells.

He felt a cold pit in his stomach, a knotting-up. The youngster had guts, was holding to it, steam pouring out from the water hitting the shells. From the far wall of the magazine he could feel the heat radiating from it.

He wanted to stop, lend encouragement, get the kid's name, make sure he was put in for a commendation, a Navy Cross at least, when this was finished, but there wasn't time, and he had to make the cold decision that if the damn thing started to light off, it wasn't his job to get killed, at least not yet. He should back away.

He pushed on down the main corridor, nicknamed Broadway, the parallel corridor on the port side being Main Street.

Broadway was the danger point now, starting next deck down. All the way to the keel the watertight doors were dogged down, crews evacuated where possible. A corpsman and chaplain had set up their "shop" in a cross corridor between Broadway and Main, six inches or so of filthy water sloshing back and forth as the ship rolled. The dead were stacked up atop each other, bodies, parts of bodies, while only feet away a corpsman, covered in blood, was struggling with scissors to cut off a man's trousers, what was left of them, which were scorched to his body. The chaplain leaned over the burned sailor. He saw the cross on the chaplain's lapel, did not understand what he was saying to the sailor.

"Hear O Israel, the Lord is God . . ." a sailor standing next to Stubbs whispered, in English.

The corpsman cut the rest of the trousers off, looked up.

"You're going to make it," he cried, "you're going to be OK. You still got your equipment. You're still a man."

Stubbs, horrified, saw that the corpsman was lying; the kid was horribly burned and torn by fragmentation that had sliced into his groin.

The corpsman pulled a morphine Syrette out of a pouch strapped to his hip, pulled off the protective cover of the needle, slapped it into the sailor's blackened arm, and squeezed it. Part of the man's burnt flesh came away with the needle.

Stubbs, horrified, yet unable to turn away, could not move.

The corpsman looked, with a penetrating gaze, at the chaplain, who was continuing to recite the prayer in Hebrew.

The chaplain, tears in his eyes, nodded.

The corpsman pulled out three more Syrettes. Those working around him were silent. He quickly stabbed all three into the tortuted man's arm, trying to find a vein.

"Hear O Israel . . ." Others were whispering it now in English, following the lead of the Jewish sailor, who had translated it from Hebrew. In the burned, blackened face of the sailor, his lips were moving, mouthing the words . . . and then he was still.

The chaplain leaned over and gently kissed him on the forehead.

"Go in peace, son."

The corpsman sat back on his heels.

"God damn it," was all he could say, head lowered. He motioned. Two sailors picked up the body and moved it to the pile farther down the corridor.

"Next," was all that the corpsman could whisper.

Stubbs turned away and pushed on, unable to bear the sight of the next man awaiting his turn, left leg gone at the knee, bloody tourniquet wrapped at mid thigh, hands and face burned.

"Not me," the boy started to cry.

The chaplain was by his side.

"Not you, son, you'll make it. What's your name and faith?"

Stubbs pushed on. The smoke ahead was thick, acrid; it was impossible to see more than a few feet, Stygian, with flashes of light, men yelling, the fire crew ahead backing up a few feet. There were two sailors dragging back a third man wearing an "asbestos joe" outfit. They pulled the hood off. The sailor inside was passed out, overcome by heat. Another sailor upended a canteen on the man's face, then pressed it to his lips as he started to come around.

Dangling electrical cables were still hot, swaying, sparking, arcing death to any who might brush against them. He turned to one of his half-dozen assistants who had been trailing behind him.

"Go forward to the next compartment. Cut the power mains there. Get replacement cables and . . ." He paused, looking at the fire forward. "Just cut the electricity. Go over to Main Street. If the fire isn't sweeping in there, find out where it is clear. Get replacement cables out of the nearest damage control locker, plug them in, and run them back across to the starboard side. Got that?"

The seaman first class was off, disappearing into the smoke.

"Gangway!"

He looked back. Half a dozen sailors were manhandling a heavy ten-by-ten piece of oak shoring. They had slings attached to it so they wouldn't lose control of the quarter-ton length of timber. At the bottom of the gangway they paused, a sailor putting his hand on the watertight hatch down to the next level, checking for heat, squatting down to look through the small glass peephole to see how bad the flooding was.

"It's OK!" he shouted, and he unscrewed the hatch and pulled it back.

"Christ," was all he said as he guided his team hoisting the timber and started down the steps to the next deck below. They were into chest deep water by the time they hit the bottom of the ladder, men cursing about how hot the water was. They disappeared from view, part of the team next deck down that was struggling to drive ten-by-ten timbers into place to shore up one of the bulkheads inward from an oil tank that was threatening to rupture, cracked already from the impact of one of the torpedoes.

He was tempted to go down with them, but felt it was time to report back in to the bridge. He went up the ladder the shoring crew had just descended.

On the fifth deck, the smoke was almost as bad. Of course, the damn stuff rose, pouring up through ventilation shafts, gangways still open, emergency escape hatches not sealed off. He went forward to the damage control center for this deck, pulling the door open, going in, assistants following before they slammed it shut.

The air inside was slightly better, drawn

down by fan from a vent up on the hangar deck. A plot board in the middle of the room was covered with a chart of the ship. The lieutenant running damage control on this deck looked up at him.

"Fire contained for the moment on this deck, sir," he announced. "But we're getting a lot of water runoff from the fires up on the hangar deck."

"How is it below?"

"We're surviving."

There was a momentary lurch; he could feel it in the soles of his feet. Something had given way below; within seconds he could sense they were taking on more of a list to starboard.

He felt isolated, only aware of what was going on here, on this deck, and what he had just seen below. He picked up a phone, heard the click. Good, it was still connected to the damage control center on the bridge.

"Stubbs here."

"Sir, Lieutenant Ferguson here," came the reply, connection barely audible. "The admiral is asking what the hell just happened down below."

"Put him on."

"Yes, sir."

A momentary pause.

"Stubbs, you there?"

"Yes, sir."

"What in hell was that?"

He could feel the soul of this ship, sensing that the list was stabilizing, but he'd have to counterflood again.

"Sir, I think it was one of the bulkheads, seventh deck. It was partially staved from the torpedo impact. It probably gave way."

He thought of the shoring crew he had watched pass just a few minutes ago. He hoped those kids were still able to get out.

"You are still saying we can hold on?"

"Hell yes, sir."

"I trust you, Stubbs," Halsey growled. "But it is chaos up here, the smoke is blinding. At least we're under the clouds so the Japs can't see us.

"Ferguson here reports they got a phone hookup running down to the port engine room." He hesitated. "It's hell down there. Can we get them out?"

Stubbs sighed. "Sir. They're under two decks of fire and boiling hot water. Besides, if we try and pull them out now, that means abandoning the only engines we still have. That shuts down all power, that shuts down the pumps, we lose the ship."

"I understand."

"I'll talk to them and explain the situation."

"Right then. Stubbs, we just made visual with *Indianapolis* and its escorts. They're coming up alongside."

"Damn good! I'll be up topside in a few minutes. Can we see if we can get them in close enough to help dampen the fires, start evacuating some of the wounded, and run some power supply across?"

"Fine then. Signing off here."

"Please put Ferguson back on, sir."

A momentary pause.

"Ferguson here, sir."

"Patch me through to the engine room."

"Yes, sir."

It took long seconds before someone picked up on the other side. He could barely hear who was speaking over the background noise of what sounded like steam blasting, men shouting.

"Just answer yes or no," Stubbs shouted, "Can you hear me?"

"Yes . . ." The voice was distant.

"This is Commander Stubbs. We are aware of your situation. I'm going to give it to you straight."

"Go ahead . . ."

"We can't get you out yet. You have two decks of water and fire above you. We cannot get to you now, but as God is my witness I promise we will."

"Christ, sir. It's over a hundred and thirty down here."

Damn, that could put a man down in a matter of minutes. He could imagine the nightmare of it, steam venting, the claustrophobia, knowing one is trapped, the terror of feeling the ship listing more to starboard. Wondering if it would just keep on rolling over, invert, and then plunge down — and then one waited, hearing bulkheads collapsing, lights blowing out, waiting for death in the boiling darkness.

"You must stay at your posts," Stubbs said slowly. "Do not try any of the emergency hatches."

He hesitated.

"And we need you. If you abandon your post, this ship will lose the last of its power. You are the only ones left. We lose you, *Enterprise* will sink."

A pause on the other side.

"Yes, sir."

"I promise we'll get you out. Call in to damage control every fifteen minutes. We'll keep you posted. Now stick with it, son."

"What the hell else can we do?" came a distant reply.

"That's the stuff."

He hung up, unable to say anything else. Chances were, by the time they did pump the decks clear — if they could pump them clear — the men down in the engine room would all be dead. They were still getting some air; the intake and exhaust stacks to the boilers had to still be working, otherwise the fires would have snuffed out by now.

It would be the heat that would kill them.

He left the fifth deck and started up to topside. He paused on the hangar deck. Fires here, damage from the first attack, were pretty well under control. The aft elevator hung down at a drunken angle. A crew was already working on it. He wondered if that was a futile gesture. It would take a shipyard with a heavy crane to lift the elevator out so that the hydraulics could be replaced, a new shaft set into place, and then the elevator deck itself replaced. It was a crazy gesture, but on the other hand, it was some kind of signal that they were working to turn *Enterprise* back into a fighting ship. For the moment, any more hands sent below would be in the way.

Amidships was now a hospital area. Once men pulled out from below were stabilized, they were brought up here where at least the air was cooler, an ocean breeze blowing gently through the open sides. A group of sailors were lined up, waiting their turn to give blood for their comrades, corpsmen matching up types and doing direct transfers.

Once topside, he pressed up to the main deck. Seeing the flight deck relative to the horizon, the extent of the list became visible and for a moment far more alarming. They were going to have to evacuate any possible positions below on the portside that could be sacrificed and flood them to keep the ship on an even keel. What was left? He'd have to get back into damage control and run down the prospects.

As reported, he could now see the smudge of smoke on the southern horizon. In spite of the lowering tropical clouds, slanting rain coming down off both port and starboard sides a mile or two out; he could just barely make out the high masthead of *Indianapolis* — a damn good old ship, nearly a battle cruiser with its armament and displacement.

He could only hope that she had enough oil on board so they could pump some across to replace the tens of thousands of gallons lost from the torpedo hits and flooding; otherwise, even if they saved *Enterprise* from sinking, she'd soon be dead in the water anyhow, along with her surviving escorts.

He turned and went back up to the bridge

to report in.

Halsey stood on the open bridge, silent, nodding as Stubbs made his report.

And even as he started to explain what was going on below, the deck bumped beneath the soles of their feet, almost as if they had struck something; a second later a blast of fire erupted out of their starboard side. An instant later the explosion changed tone, sounding like large firecrackers. Tracer streaks soared up through the rising fireball.

"What the hell was that?" Halsey cried.

Stubbs shook his head.

"I think it was one of the forty-millimeter magazines." He sighed. "It just lit off."

He thought of the young ensign leading the valiant effort to try and empty it before it blew. He wondered if anyone knew the kid's name.

"Stubbs, should I transfer my flag over to *Indianapolis*?" Halsey finally asked.

Stubbs looked him straight in the eye and shook his head.

"Sir, I hate to sound like some rotten movie line here, but I'll have to say it: Don't give up the ship."

Halsey smiled and grasped Stubbs's hand.

Chapter Ten

Hickam Army Air Force Base
December 8, 1941
14:40 hrs local time

"Any questions?"

No one spoke. Dave thought that if ever there was a ragtag group this had to be it. Three Wildcats including his own. Three P-40s, two P-36s, five Dauntlesses, which would be the core of the strike force, and three B-17s.

None of them had trained together except for the Dauntless and Wildcat crews off of *Enterprise.* The B-17 guys were fresh from the States flying the older B variant. All the fighters flew at different speeds and had different handling characteristics, and all knew after but a day and a half of battle that they were dead meat against the Zeroes.

It had actually turned into a bit of a democratic process. Struble, as senior rank, had first made noises that he would plan and lead the strike, but the army guys sided with Welldon, captain of the B-17 Gloria Ann, and without much argument Struble had deferred.

The plan was straightforward and simple. They would launch the B-17s first, followed by the Navy planes, then the 40s and 36s, which would barely have enough fuel to get there and back. If the Japs were where the PBY, which had gone silent a half hour ago, had said they were, and if they maintained their heading, then maybe this motley crew would have a chance of doing real damage to the Japanese carriers.

Altitude would be twelve thousand, a compromise between different aircraft as to most economical cruising height for fuel. Cloud cover was over fifty percent, tops up to twenty thousand; it was going to be turbulent. Welldon in the lead would elect whether to go straight through a cloud or circle around it if it looked too tough to fly through.

There was nothing more to be said.

Any semblance of bravado was gone. A Catholic chaplain had wandered over, and those of the faith took communion and absolution; those not of the faith, including more than a few who had been agnostic at best the day before, knelt for a blessing.

Engines were turning over, warming up. On his knee pad Dave had written down the primary and secondary radio frequencies, the call signal for his small group of Wildcats — it would be X-ray One — the estimated position of the Japanese fleet, and a ditching position the Navy had just handed off. A civilian interisland steamer off of Kauai had patched into the Navy frequency over at the newly established radio center, and asked if it could help out in any way. They were told a Navy sub running on the surface at flank speed was trying to move up behind the enemy group, but would not have time to do rescue operations if it was to have any chance of closing with the enemy. So it had to be the old steamer. It had been a gutsy move on their part. While helping a pilot low on fuel or shot up, they might be getting a visit from a Jap sub, but they called in anyhow.

There was an exchange of nods, the group breaking up, crews already aboard the B-17s, gunners mounted aft in the Dauntlesses.

Dave climbed up onto the wing of his Wildcat, almost into the cockpit before thinking about the fact that his feet had just left the earth, and he knew with almost utter certainty he would never walk on this earth again. An army sergeant helped him slide in and strap on the shoulder harness, tightened it, then patted him on the shoulder.

"Good luck to you, sir."

He could only nod. Why was it that most of the mechanics always seemed old enough, at the very least, to be an elder brother, or perhaps even a father? The man could not see his eyes; he had sunglasses on already since they would be flying all the way into a westerly sun — yet another advantage for the Japs.

All he could do was nod, not sure of his voice.

The mechanic backed off the wing, came around in front, hands held high indicating for him to hold position. There would be no control tower transmits. First of all, there was no longer a control tower. It had been blown out in the bombardment last night by a direct hit from a fourteen-inch shell, thus proving that the Japs had either the best gunners in the world or the luckiest. Second, the transmission just might be monitored and give advance warning. As it was, they were taking off on the north-south runway. Hundreds of men had been working all day to fill in enough of the craters to give them a halfway decent takeoff run.

They were to stay low, go over the island to the north, then turn west, keeping well out of visual range of *Hiei,* which was still surviving off the coast and could relay a report.

The first of the three B-17s, Gloria Ann, taxied out, followed by the other two, Pat's Girl and Four Aces. The nose art on Pat's Girl definitely had an appeal. The artist was good. The girl looked like Veronica Lake, her distinctive peekaboo hair style not just covering her eye but strategically placed to make sure the painting passed censors and the more prudish. The last thought on his mind would have been anything to do with that. He could barely remember how his own girlfriend looked, the sound of her voice, the smell of her hair. All he could focus on was rpms, engine heat, and manifold pressure.

Next out were the dive bombers. Struble gave him a wave as he taxied past. The lead B-17 was at the end of the runway, stopped for a moment to do the final runup; then without fanfare it powered up, starting its long rollout laden with ten five-hundred-pound armor-piercing bombs. The Navy had wanted them to haul torpedoes, but Welldon had absolutely refused on that one. They were not trained, and were too damn vulnerable going in barely above stall speed against a target that big. He had at least won that point.

The second B-17 rolled out onto the runway twenty seconds later and started its runup even before Gloria Ann lifted off.

He caught a flicker of movement and looked down. It was his army mechanic, signaling him to roll out. Chocks had already been pulled. He pushed up the throttle several hundred rpm, and the Wildcat began a slow roll; then he gave it full right rudder to turn. As he did so, the mechanic came to attention and saluted. All he could do was raise his left hand in reply, sort of a wave. He had a feeling that he was saying goodbye to the last man he would ever see.

He followed the last of the dive bombers. All the planes were doing slow weaves back and forth, with noses high. There was no other way to see forward other than to do a zigzagging weave as they taxied. It also allowed a final check of rudder controls.

Struble roared down the runway a hundred feet off to his right, a half-ton armor-piercing bomb slung under his belly. Three more Dauntlesses followed; one more to go. He pressed down hard on his brakes, ran the engine up, did a final check of magnetos and carb heater, watching if rpms dropped. If the drop was more than 150 rpms, something was wrong, and he actually prayed something would blow out, or that rpm drop would hit, which could honorably abort him from the mission.

More than one pilot in advanced training with carrier landings and takeoffs would finally hit a panic point after two or three bad landings in a row. He could not just say he was out of it; instead, he'd nudge the throttle down when doing final check, claim a problem, and be pushed over to one side, then express mystification later when it worked OK. The air boss might look the other way once, tell the guy to get some sack time and go up later — but that was peacetime.

The engine checked out. There was no honorable way out. The Dauntless ahead of him had already swung onto the runway, powered up, and gone on its way.

Though he was a Catholic, religion was something that he had let drop after his mother died when he was fourteen and his old man, in his bitterness, stopped going to church. But today he had taken communion, the first time in years, and he made the sign of the cross.

"Christ, don't let me screw up," was all he

could pray. He pushed the throttle forward and rolled out onto the runway with hard right rudder and a touch of brake to turn. He straightened out, now with a good deal of right rudder. It was not a carrier takeoff with built-in fifty-knot headwind to lift him off in just a few hundred feet. He was fully gassed up, patches quickly riveted up adding a touch of drag.

He kept right rudder in to counteract the torque and rotating slipstream. His tail came up, and he edged the stick back ever so slightly to avoid a prop strike, a touch of right aileron against the twenty-degree crosswind. Air speed up to sixty; she was starting to feel lighter. Damn crater ahead, hope they packed the dirt down tight. Work crews stood to one side, some waving their caps. He rolled through the filled-in crater. God damn . . . a rough bounce. He caught air for a second, airspeed still too slow for rotation, bounced down hard, kept stick forward. Panic now and you start yo-yoing and wind up nosing in or ground looping.

Another damn crater ahead. Stick felt right; he eased it back just an inch or so as he hit the lip of the earth-filled crater, bounced, just above stall speed, leveled it out, several feet off the ground, airspeed now building fast, crosswind causing him to drift. Not high enough to drop a wing into it, let it drift.

Airspeed now ninety-five, end of runway approaching. He hit the switch for landing gear and airspeed really began to pick up. Start to notch up the flaps, now back on the stick.

And for a brief instant he actually did feel the joy again that had first gotten him hooked on flying three years ago, when as a sophomore in college, he had joined the flying club, which just happened to be sponsored by the United States Navy.

That little contract was a million miles and eternity away from this moment. If he had known then what he knew now . . . ?

With no time to think about it, he banked to starboard to get around the raging firestorm of the oil tank farms, the wreckage that was Pearl Harbor. He had a glimpse of a ship turtled, its bottom punched through by a hit from a fourteen-inch shell. Someone had said it was the *Oklahoma.*

Coming around the far side of the smoking inferno he could see the Dauntlesses formed up already, slowly climbing, ahead of them the three B-17s, stately, huge. At least I'm not in one of those, he thought.

They were crossing up over the center of the island, same route the Japs had taken yesterday but in reverse, he thought. Plumes of smoke still soared up from Wheeler and Schofield. Down on the road below, rolling south, was a military column, trucks, and some armored cars. It made him nervous for a second. Hopefully by now some discipline regarding shooting at anything in the air had been restored. At least with these men it had. The planes stayed low, at a thousand feet. From beyond the hills to the west he could see a smudge of smoke far off, which he thought had to be *Hiei.* Was it less than eight hours ago I was over that, he wondered. And now he was going out on his third strike of the day.

He remembered reading how pilots with the RAF last year were flying six to eight sorties a day, but hell, that was different, they were up, engaged in a matter of minutes, and if the worst happened they could land on home territory or bail out and come down next to some village where civilians would stand them a pint. He had a longer way to fly on one mission than the RAF pilots were flying all day. Furthermore, flying over open water was a lot more nerve-racking. Go down out over that enormous ocean and you're shark food.

The thought of it made him think of the heavy .45 in its shoulder holster, underneath his inflatable Mae West. If I go down into the drink, can't get a life raft, then that will be it, he thought.

The column was moving into a formation. His place was with the two surviving Wildcats. One of them was not even from his old squadron, a plane that had been left behind by *Lexington* for an engine replacement. He couldn't even remember the pilot's name. Off his portside wing the P-40s and 36s came up, flanking the Dauntlesses to the west.

They were over the Dole plantation, the ground climbing as they headed for the pass, going through it, some serious buffet-

ing for a moment, trade winds rolling off the hills to the east of them, the ocean visible ahead. A couple of minutes later the 17s began their stately turns, the rest of the formation following, sliding above the north shore beach.

Damn! A few tracers went up between the 40s and the Dauntlesses. He looked down, saw the gunners. No one broke radio silence, but he knew every pilot was cursing. After a day of this, a man was tempted to just maybe do a very fast and very low flyby and strafe a few rounds, not killing them but definitely scaring the crap out of them.

The gun fell silent. They flew on, peaks to their south now shielding any possible sighting by *Hiei* or Zeroes that might be covering it. The last of the greenery dropped away; they were out over the ocean. The lead B-17 wagged its wing, turning slightly onto a heading of west-southwest 255 degrees, then began a slow climb of three hundred feet a minute, not pushing it as they hauled their two-and-a-half-ton bomb loads heavenward. He eased back ever so slightly on his stick, checking to port and starboard, wingmen positioned correctly in a V. He leaned out the fuel mixture slightly. It was a long way out there and back, and every ounce of fuel was precious. A couple of hundred feet ahead were the five dive bombers, flying in echelon, Struble in the lead position left and forward, the army fighters on their other flank.

The air was beginning to get cooler, but he kept the canopy open. He was already soaked in sweat as he knew he would be the entire flight out regardless of how cold it got further aloft.

Hickam Army Air Force Base
15:25 hrs local time

"James?"

"Huh? Yeah, sweetheart . . ."

"No, sir, it's Dianne."

More than a bit surprised, he sat up, a few of the sailors sitting on the floor of the hangar nearby chuckling.

Not thinking, he put both arms back to brace himself as he got up, and nearly fell over on his left side. Dianne grabbed him by the shoulders.

"God damn," he gasped, stump hitting the hard concrete floor, pain radiating up his arm.

She steadied him.

"They got another radio up, and, sir, Collingwood and the rest of the crew are here."

James saw his boss sitting by a table where a monster of a radio was set up, dials glowing. Joe was standing behind the unit, checking the antenna lead. Collingwood saw him sitting up, and motioned for him to come over.

Dianne helped him to his feet and without asking raised his left arm, checking the bandage, sniffing it again, this time wrinkling her nose.

"You're going to the hospital," she announced sharply, "and I'm taking you there."

"I'm OK."

"Sir," and he noticed she had dropped the James routine, "it's getting infected."

"Later."

She gave him a defiant look but then finally relented and stepped back.

He went over to the long table that someone had dragged in, and sat down on a folding chair next to Collingwood, who lit a cigarette and then handed it to James, pushing over a cup of coffee as well.

"You look like crap, James."

"Well, sir, you don't look much better," James quipped back.

He had often wondered if Collingwood only had one uniform shirt in his entire wardrobe, for there always seemed to be ash and coffee stains in the same place.

"This lad here has got us on the right

frequencies," and Collingwood nodded to Joe.

"He's a good man," James said forcefully, loud enough so others would hear. "If it wasn't for him and his friends, our asses would really be in the sling right now."

Joe reddened slightly, and nodded thanks.

James wondered for a moment if somehow they could wrangle a security clearance for him. Their entire operation in the basement of CinCPac was gone; they were going to have to rebuild a couple of hundred thousand dollars' worth of radio receivers from scratch. All their files were gone, the new IBM calculating machines that the team was just starting to get the hang of using, the darn things able to help sort coded word groups and pop out a card the size of an old dollar bill upon which was recorded the last use of that letter grouped for cross-referencing to earlier transmissions. All their translation books, all of it was gone. It'd take months before they could even have a remote chance of rebuilding and starting over.

Once things settled down he would have to suggest to Collingwood that a large detail be sent over to sweep the grounds clean, but then again they weren't the only ones in that building with closely guarded secrets not shared with others. Someone had most likely already thought of it. He looked at Joe again and sadly realized that for now he could help, but a week from now, chances were he wouldn't be allowed within a mile of any base. There was no way in hell they could wrangle a security clearance for him. He even found himself wondering if, given his own family, he might lose his security clearance as well and find himself sitting out the rest of the war stuck in some damn supply depot back in the States.

"Let's look at that arm," Collingwood said, and reluctantly James lifted it up, not letting the pain of movement register on his face.

"I need you here for a little while, and then you're going over to the hospital to get it properly cleaned and bandaged. Got that?"

"Yes, sir."

"Now, listen to this."

He threw a switch and the small loudspeaker next to the radio crackled to life.

It was Japanese. Damn, they were back in business!

It took a moment to get the feel of it; the signal was weak, distorted. Joe, back around behind them, leaned over and touched a dial ever so slightly. It came in clearer.

James looked at the lit-up dial.

"One of their naval air-to-ship frequencies."

"Exactly."

"Repeat. Ten American planes, course bearing two six five degrees. They are . . ."

The signal wavered for a second, hard to discern.

"You get that?" James asked, and Collingwood shook his head.

"He said Army and Navy dive bombers," Joe interjected softly, barely a whisper.

They looked back at him and nodded their thanks.

Joe walked away to join a group working to set up another radio.

"Our guys have already been spotted," James said softly. "Must be a scout plane watching our coast."

"Should we send them a warning?" Collingwood asked.

This was outside their game. They were cryptanalysts, not tactical air officers.

He shook his head.

"What good will it do them? The Japanese might monitor it and know we're on to them," he sighed, "and besides, those kids are doomed anyhow."

Collingwood nodded and lit another cigarette from the stub of his last one.

"Wish we had a directional antenna up, try and get a fix on them that way."

Another plane was reporting in on the same frequency, obviously far distant, barely audible, reporting no sighting, and it was turning 90 degrees to the south to start the next leg of its search. A couple of more reported in, doing the same.

From the difference in signal strength he suspected the other planes were part of the Japanese search pattern to the west of their fleet. There was nothing else, and from that he could deduct that *Lexington* had yet to be spotted. Her location was as much a mystery to him, and for that matter everyone else on their side, as it was to the Japanese.

"Stay with this," Collingwood said. "I want to see if our miracle worker over there can get us a couple of more radios set up to monitor their other frequencies."

James turned off the loudspeaker switch and worked on a set of headphones. Ever so gently touching the dial, shifting the frequency but a few kilohertz to either side and back again, picking up snippets of conversation, broadcasting in the clear, scout planes, a lot of them reporting in. And then the first one, giving another bearing on the small attack group, announced he was trailing them astern.

It was so damn frustrating. They were finally getting some information in here, but still it was only fragmentary. No one was sure, with Kimmel dead, exactly who was in charge of naval operations at this moment. As for the Army, General Short, who he suspected would not be in command much longer, was last reported down inspecting beach defenses.

All he could do for the moment was sit and listen and feel impotent while others did the fighting.

Akagi
16:15 hrs local time

They had been running back into the wind for fifteen minutes. The last of the returning scout planes had been recovered, and a new wave was going out for a final sweep before dark. If the navigator aboard the scout plane trailing the Americans was accurate in his reports, the small attack force was now seventy miles out and tracking to their south. With luck they might miss the fleet entirely.

Each of the four carriers with his task force was launching Zeroes to intercept, with a total of twenty-five committed to defending against the incoming raid. *Soryu* and *Hiryu,* not yet up to rendezvous and still trailing fifty miles to the south-southeast, were putting up all their remaining fighters, thirteen of them.

The last of the Zeroes and scout planes lifted off, and as one the entire fleet came about, returning to their westerly heading. The twenty minutes of launch time had shifted them ten miles farther to the north, shifting *Hiryu* and *Soryu* as well in the same direction.

The wind was beginning to be an increasingly frustrating factor for the admiral. Every launch and recovery required coming around nearly a hundred and forty degrees from his intended course, eating up thousands upon thousands of liters of precious oil in the process. His calculations of yesterday about the reserve available to take them to the Marshalls were becoming less and less valid. He had hoped to at least do a partial fuel transfer to the always hungry destroyers before dark. That would be impossible now, with another American strike wave coming in.

It was also impossible, of course, for him to know that the navigator aboard the scout plane trailing the Americans was indeed off by a good fifteen miles on his estimate, and that the twenty-minute run to the northeast for recovery and launch had tracked the main fleet out of visual for the Americans, but had edged *Soryu* and *Hiryu* almost within sight.

Fifteen miles northeast of Hiryu *and* Soryu, *twenty-eight miles southeast of* Akagi
16:30 hrs local time

"Damn it, they aren't here!" It was Struble.

"And that son of a bitch is still trailing us," one of the P-40 pilots interjected. "Let me go for the bastard."

"Negative on that," Struble snapped. "He'll just lead you into the clouds. They know we're coming. I want you with us."

"Just great," the P-40 pilot replied.

Dave, tense, palms sweating inside his leather gloves, kept scanning straight ahead. The damn sun was lower, straight into his eyes, giving him a headache. But that was where the Zeroes would come from.

Cloud cover was changing, the morning and midday cumulus combining into towering cumulonimbus that rose to over twenty-five thousand feet, some of them dark with flickers of lightning.

The sky ahead darkened, one of the taller clouds blocking it out. Good, it'd give them some contrast, background to search out any Zeroes, and would block out the sun. But the view below was restricted through the cloud openings, and ten minutes back Struble and Welldon had finally broken radio silence to debate whether they should drop down to three thousand feet or not, giving them better visibility of the ocean below, skimming in just below the taller of the clouds.

Struble had opted to stay at twelve, and Dave wondered if they might very well have flown right over the Jap fleet and not even seen it. But then again, the Japanese fighter pilots were aggressive as all hell; if they were near or over the fleet, they'd be bounced by now.

The towering cloud ahead looked dangerous, and Welldon's B-17 began a gentle turn to the right, northward. He could have gone either way, Dave thought; maybe he's on to something, or with luck maybe not; they'd circle past the Japs, drop their loads, and get the hell out. As it was, it was going to be close to a nighttime landing, something he never really liked. He wasn't even qualified for it yet on a carrier — and he had already heard how anything in the sky over Pearl at night was most definitely being shot at.

They were now onto a northerly heading, and Welldon, regardless of what Struble said, was going into a shallow dive, punching lower to try and get a better view.

Several long minutes passed. The storm cell was a good ten miles across. It could in fact have an entire Jap fleet hidden under it. He knew that was what Halsey would do, what any carrier commander would do if he knew a strike was inbound, and together with Gloria Ann they were definitely being followed and reported on.

Several things now happened almost at the same instant.

Welldon aboard the B-17 Gloria Ann interrupted the momentary silence. "Got a ship in sight to our north at ten o'clock!"

At nearly the same instant, from the corner of his eye Dave saw one of the P-36s just fold up, a wing shearing off, the spark of tracers and the flash of white, with a red meatball on its fuselage, silhouetted against the darker mass of clouds forward and above.

"X-ray, stay with me!" was all he could gasp as he slammed into full throttle, hitting it so fast that the engine sputtered for an instant, cylinders flooding with fuel before clearing and accelerating. Some instinct told him to pull up and bank hard. As he did so, more tracers snapped past his canopy, slashing the air where he would have been if he had continued on the same trajectory but one second longer.

He banked so hard that he rolled inverted, nose high, and as he did so he caught another glimpse of a Zero, this one cutting between two of the B-17s, knocking out an engine on Pat's Girl as it dove through. He pulled stick back hard into his gut, lined up and squeezed off a burst, another deflection shot, and the Zero walked straight into it. With the Zero flying at just over three hundred miles an hour and his four .30 caliber machine guns each firing ten rounds a second, the Zero passed through his fire, flying more than the length of a football field every second, so that only one round from each gun would impact before the enemy plane was through the cone of fire. But he was pulling back hard enough on his stick that nine rounds actually hit, walking across the top of the Zero's fuselage, blowing out a cylinder head on the Zero's Nakajima fourteen-cylinder engine, fragments cutting a fuel line, another round blowing through the top of the pilot's canopy, killing him instantly.

Dave barely saw what was happening. The Zero screamed past him, apparently still under control. He rolled out into a shallow dive between Pat's Girl and Gloria Ann, caught a glimpse of flame licking back from the inboard port engine of Pat's Girl, a glimpse of the Veronica Lake lookalike painted on her side. He pulled back up, barely hearing the radio chatter, someone, an Army pilot, screaming he was on fire and couldn't pop his canopy, Gloria Ann calling for the strike group to follow his lead, Struble cursing, then ordering his group into a shallow dive behind the B-17s.

Get above it, Dave thought, and he pulled back hard on his stick, still flying at full throttle, almost redlining the engine. He went into a climb, looked forward, to either side, up, which was now relative to his plane, back to the horizon to the northeast. Another glimpse of two Zeroes coming around hard, two trails of smoke and flame, one without doubt the P-40 with the doomed pilot screaming, mike switched on.

"Jesus . . . I'm burning! God I can't get the canopy back. Oh God!"

He felt guilt, wishing the man would switch the mike off or just die. It was horrifying to listen to.

"I see them. God damn flattops! Two, make that three . . . no, four of them!"

It sounded like Gloria Ann.

Dave continued through his climb, turning it into a loop, arcing up, over, coming back down, now back behind the heavy bombers and dive bombers. There was not enough time for Struble's group to do what they preferred, climb for a diving strike from high altitude. It was going to have to be a glide bomb run, which left them vulnerable all the way in.

A burst of antiaircraft fire ignited forward of the 17s, then a barrage. He was out of the loop, building speed. More tracers from above; the Japs were concentrating on the 17s. More hits on Pat's Girl, sparks walking up the fuselage, a Zero dropping down onto its tail, actually dropping wheels and flaps to kill off his speed.

The burst of 7.7- and 20-millimeter fire from the Zero tore into the tail and elevator assembly of Pat's Girl. Fragments flew off.

He was at long range, a good six hundred yards back, but opened up, arcing his fire in, afraid for a second his own shots were impacting into Pat's. The Zero, seeing the tracers, broke right, going into a dive as he turned, pulling up wheels and flaps. For a second he thought he had him, but then he overshot, and the Zero disappeared astern.

Christ, he'll be on my tail!

He began to jink violently, jamming in left rudder, then right, looking over his shoulder. His wingmen were nowhere to be seen.

The Zero rolled in behind him. Still at full throttle, he started into a dive, looked back over his shoulder for another second, then turned to look straight ahead. A moment of pure terror: He barely cleared the tail wheel of Pat's Girl, diving underneath the bomber and its trail of fire and debris. The Zero diverted from him and focused back on Pat, pouring in more fire as Dave went inverted, diving.

The screaming of the dying P-40 pilot abruptly ended. Gloria was back on, announcing he was starting his bomb run, the other 17s to drop when he did.

Dave pulled out of his dive at three thousand feet and four miles out from the Japanese carrier *Akagi,* a shellburst nearby marking the fact that they were firing at him.

He spared a quick glance at the enemy ship. It didn't look like the one they had hit earlier in the day. He didn't have time for a second look. More tracers snapped by his canopy. A sound of impact, and something struck the back of his armored seat so hard he felt it like a hammer blow, the 20-millimeter shell detonating, blowing out the rear of his canopy.

He pulled back hard, heading for the clouds . . . and heard Struble announce he was going in.

Akagi

Every gun on both the port and starboard side of *Akagi's* flight deck was pointed aloft, firing.

Yamamoto stood motionless, watching, and Fuchida, heart racing, watched as the first of the dive bombers began to go up, inverting, rolling into his dive . . . and his heart was actually with them.

Were the Americans insane? Five dive bombers attacking the main fleet? It was a futile gesture — and a brave one that filled his heart with admiration, even though it was his ship they had picked out to attack.

Did they know this was the flagship? he wondered.

Over Akagi

Lieutenant Commander Dan Struble lined up forward of the carrier as he went into a shallow twenty-degree dive, flak bursting around him.

To his port side he saw Gloria Ann. It was heading toward the other carrier, two miles farther on. He wanted to call for him to divert, but knew he was already on his bomb run.

Should I divert?

I can't now, he realized. If we got any chance of scoring a hit, it is now. I can't af-

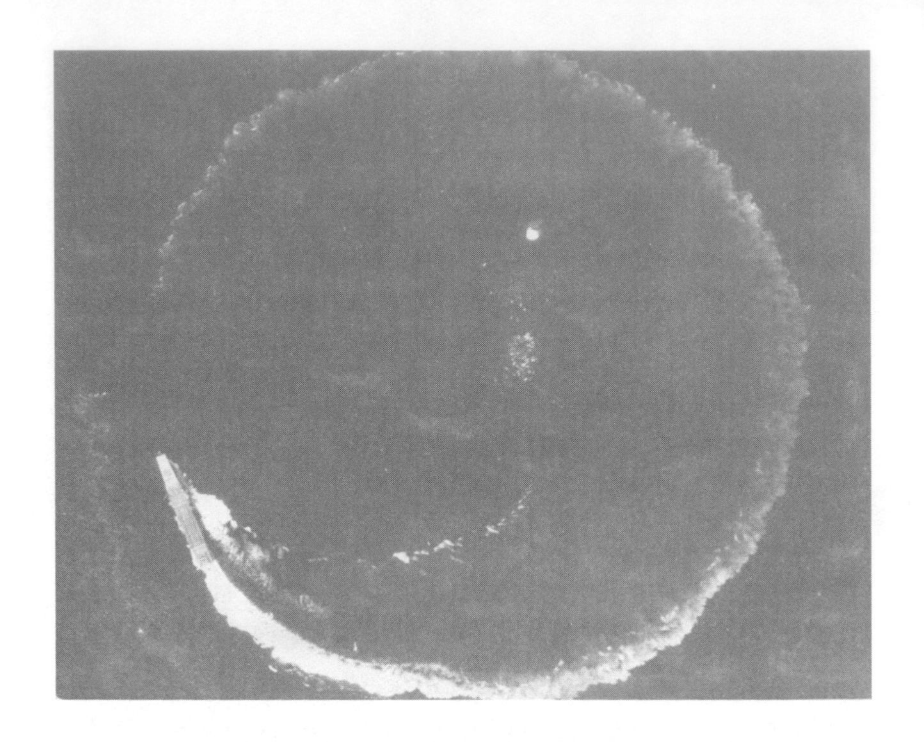

ford the extra thirty seconds to turn onto the other target. None of us will make it with so many Zeroes closing in.

The carrier was turning to starboard. He made a guess: She'll straighten out and start to reverse, and aimed for that point.

It was the last clear and conscious decision he ever made.

Three seconds later a six-inch shell burst directly in front of his plane fifty yards ahead. An impartial observer would have called it an excellent shot. Fragments tore into the Dauntless's Wright Cyclone engine, severing electrical cables, fuel line, oil lines, cracking two cylinders, a fragment slicing across the side of Struble's head, fracturing his skull, nearly knocking him unconscious.

The dive bomber lurched for a moment, skidding to port. He was all but blinded.

He was less than five hundred yards out. Release . . . but something within whispered he was dying, that his plane was dying.

"Jimmy?"

No response from his tail gunner. He wanted to apologize somehow to the kid back there, but their intercom link was gone, and he couldn't hear the kid crying. He began to recite the Twenty-third Psalm.

Akagi was turning, straightening out to shift to starboard.

Struble's Dauntless slammed into the deck, forty yards aft of the bridge, bomb breaking loose from its pinions, after plane, bomb, pilot, and gunner had smashed through the deck, burst into the hangar deck, and impacted on top of a Kate that had returned from a scouting mission and was being refueled. The spray of aviation gas aboard the Dauntless engulfed the crew working on their plane.

The bomb, now detached, crashed through two more decks — even as the wreckage of the plane and its dead pilot and gunner skidded off the hangar deck floor, spreading a plume of wreckage. The bomb failed to detonate. The detonator had rested for over two years in a storage bunker, moisture slowly doing its work, corroding the assembly for the plunger. It should have been opened, if need be greased, and checked before being screwed into the bomb, but the sergeant responsible was dead, killed in the bombardment, and his replacement was just told to screw it in, there was no time to waste, and he had not checked to make sure the detonator plunger worked smoothly, so that the impact failed to release it.

But for Commander Struble and his gunner, that no longer mattered, or ever would matter. His plane, however, had nevertheless taken *Akagi* out of the fight.

"Jesus Christ, Skipper, you see that?"

It was Gary, his ball turret gunner, who was supposed to be watching out for Japs underneath while at the same time reporting their bomb fall.

"Did we get it?" Welldon shouted.

"Negative, Skipper, short."

"God damn it! I told them we ain't worth shit against a fast-moving ship!"

"Skipper. One of the Dauntless bombers, it deliberately crashed into the other Nip carrier. Look at it burn!"

"Everyone shut the hell up, watch our own patterns!" Welldon shouted, but nevertheless he did spare a glance to port and caught a glimpse of a spreading fireball on the other carrier, with two bomb splashes to either side of it.

"Where's Pat's Girl?" he asked, even as he put his B-17 into a harrowing sixty-degree bank to starboard, turning away from the two enemy ships.

"She's gone, sir." It was Carl, his top gunner. "Didn't you see? His wing just folded up."

"Any chutes?"

"Yeah, as if that would help. Shark food."

"Christ, if we were fighting the Krauts, at least we'd come down on dry land," someone else chimed in.

"Everyone shut the hell up. I want a strike report!"

"No go, skipper," Gary came back. "Pat never dropped. We fell short by a hundred yards. The damn Jap maneuvered out of the way. I don't even know where the hell the other plane is."

I could have told them what would be the results, Welldon thought. But that didn't matter now. It was getting the hell out of here that counted, and he aimed straight for the nearest cloud. Thunderstorm or not, it was better than facing the damn Zeroes again.

As he leveled out he caught a glimpse of *Akagi.* Gary was right: it was indeed burning fiercely. He wondered if whoever had dived into it had done so deliberately or as a desperate dying act. Well, if they ever figured it out, he'd most likely get the Medal of Honor and they'd claim the ship as sunk. As for the rest of them, no one would remember or care.

Dave popped back out of the cloud, and saw the last few seconds of Struble's dive into the carrier. The sight of it left him stunned. Why? He knew he was pissed off over missing one strike and the electrical release failure on the second strike leaving him without a bomb. But commit suicide? After taking the antiaircraft hit, he should have released, pulled up, and bailed out.

He barely knew the guy, and yet had looked up to him as some sort of ideal, a guy without fear, what they were all supposed to be.

The two surviving Dauntlesses dropped, both bombs short, pulled out and away. The P-40s and 36s, or indeed his own wingmen, were nowhere to be seen.

Above he saw a B-17. A Zero popped out

of the same cloud he had been in but seconds before, swinging in underneath the 17, nosing up to fire at him.

This one, at least for a few brief seconds, was absurdly easy. All he had to do was pull stick back — he was on his six, two hundred yards out — and then squeeze.

The Zero's pilot didn't even have a second to react before his starboard wing root erupted into flames, the plane rolling over, canopy popping, the pilot tumbling out, so close that for an instant he feared he would ram the man, catching a glimpse of his face as he fell past, chute beginning to deploy.

That simple?

"Thanks, Wildcat!"

It sounded like Gloria Ann, he wasn't sure. For only seconds later he was in the same position as the Zero he had just dropped, tracers cutting into his wing.

Terrified, he pulled hard stick, rudder, and rolled back into the cloud.

He continued to turn for several seconds, his compass tumbling, artificial horizon upside down, then inverting around, stabilizing, telling him he was in a steep dive. He followed the instruments, pulled back, chopping throttle as he did so. He had been drilled for countless hours to trust the instruments, never what his body was telling him, even though his inner ear, jumbled and rejumbled, was sending a signal to his brain that he was in a vertical dive, while the instruments said he was leveling out in the turbulent gloom of the cloud.

He trusted the instruments and leveled out, turning back on a heading of 85 degrees. He prayed that the fuel indicator was off even as he switched from starboard to port tank. He was down to a half a tank on port side, starboard was virtually empty. If these instruments were reading true, he'd barely make it back to Oahu, and he leaned out the mixture until the engine was barely firing.

He did not know that of the sixteen planes that had launched, four were struggling to get back home, and that of all the planes that had launched from *Enterprise,* his fighter and two of the Dauntlesses were the only ones left in the air. Nor did he know that he was the first ace of the war. All that he knew was that in those darkening clouds it was both lonely and terrifying.

Akagi

The three of them, Yamamoto, Genda, and Fuchida, were leaning over the railing, looking aft, the entire stern of *Akagi* engulfed in flames.

No one spoke, watching as fire crews were already snaking out lines, spraying water and foam toward the huge hole torn into the deck aft of the bridge.

"Sir!"

It was one of his staff, and Yamamoto nodded.

"Sir, damage control reports the American plane crashed through to the hangar deck. So far we've lost eight of our planes below, but we think the fire can be contained. Amazing, sir, the enemy bomb has been found two decks farther down, it did not explode. We have several men on it now, working to remove the fuse."

"That explains it," Fuchida interjected softly. "I thought the damage should be worse."

"The gods were with us," Genda replied.

Yamamoto sighed, looking back at the hole torn by the crashing Dauntless.

"The Americans have bushido," he said softly. "Anyone who thinks differently now is a fool."

CHAPTER ELEVEN

Hickam Army Air Force Base
December 8, 1941
17:25 hrs local time

He sat back in his chair, light-headed, definitely feeling shaky. Evening sunlight slanted in through the open hangar doors, actually rather unearthly and beautiful, colors distorting due to the gloom of smoke hanging over the base.

All had heard the running commentary of the battle an hour past, stood silent, some in tears as the dying pilot's screams burst from the loudspeaker, a scattering of cheers when Gloria Ann reported that one carrier was hit and definitely burning, and then silence again when he reported how it had been hit.

James had tried to stay focused on the Japanese transmissions. Four carriers sighted by the B-17 — they had definitely struck the main fleet and perhaps damaged at least one. Both could detect a certain level of stress when one of the Japanese carrier radio operators sent a message in the clear, ordering all their planes aloft to divert to other carriers.

He and Collingwood talked it over.

"Maybe," James finally ventured, "they split last night, those two carriers a southern force, perhaps detailed to protect the battleship, explaining their aircraft presence over it before any of our forces hit at dawn. That's the one Halsey launched his second strike against. The picture just might fit."

James sketched a rough map out on a piece of scrap paper.

"If so, it means six carriers. One might have been sunk. We know we damaged another," Collingwood replied. "It just might even up the odds a bit for *Lexington*."

It had started a running debate. Being the only outside radio link on the base, the hangar was rapidly assuming the air of a headquarters. A couple of one-stars were in there now, along with a good scattering of colonels and others, all debating what the data meant, what was the next move. Several of them were behind James, listening in. He did not recognize a single one of them, and instinctively he shut up, but the debate was on.

At that moment it struck him just how extraordinarily vulnerable they had been and still were. There was no clear chain of command. General Short was supposedly running the show as the senior ranking military official on the island, but where he was no one could say.

It reminded him, chillingly, of some of the confidential reports he had read analyzing the French collapse a year ago. How their commander-in-chief was safely billeted at a chateau just outside of Paris, with one, exactly one land line linking him to the front lines, and no radios since no one trusted them against German monitoring, as if any code they might create would be cracked in minutes. It might have worked in 1918, where an advance of but a mile was trumpeted as victory, but in a modern fluid war, where the front was shifting fifty to seventy-five miles a day, it had doomed them from the start.

Are we France now, he wondered, as Collingwood lit him another cigarette and passed it over, while the generals and colonels behind them argued as to just how many Jap carriers were still out there and if they would be back tomorrow. The point was moot anyhow. From what they had listened to earlier, the island no longer had a single plane capable of offensive action other than one, perhaps two, shot-up B-17s and maybe a couple of Dauntlesses.

"You know something?" James sighed, while the argument behind them continued. "Maybe we hit the wrong target just now."

"What the hell do you mean?" Collingwood asked.

"Think about it. Our guys are sweating out the oil supply if *Enterprise* is still out there. There's no way it will come back here if it is still alive. Hell, the channel might be blocked for days regardless of what they say, and then what is Halsey supposed to do, just sit out there? Just hang a 'kick me' sign on him for the Jap subs. He needs oil to get back to the States."

"So what are you getting at?"

"Their oilers. We know they don't have many. Suppose our guys had targeted them instead. They'd even be easier to hit, slower with fewer guns, one good shot and boom the thing just tears apart. Do that and the Japanese fleet might be screwed."

Collingwood stared at him intently for a moment and sighed.

"Wish the hell we'd thought of that earlier" — he paused — "like yesterday and somehow communicated it.

"Try convincing them now," and he

pointed back to the staff officers fruitlessly arguing behind them, "and besides, we don't have anything left to hit with."

James half lowered his head, frustrated, angry, numb with exhaustion. The pain in his arm was getting worse by the minute.

The brass behind him could argue all they wanted, he just felt an infinite exhaustion. It was time to try and go home.

"I'm leaving," he announced and tried to stand up, and next thing he knew he was back in the chair, his legs giving out.

"Dianne!"

She had been sitting against a hangar wall, head down, dozing, but was awake, wiping her eyes as she came over to Collingwood.

"Would you help Commander Watson here to the hospital?"

"Yes, sir."

"I don't need a hospital."

"It's an order, James," Collingwood said, "so let's not play any more silly games about this, or I'll pull one of those generals over there into it to back me up."

"I'll be back tomorrow," James announced. "We've got to start rebuilding a decoding center here, or somewhere."

"Sure, James, now go."

He nodded and stood up. Dianne gently put an arm around him, and they started toward the open hangar door, Collingwood by his side. He had a vague recollection that last night he had parked his Plymouth up near CinCPac. Damn, that was a couple of miles away.

"Dianne, you know where the hospital area is set up?"

"Yes, sir, I think so."

"Take that car over there," and he pointed out a battered DeSoto, and fished the keys out of his pocket. "If they release him, take him home, then you go home too and get some rest. I'll see both of you tomorrow."

She helped James get into the car, slipped into the driver's seat, and got it rolling, driving around piles of wreckage. She had to back up off a street that was closed, with water from a broken main spraying twenty feet into the air. A Shore Patrolman told her there was an unexploded fourteen-inch shell down in the hole. It was obvious he was not pleased with his assignment; he looked back over his shoulder nervously as he gave directions for getting around to the base hospital area, set up in a row of barracks.

She backed up, turned the corner, and then slowed.

"Merciful God," she whispered, and

pulled up onto the curb, turning off the engine.

James, eyes half closed, stirred and looked out the window.

The lawn area in front of the hospital looked like something that reminded him of old photographs of the Civil War. Three long rows of bodies were laid out on the lawn, covered with blankets, sheets, old tarps. A team of stretcher bearers was setting a body down even as he watched, lifting him off the stretcher, pausing for a moment. Then they picked up the stretcher and went back into the barracks hall.

Dianne had the door open.

"Come on, sir, you've got to go in there. At least let them get some sulfa on the wound and we'll get out."

He tried to smile, as if he wasn't afraid, but suddenly he was terrified. The memory of the amputation of his hand while he was still awake came back. The local anesthesia had barely blocked the pain.

He leaned against her as they started for the barracks door. On the opposite side of the lawn, more than a hundred men were waiting, some lying on stretchers, others sitting, a few standing. Every kind of injury imaginable confronted James. Men cradled broken arms. Some looked as if they were not hit at all, but just sat or stood, eyes vacant. Others rocked back and forth, clutching their stomach, chest, head, a leg, or what was left of a leg, and there was a universal moaning, crying, occasional screams.

He stopped, unable to move another step.

"Stay right here," Dianne said, and she let go of his side, going up to a female nurse who was bent over a stretcher case. A corpsman by her side was cutting back the man's uniform jacket, revealing a hole in his right chest, blood leaking out with every breath.

"Priority!" she shouted. She marked a number on the wounded man's forehead with a grease pen and motioned for a stretcher team to pick him up and take him inside.

The doorway was open and James could see in. Though it was still daylight, bright incandescent lamps were set up inside. At least a dozen surgery teams were at work, with mess hall tables now surgical tables.

The sight of it made him feel weaker, as if he were going to faint.

"Sir, she wants to look at you."

It was Dianne, and by her side the female nurse. Her uniform might have been sparkling white once; now it was literally caked with dried blood and fresh blood, as if she had just staggered out of a slaughterhouse — which, he realized, this actually was. The woman would normally have been very pretty — tall, jet black hair tucked under her cap — but now her eyes were hollow, dark circles, and a nervous tic was causing an eyelid to flutter.

"Let me see the arm," she said woodenly.

He raised the bandaged stump up.

"You lose this yesterday or today?" she asked, almost matter-of-factly, as if asking him about the weather.

"No. The hand was amputated four years ago. He was hit on the *Panay,*" Dianne said. "The stump was hit by shrapnel or a bullet yesterday morning."

The nurse nodded.

"*Panay*? What was that?"

He couldn't reply.

She took his arm, and he winced as she raised it, sniffed the bandage, nose wrinkling, then let the stump go. She put a blood-caked hand to his forehead.

"Sir, it's infected and you're running a fever," she said. "I'm marking you low priority. Take a seat on the lawn," and she started to raise her grease pen to write whatever was the code for his case on his forehead.

He stepped back.

"How long?"

"What?"
"How long do I have to wait?"
"Sir, there are other men a lot worse off than you."
"I don't mean that," he snapped back, sensing that she was interpreting his question as some sort of appeal, or an attempt to pull rank to be treated first. "I just want to know when you think someone will look at it."
The girl sighed, and it struck him at that instant that she was in shock, in a way as wounded as the men she was tending.
"It's OK," James said softly now. "I know these guys are ahead of me."
"Maybe tomorrow morning, sir," she finally said, and her voice was brittle.
"Can you get us a couple of sulfa packets?" Dianne asked. "I was training to be a nurse once; I'll take care of him."
"Sure," and she motioned to a corpsman who was on his knees, using forceps to pull out a piece of shrapnel from a marine's forearm. The man was grimacing; obviously the hasty operation was being performed without any painkiller.
The nurse turned and walked away, going over to a stretcher that was being carried up the walkway. She stopped the team for a moment, gave one quick glance at the man

lying on it unconscious, wrote a number on his forehead, and gestured over to a grove of palm trees. There were a hundred or more men lying under those trees, a lone chaplain with them; it was obviously the dying place, where those triaged off were placed until they died.

Dianne was back by his side. "I got some sulfa. Let's get the hell out of here, sir. I'll take you home."

They started back to the car.

"Dianne?"

She slowed, looked over her shoulder to the young second lieutenant who was calling to her. His arm was in a sling, his forehead bandaged, his nose swollen — it looked broken — and his face blistered, except around the eyes, clearly where flight goggles had protected them.

The young officer came up to them.

"Adam? Good lord, are you OK?"

"Sure, Dianne, sure."

"What happened to you?"

"Got shot down, that's what happened. Crash landed, broke my damn nose. Medic said I might have cracked my noggin. I'm waiting to get x-rayed."

His voice was slurring. James could see the young pilot was badly battered.

"I'm sorry, Adam," and she leaned up and

gently kissed him on the cheek. He winced a bit but forced a smile.

"Jeremiah, how is he?" she asked — and in that instant, the look in his eyes, James knew. For the moment he forgot his own pain, and with his good hand reached out to grab Dianne's.

"Oh damn," Adam sighed. "You didn't hear about it?"

James squeezed her hand tight.

"He's dead, Dianne. Got shot down yesterday afternoon."

She froze in place, and then strangely, actually laughed softly.

"No, not my Jerry. He always said he was the best, you know that, Adam."

"He was the best, the best we had," Adam whispered. "I'm sorry, Dianne. Word was he went at it alone in one of those obsolete crates, a 36, against the entire third wave. Gave the first warning, then went in alone."

"So you didn't see him?" she asked softly. "His body, I mean."

"No, sweetheart," Adam sighed. "He crashed out to sea, no chute."

"He could have made it to shore somewhere, that would be like my Jerry."

Adam said nothing, only lowered his head.

"Take care of yourself, Adam," she whispered.

"Come on, James," and she started to walk back to the car, James still holding her hand tight.

"I'll drive," James said.

"What?"

"I'll drive, Dianne. It's OK."

"Yeah, sure."

Ignoring his pain, he helped her get into the passenger seat, went around to the driver's side, and got in. For a moment he cursed his sense of chivalry. It was going to be hell shifting gears.

"Can I have the keys, Dianne?"

She reached into her purse, pulled them out, and handed them over without saying a word. He made eye contact with her.

"Dianne?"

"What, sir?"

"He's gone. I heard the report when it came in yesterday. A lone P-36 spotted the Japs, said he was closing to attack, and then radio contact was lost. I'm sorry. I had no idea it was your boyfriend flying that plane. I would have told you if I had known."

She didn't reply.

"He died a hero, Dianne. He gave us ten extra minutes of warning, enough to get our defenses ready."

He felt foolish saying what he had just said. Did dying a hero really matter to a woman, any woman who had lost a lover, a son, a husband?

And then she dissolved into tears, sobbing, leaning against his shoulder. He put his good arm around her for a moment, hugged her as he would a child.

He finally let go of her, started the car, and left the place of sorrow.

They drove in silence, except for her muffled sobs.

There was surprisingly little traffic on the road out of the base, though he had to gingerly weave around more than one wreck and backtrack around a blocked-off street, cratered by a bomb or a shell. Every shift of the gears was agony, as he braced the steering wheel with his legs, injured arm nestled into his lap.

Once out of the base the streets were all but empty. National guardsmen were posted every few blocks. A couple motioned for him to stop, but he didn't slow down, and at the sight of his uniform and then his handless arm, which he deliberately rested on the rolled-down driver's side window, they let him pass until he was onto Pali Highway.

A roadblock and long frustrating minutes of inching up to the checkpoint.

Again some national guardsmen; a sergeant came up to the window and looked in.

"Identification, sir?"

He took his hand off the gearshift, fumbled to his breast pocket. Damn, his wallet was gone; he must have dropped it somewhere, he couldn't remember.

"Sergeant, I've lost my wallet."

"What about her?"

She didn't move, face turned away.

"Sergeant, she just found out her boyfriend was killed, a pilot. Damn it, I'm wounded, I'm ordered to go home, and home is up that road."

The sergeant looked at the blood-soaked bandage covering the stump and nodded.

"Sir, we're not supposed to let traffic over the pass to Kaneohe. Civilians are being evacuated to this side of the island in case the Japs try to land there."

"I know. I moved my family out last night. I'm just going up the road a mile then turning off."

The sergeant hesitated then nodded, stepped back, and saluted.

"OK, sir."

And he motioned to the half-dozen men who blocked the road ahead to let him pass.

He eased the clutch out, struggled to get into first gear, drove up the empty road, and finally turned onto the street where Margaret's cousin lived. He was barely into the driveway and the door was open, Margaret flying out the door and down the steps, her mother hobbling behind her.

She pulled the door to the car open, and he winced.

"James?"

"I'm OK, just a little shaky. If you could help her out, I'd appreciate it."

Margaret looked in through the open window. Dianne was not responding, staring off.

"Her name is Dianne." He lowered his voice though he knew she'd hear. "She's one of our staff. She just found out her boyfriend was killed."

Dianne looked over at him, eyes defiant.

"He could still be alive out there."

James nodded, saying nothing, not sure what to say.

Margaret went over to the other side of the car, opening the door while James got out. His mother-in-law came up to his side and actually put a supportive arm around him.

"My poor boy," she said in Japanese.

"Sir."

He looked across the hood of the car. Dianne was standing there, staring at him coldly.

"You never told me you were married," she hesitated, "to one of them."

"It's OK, honey," Margaret said calmly. "Let me help you inside."

"Don't touch me," Dianne snapped. "Get him inside. Whoever did the bandaging didn't know what the hell they were doing. I'll take care of it."

James caught Margaret's eye. He could see the tension boiling up; he subtly shook his head, and she nodded. His mother-in-law said nothing, but then finally broke the moment by starting back up the stairs, alone, not looking back, Dianne following her.

"Who is she?" Margaret whispered. Beyond the insult of the moment, he could sense a bristling. Was it because of the obvious racial insult, or because a woman who she knew nothing about, and now found out had been working alongside her husband for nearly a year, was exceedingly attractive, even in her wretched, disheveled condition?

"As I said, she's a civilian assistant to Collingwood. Her boyfriend was a fighter pilot. He got shot down yesterday, reported killed in action."

"Poor girl," but James could sense there wasn't much compassion in Margaret's voice.

"Things here OK?"

"No," Margaret replied coldly. "Someone drove by earlier, saw mom and me outside, and called us f-ing Japs. There have been rumors all day. Two men executed down on the beach, supposedly spies, rumors of lynch mobs downtown hanging a kid accused of signaling enemy ships with a flashlight. Men being rounded up and taken to jails. No, things are not OK."

"I'm sorry, honey, tensions are pretty high right now."

"What next?" Margaret replied. "A concentration camp? That's the rumor going around."

"Just damn rumors" was all he could say, as she helped him up the stairs and into their cousin's house.

"Sit him down at the dining room table," Dianne said, as if giving an order, "then boil a couple of towels, a sheet, some scissors, tweezers, a sharp knife, thread and needle."

"My mother knows what to do," Margaret replied, still trying to sound polite.

Her mother said nothing. She was already in the kitchen and came out a moment later with everything Dianne had requested.

"I was prepared for him to come home," she said slowly, looking straight at Dianne.

"Did you boil everything then keep it covered with something sterile?"

"Young lady, I was tending to injuries out in the pineapple fields before you were born," Nan replied, and now there was a note of sharpness in her voice.

"Well, you didn't do a good job on the commander here. It's infected."

There was a momentary standoff. James actually felt torn. This was his family, and yet he could understand the grief, the rage this girl was feeling. But still, this was his family.

"Dianne," he finally said, stepping between the two, turning to face her. "I know you are hurting about Jerry. We all have lost someone. But please don't take it out on my mother-in-law or my wife."

She looked at him coldly. "I can leave if you want, sir."

"Where's home?"

"Over in Kanoehe."

"You heard what the sergeant said back at the roadblock. It's sealed off for now."

Tears started to stream down her face, but there was no sob, no shuddering.

"Jerry might be over there. He was the best. He could have swum to shore or been picked up. And besides, he could outfly any damn Jap."

"You can't go home now," James replied, keeping his voice low, even. "You are welcome to stay here."

He hesitated.

"But in my house, Dianne, I don't want to hear the word 'Jap'. "

She stared at him, tears flowing. "I think I'll go back to the base, sir."

"Young lady, lie down on the sofa. I'll get you some tea with something in it once I've taken care of James."

It was Nan coming up to Dianne's side.

Dianne looked at her coldly, but Nan stared at her comfortingly and repeated in a welcoming voice, "Come on now." Then Dianne just simply broke, and Nan put her arms around her. Dianne, far taller, cradled her head on the old woman's shoulder, sobbing.

Nan led Dianne over to the sofa, sat her down, helped her put her feet up, even taking off her shoes, and the girl turned away, facing the wall, crying softly.

Margaret came into the room with a blanket and covered her, and James felt tears come to his own eyes as he watched the three women. How completely different war was for them, he thought. And there was fear as well. If things got worse tomorrow, if another strike hit — and he far better than most knew just how utterly defenseless the island now was from attack by air or sea — would there be an escalation? Would some idiot set off a lynching frenzy? He knew the story of the two men being shot was not a rumor, but it had not been an execution. The kid being lynched, that had not been reported on the base, but he could easily imagine it happening. And the concentration camp? He didn't want to think about that prospect.

"Sit down, son."

His mother-in-law motioned to the dining room table, where she had already spread out a towel. She deftly cut the bandage off and he could not help but flinch as she peeled it away.

She whispered something in Japanese, he couldn't quite catch it, and Margaret was up by his side.

He looked down at the stump. It was swollen; the edge of the wound she had stitched up was puckering, red, a slight discolored discharge leaking from it.

"It's infected," she sighed. "James, why didn't you go to the hospital?"

He shook his head.

"Mom, you don't want to know what that

place was like. There's thousands of guys hurt worse than me."

"I'm going to have to cut it open and clean it out again."

"Shit."

"Watch your language," she replied, trying to force a smile.

"Let me help."

He looked over his shoulder. It was Dianne standing behind them.

"I was studying to be a nurse. I've helped with worse than this before."

His mother-in-law hesitated, then nodded. He could feel Margaret's hands on his shoulders tighten up ever so slightly. She wasn't happy about this, but he said nothing as Dianne went into the kitchen and scrubbed her hands for a couple of minutes before coming back out, not bothering to dry them, just shaking them to get the moisture off.

She looked at the wound, and James remembered what she had said earlier, that she had quit the training program because she had a weak stomach.

He felt decidedly weak himself as his mother-in-law carefully cut the stitches off. The wound opened up slightly.

"This will hurt," she said, and she spread the wound open. The pain was electric rushing up his arm. For a moment he thought he would faint, as his vision narrowed.

"Keep it open, I'll clean it out," Dianne said, picking up a torn sheet from the tray his mother-in-law had brought out, and she swabbed the wound clean, fresh blood beginning to leak out near the stump of the bone.

"Did you probe for any fragments?" Dianne asked.

"I didn't see any."

Dianne picked up a pair of tweezers and looked at Margaret.

"You better hold him tight. This will hurt but I have to do it."

James nodded, bracing himself, and he felt the tweezers slipping in. He arched, cursing, Margaret holding him down.

"I think there's a bullet or fragment in there," Dianne said.

He felt something grating, dear God this was bad . . . He could barely focus. It was as bad as the amputation; at least then they had him shot up with a local and some morphine. He regretted his bravado; he should have stayed at the hospital.

"Got it," and she was holding a metal fragment with the tweezers, a small jagged piece of steel, about the size of a dime.

"My God," Nan whispered.

She let the tweezers drop on the table, reached into her purse, and pulled out two packets of Sulfa.

"Pour sterile water in, clean it out good. Then pour these in across the inside of the wound. Then carefully stitch it up. Cover it with sterile gauze and bandage it lightly, then we can check it again in the morning."

"You are an excellent nurse," Margaret whispered. "Thanks."

Dianne was already halfway into the kitchen.

"No, I'm not. I went to school one semester, kept throwing up. Saw that probe thing in a Dr. Kildare movie."

She raced the last few feet to the kitchen sink and began to vomit, and then started crying again.

Margaret poured him a stiff drink, which he gulped down even as Nan stitched the wound closed again. Margaret gave him another drink, and then she helped him to a bedroom, where as if he were a child, she helped him undress.

She kissed him on the forehead, told him to go to sleep, and left the room, the door still open. He could hear crying out in the living room.

The window was open to let in the cooling breeze. The air was pure, but he could still hear, and sleep would not come. Distant rumbles of explosions, a siren of a cop car or an ambulance, someone shouting in the distance, a couple of gunshots . . . and out in the living room he could still hear soft voices and crying.

A distant flash reflected on the opposite wall of the room; long minutes later there was a faint rumble, but in spite of the pain, exhaustion and the liquor had taken hold and he was asleep.

Aboard Hiei
31 miles southwest of Oahu
17:52 hrs local time

Captain Nagita never heard a warning. No one saw the four torpedoes, fired from but a thousand yards out, streaking in. One circled wide — yet another failed gyroscope in the American Mark XII design. The second hit fifty yards forward of the stern. Those directly on the other side of the bulkhead heard the terrifying bang of its impact, but there was no explosion; as with so many of the American torpedoes, its magnetic mechnical detonators failed. But numbers three and four struck amidships, and the fourth one, just under number two turret, did detonate.

During their long day of struggling to

survive, Captain Nagita had first been filled with pessimism. The air strikes had all but finished off his beloved ship, and yet somehow, his damage control teams had managed to keep her afloat and even stabilized the list.

There had been a buildup of deadly fumes below decks during the afternoon, and yet he had ordered full watertight integrity to be maintained, anticipating at least one more air strike from the island, or an enemy carrier. A brief coded message had been sent from Yamamoto, wishing them luck, but also saying they must rely upon their own guns since there were no longer planes to spare for her protection.

He had sworn a solemn oath that if he ever got his ship out of this, when he returned to Tokyo, he would try and find a way to reach the Emperor himself to denounce this flagrant abandonment of one of Japan's most precious lines of defense, the guns of a battleship, recklessly thrown away by a commander obsessed with airplanes.

But with dusk settling, as he listened in on radio reports of a final and feeble American attack on *Akagi,* he felt assured that there would be no more air strikes, though the threat of submarines was all but certain. At least one of the Imperial fleet's own subs was now slowly circling him, helping to stand guard, though. And a half hour ago he had ordered watertight conditions above the flooded-out zone of the ship to be unsealed, ventilator fans turned back on, to clear out the noxious fumes which had killed dozens of his men fighting to contain the still-smoldering fires.

The flash of the fourth torpedo blew into the bowels of the ship, having first burst through a fuel blister that had been drained out, the precious oil pumped over to a port-side fuel tank to help with counterbalance. The explosion was not contained by the bunker oil, which would not have flash burned, and it therefore broke into the main compartments of the ship, racing through an open corridor. There was a momentary wave of thousand-degree heat that incinerated a score of men caught in its path and in that one-second burst blew into a doorway open to a magazine of five-inch shells. The magazine was nearly empty; most of the ammunition had been expended during the night bombardment and antiaircraft fire repelling the air attacks. The shells were standard. The huge brass cartridges were kept open, and the number of prepackaged powder bags called for were first stuffed inside the cartridge by a loader, then another man fitted the actual shell atop the cartridge, sealing the unit shut, and set the fuse. It would then be loaded into a hoist that took it up topside to the gun turret.

Nearly half a ton of powder bags were exposed, either inside open shells or in racks, some properly sealed, some opened during the heat of battle and then not secured afterwards as crews turned to damage control. The junior officer in charge of that magazine was new to his post and had not followed correct procedure to secure the magazine and properly dispose of two powder bags that had broken open in the heat of action, during which his crew was expected to prepare and put in the hoist up to eight rounds a minute. The broken five-pound bags were now resting on the floor.

The torpedo flash burst into the open doorway of the magazine, open because the air was being vented out, and scant milliseconds later the two open bags of powder flashed, setting off a chain reaction within the room so that even as the explosion from the torpedo reached its limits, the partial vacuum left in its wake now caused a back-flash of flame. The explosion from the five-inch magazine crashed through two bulkheads and into the main ammunition hoist for number two turret. Topside, not only the bulk of the turret, but the deck itself provided so much armor that a direct hit from an incoming shell or 500-kilogram bomb most likely would not have penetrated into the hoist for the three-quarter-ton shells and powder bags.

But six decks down, the explosion met little resistance. It blew into the hoist, most of the fire and heat soaring up, but enough going down that it flashed into one of the four main magazines for the fourteen-inch guns.

The two aft turret magazines had been flooded as a precaution, but not the two magazines forward.

Captain Nagita barely had time to register the fact that they had taken at least one torpedo hit, and then the entire forward half deck of the battleship *Hiei* burst asunder, the fireball, like that of the *Arizona,* racing thousands of feet heavenward.

Unlike with the *Arizona,* there was no mud only thirty-five feet down to settle into; they were in nearly two hundred fathoms of water.

The explosion raced down the main corridors, through open doorways, up and down ventilation shafts; anything that could burn — secondary magazines, wood, bedding, paint on the walls, uniforms and the men wearing them — flashed.

Even before the last of the debris from the main explosion had finally splashed into the ocean, *Hiei* was going down, its captain and all but a hundred or so of its crew dead. A few compartments aft near the stern, with watertight doors secured to contain smoldering fires in the next compartments, actually held, the men behind them surviving, along with a couple of dozen men laboring in the starboard side engine room. For them, the force of the explosion hit with such violence that most were knocked unconscious, the rooms they were trapped in as black as the deepest cave, except for the dim glow of a few emergency battle lamps that still worked.

The aft end of the ship, in spite of the thousands of tons of water still on board from the hits, and counterflooding, for a brief instant actually lifted clear of the ocean and then plunged down, as if pulled into the ocean by a primordial monster concealed beneath the waves.

The wreckage of the ship started its long dive to the bottom, internal explosions still igniting, but the increasing pressure of the water flooding in containing the burst.

The few men still alive and tragically still conscious might have grasped what was happening. What had been a forward bulkhead was now the floor they lay upon. As the ship reached a depth of four hundred feet, the overpressure of the ocean caused the remaining bulkheads to implode, those farther forward bursting first. Those farthest aft could hear the implosions marching closer and closer, like the sound of terrible iron shutters being slammed shut, crushing all within.

Those who were Buddhist called upon his name, some called for their mothers, a few, secretly Christian, called upon Christ. And then their bulkheads collapsed as well. At that depth the water pressure was over four hundred pounds per square inch. Life was crushed out before they even had time to drown.

U.S.S. Gudgeon
17:55 hrs local time

The cheering finally died down.

"Boys, we got ourselves a battleship," Captain Lubbers announced over the public address. "Now secure for silent running. Those destroyers out there will be pissed as hell."

There was still some back slapping, handshakes all around. All knew that if their cruise had been cut short by but two days (they all had groaned when told they were staying out to sea) they would have been inside Pearl Harbor yesterday. Now it was payback time instead.

As all hands quieted down, the sound echoing through the ocean rumbled past their hull, sound traveling far quicker and farther at sea.

There were muffled explosions, and then a strange metallic sound, almost like a tin can being crushed under foot.

"Bulkheads collapsing as she goes down," one of the torpedo men forward whispered.

There was a moment of silence, then that crushing tin can sound again, louder.

"Poor bastards," someone said softly.

"The hell with them, they started this," a petty officer replied coldly.

Hickam Army Air Force Base
17:59 hrs local time

The engine was rough, sputtering. According to the fuel gauges, he was empty. His mixture was set so lean it would barely fire at this altitude.

David spared another quick glance to the southwest. The fireball that had been there minutes ago was gone; the only light now was twilight of the setting sun. He didn't give it another thought. He was trying to stay alive, and anything beyond that was blocked off.

He was lining up on the base leg of the pattern; amazingly, there was now a radio hookup, clearing him to land on runway three. He pulled full flaps, trying to keep his approach so high that if the engine cut, he still had enough air speed to nose over, go into a glide, and reach the threshold. In a few more seconds he'd be there. He held off on landing gear until safely within range — too much drag otherwise.

Behind him were two Dauntlesses, both more or less shot up, but not declaring an emergency, and a B-17, Gloria Ann, that incredible lone survivor after but two days of war. She had two wounded and one dead on board, but was told to stay in pattern so the small boys could land first, their fuel nearly exhausted.

"This is X-ray One, on final," and he banked over hard, leveled out, throttle back, flipped the switches for landing gear. Keep the nose down.

"X-ray One, your landing gear is not deployed!"

He spared a quick glance down at his instrument board. One gear was showing green, the other no light at all.

"I got green on one."

"No gear, break off and go around."

The hell with that. He could smell the engine burning out from the far too lean mixture. He was running on fumes; break off now and he'd wind up plowing into the wreckage of the bases below before he could even get back into the pattern. His landing gear was shot up, and circling wasn't going to change a damn thing now.

He angled to one side of the landing strip; thank God this one was wide, at least two hundred feet across.

"X-ray One, go around!"

He didn't even bother to reply. Felt ground effect begin to kick in as he began to level out ten feet above the runway, air speed dropping, back stick, don't yo-yo, little more back stick, his battered Wildcat floating for a hundred yards and then a gut-tearing screeching as the aluminum under-belly hit the concrete. The nose dropped, props striking, instantly stopping, bent back. He began to skid sideways, part of his starboard wing shearing off as the Wildcat looped on its belly. He braced; the impact was hard, blurring his vision . . . and then silence, except for the wailing of an ambu-lance siren, two vehicles racing over, one a truck with a roughly painted red cross on its side, the other a crash wagon, an asbestos

Joe riding on the sideboard, jumping off even before the truck rolled to a stop, the man leaping up on to the portside wing, climbing up to Dave's side while two others ran to the front of the plane and began to hose the engine with fire retardant.

The asbestos Joe, looking like some kind of spaceman from a Flash Gordon serial, reached in, unsnapped his harness and pulled him out of the cockpit.

"You injured, sir?"

"Don't think so."

They were on the ground, his rescuer guiding him a safe distance back from the Wildcat, which seemed like a dying friend, engine ticking from the heat, hissing from the fire retardant striking hot metal, its lifeblood, oil and hydraulic fluid, pooling out underneath it.

And he suddenly felt heartsick. She had been his plane. When first she was given to him, just a month ago, and he had made his first landing on the *Enterprise,* he'd go to the hangar deck at night, walking around her, running his hands along her side, as if she were a lover whom he could always trust and who in turn could trust him. He had believed that together they'd always come back. She had been something living to him, and now she was dying.

An army mechanic came up, chewing a wad of tobacco, took a long look, and shook his head.

"Junk pile for spare parts now."

Dave looked at him coldly.

"You just screwed up fifty-three thousand dollars, sir."

"Get the hell away and leave me alone," Dave snapped. The mechanic, still shaking his head, walked away.

A tractor rolled up and turned. The mechanic and two other men ran cables out, sinking hooks in through the cowling to the engine frame.

"Take her away, Charlie," the mechanic shouted. The tractor revved up. He wanted to scream at them to stop, to leave her alone as she died, but she was blocking part of the active runway. The Dauntless behind him had aborted and circled around. Gloria Ann, higher up, was circling the field, popping off another red flare to indicate wounded aboard.

His plane emitted a harsh metallic cry as they began to drag her away, bits of aluminum undercarriage and part of a tire left behind in her wake, trailing oil, hydraulic fluid, even a faint whiff of av gas. They dumped her at the edge of the runway, disconnected, and the tractor drove off. To either side were other dead planes, some of them completely burned out, others being dissected, like bodies on an autopsy table cut open for parts, or maybe in some vain hope that, Frankensteinlike, life could be jolted back into them.

The Dauntlesses came in, rolled out, and last came Gloria Ann, silhouetted by the western twilight, most of her vertical stabilizer and rudder shot clear away, holes punched through the length of the fuselage. She came down with a hard bounce, lifted, seemed to hang in a dangerous stall, nosing over slightly, came down hard again on two wheels, tires shrieking in protest, and then rolled out. The meat wagon that had been beside his plane was now racing down the runway, siren echoing.

He stood by his plane, took off his leather helmet, unsnapped the seat parachute, and just let it drop to the ground, lifted off his yellow Mae West, let that drop as well, and opened his shirt, letting the cool breeze envelop him.

"Sir?"

It was the damn pesky intelligence officer from earlier, clipboard in hand, the colonel who had sent them out by his side.

He didn't reply, didn't salute.

"Just a few questions," the colonel said

softly, "then we'll leave you alone for now."

He nodded.

"We heard that a dive bomber crashed into one of the Jap carriers."

"Yes, that's right."

"Who?"

"I think it was Struble."

"Was it a controlled crash?"

"What?"

"Did he deliberately fly it in?"

Something told him they were looking for a hero. He didn't know. Dan could have already been dead; the shell burst had pretty well hit him head on.

"Yeah, he flew her in," he finally replied.

"Can you identify the carrier?"

"*Akagi,* I think."

"Was it the same as the carrier hit earlier?"

He looked at them, tried to picture the glimpse of the first carrier, but he was down low then, skimming waves, trying to cover the Devastators, God save them, those poor bastards.

"I don't know. I'm sorry."

"One more question, sir." It was the lieutenant, but the colonel put his hand on the lieutenant's shoulder.

"Later, we can do it later."

The lieutenant, a bit embarrassed, walked away, heading up toward where the two

Dauntlesses had taxied off the runway.

"Need a cigarette, son?" the colonel asked.

Dave nodded. Yeah, I started smoking this morning, he realized.

The colonel lit one and handed it over, reached into his breast pocket, pulled out a flask, and handed it to Dave as well.

"Take a good long drink."

Dave did, almost as if ordered. Unlike most pilots, he had never joined in the riotous drinking bouts when on leave. He had rarely had anything more than a few beers. But he took the flask, downed two long gulps, coughed a bit between the smoke and the burning of the whiskey, and handed the flask back.

"Son, I think you should know something."

He looked at the officer, face barely distinguishable now in the deepening twilight.

"You're an ace. First of the war. Radio reports state you dropped two Japs this afternoon. Reports of other pilots say you got three in the other two fights. The whole nation will be hearing about you, son. You better be ready for it."

"Who said I got five?" he asked, confused. It was all so damn confusing . . . too much to take in now.

The colonel hesitated.

"Struble for one witnessed two of your kills and reported them earlier today."

"I don't remember," was all he could say, "and besides, like I said, Struble is dead."

"I know."

The colonel squeezed his shoulder in a fatherly gesture and walked away, leaving him alone with the wreckage of his plane.

He was alone, soft tropical breeze touching him, cooling, gentle. He sat down, sinking into the shadows, hands touching the warm earth, recalling boyhood days, lying on the ground, watching the clouds, wondering how angels saw them, a few memories, a precious few, of girls by his side, playing at almost making love, snuggled together on a sunlit hillside, concealed in the high grass.

It was a life, a world, remote, gone forever. He began to shake, too many images flashing in his mind, like a film projector gone berserk, running insanely fast, film spilling out: Struble, Gregory, a glimpse of a white plane, red sun on fuselage. Did I kill that man? The P-40 pilot screaming as he burned . . . Turn off your damn mike! *Enterprise* — were they still alive . . . Am I still alive?

He felt as if there were two of him sitting

there. There was him, the me of this moment, shivering, stinking of sweat, vomit, fear, and yes, feeling a strange, detached, primal joy. I am still alive, the rest are dead, but I am still here, still breathing. I am alive.

And there was the "other." Someone who was him, who just two days ago could laugh as he darted between sunlit clouds, and could look heavenward, high up, all so high up where the air was so thin and pure, knowing at that moment there was not another living soul who saw the world as he did. A boy who could laugh, smile, dream of his girl by his side in the darkness, memories of home, Midwestern pastures and distant horizons.

That boy was someone else, who at that moment arose out of him, and without looking back, walked away, into the darkness. He would be lost out there forever, a fading memory, wandering alone — and he would never return.

Dave lowered his head and silently wept.

Chapter Twelve

Enterprise
145 miles east-southeast of Oahu
19:15 hrs local time

Commander Stubbs, Admiral Halsey by his side, stood on the deck of their beloved *Enterprise,* still listing at nearly eight degrees to starboard, Stubbs with megaphone in hand.

The heavy cruiser *Indianapolis* lay thirty yards off, precisely matching speed and course, a dozen lines and cables linking the two ships — electrical cables to provide additional power for pumps, bosun's chairs for the transfer of the less critically wounded and slings for the stretcher cases, hoists for the transfer of portable pumps, foam generators, and medical supplies.

Indianapolis had swung in alongside at nautical twilight and Halsey had already announced that regardless of the condition of *Enterprise,* she was to cast off and move away just before moonrise in a little less than four hours.

The Japs had a fix on them, and submarines might be closing in, like hyenas circling a wounded beast, ready to dart in for a kill. He would not risk what was now one of the two heaviest ships America still had in the entire Pacific.

To his dismay, *Indianapolis* had informed them that they had little fuel oil to spare, having engaged in high-speed maneuvers prior to the war warning.

Halsey now was facing a choice perhaps even tougher than his decision of the night before to turn north and alone seek out the entire Japanese fleet, with the forlorn hope that he just might get a first strike and a killing blow. Do I go back to Pearl or turn due east and run for the West Coast?

The second choice was damn near impossible now. Even if they did survive the night and contain the fires still raging below, somehow block off the holes cut into their hull by the torpedoes, pump out the decks above the starboard engine room, where miraculously the crew trapped down there were still alive and thus keeping the ship alive, and somehow make speed again on two or three of their four screws — even with all that they would run dry a thousand miles off the coast, and the accompanying destroyers would have lost steam long before that.

Enterprise had hemorrhaged out too much precious fuel oil, and a good portion of the rest was now polluted with seawater due to emergency counterflooding. Still, Stubbs had announced they might be able to pump out the contaminated fuel and somehow distill out enough of the water so that what was left could burn.

And, yet, if I turn back toward Pearl? What guarantee was there that tomorrow, the Jap fleet in its entirety would be waiting for him? Though the Big E was one hell of a fighting lady, even with his pride in her, he knew that one more hit would most likely prove fatal, especially if it was a torpedo. Even if the Jap fleet was no longer near the island — and a gut instinct told him they would not be — they undoubtedly were facing fuel issues as well, and that meant they were most likely steaming westward, to some reserve tankers positioned in the Marshalls. Nevertheless, the waters would be crawling with their subs, and making ten knots or less, the carrier was easy prey and they would go for it.

Once into Pearl, then what? Their radio contacts were coming back on line, one of them a definite link to the mainland. They were not yet encoding, but at least speaking cryptically. Some smart guy had come up with the idea of using Hungarian, figuring that was a language that, at least within the Japanese fleet, no one would have a clue about. They had a native-born speaker on the island and back on the mainland they had scrambled and found someone who could speak it as well. Thank God one of the messroom stewards on board the *Enterprise* was born in Budapest, knew the lingo, and had suddenly found himself in the CIC, providing translation.

Even then they spoke cryptically. The whole world could listen in if tuned to the right frequency. Tokyo would figure it out soon enough and find someone, most likely from the embassy of Hungary, now a tacit Axis ally, who would help them out.

Mention was made that the "big bathtub" broke. That was easy enough to figure out. Number one drydock, the only facility that could contain *Enterprise,* or for that matter *Lexington,* was out of operation. The primary damage below the waterline would be impossible to repair at Pearl without that dry dock.

A civilian radio station, the damn fools, had already broadcast that the oil tank farms were ablaze, but then again that didn't need any coding; the Japs clearly must have known that.

It was even doubtful if they could clear the main channel, according to a report that "a key was broken off in the lock and it couldn't be opened."

There had been some head scratching on that one, the mess steward swearing he got it right, until one of the radio operators figured it out. The various channels of Pearl Harbor were referred to as lochs, and it must mean the main entryway was blocked by wreckage.

So, no sense to turn toward Pearl, run the gauntlet of subs, and then find themselves sitting five miles offshore, unable to head in, perhaps for days.

Pearl was out, but there was one tragic point to that besides trying to save the ship. At least three hundred men on board were dead, another five hundred injured, many of them badly burned. Every surgeon and corpsman on board had been frantically at work since dawn. One of the doctors from *Indianapolis* had already transferred over, along with cases of plasma, sulfa, morphine, and anesthesia, but it was still nowhere near enough.

If they took the long road back to the

States, it'd take at least two weeks or more, and of those five hundred, many would die who could have been saved, and even those who were saved would be in agony.

He had ventured below deck an hour ago, making a stop at one of the triage centers. Across all the years of his career, those had been the toughest minutes. At least fifty men had been "set aside," too badly injured to be saved here, though back on the mainland, with enough doctors available, some most likely would make it.

Most were unconscious or doped with increasingly scarce morphine. But some were fully conscious. No amount of morphine would be able to deaden the agony of flash burns, or the parboiling of human flesh from blasts of superheated steam from ruptured lines.

He tried to make eye contact, speak a few words of encouragement, and tell them how proud he was of them. Some could not reply, and some looked at him vacantly as if no longer knowing who he was. One had asked him to write his mother, and he promised he would, a petty officer taking down her address on a napkin, which he had put in his breast pocket. The toughest one, though, was an old hand, a chief petty officer, whom he had some recollection of from years ago, but now it was nearly impossible to recognize the man, his face so contorted with pain. The petty officer held his hand up and Halsey had knelt down by his side to take it.

"I'm proud of our Big E, sir," he gasped, "and, sir, I'm proud of you. Don't give up the ship."

He could not reply, merely nodded, squeezed the man's hand and moved on. Once out in the corridor, he struggled not to break down. Too many were watching. He fought the exhaustion; he had had less than four hours sleep in the last two days. After the risky maneuver with *Indianapolis* was finished, maybe then he would go to his cabin, close the door, and try to block things out for a few hours.

A heavy jet of water burst from near the stern of the *Indianapolis,* just barely visible in the starlight. There was the red glow of battle lanterns, shining against the side of *Enterprise,* penetrating in through the hole just above the waterline where a torpedo had hit. Another hose stretched from the *Indianapolis* opened up, aimed at the still-smoking machine shop on the hangar deck, its power and volume far exceeding the overstressed fire pumps on board ship, freeing up electrical power which Stubbs, turning to an assistant, ordered should now be transferred to one of the drain pumps fighting against the water flooding in from the aft torpedo hit.

"Sir."

Both turned, it was a seaman first class, breathing hard, uniform blackened, soaking wet and stinking of oil.

"Go ahead," Stubbs replied.

"Lieutenant Anderson reports that the last of the aviation gas, except for a thousand gallons safely secured in a forward tank, has been jettisoned overboard. Ventilators are working now, pumping out the fumes overboard as well."

"Very well, and congratulate the lieutenant on a job well done."

"Yes, sir, thank you, sir."

The seaman saluted and started to run back across the deck, disappearing into the dark.

"One less worry," Stubbs announced.

Ruptured av-gas tanks were perhaps the biggest fear on board a carrier. Fuel oil could burn, but rarely would the fumes explode. The hundred-octane aviation gas, however, was nothing less than a giant bomb below decks. Not only would it burn like an inferno if ignited, but if a fuel tank was ruptured and the fumes blown through the ship, and a single spark hit those fumes, and the mixture between gas in the air and oxygen was just right, the explosion could be more deadly than any bomb ever dropped. It could sink them, and from the battleship admirals' side, had always been one of the main arguments against putting trust in a carrier, which could never sustain any kind of damage and survive, let alone return to the fight.

She had been hit twice this morning and still launched a second strike, she'd been hit again, and by God, she would survive.

"Stubbs, can you get us back to the West Coast?" Halsey asked.

"Sir?"

"You heard me."

"So Pearl is out, sir?"

"Unless that Hungarian mess steward later proves to be a damn idiot or some sort of Nazi agent helping out the Japs, we both know our chances of making it through their subs back to the island are not that good.

"There's a chance they still might be within air range of the island and they'll be on us like flies on" — he hesitated, no way in hell was he going to compare his ship to a heap of cow flop — "well, like carrion buzzards. The channel is most likely still blocked, and even if we get into the harbor, the main drydock is gone. So it's the drydock at San Diego or nothing."

Stubbs stood silent, thinking it over.

"Our fuel?"

"You promised you could figure out a way to distill out the seawater from the fuel that's polluted down to the point where we can use it in the boilers."

"I'll try, sir, but we'll burn fuel like mad to heat it enough to cook off the seawater, so it's only a partial tradeoff. I'll work up the calculations, though."

"You saying we can't make it?"

"What about the destroyers? They'll be dry in a matter of days."

"Then we abandon them," Halsey said coldly, "transfer their crews aboard, and then sink them if need be."

"Can we raise an oil tanker for a rendezvous, sir?"

Now it was Halsey's turn to hesitate, to balance the risks. He knew the tanker *Neosho* was somewhere out at sea between Hawaii and San Francisco.

We turn east, stay out of the main shipping lanes. The random chance of a Jap sub finding them was remote in another day or so. Broadcast a request for an oiler and set a rendezvous point. There might be a wolf pack of them sitting there waiting rather than the oiler.

"I'll think about it," was all he said.

Stubbs nodded.

"If you can keep her afloat, Stubbs, I'll get us to the Coast, somehow."

Stubbs could not help but smile and extend his hand, which Halsey clasped warmly.

Akagi
230 miles west of Oahu
19:50 hrs local time

Those gathered around him in the small conference room were silent, some from exhaustion, others obviously from depression. In a sense it was understandable. They had been at nearly continuous battle conditions for two days.

Their first two blows had been nearly bloodless victories, but the task then, especially with the realization of the utter, insane failure of the Foreign Ministry to deliver the declaration of war before the attack at Pearl, had required that he must continue the attack now, while the Americans were still reeling. They had to be like the sumo wrestler who nearly had his opponent off balance, but now had to push the rest of the way, regardless of exhaustion.

The third strike had come at a price, a loss of planes equal to that of the first two raids together, but the damage inflicted had been worth that price.

It was the results of today that had worn his men down, changing their exultation to this state of worried exhaustion.

Yamamoto settled back in his chair, scanning the faces. Kusaka, the chief of staff to Nagumo, whom he had kept on . . . Yamamoto knew of course that pessimism would emanate from him, perhaps now infect others, and he debated yet again whether perhaps he should just relieve him of his post now. No, he was already an enemy and well connected politically. There would be tough questions enough to answer in Tokyo once this campaign was finished. Removing Kusaka, thereby removing him as well from any potential connection to the inevitable further losses, would in fact enhance the man's influence in Tokyo.

Genda and Fuchida were their typical selves, though he could sense their frustration and grief. Commander Kijuru, the damage control officer for *Akagi,* was blackened, head half lowered. Perhaps for him more than anyone in the room this had been the longest of days.

"The loss of *Hiei* was tragic. All of us

mourn comrades lost," he said, opening the meeting and going straight to the point without any of the protocols of a few minutes of personal talk, his inquiring as to the health and condition of those gathered.

"That is the price of war. To repeat again an Americanism: one cannot make an omelet without breaking eggs. When this campaign was first planned and war-gamed, we concluded that upward of half our aircraft would be lost in the opening move, and one or more carriers as well. We, therefore, are far ahead of the game."

"Sir, the loss of a battleship is, in my mind, not just a playing piece of a game; it is one of the most valuable assets of His Majesty's power," Kusaka replied sharply.

"Are battleships so precious that they are like ancient swords?" Yamamoto snapped. "A weapon so precious that it just hangs on the wall of its owner's home, and even if the owner is attacked, is too precious to be drawn and perhaps nicked? That is the attitude I hear.

"War is risk; war does not mean we are destined to bloodless victories. Whatever harm the Americans have inflicted upon us, we have leveled back a hundredfold."

"And yet we lost the *Hiei,*" Kusaka replied with intensity. Frustrated, knowing exhaustion was overwhelming him, he could not let it pass.

"The *Hiei* delivered tremendous damage to the American bases before she was hit. She took out several of their destroyers and a cruiser. She shot down dozens of their planes. And, I must add, she absorbed a first air strike that could have destroyed one or more of our carriers."

"And you rate the destruction of a carrier as more tragic than the loss of His Majesty's battleship?" came the heated reply.

"Yes I do!"

"I shall remember that," and the threat was clear.

"Remember it then," Yamamoto snapped angrily. "Yesterday morning our planes put out of action eight of their battleships, the entire fleet which we had once feared would disrupt our strategic moves to the south. Our southern fleets are now free to move without fear. I think that shows the future of where the true strength in naval battle now rests.

"*Hiei* died gallantly. Her memory will not be forgotten. She inflicted far more damage than ever dreamed possible. She allowed our planes to track their *Yorktown*-class carriers and sink one, possibly two of them. If we believe a sword to be so precious it cannot be drawn and risked in battle, then why even have the sword?"

Kusaka bristled but did not reply.

He shifted attention to his damage control officer, Kijuru.

"Our status?" he asked coldly, trying to contain his anger at Kusaka.

"Sir, we will be ready to resume operations by morning."

"Excellent work."

"Sir, what of *Soryu*?" Kusaka asked.

"It is not good," Genda interjected, sensing that he should somehow intervene to prevent another explosive confrontation.

Yamamoto looked over at him, as if sensing Genda's reasoning.

"Go on."

"We received a coded report twenty minutes ago. *Soryu* is stable but cannot yet be counted on to be ready for battle. For the moment it is out of the fight. Its surviving planes are aboard *Hiryu*. Even then, between what were the strike forces of two carriers, they can now only muster fifteen bombers and twelve Zeroes for action."

Yamamoto made no reply; he already knew some of the details, having looked over Genda's shoulder while the telegraphed report had been decoded.

"How many total planes can we have

ready for an offensive strike at dawn?" Yamamoto asked.

"Sir, at least a hundred and ten, with sufficient reserves held back for air cover over the fleet, search operations, and as a secondary strike if required. I suggest that the reserve be the planes on *Hiryu.* They have fought enough these last two days."

He sat back, closing his eyes. There was no need to even look at the charts.

By morning they would be well out of range of Oahu, though perhaps if any American B-17s were left, an attack could be expected; however, that plane, though proving to be highly effective at scouting and spotting at sea, was woefully inadequate for strikes against fast-moving ships.

"Our oil supplies?" he asked, and that was definitely Kusaka's territory.

"Barely adequate now for reaching our reserve oilers in the Marshalls. The number of reversals of course today in order to launch and recover planes consumed far more than we had planned."

Yet again the damn reproach just barely concealed. But he was right. The northeasterly winds were blowing exactly opposite the course desired. Coming about, speeding up to launch and recover, then reversing back onto course had nearly doubled the intended distance traveled today, and still they were less than two hundred fifty miles away from Oahu.

If indeed there was still an American carrier or carriers to the west, the damn wind favored them, since they would be steaming into it.

Also, the question now was how to deploy the fleet. Concentrate? *Soryu* would not be operational tomorrow; it needed to be covered while its planes were out of action. But concentration meant contracting the search range. Or spread the force into three groups of two, or two groups of three? Keep them within mutual support range, but spaced a hundred miles apart, thus extending search ranges out over an additional fifteen thousand square miles of ocean or more.

One side of him reasoned that whatever forces the Americans had just might try to swing north, to avoid engaging the superior numbers they knew they would be facing. The second argument was that they might try and swing south. Though his pilots were certain they had sunk one carrier to the south and perhaps two, the reports might not be accurate.

The ships to the south were definitely *Yorktown* class. A bombardier with a hand-held camera had photographed one of the carriers. It was their number six, the *Enterprise.* But there was no hard evidence that the *Yorktown* was in the Pacific. Intelligence reports just before the fleet had left from Japan indicated the *Yorktown* was definitely on the East Coast of the United States. Could it have moved out here by now, or were the intelligence reports wrong?

The numerous reports that they had built their plans around were clear on the fact that only one *Yorktown*-class carrier, the *Enterprise,* was currently based at Pearl Harbor, along with the two older and far bigger carriers, *Saratoga* and *Lexington.* Not a single debriefing of the crews in the strikes to the south had indicated sighting those two ships clearly and unmistakably.

It meant to him that *Saratoga* and *Lexington* were still to his west. If it was those two carriers (in a sense, the sister ships of *Akagi* and *Kaga;* both of them had originally been laid down as battle cruisers but because of the Washington treaty changed instead to carriers), the Americans might very well be able to match us in number of planes tomorrow.

That realization decided it. He must keep the fleet together.

The question now was their direction.

North to avoid us? South to try and link up with the American ships known to be in that area, perhaps even a surviving carrier? Or would they come straight in, seeking a fight?

I would seek out our main force, he thought, calculating it off of the position reported from their final attack of today.

We will be the target they'd seek. If roles were reversed, it would be the one my first instincts would tell me to seek. And for that very reason alone, I would assume a shift, moving the damaged carrier into the center, protected by the others. It had been war-gamed out before when the older doctrine of matching but two carriers and no more had been changed by him to combining six, and perhaps someday even eight or ten. If one is damaged, ensure that it is protected by the others. And in reality we have two damaged ships; though his beloved *Akagi* could launch, it was still wounded and not able to sustain any more serious blows. As it was, both ships would need to be docked for several weeks or more for repairs back in Japan.

Keep the group together then, assume the Americans will come seeking us. *Tone* and *Chikuma,* his two seaplane cruisers, could be positioned to either flank, north and south, and arc outward with their long-range search planes covering the southern and northern flanks, while the six carriers in the middle with the battleship *Kirishima* moved westward at reduced speed to conserve fuel. Then, if contact was made to either flank, he could turn and run at high speed, at least for several hours, to engage. If the enemy was straight ahead there would have to be contact, of that he was all but certain.

Someone coughed. It was Genda. He opened his eyes and saw that they were all staring at him. It must have appeared as if he had fallen asleep. He looked at his wristwatch. He must have been sitting thus for thirty minutes or more, no one speaking, and wondered if he had indeed dozed off for a few minutes, Genda's cough a polite wake-up call.

"Order *Soryu* and *Hiryu* to close on our position as we steam due west throughout the night at ten knots to conserve fuel. Before dawn we will position the carriers in a broad circle around *Soryu* to protect her with *Kirishima* nearby to provide additional antiaircraft coverage.

"*Tone* to move north, seventy-five miles north of our flank, *Chikuma* to do the same to the south, launching their search planes at first light, their pattern to be in a half circle west to east. One hour before dawn *Zuikaku* will turn about into the wind and launch its search planes, and use its remaining bombers as search planes as well. They will depart fully armed, their pattern to be northwest to southwest, overlapping the pattern of the cruisers. All of *Zuikaku*'s fighters to be launched as well to provide cover over the fleet. Once fully launched, *Zuikaku* will steam at best speed to rejoin the main group.

"Any questions?"

Genda, as chief of air operations for the entire task force, was rapidly jotting down notes, looking over at a sheet that listed the number of ready aircraft on each of the carriers.

"Sir, our numbers of attack aircraft will be cut by one quarter if *Zuikaku*'s role is to provide search and cover. We'll have less than a hundred aircraft available for offensive operations."

"I'm aware of that."

"And if the Americans have two of their *Saratoga*-class carriers out there, we'd actually be outnumbered."

"I am aware of that as well. Your point?"

"None, sir," Genda replied cautiously. "I just wished to state the facts as your air officer."

"Thank you, Commander Genda."

"Are there any other questions?"

Fuchida stirred, cleared his throat, but said nothing.

Yamamoto smiled.

"Yes, I am lifting the ban on flying for my eager strike leader," Yamamoto said. "It is just that you must promise to return safely. No more foolhardy leadership such as I heard about on the third strike at Pearl Harbor. Do we understand each other?"

"Of course, sir," Fuchida said with a grin. "And nevertheless, I promise you two carriers sunk tomorrow, sir."

"Let us hope it is their carriers and not ours," Yamamoto replied softly. "Now, an order for all of us. Sleep."

He looked at his wristwatch again.

"Six hours for all of us, at the very least. We shall need it tomorrow."

A nod indicated the meeting was over, and the staff filed out of the office.

He unbuttoned his formal uniform jacket, took it off, and laid it over the top of the chair where Genda had been sitting. As he did so he looked once more at the charts spread out on the table.

It had been a close-run battle today. Though he wanted to claim complete victory, the sinking of one, perhaps two of their

Yorktown-class carriers, he knew he could not, though staff back in Tokyo, once reports were sent in, would trumpet that. It was a disease he knew was endemic to both the Army and Navy in Tokyo, to become flush with success and overstate the results without absolute confirmation. It led to overconfidence. It was possible that in reality, he had taken the harder pounding today, with *Soryu* stable but out of the fight and *Akagi* damaged. If the gods had not intervened, and the bomb carried by the heroic American pilot had exploded rather than being a dud, it could have been two carriers out of action, *Akagi* perhaps even sunk, given that the hangar deck had been crammed with fully loaded strike planes.

Regardless of all their planning, it was proving that upon such random chances victory or defeat at sea often played out.

War itself was indeed random chance, and to his gambler's heart, it was part of the appeal.

Tomorrow chance must play to our side. If they do indeed have both of their *Saratoga*-class carriers to our west, we must find and sink them before they find us.

He stretched out on a cot in a corner of the room, not even bothering to turn off the light, just making sure first that the blackout curtains were properly drawn and secure.

He could feel the slow, steady beat of the engines far below, *Akagi* moving nearly with the wind and a following sea.

There was barely enough oil for one more fight. He had hoped it would have been today that finished it. It had not been. If he was forced to come around several times into the wind and run defensively at flank speed against incoming attacks, the situation with oil would become extreme. It might prove necessary to order one or more of the reserve tankers out of the Marshalls to meet the fleet the day after tomorrow — a risky move, given that reports had come in that the first attempt to take Wake Island had failed. That base was still in American hands, and Midway, as yet untouched, was dangerous as well. The fleet would have to thread between the two to reach the Marshalls. Sending a lone tanker without escort to meet them was a risk he would have to ponder.

Yet another gamble.

Draw that card tomorrow when it is time, not before, he thought, and within another minute, following his own orders, he drifted off to sleep.

Three hundred miles northwest of Oahu
22:40 hrs local time

Rear Admiral Newton walked the open deck of *Lexington,* rising, dropping in a slow rhythmical roll, the Pacific living up to its name this evening after so many days of rough seas, long gentle swells that if one was in a bunk could somehow carry one back to a long-suppressed memory of a cradle rocking. Though he was not even conscious of it as he walked, he wondered if perhaps that was part of the reason men could so love their ships, speak of them as "her," for that gentle rocking carried with it a primal memory, an ancient rhythm of peace.

The stars were out in all their splendor; moonrise was still an hour away. Once this was a time to be enjoyed when standing watch in such a sea. Now in this new world, it was a time when lookouts would be doubled, tensions rising, for a low moon rising could silhouette a ship to a lurking submarine stalker, giving to him that momentary advantage when he could slash in and kill.

But for now, only the stars were out, Orion high in the southeastern sky, the hunter — and we are the hunters now.

He moved between planes, Devastators

parked farthest aft, next in position the squadron of Dauntless dive bombers, and then the marine squadron of Vought Vindicators that had been slated for delivery to Midway but were now still on board.

Just before dawn that entire squadron would launch as the Task Force's scout planes. They were as antiquated as the Devastators, and having monitored some of the reports from the battle between *Enterprise* and the Japs, he had surmised the chances of the Vindicators surviving as a primary strike weapon were next to nothing.

He slowly walked between the folded-up wings of the planes. In the darkness deck crews were still at work, the only illumination dim red battle lanterns and red-covered flashlights. On the hangar deck below, those planes that for various reasons had problems — a bad magneto, a leaky cylinder, a balky landing gear, or just simply some damn "gremlin," as the men called them — were being tracked down and repaired and would be spotted up to the deck later. Sherman had announced that every single available plane must be ready for launch. They would only have one good shot at the enemy, and he wanted that to be with everything *Lexington* could possibly put into the air.

Newton moved farther forward. The ready Wildcats were spotted into place, wings down. Though night carrier flights were rare, with few pilots yet qualified, after hearing how the Japs had used scout planes to coordinate their bombardment of Pearl Harbor, he would not put it past them to have them out searching once the light from a three-quarter moon illuminated the seas.

In the cockpit of each Wildcat sat a deck crewman, ready at an instant's notice to start the plane up, the pilots trying to relax, ordered to stretch out and take it easy in the darkened first squadron ready room just inside the bridge so as not to diminish their night vision. He knew those boys most likely were not sleeping. Who could?

In the darkness on the deck few recognized him as he passed. He bumped into one sailor who was coming out from under the wing of a Wildcat, who grumbled, "Damn it, hey, watch it Buddy." He chuckled, "Sorry," and moved on.

He went farther forward, walking near the port side gunnery positions. The gun crews were standing down, but ready for alert. The old 1.1-inch guns each had one man on them now, ready to switch on the electrical power, connect into the fire control center to get the weapon ready in a few extra seconds, until his resting comrades reached the position. Spray covers had been removed from breeches and muzzles, the ready ammunition racks behind each gun filled.

He reached the forward edge of the deck, walking over the huge painted number 2, and stepped up to the white safety line across the forward edge of the bow. He stood alone. They were running at ten knots, heading nearly straight into the northeasterly breeze, the wind thus a refreshing twenty knots, whipping his light jacket.

The water ahead was churned over, foaming. It was the wake of the destroyer running half a mile ahead, a lone red light, hooded so it could only be seen from nearly directly aft, marking its stern, barely visible. But against the horizon, in the starlight, he could just about make out the deeper darkness of its outline. He was angered for a moment by a brief flash of light, some darn fool not yet used to wartime discipline opening a porthole, or door, not ensuring first that the blackout switch would automatically turn off the interior light as the door was opened. It went dark again.

He hoped someone on board noticed it and the offender was hauled before the captain. There was more than enough experience now from the Atlantic, stories of ships being lost to submarines because of such slackness.

We've trained for this for years, and tonight is real, he thought. Of course some, including himself, had served in the Atlantic during the last war, but everyone knew that the show was already winding down. There had been a handful of skirmishes against German subs, true antiques when compared to what was out there now, but never a major ship-to-ship action, let alone what was being contemplated for little more than eight hours from now.

This is the first for all of us. I'm still awake, unable to sleep. He doubted if more than a stoic few aboard this ship, or their escorts, were asleep, even though all hands, except for the ready crews, night watch, and extra lookouts, had been ordered to stand down and try and get at least four hours.

Most were undoubtedly in their bunks, in the darkness staring at the ceiling, some praying, and some whispering back and forth to each other. He had passed the word that the radio reports coming in from *Enterprise*'s strike teams be broadcast throughout the ship. He wanted them to hear what they were facing. Perhaps it had been a bad move, given the total annihilation of the Devastators. He almost regretted their knowing the fate of their comrades, but now was not the time to pull punches with his men, to swaddle them. It was time for them, for an entire nation, for all Americans, to face the brutal realities of war, to know what they were fighting, what they must face, and that yes, tomorrow some of them would indeed die.

Something in his gut told him that this might be Lady Lex's last night upon the waves. Odds were most likely three to one, but could be as high as six or seven to one. No one yet had a truly accurate fix on their numbers. Sherman's XO, though a bit embarrassed to take the position, fearing he'd be seen as a coward, argued vehemently for them to turn away and just evade the Japanese fleet for now, to save their "Old Girl" for later battles. If *Enterprise* was indeed gone, they were the only carrier left in the entire Pacific, except for *Saratoga,* which was still on the West Coast.

There was a logic to his argument, even as it was evident that the XO personally was against it, playing the role of devil's advocate, and it caused a momentary pause in their conference at 1800 hours, as the ship stood down from full battle alert, half of the crew sent below to get their first hot chow of the day.

For generations, the moment of battle at sea had been joined, both sides had a fair assessment of the other. Destroyers, or frigates and sloops of old, had scouted out the battle line of the enemy, counted ships, their ratings, guns aboard, even their names. As battle lines drew closer, the two- and three-deckers could see each other, pick their targets, and know what they would strike and what they would be struck with in return. Often commanders even knew exactly who was leading on the other side, had perhaps even been friends with them, and could be friends with them again, given the way alliances so easily changed in the days of kings and sailing ships.

This was all so different. Earlier this day the first carrier-to-carrier battle in the history of warfare had been fought. It had been a matter of confusion, random chance, flights lost, targets missed or accidentally found. Neither side knew the numbers, the strength, even the ships of the other. It was like two pugilists fighting in a darkened arena, perhaps catching brief glimpses of the other in flashes of light. Captains and admirals did not even see the enemy, forced to rely on the reports of young men, some in reality barely trained, often shaken, some wounded, others in shock.

It was thus that he and Sherman had made their decision. There might be but three Jap carriers out there, and if so, they knew their offensive numbers had to be down with the losses sustained over Pearl and in the strikes on *Enterprise.* If so, they might even have a slight edge in numbers.

On the other hand, there might be six or more carriers out there. If so, they would most certainly be overwhelmed, even if they got the first strike in and sank or crippled one or two of the Japanese.

Two nights ago he would have been far more confident. That confidence was shaken after hearing about this new fighter, this sleek high speed "Zero" they had on their carriers. Naval intelligence had assured him and Halsey that the Japanese carriers still flew their older "96" models, which the Wildcat could at least match up against. This failure of intelligence was as damaging as all the other failures in intelligence. He knew that every Devastator crew member on board was already giving himself up for dead.

And he could not even reassure them with the numbers they would actually face come morning.

Three carriers or six? Two paths. His history classes so long ago at the Academy taught all of them about generals and admirals on the edge of a stunning victory, pausing, believing their foe was still superior while in fact he was reeling back and needed but one more blow to finish him. Afterward when history showed the truth, that general or admiral was haunted for the rest of his life by the thought that he could have won a battle, perhaps even a war, if he had only shown the guts and determination to risk all, like Meade at Gettysburg, who could have finished the war that day if he had attacked after Pickett's Charge went down to defeat. And yet, on the other side of that equation was someone overconfident, pushing in, and going down to tragic defeat, forever haunted by the folly of his decision, and the realization of so many lives lost through his futile action, like Lee himself at Gettysburg, when he ordered Pickett in.

And there was another element of the equation. In the morning his boys would, for the first time in their lives, actually fly into combat, while their opponents were already well seasoned, some undoubtedly from the war in China, but all of them hardened by two days of operations. Regardless of how many hundreds of hours of training a pilot, or any soldier, had, the shock of just one hour or even minutes of battle taught far, far more about survival, about killing versus being killed. In that the Japs most definitely had the edge. On the other hand, the Japanese pilots were also tired from their long trip across the Pacific and their three sorties against Pearl Harbor and then yesterday's action against *Enterprise.* Maybe that exhaustion would cut some of their advantage in superior technology and training.

Such logic, though, or worries about superior planes or pilots, must not make him hold back now. If he let his concern show, it would infect this entire task force. I must project confidence, especially to those few who will directly face the enemy tomorrow alone in their planes.

The eastern horizon was beginning to glow brighter off the starboard quarter. He stood silent, hands in jacket pockets, wishing suddenly for a cigar or cigarette but knowing he could not light one out here. The moon started to break the horizon, a golden shimmer stretching across the gently rolling waves, the light illuminating the outline of a destroyer a mile off.

He could hear the PA crackling to life, the call for extra lookouts to report, to ensure watertight security below decks, a bit of a surge as speed picked up from ten to fifteen knots to give them a little more maneuvering capability, to lessen their vulnerability to a torpedo attack. Aft, two plane engines turned over, warming up, then throttling back to idle, ready now for launch if the Japs had a night scout plane somewhere up there and it was spotted. The moon was clear of the horizon. His task force was up to fifteen knots, tracking north-northeast, and in two hours would shift to east-northeast.

Neither he nor his rival knew that the two task forces would slip past each other in the night, barely a hundred miles separating them from each other.

He yawned, turned his back, and started back down the deck, passing without comment a small knot of sailors who stood in a circle. Whispered conversations were going on, gallows humor, betting on whether they would be dead, swimming, or still on this deck tomorrow night. The agreed-upon odds were at the very least swimming, but "we'll take a few of the bastards with us down to the bottom."

He was tempted to wander over, place his own bet, for morale purposes, of course, that they'd still be standing on this deck, counting off how many Jap carriers were sleeping with Davy Jones, but he moved on. It wasn't his style.

It was time to get some sleep.

Chapter Thirteen

Honolulu
December 9, 1941
04:30 hrs local time

James awoke with a start, bedsheets soaked with sweat, disoriented, the nightmare still half real. *Oklahoma* was rolling over and he was inside, going over with her.

He sat up, shaking, a shot of pain coursing up to his shoulder when he tried to rest the stump of his hand on the bed.

"Damn!"

He had to go to the bathroom and swung his feet off the bed and on to the floor. He was still disoriented, thinking he was home, not at his cousin's house. He nearly walked into a wall, then tried to open a closet door.

"James?"

In the shadows he saw Margaret sit up; she had been slumbering, curled up on a chair.

"You OK?" she asked.

"Need the bathroom," he announced.

She switched on a light.

"Turn that off," he gasped, and she did as ordered. He looked out the open window. The city was supposed to be under blackout, but power had been restored to some quarters of the town, light streaming from more than one window. Not that it really mattered; to the west, the fires from Pearl and Hickam, the oil tank farms, still flickered and glowed, a target that could be marked twenty miles out to sea.

"This is absurd," she announced. "I don't need you banging into walls," and she switched the light back on, then went over and drew the curtains shut.

She opened the bedroom door, and motioned him down the hallway, ready to go with him into the bathroom if need be.

"I can do this myself," he announced, a bit embarrassed, and went into the bathroom and relieved himself. With the light switch on he looked in the mirror.

Damn, I look like hell, he realized: hadn't shaved in days, eyes dark rimmed, face a bit gaunt, pale. His mouth felt gummy, disgusting. He opened the medicine cabinet, found a can of tooth powder, held it with his right hand, pried the lid off, then just held it up and shook some of the powder into his mouth and swished it around, spitting it out into the sink. He turned the water on; barely a trickle came out, brown, almost muddy looking, and he realized the tank for the toilet was just barely filling as well. Blown water mains; pressure was still down.

He switched off the light and came back out into the hallway.

"Open your mouth," she ordered and popped a thermometer in, guiding him back to the bedroom, where the light was still on, pointing for him to sit on the bed.

She checked the thermometer a couple of minutes later.

"Just over a hundred," she announced. "You're still fighting the infection. Now get back in bed."

He shook his head.

"Back to the base."

"James, don't be absurd."

"I'm not. How many Japanese translators and code readers do they have down there?"

"I don't know, you never told me about your work, but I'd guess there are enough on duty. You've done your part, now for God's sake, get back in that bed."

He shook his head.

"I have to go back," and he looked at her sharply. "Now help me get dressed."

She sat down by his side, gingerly took his

arm, raised the bandage to her face and sniffed.

"Smells a bit strange."

"It's the sulfa. I'm feeling better; it isn't throbbing like it was before."

He was half lying. It still hurt like hell, but the pain did feel a bit different now. With the fragment of God knew what pulled out by Dianne, the throbbing sensation was gone, though the infection was still there. The fragment, what was it? Part of *Arizona* when she blew? The thought made him sick, hating the memory of that moment. And I want to go back down there?

Take a day or two in bed, his weaker and yet more sensible half whispered. And besides, given the tensions in the city, he wanted to stay here, look out for Margaret and her mom. Lord only knew what had transpired in the city during the night. He had heard more than one story about lynching of Negroes in the South and Midwest not all that far in the past, more than a few of his comrades in the Navy talking about witnessing such things, and an unpleasant few obviously not caring, or even joking about it. Were we capable of that here, now? Could there be some in this town who would trigger a "Crystal Night," as it was called in Germany, and run riot against

Japanese civilians?

Without doubt there could be the same here if that darkness was allowed to fester, the same as an infection, and then spread. He looked at Margaret, her jet-black hair, the oriental cast to her eyes which had so bewitched him when first they met, and which still after twenty-one years could steal his breath away. Some would now call them the eyes of the enemy.

If that is how this war turns, then God save us all. Perhaps I should stay here. If things turn ugly, I can at least protect them.

And yet if I let that fear keep me here, what will I think later? I'm needed down at Pearl. I at least did something useful yesterday, even if only for a moment. If their boy was still alive, chances were he'd be in the Navy now. Kids his age had died by the thousands these last two days; more would die today. I've got to do something.

"Help me get my jacket on and make up some kind of sling."

"Damn your stubbornness and sense of duty," but there was a touch of a smile as she whispered to him.

She went out to the hallway, fished through the linen closet, came back a moment later with a towel, folded it into a triangle, and making a sling, helped him slip his arm into it. He tried not to grimace or react to the pain.

"To hell with the jacket," she said. "It's a filthy mess anyhow, they'll know you're an officer from your hat. Now let me make you some coffee."

Together they went down the small corridor into the living room. On the sofa his mother-in-law was sitting upright, and for a second he wasn't sure who the other person was, head nestled in the old woman's lap. It was Dianne, blanket half off her. In the moonlight he could see her tear-stained face. She was fast asleep. He had to admit she did look beautiful, and he could understand Margaret's initial reaction, even before Dianne's bitterness toward the Japanese was voiced. His mother-in-law smiled sadly and made a shushing motion with a finger raised to her lips.

They went into the kitchen.

"She cried for hours," Margaret whispered, "wanted to leave, to walk home, insisting her boyfriend might still be alive and looking for her. Mom stuck with her, even when that girl really let loose with some pretty rotten things about us."

Margaret hesitated.

"I think I would have thrown her out, but Mom took it. At last she just collapsed in tears and went to sleep. I think Mom has been up all night like that."

"Dianne is a good kid. Try not to take what she said too hard."

"You like her?" and he caught a slight edge of accusation and tried to step around it.

"Collingwood thinks the world of her. She comes from good family. Her father was in Annapolis, an instructor when Collingwood was there. She passed the security check with flying colors."

He realized he was being a bit too enthusiastic about her and fell silent.

"I bet Collingwood likes her," Margaret replied softly, even as she measured out the coffee into the percolator, filled the pot with water, and put it on the stove. Fortunately it was electric; those using gas had been cut off.

Registering a bit slow, he finally caught on to the implication in Margaret's comment.

"Come on. Old Collingwood is a decent man, loves his wife as much as I love you. Dianne's a kid, not much older than Davy would have been."

"How come you never talked about her?"

He drew closer, put his good arm around her waist and drew her closer.

"Think about it. I never said a word about

work, period. We were all under strictest orders; it was the most secret operation in the Navy. The fact that she got a security clearance to work in our office says something about her character. Her boyfriend was a pilot, and there's nothing else to tell."

He thought of the blown-out wreckage of CinCPac headquarters. The thousands upon thousands of pieces of paper floating around, scattered across the lawns, top secret documents, coding books. Hell, we're going to have to rebuild all of that.

He could sense her relaxing a bit.

"Sorry, just so you know how it is."

"Sure."

He suddenly realized that there were just the four of them in the house.

"Your cousin Janice, is she OK?" he asked a bit nervously.

"She called from the fire station right after you fell asleep. She's staying there for now, helping with blood transfusions. God, James, she said it's a madhouse. They're so desperate they're sterilizing milk bottles and using them to store blood. There's so many wounded at the bases and in town. I've got type A; I think I should go down."

He violently shook his head. The last thing he wanted was his wife walking around alone out there.

"Not on your life. Stay here and keep an eye on your mom." He didn't add Dianne's name into that equation.

"You've got your duty, I've got mine," she replied sharply.

"Wait until I get back, then I'll drive you down. Is that OK?"

She reluctantly nodded in agreement.

The coffee began to percolate. She offered to make him some eggs and bacon and he refused, just settling for toast. He was afraid if he ate anything more, his stomach would rebel. In spite of his bravado, he was feeling a bit lightheaded and nauseated.

She poured him a cup, leaving it black, no sugar or cream, as he preferred it, as nearly everyone in the Navy drank it. The toast filled his stomach a bit, settling it down.

As they opened the front door he looked back at his mother-in-law. She smiled at him, and then looked down at Dianne, who was still asleep, not wishing to move and disturb her.

"Keep an eye on her," he whispered, "and try to get her to stay here till things settle down. She can't go home, and she needs someone to look after her."

The old woman smiled, and he felt such a wave of love for her he tiptoed back over and kissed her lightly on the forehead.

"Be careful, my son," she whispered in Japanese.

"Of course, Mom," he replied, in the same language.

He went outside. Not yet dawn to the east, moon fairly high in the southern sky, to the west, the flickering glow of fires still raging.

He slipped into Collingwood's old DeSoto, realizing again it was going to be tough to drive with one hand, but he had made it up here, he'd make it back.

Margaret closed the door of the car and leaned into the window, kissing his forehead.

"You still have a fever. If it starts to get any worse, you come home immediately."

"Of course."

He looked into her eyes and hated to say it now.

"You have the gun."

She nodded.

"Things should be OK. But if something goes wrong . . ." He paused. "If an invasion starts and I can't get back, don't resist. Chances are you'll be left alone."

Memories of what Cecil had told him about Nanking drifted up, what he had seen as well in China. She was American, so was her Mom, but if they were invaded, their race might protect them.

But will their being American protect

them from us? he wondered sadly. It will have to be enough, he thought. If not, then this is no longer a country worth fighting for. A horrifying thought as he looked back to the west, the fires from the oil tank farms still soaring into the night sky.

"Just be careful. Stay inside. There are enough decent folks around here, nothing is going to happen."

She nodded, saying nothing.

"I'll be home at the end of the day, I promise."

She leaned in and kissed him.

He forced a smile, shifted the car into reverse while bracing the steering wheel with his knees, and backed out. He shifted into first and started up the hill and then out on to Pali Highway, the glowing of the fires to the west almost as bright as a rising sun.

The White House
December 9, 1941
09:30 hrs local time

It had been a tough night for sleep. The President had been tempted to ask for a mild sedative, but decided against it. If some new crisis hit that needed a decision he had to be instantly alert.

He dressed and had breakfast in his

bedroom. One of his Secret Service agents rolled him into his office and left him alone. His secretary had placed his datebook on the table, opened to the day's scheduled events. Several had been crossed out, replaced with more pressing matters: meetings with Marshall and Stark in an hour and a half for a briefing update. There was also a single typewritten sheet, a briefing paper, one or two sentences highlighting what had transpired during the night.

No contact with *Lexington.*

No contact with *Enterprise.*

Pearl reports monitoring Japanese report claiming one *Yorktown*-class carrier (*Enterprise*) sunk, one damaged.

Sighting of German submarine off of Newfoundland coast reported. Attacked by USN destroyer, aided by Canadian destroyer escort, no confirmation of results.

Strike report from Pearl confirms battleship of *Kongo* class, most likely *Hiei* (36,000 tons), sunk by submarine 5:00 p.m. Hawaiian time.

Strike report from Pearl confirms one Japanese carrier of *Soryu* class (18,000 tons) seriously damaged. Second Japanese carrier, perhaps flagship, struck by one dive bomber, its pilot deliberately crashing his plane into the ship. Recommendation will be forthcoming for appropriate decoration for pilot.

Report from Pearl confirms one pilot shot down five Japanese planes in one day. Recommendation for decoration forthcoming.

Report from Pearl, three aircraft from *Enterprise* recovered there.

No new information from Manila.

No new information from Singapore.

Hong Kong has surrendered to the Japanese.

He continued to scan the report while sipping his coffee. Two Medals of Honor, he thought; the nation needs heroes as soon as possible, and those two fit the bill.

There was a knock on the door and it cracked open. It was Eleanor, and he smiled, motioning for her to come in. She came around to the side of his desk and scanned the datebook as she rested a hand on his shoulder.

"I see the luncheon with your mother and me has been canceled," she said quietly.

"Priorities of war now," he said.

She nodded, picking up the night report, looking it over.

"Do you think the Japanese report is accurate? Why no word from our aircraft carriers?"

"Security. If the *Enterprise* is still afloat, a single radio transmission could be monitored and tracked. The same with *Lexington.* Maybe later today we'll know for certain."

"What do you think?"

"It sounded like *Enterprise* took a terrible pounding yesterday." He paused. "If Pearl is reporting only three planes from that ship landing there, it could indicate *Enterprise* is sunk and orphan planes are all that is left of her."

"God save those boys," she sighed. "How many are aboard a carrier?"

"About two thousand men."

"Nearly half as many dead, then, as reported from Pearl Harbor so far."

He nodded, saying nothing.

She put the report down. He shifted a bit uncomfortably in his chair, lighting a cigarette, a subtle signal that he wanted to be alone for a few minutes before the day started.

"I wanted to talk with you about something over lunch," she finally said.

"Let's do it now, Eleanor, but I'm sorry, it will have to be brief." He looked up at her, trying to smile as he said it. "I have meetings starting in half an hour."

"This is important, Franklin. We're already hearing rumors about anti-Japanese propaganda," and she unfolded a newspaper that she had kept in her left hand and laid it upon his desk. It was a political cartoon, a crude caricature of a leering "Jap," buck-toothed, with thick glasses, laughing as he plunged a samurai sword into Uncle Sam's back. A decapitated body, labeled "China," lay at the "Jap's" feet.

"How all Japs fight," was the caption.

It was stunning how quickly the mood of America had changed. When the *Chicago Tribune* had leaked the secret plans for Rainbow Five, on December 4, their political cartoon on the front page was a worried "Midwest," Illinois represented by an Abraham Lincoln–looking character, staring towards Washington, D.C., and written above the image of the White House and Capitol was the caption "War Propaganda!" Now but a few days later it was a caricature of Uncle Sam getting stabbed in the back. What they had decried but days before as propaganda had finally been realized as reality.

"So?"

"Franklin, it's no different than the Nazi pictures of Jews. I don't want to see this of us."

"People are angry. It was a stab in the back."

"Franklin. Fight their government and their military yes — but this? It could spread. There are already calls for every Japanese citizen in America to be rounded up and put in concentration camps for the duration."

"Eleanor, one thing at a time."

"Bad enough that we are calling on Negro soldiers to be drafted while back home they are less than third-class citizens but are now expected to fight anyhow. Hatred of the Japanese . . . If you don't say something, at least about those living here, it could get out of control. We say we're fighting to defend democracy and against racism. We have to live up to that."

He looked up at her. She could be so damned determined. He knew how polarizing she was politically. It seemed half the country adored her, the other half grumbled she was "that communist agent" inside the White House.

He finally nodded.

"I have a press conference in twenty minutes. I'll make some kind of statement about not letting our passions run away, to remember we're all Americans. Will that satisfy you?"

"For now," she said, with a trace of a smile.

She patted him lightly on the shoulder and left the room.

He sighed, lighting another cigarette.

He knew she was, after all, right. He loathed racism as much as she did, but had to face far more bluntly the political realities of the moment. She wanted to push for more legal protection of Negroes in the South, and yet the solid Democratic base in the South would melt away like ice in July if he pushed that agenda too hard.

Perhaps, in a strange twisted sense, this war might actually help to serve that purpose. As the Civil War had finally brought Lincoln around to the need for liberation and the Thirteenth Amendment, something he never could have openly supported in 1861, perhaps this war would do the same. If Negro soldiers stand, fight, and die alongside white comrades, how can equal rights still be denied if victory is finally achieved? If the first reports about Japanese fifth columnists in Hawaii and California are finally proven false, that except for a few rotten eggs they are indeed loyal Americans, the issue there will go away. But if evidence provided otherwise, he knew it would be nearly impossible to resist the political pressure, perhaps even necessary if only for the protection of the Japanese-American citizens themselves.

It was going to be a long day, he realized, but an interesting one, and he began reviewing briefing papers, thinking about how he would handle the press in a few minutes. Confidence, always display confidence and determination. At even the worst of moments we must never falter. Otherwise how can I expect young men to go out and die, as did the pilots of *Enterprise* yesterday, unless they know that back here, we are behind them 100 percent, believe in them, and believe in ultimate victory.

Then he stopped and reflected. Was *Enterprise* still afloat? And *Lexington*? He looked at his wrist watch. First search planes were most likely going out now for both sides, seeking, and the first one to find and strike would almost certainly win.

He lowered his head and began to pray.

Akagi
05:40 hrs local time

With binoculars trained on *Zuikaku,* steaming at flank speed into the northeasterly breeze, he could barely make out the silhouette of the ship to the northeast, outlined by the beginning of nautical twilight.

The first of the *Zuikaku* search planes lifted clear of the deck. The second one followed twenty seconds later, another twenty seconds after that. As each plane built up speed, climbing, it turned. A couple of minutes later one of them flew directly over *Akagi,* rocking its wings in salute. Deck crews looked up; a few took off their caps and waved. Not the wild enthusiasm of two days ago, when the first strike wave started its launch toward Pearl Harbor. The men were too exhausted now for that.

That search plane continued on its track to the northwest. The dozen planes sent aloft by *Zuikaku* would fan out on tracks north-northwest to south-southwest. *Tone*'s six seaplanes, with pilots and spotters on board well trained for this kind of mission, would cover the arc northwest to east-northeast. *Chikuma* to the south would do the reciprocal from southwest to east-southeast.

Zuikaku's Zeroes would launch next, ten planes to provide cover over the fleet, two of them to trail astern, watching back toward Oahu, which was now over three hundred fifty miles away. The only potential threat from that direction was perhaps their B-17s or PBYs, if any had survived. Still, it would not do to have a land-based plane locate the fleet for the American carriers.

Ten minutes later the last of *Zuikaku*'s planes launched. The carrier came about sharply, the interval of launch having separated her from the rest of the fleet by over ten miles, and began to race at flank speed back to rejoin the protective circle half a dozen miles across.

No one aboard that carrier ever noticed the four torpedo wakes that crossed astern by four hundred yards where she would have been if she had continued on the same course but for one more minute. Nor did any ship monitor the frustrated radio report from the American sub, which had been engaged in a stern chase on the surface for the last two hours, the captain all but giving up until almost, it seemed, heaven sent, the one Japanese carrier had come about and begun to steam straight toward him, illuminated by the moonlight, caught visually in the powerful night binoculars mounted on the minuscule bridge of the sub.

His message of coordinates had been sent repeatedly and had been heard.

Lexington
05:50 hrs local time

"You have your coordinates. You know your targets. Go for the two largest of their carriers. Ignore anything else, especially their damn battleship. We want carriers. If you get hit, and can't make it to your primary, then attack whatever you can."

Admiral Newton leaned against the back wall of the ready room, saying nothing as Captain Sherman finished his comments.

"Remember, we've got a sub trailing them. If you get too badly shot up to make it back here, turn east, send out a distress signal, and try to ditch. We are not going to leave you out there the way the Japs do with their men. We will get you back, I swear that to you. We will get you back."

As he spoke, Newton could see him paying particular attention to the Devastator and Vindicator pilots. Morale with them had gone to hell during the night. The Catholic chaplain reported that every last man from that squadron had come to him or his Protestant counterpart for communion or general absolution, with all leaving farewell letters.

"Pilots, man your planes!"

Sherman stepped away from the podium and hurriedly tried to shake the hand or pat the shoulder of each man heading out the door.

The room emptied, and Newton came up to the captain's side. He could see tears in

the man's eyes. Rather than go up to the bridge, they followed the last of the pilots out into a roaring cacophony of noise. Every engine was turning over. Backseat gunners for the Dauntlesses and Vindicators were already strapped in, as were gunners and bombardiers aboard the Devastators.

The combat air patrol of six Wildcats was already aloft, circling high above the fleet. The first of the Wildcat escort fighters began its rollout. Orders were to launch every fifteen seconds, and even before the first plane had cleared the next one started its roll. The yellow-shirted launch director dramatically crouched down, pointed

straight forward for each plane, watched it for a few seconds, making sure it was accelerating, keeping alignment to the center line, and able to clear even if it should lose an engine, then turned his attention to the next plane in line.

The Dauntlesses were parked nearly amidships, 1,200-horsepower Wright Cyclone engines howling at full throttle, a hurricane of noise. It was so overpowering that one could actually feel it coursing through every fiber of the body, the thunder of a nation aroused. Wheel chocks were pulled on the lead plane of the squadron, and it began its roll forward, slower than the Wildcats with a half ton armor-piercing bomb slung to its belly. Every bomb had a message chalked on it:

"Eat this, Togo."

"Remember Pearl Harbor!"

"See you in hell."

And more than a few that no stateside censor would allow to be printed in the papers.

Newton had to brace himself against the side of the bridge as the back blast from the powerful engine of the Dauntless next to him started its rollout. He saw the young tail gunner looking straight at him.

Perhaps the toughest job of all, he thought. At least a pilot had some sense of control of his fate. The kid in the rear seat was just along for the ride that he might return from, or might not; that was in the hands of his pilot and God. Newton stiffened and saluted the kid, who just continued to stare at him, braced for the takeoff.

Next came the Vindicators, needing a lot more deck space with their far less powerful 825-horsepower Twin Wasp Junior engines.

Marine pilots as well — recovery for them, if they got back, would be tough; none of them were qualified for carrier landings. If war had not broken out, they'd be on Midway today. Their original mission had been to fly off of *Lexington* and land at Midway to reinforce the garrison.

He looked back to where the Devastators were moving into position, wings being locked into place. Then he heard shouts, a commotion forward, and caught a glimpse of a Vindicator angling off the deck to starboard, torquing, starboard wing dropping as it skidded, staggering off the side of the ship fifty feet short of the bow, edge of the wing clipping the gun deck. It rolled up onto its side, seemed to be hanging in midair as *Lexington* continued to race forward at flank speed of over thirty-five miles per hour. Rolled onto its back and then disappeared.

The plane launching behind it skidded slightly to the left, appeared almost to be doing a repeat of disaster in the opposite direction, then straightened out and lifted off.

An explosion rocked the ship. Running up to the side of the bridge he could see a huge column of water erupting skyward fifty yards off their starboard beam, the bomb detonating, fragments of plane going up with it.

"I want a damage report from below," Sherman shouted, and one of his aides ran off.

The Devastators finally began their roll-out, while overhead the squadrons slowly circled, forming up, struggling for altitude. A ninety-plane strike was ready to go once the last of the lumbering torpedo bombers were aloft.

He watched each of them go, the deck almost empty now, hundreds of men, their jobs done, watching, some subtly gesturing as if by the motion of their hands they could help lift the old planes into the air, others saluting, a few waving and cheering.

The last of the Devastators lifted off, and suddenly there was just silence, except for the whipping of the forty-five-knot wind blowing down the length of the deck, *Lexington* already beginning to slow, turning from its northeasterly heading to a course due south at fifteen knots.

"Sir!"

Newton broke away from his thoughts, looking aft to the circle of foaming water, now a couple of miles astern, where the Vindicator had crashed. A destroyer circled around it — a futile gesture really, as if the two men aboard her could have somehow survived the impact, let alone the explosion of the bomb on board.

It was a seaman first class, standing stiffly.

"Go ahead."

"Sir. Combat Information reports radar detecting an inbound, twenty miles to the southwest. Two of the Wildcats have already been ordered to intercept."

For a moment he was tempted to tell Sherman to countermand the intercept order. It was most likely a Japanese scout plane. Perhaps it'd miss them, but the presence of the Wildcats would by their mere presence confirm the existence of this carrier and its possible location.

He looked at the sky, brightening by the minute. There was a scattering of low-hanging stratus, morning mist rising off the ocean, but no buildup yet of cumulus or the towering cumulonimbus of later in the day, which might conceal beneath it an entire fleet.

Sherman went into the bridge and up the steps to the Combat Information Center, room bathed in red light, still under night-time conditions. He followed.

The radar screen, small oval wonder, its magic images impossible for him to interpret, flickered green. The operator, seeing the approach of the admiral and captain stiffened, then pointed to a wavy point in the lower corner, hard to discern with so many other points and lines appearing and disappearing.

"That's it, sir. He must have been flying low and then started to pop up. Definitely tracking from the west-southwest, and heading straight toward us."

Even within the confines of the CIC, he could hear the thunder of the strike wave, having formed up, now tracking southwest, bearing 220 degrees, toward the position of at least four carriers reported by the submarine. The search plane was from nearly west, behind them.

Were their carriers closer? Should part of the wave be diverted to scout it out?

A radio loudspeaker crackled to life. It was one of the Wildcats reporting a visual, a Japanese float plane. They were closing to engage.

At nearly the same instant one of the radio operators turned to announce a transmission on a Japanese frequency, loud, extremely close — most likely the scout plane calling in their position.

"We better get ready," was all Sherman had to say, turning away and heading up to the bridge.

Fifteen miles west-southwest of Lexington

"Confirmed. One *Saratoga*-class carrier, half a dozen escorting ships."

Damn!

His pilot went into a sharp banking turn, diving. He had caught a glimpse of movement, an American plane.

"We are under attack! Repeating coordinates!"

The spotter looked again at his navigational clipboard. They'd been aloft for little more than twenty minutes. *Tone* was thirty-five miles away, so close there was a chance that smoke from the American ships could be spotted and closed on at full dawn. He could clearly see dozens of American planes aloft moving across the eastern horizon, outlined by the early light of dawn.

He was barely able to get the message out one more time, warning as well that an American strike wave was outbound, apparently bearing south, before the combined firepower of two American Wildcats slashed into the fuselage, wings, and cockpit, killing both him and the pilot.

In flames, the plane rolled over on its back and dove into the sea.

Akagi

05:55 hrs local time

Admiral Yamamoto turned away from the seaman still clutching the flimsy sheet of paper, noting the coordinates radioed in by the scout plane, which had just gone off the air, obviously shot down, and gazed at his signals officer.

"Pass the order and radio immediately, all ships. Turn to a heading straight into the wind, 050 degrees. Launch all aircraft immediately, strike aircraft to receive coordinates momentarily."

"Radio?" Genda asked.

"They know where we are," Yamamoto snapped. "We heard their transmission from Pearl, in spite of whatever damn language it is they are using, and part of the message sounded like it was reading off numbers, coordinates of longitude and latitude. We can't waste a minute with flags or Morse blinkers. Send it now! Helm, bring us about to a heading of fifty degrees, order flank speed."

He strode over to the chart table, scanned it, circling a spot with a pencil.

"They're to our northeast! They must have slipped around the flank during the night, and *Tone* is less than thirty-five miles away!"

He looked back at Genda.

"It is them; it is their remaining carrier fleet! Order all planes to launch." He looked again at the chart. The American planes were slower but were already aloft.

"We have forty-five minutes at most."

Genda saluted and dashed from the bridge. *Akagi* was already responding to the helm, and even before general quarters sounded, all knew that something was up, already heading to their stations.

"Sir!"

He looked up from the chart. It was Fuchida, standing there eager, already dressed in a flight suit, almost trembling like a racehorse just before the gate opened.

He felt a surge of trepidation. This man was too precious to lose now. His experience of leading at Pearl, both the successes and failures, had to be thoroughly reported, rewarded where necessary. Already he had planned for him to be moved up to a position parallel to Genda's. And beyond all that, he was almost like a son. He loved this eager pilot, and the thought of sending him to his death caused a surge of pain.

And yet he could not say no to such a samurai.

"Go then!"

Fuchida grinned, saluted, and started to leave.

"Wait."

There was hesitation in Fuchida's eyes as he looked back, almost fearing that the admiral was about to reverse his approval.

"Not in a torpedo bomber. Besides, yours is gone."

"What then, sir?"

"Take one of the Zeroes. One with a radio so you can lead. Stay out of the dogfighting, keep above the enemy fleet. I want the attack coordinated, well directed, and reported on accurately. There was too much confusion yesterday. I demand that you come back and report."

He could sense the touch of frustration.

"No compromise. You can fly, but you are to lead as a daimyo of old, not to draw a sword and fight. You are to lead."

"Yes, sir."

Yamamoto extended his hand.

"Go, my son, and may the gods protect you."

Fuchida seemed overwhelmed by emotion, as if almost ready to embrace his admiral. He drew back, saluted, and sprinted down the stairs to the deck.

On the flight deck, planes had already been spotted into position. Crew chiefs were in cockpits, engines beginning to turn over, warming up as *Akagi* swung around from a westerly heading to northwest, the quartering breeze blowing the exhaust from the planes across the deck. The dark horizon to the west was being replaced by early dawn to the east.

He could see other ships beginning to turn. Signal pennants were going up from the flying bridge of *Akagi* giving the coordinates of the American fleet as last reported, Morse blinkers relaying that data as well.

Pilots were pouring out of the ready room, Fuchida in the lead, running to the portside wing of the lead Zero.

They were now running fifty degrees north, speed still picking up, past twenty knots, the glorious old ship surging ahead.

He knew he'd burn more fuel in the next hour than in an entire normal day. It would make the margin to reaching the Marshalls slim indeed, but this was the gamble of war. One solid strike and the mission would finally be accomplished. Then he could afford to limp slowly toward the tankers and their invaluable replenishment.

He turned his binoculars to the south and could barely make out on the horizon the wounded *Soryu,* with *Kirishima* steaming astern. They were now turning as well. He debated whether they should move on west ahead of the others or not, but decided against it.

"Hoist the Z flag," Yamamoto announced, and a moment later that legendary banner unfurled from the highest mast, a cheer erupting on the deck.

He caught a last glimpse of Fuchida standing in his cockpit, looking back at him, saluting, then sliding down, crew chief helping him to buckle in, then jumping off the wing. The forlorn pilot whom Fuchida had replaced stood dejected to one side, obviously humiliated, head lowered.

The launch director, standing on the deck,

holding signal flag aloft, waved it in a tight circle. Fuchida revved up his engine, and smoke whipped out of the exhaust pipes. At the signal the deck crews pulled back the wheel chocks. With a leap the Zero started forward into the wind, tail up in a matter of seconds, rudder angled against the torque, and he lifted off well short of the bow, plane after plane following, while strike waves from the other carriers, but minutes later, started aloft as well.

USS Thresher
06:15 hrs
They had stayed submerged since their failed attack on the Japanese carrier, and to the captain's utter frustration, the enemy fleet was pulling away, his old tub unable to match their speed while submerged in a stern chase.

But now?

"Repeat the signal in the clear, damn it," he snapped, not taking his eyes off the periscope.

"Entire Jap fleet coming about and launching aircraft. Give our coordinates again and keep repeating!"

Hickam Army Air Force Base
06:17 hrs

The drive into base had been tough, but he had managed it. More roadblocks were up, manned by national guardsmen. One near the base was a heavily manned position of regular infantry from the Tropical Lightning Division, Schofield Barracks. It was sandbagged, with two .30-caliber water-cooled machine guns posted. Margaret had found his wallet, tucked into his uniform pocket after all, and he had it out. The sight of his arm in a sling, amputated hand obvious, ID held up, had won through. Near the base entrance a lieutenant in charge had even ordered one of his men to drive the commander the rest of the way in, for which he was damn grateful. He was feeling lightheaded and now a bit foolish over his earlier bravado.

"Sir, you lose that in the fighting on Sunday?" the corporal driving him had asked, after several sidelong curious glances.

"No. I was on the *Panay* when I lost my hand. Got nicked by some shrapnel, though, when *Arizona* blew."

"What's the *Panay,* sir?"

He did not reply. It was a question asked him hundreds of times since 1937, and he was sick of it. Damn it, didn't they now know?

His driver got him to what was now the radio center for both Hickam and Pearl. As he came into the open hangar, there were nods of recognition. He saw Joe, apparently at work for over a day now without sleep, with several of his ham operator friends, rigging up yet another set. More than twenty radios were up and running, antennas crisscrossing like a spiderweb high up in the rafters of the hangar.

He was glad he had come. Collingwood was passed out, asleep on a cot in the corner. Lacey smiled and handed him a mug of coffee.

"Something's up," she said, pointing to the radio that he knew was monitoring a frequency used by the Japanese fleet.

He sat down by the operators, who motioned for him to pick up a headphone set. He started to listen in.

They weren't coding. The message was in the clear, chatter between scout planes already aloft, and then the frantic report of the plane that had located a target before being shot down.

"Who's in charge here?" James shouted, looking back from the radio.

An Army brigadier came over.

"I am," was all James got. "Who are you?"
"I'm Commander Watson. Until all this happened I was with cryptanalysis and monitoring for CinCPac."
The brigadier eyed him for a few seconds, noticing the sling.
"I heard about you. OK, what's up?"
"Relay this to our fleet. They definitely have been spotted and should expect an attack. Damn, does anybody have charts around here?"
He half stood up, looking around, but there wasn't a nautical chart in sight.
Yet more information came in a few minutes later from a sub, a report that it had been trailing the enemy fleet. James called for its data, too, to be relayed to the strike force. If anyone had good navigators on board who could pinpoint a location, the subs did.
In a sense he felt part of it all now — he was doing something to hit back — but at the same time he felt impotent, like a spectator in far away bleachers while the real game was played out beyond his reach.

Thirty miles north-northeast of Akagi,
ninety miles southwest of Task Force Eight
06:30 hrs

The two opposing waves could actually see

each other, the Japanese attack force, a hundred and twenty-two planes, tracking ten miles to the west of the ninety-two planes of the American force heading in the opposite direction.

Fuchida looked at them hungrily, fighting the temptation to lead one squadron over, to slash in. It would only take a few minutes to close upon them, standing out clear against the sunrise.

But his orders were firm. The few Zero pilots with radios begged to be cut loose, but he ordered them to stay on track, to protect the strike force, which was still not in any semblance of formation, raggedly attempting to form up.

Attrition of the last two days had cut some squadrons down to just five or six planes, and he had broadcast in the clear for all dive bombers to form into a single group on the lead *Akagi* pilot and the same for the torpedo bombers. It was taking time, precious time, as they slowly climbed for altitude.

He then radioed back to *Akagi* to expect an attack to hit within fifteen minutes at most — then led his group on.

Lexington
06:35 hrs
The CIC was a room of barely contained chaos, every radio operator at work, jotting down messages, shouting for assistants to pass them up, orders being given back.

Newton and Sherman stood in front of the Plexiglas plot board, watching as two seamen on the other side traced in information, symbols, tracking lines.

Radar and radio reports both confirmed an inbound wave of Japanese planes now eighty miles out: a report of a sighting of a Japanese cruiser to the southwest, thirty miles out, closing in their direction, and a report relayed in from Honolulu stating it had monitored Japanese radio signals confirming a strike launch ordered from what was believed to be the *Akagi,* most likely their flagship.

"Radio the boys, that's their primary target," Sherman announced. "They should know what the hell they look like. I want the *Akagi.*"

"*Kaga* looks almost identical," Newton said softly.

'Then tell them to sink the first bastard and then the other," Sherman replied coldly, and Newton smiled.

Akagi
06:45 hrs
"Enemy planes sighted!"

Helmets were being passed around, and Admiral Yamamoto and Genda, by his side, took theirs and put them on. Binoculars raised, they could see the incoming wave, ten miles out, already with smoking trails as the defending fighters swarmed in on them.

He tried to count their numbers. Several score at least, coordinated this time, in tight formations.

In line of battle *Kaga* and *Akagi* were in the center. Three miles to the north were *Zuikaku* and *Shokaku.* Three miles farther to the south were *Hiryu, Soryu,* and *Kirishima,* their ring of eleven destroyers broken into three groups, five to the central group, three each to the other two.

Antiaircraft guns from the northernmost group began to open up, dark splotches staining the morning sky. The enemy planes pressed on, their torpedo bombers beginning to drop altitude, all aimed straight at *Akagi.*

"They're coming for us," Genda announced, "ignoring *Zuikaku* and *Shokaku.*"

"It's what I would have ordered them to do," Yamamoto replied.

Another two minutes. The heavy guns on

both *Kaga* and *Akagi* opened up, though *Akagi*'s rate of fire was vastly slower due to damage below and the ditching of ammunition overboard while fighting the fires.

The attack was coming on fast. A dozen or more planes were tumbling from the sky, trailing smoke, a few parachutes blossoming. Several Zeroes focused in on the torpedo planes, slashing into them, while high overhead the dive bombers continued on, now well past *Zuikaku* and her sister ship.

Akagi started to heel over to port, the helmsman, as ordered, going into evasive maneuvers. A destroyer nearby nearly rammed into her bow, just barely avoiding collision as it turned aside.

"There are more of them than last time," Genda announced heatedly. "A lot more. This might be two carriers hitting us at once."

He focused on the lead dive bomber. Different design, looked almost like one of their Devastators.

"That's a Vindicator," Genda announced, as if reading Yamamoto's mind. "They're usually land based."

As the first two dive bombers began their wing over, they exploded, one after the other, a Zero diving past them. Two more began their dives. One of the Zeroes cartwheeled, wing sheared off.

Akagi was heeling hard over in a violent full turn to port.

He saw the Dauntlesses moving into position up high, puffs of smoke from antiaircraft shells, a mad confusion of aircraft.

Three of the Vindicators were shrieking down, their aim good. The three released fairly low before pulling out. One had its wing shearing off, either from a direct hit or overstress. But the bombs winged in, the first bursting a hundred yards off the bow, the second fifty yards from the port-side bow, but the third clipped the front of the landing deck, punched through into the depths of the ship, and blew.

We might survive this, we might survive this, Yamamoto silently chanted. This bomb burst did not feel that bad, some splintering of the deck forward. Fortunately the hangar deck was empty of planes.

But now the Dauntlesses were coming in, and he sensed this would be the moment.

There were at least fifteen of them, six winging over, the others appearing to hold back. It must be a good commander up there, ready to divert the others if the first wave hits us hard.

They were still turning hard to port, the bombers winging down, guiding straight in.

Two more were hit, the bomb of one exploding right underneath the plane, taking out the plane behind it. But still they pressed in, two more bombs visible through the smoke.

There was no need to be told to duck. He crouched down low and felt the two sharp impacts, the explosions erupting somewhere down deep within.

"More!"

He gazed up. The rest of the attack group was coming in and he knew that his beloved comrade, the first fleet carrier of His Majesty's Navy, was now in mortal peril.

The Americans came on relentlessly, more bombs dropping. Another impact, and this one astern, close enough that he felt the heat of the blast washing over the bridge. A loud screaming: a Dauntless, out of control, tumbled, barely cleared the bridge, and then disappeared astern, crashing in their wake.

He stood up. Fires were burning the length of the deck, soaring up out of impact points, and he could feel their speed slacking off.

"American torpedo planes!"

Genda pointed to port but the smoke was so thick he could not see them.

Heavy gunfire. An American plane appeared through the smoke, skimming the

deck forward of the bridge, a Zero on its tail tearing into it, an American Wildcat behind the Zero, both Devastator and Zero bursting into flames, the Wildcat breaking away but it too now going down as antiaircraft fire tore off the aft fuselage of the planc.

The intense bravery of all three pilots struck him, held his awed attention. A second torpedo plane came out of the smoke, crossed over the deck, and dropped back down as it cleared and skimmed off over the ocean. Hardly a gunner on the starboard side fired at it, their concentration still focused aloft.

He caught a glimpse of four more bombers, dropping down, heading toward *Kaga,* then they were lost in the smoke.

And then the double impact as two torpedoes struck nearly side by side astern, the force of the explosion throwing him back down, helmet cutting open his brow as he fell to the deck.

Genda was by his side, helping to pull him back up, shouting for a corpsman. He waved him off.

"I'm fine. My ship. Find out about our ship!"

Akagi was still turning to port, but already slowing even more. From the starboard side exhaust stack a deafening burst of steam exploded out, indicating boilers were being flooded. A moment later he could sense the list beginning.

And then there was a momentary silence, except for the hungry crackle of the fires sweeping the deck, an alarm sounding somewhere, men shouting — but the thunder of the guns, the shrieking roar of the planes was gone.

They circled through one hundred eighty degrees, turning, helmsman shouting that the engine room was not answering. As they turned across the wind, he caught a momentary glimpse to the northeast. The surviving

American planes were forming up in the distance, streaking away, bursts of antiaircraft fire from the escorting destroyers following them, a few Zeroes still in pursuit.

But the damage had been done. He could feel the list increasing, speed dropping away.

His damage control officer, cradling what looked like a compound fracture to his arm, bone sticking out just above the elbow, stood before him, pale faced.

"Sir, nothing is answering below. I have verbal reports of the hangar deck swept by fire, port-side engine rooms flooding, uncontrollable flooding below. The forward hit ruptured plates on the bow, and water is flooding in there as well. I've ordered counterflooding, sir, but . . ."

He lowered his head, barely suppressing a sob.

"Go on."

"Sir, I think you should transfer your flag."

A huge explosion erupted forward, fireball white hot. Obviously an aviation gas tank exploding, the explosion consuming fire crews that had been trying to train fire hoses into the hole punched by the bomb. That hole was now buckling back the entire forward deck of the ship.

The list was continuing to increase; it was past ten degrees.

He could see *Kaga* now. She had not been hit and was still steaming at full speed, coming around to run alongside her sister ship.

He swept the bridge with his gaze. Another explosion, this one astern: vents of steam pluming up, an indication of boilers flooding or major steam lines letting go.

Electrical lighting on the bridge flickered down, winked off. Emergency battery-powered lamps turned on their faint beams, piercing the gloom of smoke.

Akagi was dying.

"Order the crew to abandon ship," he said quietly. "Signal destroyers to stand by to pick up survivors."

Genda, openly crying, saluted and started to turn away.

"Sir, your flag. You are transferring, of course."

He forced a smile.

"I'm not some suicidal fool, my friend. Of course I am transferring, but first let us get our valiant men up from below. Only then will I leave."

He paused.

"And, Genda, make sure you retrieve the Z flag. Admiral Togo's spirit would never forgive us for leaving it behind."

Over the Lexington
07:12 hrs

Tears of rage clouded Fuchida's eyes. The battle report from *Akagi* was evident as he tuned in to one of the American frequencies, the pilots exulting. "Scratch a Jap flattop!" one of them shouting. "It's *Akagi,* I tell you. Look at that son of a bitch burn. Good work, McMullen! Danny, you put it right down the bastard's throat!"

The enemy target was visible ahead. Definitely one *Saratoga*-class carrier. But only one? Surely both had to be here, for the battles of yesterday indicated they had engaged only *Yorktown*-class carriers.

Regardless, the target was his, and this time he would make sure it was taken.

"All planes!" he announced, switching on

his mike. "Attack the carrier and the carrier only! Attack!"

He wanted to add, avenge the *Akagi,* but did not want that thought to cloud any of the pilots from his ship, nor reveal more if the enemy was listening.

The torpedo planes were already down low, dropping in fast. The bulk of the American fighters and his own escorting Zeroes were already entangled with them.

The twenty-seven Vals of the strike force, though broken up into four attack groups from the various carriers, began to wing over, one after the other. How he wished he could go in with them, but his admiral had given him clear orders and he felt compelled to obey.

Lexington

"For that which we are about to receive . . ." Sherman whispered, watching as the long, apparently endless stream of dive bombers began their runs.

Within only a few minutes, five bombs had smashed into the deck of the old Lady Lex. Three minutes later three torpedoes were into her port side, all of them near the bow, one of the explosions bursting a main aviation gas tank. Several thousand gallons spilled out before it suddenly flashed and

exploded in a huge secondary that lifted off the first forty feet of decking, and blew out more of the bow below the waterline.

However hard they had been hit, they had also hit back. At least thirty of the attacking planes had reportedly been dropped by excited Wildcat pilots and gunnery crews. It was damn small compensation.

Damage control reported that the forward hundred feet of the ship was torn wide open, while a bomb hit aft had punched clean down to the port side turbine, blowing it apart. That had shut down one of their props completely. Secondary blasts were cutting through both port and starboard

engine rooms.

She was already going down at the bow, flooding so rapidly that it made him think of the stories about the *Titanic,* which had been torn open forward, stern lifting out of the air until the ship rose nearly vertical before sliding beneath the waves. At the same time the *Lex* was taking on a sharp list to port, so rapidly that panicked sailors were already abandoning positions below, afraid they would be caught below decks if the carrier rolled over and turtled.

He was responsible for the lives of over two thousand men on board, though only the good Lord knew how many were still here and how many were already dead.

With half this damage, if just below the water line from the torpedoes, or just the bomb hits, he could have put their backs to the wall and ordered a fight to the finish to save this ship. He had never been on a sinking ship before, but all his knowledge and instincts told him that *Lexington* was dying, and would either go down bow first or roll over.

He sighed, looking over at Admiral Newton, who without comment just nodded in agreement.

"Prepare to abandon ship," he said softly. "Order destroyers to come alongside to take on survivors. Make sure all wounded are properly evacuated. I want no one left behind."

The intercom system was entirely knocked out, but the order was passed by mouth, shouted down from the bridge, to fire crews battling the blazes, and then down below, where already men were sensing the inevitable and beginning to stream up to the deck.

Honolulu

The mood in the hangar was electric. Radio operators were monitoring both Japanese

and American frequencies, shouting out reports, everyone cheering with them when the cry went up, "Definitely scratch a flat-top. *Akagi* is burning bow to stern!"

There were backslappings, cheers, a delicious taste of vengeance at last after the heartbreaking confusion of yesterday's battle of inconclusive reports, and the gut-wrenching sight of the few battered planes returning, pilots numbed with shock.

The voices on the radio sounded exuberant even though squadron leaders were now beginning to report in the heavy toll exacted for their kill: nearly all the Vindicators and Devastators gone, but still, they had made a kill, and once the survivors were refitted and refueled, they would go out and take another of the four carriers reportedly sighted, of which one was definitely finished.

And then the reports from *Lexington* came in, and then suddenly just went off the air, until one of the ham radio operators announced he had communication with a Wildcat flying combat air patrol. The man's voice was breaking.

"She's going down. God damn, they got her, she is going down."

The gathering in the hangar instantly sobered. There had been hope against hope that *Enterprise* and the attackers from Oahu had perhaps sunk two of them and that maybe there were only two or three left and *Lexington* would finish the lot. But the retiring strike wave reported confirmation of at least three carriers still out there, one pilot chiming in that he had seen two more, farther to the south.

"We don't have a single carrier left in the entire central Pacific," Collingwood whispered, awake because of all the confusion and now sitting by James's side.

"What about the orphans?" someone asked, a pilot standing to one side, eyes hollow, hands in pocket. James looked over at him, didn't recognize him, and saw a squadron insignia on his sleeve indicating *Enterprise,* the name Dellacroce stenciled on his shirt.

"Order them back here," General Scales, who had taken command of communication, announced.

There was a moment of silence. Nearly everyone in what was now called the "radio shack" was Army.

"Who knows ranges here?" Scales asked.

The lone *Enterprise* pilot stepped forward.

"I flew Wildcats," he announced.

"Your name, son?"

"Lieutenant Dellacroce."

Scales looked at him appraisingly and then actually went over and shook his hand.

"Heard about you. You're the pilot who nailed five Japs yesterday. Proud to shake your hand, son. You are America's first ace in this war. Word's already out that you're being put in for the Medal of Honor."

Dave took his hand, but there was no warmth, only a distant gaze, and James, like so many others, saw and understood that gaze. He was in shock.

James stood up and went over to Dave's side.

"Tell us what your planes can do. Can they make it back to here?"

"The dive bombers, if fully fueled out,

have a range of fifteen hundred miles, but that's a bunch of civilian-time baloney. Cut that in half for wartime flying, and that is with no damaged fuel tanks. They just might make it. Wildcats, twelve hundred miles, but again, cut that in half, two-thirds if they've been dogfighting for fifteen or twenty minutes. A few might make it in."

"Get the pilot from *Lexington* on the radio," Scale said. "All birds from *Lexington* to head for Oahu or splash down near that civilian freighter off Kauai."

Lieutenant Dellacroce turned and walked out of the hangar, gaze fixed on the western horizon, where he knew yet more of his comrades were dying, or nursing in damaged planes. He felt nothing other than infinite weariness.

Akagi
08:10 hrs

"Sir, you must leave the ship now!"

Yamamoto barely heard him, absorbed in other thoughts. Memories of the first time he had walked her deck, even before launch, dreams of what she would be, the backbone of a new modern navy for Japan, his own times aboard her in various command positions, and now this last time as admiral.

He knew her as intimately as he knew his

own children. He had seen her grow and change. He had seen the early rickety biplanes taking off from her deck, and then this morning, in her final strike, sleek Zeroes, Vals, and Kates.

Another explosion rumbled up from below, and he could see the look of concern in Genda's eyes. Tucked below the air officer's arm was a folded canvas bag.

"The Z flag?" Yamamoto asked, and Genda nodded.

"Any still on board?"

"Just those waiting for you, sir."

"Have all wounded been properly evacuated?"

Genda hesitated.

"Well?"

"Sir, I regret to say that there are still some men trapped far below decks, fires and flooding above giving them no escape. Men too critically injured to be moved," he sighed. "Sir, they can't be evacuated. Moving them will kill them anyhow. They beg to go down with their ship."

He sighed and for the first time in a very long time, others saw tears openly coursing down his weathered cheeks.

"If I leave them behind, what will others say?"

"You have done all that you can possibly

do, sir," Genda replied heatedly. "Remember you yourself said that you would not tolerate the utter foolishness of commanders insisting they go down with their ships. You must now set that example!"

Genda reached out as if to grab his arm but an icy stare caused him to hesitate.

He turned for one look back from the bridge. *Akagi* was now listing over thirty degrees, the starboard side of the deck awash. A last few were still going over the side just aft amidships, where there was a hole in the fires that entirely engulfed both bow and stern. Two destroyers were close alongside, cargo mats draped over into the water, oil-soaked men looking like black ants climbing up them, while launches were in the water picking up the injured and those too weak to climb. Another destroyer trailed astern, picking up men going off the aft end of the ship.

"Let's go then," he said softly and went back through the bridge, which was now empty except for a few of his loyal staff and his personal steward. He hesitated.

"My lighter and cigarette case?" he asked, and his steward smiled, reached into his pocket and pulled them out. The lighter, an American Zippo, keepsake gift from an American captain whose name he could no longer remember; the cigarette case, won in a card game years ago, back at Harvard.

He went out onto the deck. Several firefighters were waiting. They tossed asbestos blankets to him and Genda, draping them over their heads to ward off the intense heat, the blaze consuming the deck. Another explosion lit off below; the ship lurched, as if trying to rise out of the water. Another explosion rippled after the first one; what had been the forward elevator unhinged, lifting up thirty or more feet into the air. The fire crew pressed in around their admiral as fragments and burning pieces of deck came raining down.

The deck was slick with water and firefighting foam. It was nearly impossible to keep his footing, and he slipped, nearly sliding off and into the gun deck, its railing already beneath the water, which was black with oil.

A destroyer was lying fifty yards off, dangerously close if the ship should actually pitch up over and start a death roll. A few cables were slung across, a stretcher case being transferred, and the firefighters directed him to one of the lines. There was still a wounded man waiting to be transferred, face bloated from steam burns, eyes swollen shut.

"Him first," Yamamoto announced, and no one thought to argue, waiting a few tense moments as the sling was run back over, the stretcher secured.

Water was now lapping up onto the side of the deck. Below came an endless cascade of crashing, as lockers, mess gear, plates, tools, anything that could move was breaking loose, each additional pound of weight shifting *Akagi* further off balance, adding its mass to the water still pouring in through the holes slashed by the torpedoes.

He could tell she was going.

He looked at Genda and forced a smile.

"Time to go, forget the line," and he motioned to the water now lapping but a few feet away.

Genda hesitated.

"I am the last one off," he announced sharply. He turned to the fire and rescue crew, who were preparing to run the transfer line back from the destroyer.

"Into the water, my men. Your duty here is done."

They hesitated, a few even bowing, refusing until their admiral went first.

"Now! I won't leave until you do."

There was hesitation, and the half dozen men stepped off into the oil-slick water and started to swim toward the destroyer. Genda looked at his admiral.

"You promise you will follow. If not, sir, I could never live with the shame of leaving you. I will kill myself if you do not come with me."

He smiled.

"I can't allow you to do that. All right then, together, but you take the first step and try and keep our Z flag out of this muck."

Genda stepped off into the water and he followed suit.

His life belt kept his head well above the water, but the slapping of the choppy water between the two ships splashed oil into his face and eyes, stinging them. It was hard to see as he swam the few strokes over to the destroyer. When crew members aboard realized who was approaching, several jumped in, coming to his side, and he shouted for them to first help Genda, who was floundering, trying to keep one hand above the oil-slicked water, clutching the canvas bag containing the Z flag.

Together they reached the netting, and eager hands pulled him aloft and onto the deck of the destroyer, whose captain stood at rigid attention, saluting the admiral, his white uniform now stained black with oil.

"I am transferring my flag to your ship,"

Yamamoto said formally.

"I am humbled and honored by your presence, sir."

"We're the last. May I suggest cutting away lines and moving away," Yamamoto ordered.

Seconds later the lines were cut. The engines slowly revved up, helm put over gently to turn away without swinging their fantail into the dying carrier. He could sense the sighs of relief by all aboard.

Akagi loomed like a giant above them. With the angle of list, the bridge all but towered directly above the small destroyer, threatening to engulf it if the ship should roll, the heat of the inferno consuming the carrier so intense he actually had to shield his face. A sailor offered him a basin of fresh water and a white towel. He made it a point of first passing it to Genda, who rinsed out his eyes, wiped his face somewhat clean, and then with a bow passed the soiled towel back to Yamamoto, who did the same. The sailor took the towel back, clutching it as if were now some honored, historic heirloom.

They were making way, standing a hundred yards off, then a hundred and fifty.

Another explosion, this one bursting somewhere below the water line, flame and a geyser of water soaring up, the great ship lurching; then more explosions, louder. He sensed it must be the torpedo or bomb lockers far below, their detonations ripping out the keel of the ship.

She started to settle, list now over sixty degrees, and then the death plunge began, deck nearly vertical so that for a moment it looked as if she would indeed roll over, and then this beloved ship simply died, like a beloved dog that drew a final breath and then slowly laid its head down. Resting on her starboard side, stern angling down slightly, *Akagi* settled deeper and deeper, great blasts of air, steam, and smoke venting out her starboard side, water foaming.

To his horror he saw a few men were still on board after all. Somehow they had made it up to stand precariously on what had been the side of the ship, perhaps blown clear out by the blasts of air escaping the ship. One of them actually appeared to salute. A sigh, a cry went up from all those watching and Yamamoto, crying unashamedly, saluted back. In spite of his belief in the absurdity of the tradition of a highly trained officer feeling compelled to die with his ship when rescue was but yards away, he felt a wave of guilt for leaving those who had been trapped aboard.

And then she was gone. Oil and smoke

bubbled up from the foaming sea; a moment later explosions rocked the destroyer as they tore through *Akagi* even as she started her long slide down to the ocean floor. Then there was nothing but an oil-slick sea, wreckage bubbling up, and the vast ocean had claimed another victim of the war.

A bugler on the destroyer sounded a ceremonial flourish, a salute to the fallen. All bowed their heads, and nearly all wept. A lone Zero came down low, skimming over the water, and then pulled up, rocking its wings in salute.

Over Akagi

Fuchida wept with them. The strike wave that had destroyed *Lexington* was returning, and those who had flown off their beloved *Akagi* were being ordered to land on any carrier available.

But he could not leave her yet as he pulled up from his salute, circling one more time before breaking toward *Kaga,* to go into the landing pattern . . . and then he saw it. A thin, almost invisible wake was closing in on *Kaga* but two miles ahead.

"Submarine two miles off *Kaga*'s bow!" he shouted, sending the message in the clear, and he dived over, lining up, and began to strafe. With luck perhaps one of his twenty-millimeter rounds just might strike the periscope, but at least his gunfire would mark the position.

USS Thresher

"Shit!"

"Dive! Take her deep!"

Captain Lubbers slapped up the handles of the periscope, stepping back, a petty officer hitting the periscope down button. There was a vibration — something had hit the periscope. *Thresher* started to arc down.

Another minute at most, and he could have put four fish into that other damn carrier. It had been coming straight at him.

"Damn it!"

Through the hull he could hear soft thumps, explosions. He cursed that damn Zero, which he had only caught a glimpse of, as water began to foam up around the periscope lens.

"We better get ready. They've spotted us," was all he said, heading down from the periscope room to the main deck.

"Did you get that signal out about the Jap carrier sinking?" he asked, looking over at his radio operator, who grinned, nodded, and gave him a thumbs-up.

"Wish it'd been us that did it," he said

bitterly, his attention turned away to his sound detector, who announced he had something inbound, sounding like a destroyer.

With those fat carriers out there, they were going to be swarming all over him, he realized bitterly. Angling down now through a hundred feet, his firing solution on the carrier lost, he raged in silent frustration. Without doubt the fattest targets of the war had decided to steam straight at him. He should have fired earlier, instead of electing to wait until range was down to two thousand yards. And now the moment was lost.

But at least he had had the pleasure of watching the other Jap go down, and even as they dived they could hear the distant rumbling of the huge ship, as it sank into the depths, bulkheads collapsing, explosions rumbling, the noise so loud it all but drowned out the sound of the approaching destroyers that would doggedly follow him and drop depth charges for the next two hours.

CHAPTER FOURTEEN

Lexington
December 9, 1941
09:55 hrs local time
"I think there's supposed to be some tradition that I'm to be the last one off," Captain Sherman announced, trying to put a smile on, though the anguish in his voice was obvious.

"Fine then, you got it," Admiral Newton replied.

The old Lady Lex was heavy down by the bow, water now beginning to pour in through the huge hole blasted there by the secondary explosion of the aviation gas. As the thousands upon thousands of gallons of seawater began to cascade in, the ocean did what the firefighters could not, dousing the flames eight decks below. Vents of hissing steam and smoke roared back up.

A destroyer and cruiser lay off her side. Dozens of launches were in the water, pick-

ing up survivors. The last of the sixteen hundred men were leaving four hundred of their dead comrades behind.

He walked to the edge of the deck and noted something strange. There were rows of shoes; for some reason men had taken them off before jumping off. He looked down at his old "brown shoes," proud symbol of a naval aviator, and opted to keep them on.

It was roughly a twenty-foot drop. *Lex* was going to go down bow first, rather than rolling over, though the list to port was significant, otherwise it would have been a nearly deadly eighty-foot jump.

A hundred or more ropes dangled over the side. More than a few of his men had decided to try and climb down rather than take the jump, but the ropes were now so slick with oil that such an attempt simply resulted in bad friction burns to the hands.

He took his flag and handed it to his steward.

"Can you manage this?" he asked.

The steward smiled, saluted, set down a duffel bag, and stuffed the flag inside. Admiral Newton asked for the same regarding his flag. The duffel bag had two Mae Wests secured to it.

Sherman looked back toward the bridge, the famed silhouette unique to *Lexington* and *Saratoga.* Fires, boiling up from the abandoned engine room, were pouring out a soaring plume of black smoke from the stacks, and the bridge itself was aflame now.

He could feel the list increasing under his feet as the bow slipped deeper beneath the waves, and as it did so the distance to the water actually began to increase where they stood.

"Over you go, gentlemen," Sherman announced, and he even gave Newton a bit of a shove as the commander of the task force leapt off, steward and the last of the bridge staff following.

He paused a moment, looking about, wanting to make sure he was the last able-bodied man off. He saw a couple of jumpers farther aft, cradling between them a wounded comrade, an "asbestos Joe" sitting on the edge, kicking off his bright leggings and then slipping off the side, hitting the water and surfacing. He was about to jump when he spotted a chaplain who was coming out of the smoke, walking backward slowly, looking toward the inferno amidships.

"Come on, Padre! Over with you."

The man looked at him, face tear streaked, and actually shook his head.

"Padre, now!"

"I had to leave four men down there," the priest cried, a sob shuddering through him.

There was a moment of horror at the implication that the padre was looking for help, that he'd have to go back.

"They were dying, we couldn't move them they were so badly burned. I gave them last rites." He began to sob. "They told me to go. Two of them were brothers."

He was clutching a sheet of note paper, names and addresses scribbled on them.

"Padre, you staying won't change it for them," Sherman said, his own voice husky with emotion. "Now come on, jump with me."

The padre stood next to him, hesitated, and shook his head.

"Damn it, Father, you don't go, I don't go. The Lord is with them now, we can't do anything more for them."

He pointed to the paper crumpled up in the priest's hand.

"Give that to me."

The priest did not resist as Sherman took the sheet of paper and scanned the names: two seamen second class from Millburn, New Jersey, a lieutenant from Texas, a petty officer — merciful God, he recognized the name, an old hand on *Lex* from the engine room.

He folded the slip of paper up and stuck it into his pocket.

"Find me after this and we'll write the letters together. OK?"

The priest nodded.

Before he could say another word, Sherman forcefully shoved him over the side. He spared one final glance back, saluted the bridge, the American flag still flying above it, turned, and jumped.

Minutes later he was on the deck of the old cruiser *Chicago*. Picked up by their launch boat, Newton had preceded him up the netting. He had hung on to the padre, pushing him into the launch first and then up the net, just to make sure that the distraught priest did not do anything foolish and try to go back.

Ritual was followed as he was piped aboard, returning the salute of *Chicago*'s captain, who greeted him and shook his hand.

"Sir, *Portland, Astoria,* and two destroyers are currently engaged at long range with a Japanese cruiser to our southwest about twenty miles from here."

Newton, black with oil, but face wiped clean, already had binoculars up, trained aft, and even without the binoculars Sherman could see *Astoria,* hull down on the horizon, flashes of gunfire.

An explosion rocked *Lexington,* and his attention was focused back on his ship. Her stern was rising rapidly. It seemed impossibly high out of the water, surely her back would break from the strain but she held together. And then ever so slowly she began her death slide, going down at the bow, flags still flying.

A shiver went down his back. The *Chicago* was noted for its band. Only a handful could be spared, a few brass and woodwinds, the rest of them at crucial battle stations. They began to play the old Navy hymn.

> "Eternal Father, Strong to save,
> Whose arm hath bound the restless wave . . ."

The priest began to sing, others joined him. Sherman, too, choked with emotion, joined in.

The *Lexington* died as a lady, slipping away quietly. More than a few around him were crying as they sang.

The first stanza of the hymn finished, and a lone trumpeter now blew "Taps." For so many that was what did them in, tears flowing down oil-streaked faces.

He thought of the four men below still alive, wondered how many in fact were still alive within her, trapped beneath flooded compartments, fatally wounded, comrades in anguish to be leaving them behind. He thought of the note in his pocket, how he could explain this to the parents of the two boys, what lie would he tell them to give them comfort.

"Dear God, grant them a peaceful death," he whispered.

Her stern disappeared beneath the

waves . . . She was gone.

There was a moment of silence, the last note of "Taps" echoing out over the ocean, distant gunfire rumbling across the waves.

Honolulu
10:05 hrs local time

Dianne stirred from her slumber and awoke, disoriented for a moment. Where am I? The question so many always asked when awakening in a strange place, made infinitely worse when seconds later the memories of the day before, the horrible reality of it all came back to her consciousness.

She sat up.

The house was quiet. She couldn't remember their names, the names of James's wife and mother-in-law. She did remember they were Japanese. Where was James?

She called his name, trying to sound formal now. "Commander Watson?" No response.

She stood and walked into the kitchen. There was the smell of fresh coffee, some toast on the table as if waiting for her. She poured a cup, looking around.

She actually had known very little about James until this last day. He was a commander, a married man, ring evident, always kind and polite to her in an almost fatherly way. She had heard about how he lost his hand in the *Panay* incident, had been a college professor.

She nursed the cup of coffee: Kona beans, yet another reason she loved living in

Hawaii — at least up until two days ago. She walked back into the living room, noticed the sofa where she had slept, and then the recollection came back of an old woman holding her as she cried, whispering softly, singing something to her as she drifted off to sleep. Singing in Japanese, but the words had the feel of a lullaby. Incongruous, a .38 revolver rested on a side table. While I slept, she thought, these Japs had a gun.

God damn, why did that old woman have to be so nice, she thought.

She heard something outside, shouting. She walked to the door and opened it.

"Leave that boy alone!" Margaret screamed. If not for her mother, she would have gone into the middle of the fray. Instead, she was holding back, standing at the edge of the curb.

She had tried to stick to her promise to James not to go outside. She and her mother had had breakfast, deciding to let the woman on the sofa sleep, not quite sure what to do with her when she woke up. Margaret still felt a bit leery of her, realizing she was being foolish; if ever there was a loyal husband it was James. It was just that the girl was so darn pretty, even in her shocked, disheveled state. Her mother actually pitied her, in spite of the more than one foul racist comment that had spilled out in her hysteria, as she sobbed that all Japs would burn in hell.

"Suppose it was Chinese that killed our James," her mother had argued, the two of them whispering together in Japanese after James had left and she had gently slipped Dianne's head from her lap to a pillow. "How would you first feel? Remember your papa couldn't stand the Spanish. Men are sick over such crazy things; it infects us too."

They had decided to just let her sleep and had quietly worked around her. Margaret's cousin had yet to come home, nor called since yesterday. All radio stations were off the air, there was no newspaper, they were in a vacuum, except when they looked out the windows and could see the fires still burning down at Pearl and in downtown Honolulu.

And then they heard the commotion.

Someone shouting and yelling. She had looked down the street. It was fifteen to twenty men and a couple of women, most of them obviously drunk, weaving their way up through the neighborhood, cursing, yelling, and in their midst they had a rope around the neck of a young man, actually more likely a boy of not much more than sixteen or seventeen, face bloody and puffy. He was Japanese.

That had set her mother off, and the old woman was out the door and down the steps, shouting for the mob to let go of the boy.

Some of the neighbors were out, watching, others nervously peeking out from behind half-closed shutters or doorways.

"Come on out, you goddamn Japs!" someone was screaming. "We got one of your murdering sons of bitches!"

The neighborhood was primarily nisei. An old man came down his walkway, shouting for the men to leave the boy alone, and to Margaret's horror one of the drunks punched him in the face, sending him sprawling backward.

Some more neighbors were coming out, almost all of them women; old men, frightened children ordered to stay inside. Their men were gone, many called up with the national guard units, or at work. More than a few were married to Caucasian sailors and soldiers, like Margaret and her cousin, with husbands and sons in the middle of the fight — and more than a few would receive telegrams in the days to come.

One of the drunks had several rocks, and

he threw them at the old man's house, breaking a window, the sound of it shattering sent a cold shiver through Margaret and made her think of the infamous Crystal Night of Germany. So it was beginning. . . .

The drunks were laughing, cursing, shouting that the boy was a pilot they'd caught.

Margaret drew closer, could hear the kid pleading in perfect English that he worked for Western Union as a messenger.

There wasn't even a vague semblance between his blue uniform and that of any Japanese sailor, soldier, or pilot.

"Let him go, you damn cowards!" Margaret screamed.

"Let him go?" a drunk, breath stinking, potbellied, scrawny-looking like a scarecrow, unshaved, was up alongside her, and shoved her back so that she nearly lost her balance.

"Let's string the son of a bitch up right here. Let the other Japs watch," someone cried, and the small mob started to move toward a tree with an overhanging branch.

"Hey, I've always wanted to try one of 'em," another drunk shouted, and he pointed toward Margaret. "Heard they put out real good."

"Go for her, Steve," one of the mob shouted.

The drunk, leering, stepped towards her.

Her kick caught him in the groin; he doubled over with a gasp, collapsing back.

Several of his friends now turned toward her and she backed up, three men closing in, her mother screaming . . .

The bark of the .38-caliber pistol roared out. The three advancing toward Margaret froze.

Dianne stood on the porch, pistol held high, cocked it, and leveled the weapon at the three.

"I'll kill the next son of a bitch that moves!" she cried.

There was a frozen tableau. The three that had been coming toward Margaret, the dozen or so who had been struggling vainly to toss the rope up over the limb of the tree. A couple of the men with the lynch mob had guns in their hands; one of them started to turn toward Dianne. She swung the revolver and pointed it at him.

"Move and I'll blow your head off, you filthy bastard," her voice breaking. "And God damn you, I know how to do it. My boyfriend is a pilot and he taught me how to shoot."

Ever so slowly Dianne came down the three steps from the front porch, moving toward Margaret and her mother.

"Get inside," she hissed.

The two women backed up, got behind Dianne, but refused to retreat further.

"I'm staying with you," Margaret snapped, and then she looked over at the mob around the boy.

"Now let him go!"

More neighbors were gathering, coming over to join the three in support.

One of the drunks, apparently some kind of leader of the group, started towards Dianne. He had a pistol in his hand, his other hand up, and he was actually grinning.

"Come on, blondie, put the gun down. What are you doing defending these Japs anyhow?"

"Let the boy go!" Margaret screamed.

"Shut up, bitch," the leader shouted.

The roar from Dianne's pistol snapped out, spinning the man around, dropping him to the pavement, screaming, clutching his shoulder. She cocked and now trained it on the rest of the group.

"Who's next?"

The wounded man was rolling back and forth, screaming for them to kill her. The rest of the group was frozen. Several started to back away, turned, and ran.

From up on the corner to Pali Highway a pickup truck came around the corner, tires squealing. Margaret's heart froze. She saw guns sticking out of the back of the truck.

Oh God, it's starting, it's really starting!

She tried to grab Dianne by the shoulder, pull her back. The mob looked up at the truck, a few shouting, laughing that friends were coming to help, and another crying a foul oath as to what he was going to do to the traitorous blond bitch.

The truck skidded to a stop. Three national guardsmen armed with Springfield .30s leapt off the back, one of them a nisei, led by the driver, an elderly sergeant.

Without hesitation the three enlisted men leveled their rifles straight at the group, the sergeant with .45 semiautomatic drawn, expertly poised.

"All you drunk sons of bitches, back off right now," the sergeant shouted.

There was still a frozen moment.

"Let go of that boy now or we shoot! I'm giving you exactly three seconds!

"One . . ."

The mob began to break up.

"Two . . ."

They turned and started to run back down the street.

"Three!"

The sergeant raised his pistol and fired it twice, and now what had once been a mob was running in blind panic, facing a gauntlet of taunts from those lining the street.

Dianne, who had been standing rock solid, suddenly just seemed to dissolve, shaking.

The sergeant looked over at her, approaching cautiously, making a point of lowering his pistol.

"Ma'am, please lower your gun."

She did as ordered.

"Now carefully uncock it."

She put her thumb on the hammer, pulled the trigger, and let the hammer slowly drop back into place.

"That slut shot me!" the wounded man, still twisting in agony, cried.

The sergeant took it all in: the badly beaten boy, a couple of women from across the street helping untie him from the rope that was already around his neck, the kid shaking uncontrollably, sobbing, the drunk that Margaret had kicked still in the gutter, clutching himself in agony, the wounded man.

The sergeant walked over to the wounded man on the street, and then stepped on his wrist, forcing him to release his pistol, which he picked up.

"Shut your goddamn mouth or I'll do it for you," the sergeant snapped, sticking the pistol in his waist belt.

He walked up to Dianne.

"What happened?"

She couldn't speak, she was shaking so hard.

"They were going to lynch that boy," Margaret cried. "Look at the kid, he's a Western Union boy for God's sake. They said he was an enemy pilot."

Her own voice was breaking.

"That scum in the gutter tried to rape me, so I kicked him where it hurt."

The sergeant could not help but let a flicker of a grin cross his features.

"It got ugly and then my friend here," and she put a hand on Dianne's arm, "saved us. She had to shoot that one man, he was getting set to shoot her."

Margaret hesitated.

"Dianne's boyfriend was a pilot; he was killed in action on Sunday. She works with my husband, a naval officer, and was staying here."

The sergeant looked at her, nodded, and then looked back at the wounded man in the street.

"Load that son of a bitch up," he snapped. "We'll take him in."

The women who had been helping the Western Union boy were bringing him over.

He was badly bruised, obviously terrified.

A second car came around the corner, more guardsmen getting out, a captain leading the group.

"What's going on here, Charlie?"

Charlie nodded to Margaret, went over to the officer, the two huddling for a moment, the captain taking it in with a sharp gaze as the sergeant whispered to him.

She could sense these two knew each other well, perhaps were close friends in civilian life. She sensed that the older sergeant was actually the real leader of their rescuers.

The captain nodded and first went to the terrified boy.

"Son, you'll be OK. No one is going to hurt you. I want to take you into the hospital and get you checked. Do you understand me? Then we're going to find out who the rest of these scum are and have them arrested for what they did to you."

The boy couldn't speak, but just nodded his head.

Two soldiers helped the boy back to the command car. Another two hoisted up the wounded drunk, who yowled with pain as they dragged him off and unceremoniously dumped him in the car as well.

The captain came up to Dianne and actually saluted.

"Ma'am, I'm sorry about this. One of two things can happen. I take you in, there are reports to file, charges pressed, that piece of slime there might try and press countercharges back. Your name will get out, and I hate to say it, but there are more than a few like them out there today that might bother you later. This is the third incident I've had to deal with so far today."

"Or you forget about her," Margaret interjected.

The captain smiled.

"Ma'am, I don't know who you are other than one hell of a brave lady. Do we understand each other?"

Dianne forced a smile.

He put his hand on her shoulder and squeezed.

"I'm sorry about your loss. We've all lost someone, something," and as he spoke he looked back at the street, the coil of rope. "God, we've all lost something if we turn to this."

He saluted her again and turned away.

"Sergeant, stay here and post a guard on this street."

The sergeant smiled, saluted. The command car with the wounded drunk and the terrified boy backed out of the street and on to the highway.

"OK, folks, let's get back inside," he announced. "The show is over. You're safe, I promise you that by God."

"Hey, I know you, Steve, you piece of shit," the sergeant said, dragging the man still in the gutter up to his feet. "You say a word about this, you come back around here, and I'll finish the job."

He gave him a kick to the backside as the injured man, still clutching himself, staggered off down the street.

Margaret took Dianne by the shoulders and pointed her back toward the house.

The three went inside, closing the door. Dianne was no longer shaking; she was remote, stoic.

"Dianne, please give me the gun. Best we hide it for now."

She held the weapon tight.

"Not for a while. They might be back."

There were distant gunshots. All three looked back toward the open window, but the sergeant and his men were out in the middle of the street, obviously not concerned, standing in a circle, and smoking.

"I'll make those boys some coffee," Margaret's mother announced, and she went into the kitchen.

Margaret stepped in front of Dianne and

put her hands on her shoulders.

"You were so wonderfully brave out there."

"No, I wasn't, I was terrified."

"Why did you do it?"

Dianne tried to force a smile.

"I like your mother," was all she could say, and then both were in each other's arms, crying.

Enterprise
10:55 hrs local time

"Sir, it is my pleasure to report, all fires are out, watertight integrity is holding."

Admiral Halsey, dozing, stirred from his seat, looked up at Stubbs standing before him, and smiled.

"Good job, Stubbs."

"Sir, we got five boilers up and running."

"The crew trapped in the engine room?"

"Reached them a half hour ago." He paused. "Sir, half of them were dead from the heat, the others barely alive, but by God they kept us running. We pumped out sections of the two decks blocking them, and have a replacement crew in their place now."

"Good, damn good," Halsey sighed. "I want to go down to sick bay, shake their hands, God bless them."

"It was hell down there, sir," Stubbs

sighed. "I went in with the rescue crew. How they stayed alive in that inferno is beyond me. It would have driven most men insane."

"Most everything this last day could drive men insane," Halsey said. "It's called war."

Stubbs could not reply.

Halsey stood up, stretched, a bit embarrassed to realize he had indeed dozed off, and been asleep in his chair since sometime before dawn. His bridge crew looked away, as if abashed that their boss was realizing they had stood watch over him, not letting anyone disturb him when he had finally collapsed. An old petty officer had placed him in the captain's chair and ordered everyone to leave him alone for a while.

And across those hours the survivors of *Enterprise* had fought to contain the last of the fires, shored up bulkheads about to burst, manned pumps and fire hoses, balanced the ship back to a reasonable list of but four degrees to starboard, then fought to block off flooded passageways. Then they had to fight their way down through two flooded decks to secure leaks so that a way could be found to the blocked-off engine room, their only source of power and hope of survival, and to rescue the forty-one men still alive down there who were keeping *Enterprise* alive.

Towlines to two destroyers had been cast off fifteen minutes ago, and *Enterprise* was under way on her own, making eight knots, due east. Forward was *Indianapolis* with her small group of destroyers, ringing the crippled carrier. Their own surviving destroyers and cruisers were matching speed except for two, one to either flank, that were sweeping wide at fifteen knots, searching out any potential threats from subs.

"Our position?" Halsey asked.

"We're three hundred and ten miles southeast of Oahu, sir, making eight knots," Stubbs replied.

He nodded.

"Any sign of the Japs?"

Stubbs looked over at the chief petty officer who had loyally been standing watch over "his" admiral while he slept.

"Sir, we monitored a fight, just after dawn, three hundred miles west northwest of Oahu. It was *Lexington.* Newton and Sherman got one of their carriers, confirmed as *Akagi.* Apparently it was their flagship."

"Damn good," Halsey said, "though Newton will never let me live that down, getting a kill like that."

"But, sir, they got the *Lexington.* She went down just about the same time as *Akagi* was sunk."

"Christ."

He lowered his head.

"Newton, Sherman?"

"No word yet on survivors, sir. Just a report radioed in from *Chicago* saying that flag had been transferred. Knew that meant *Lexington* was gone. Jap radio traffic was confirming the sinking as well."

He looked down at the flame-scorched deck of *Enterprise,* devoid of even a single aircraft.

"That leaves us the only carrier in these waters," Halsey announced.

No one spoke. The only carrier, but fought out, barely afloat, limping off from the scene of battle.

"Any more attacks on Pearl, or the islands?"

"No, sir. Last sighting of the Japanese fleet, they were steaming due west at fifteen knots or better."

"They're pulling out," Halsey said. "It's over for now."

They had to be pulling out, he realized. We've sunk two, maybe three of their carriers. They punched us hard, but we punched back at last, damn it. They were most likely low on oil and would make a run now for the Marshalls. But they would be back, of that he was certain. And we have to be ready for them, he thought with deep determination.

"Our oil supply, sir," Stubbs finally said, interrupting his thoughts. "We definitely will not make it to the West Coast. Half our oil aboard was lost yesterday; half of what is left is mixed with seawater that will have to be distilled off. *Indianapolis* reports they are down to forty percent. Our destroyers will run dry within three days, though they can calve off of *Indianapolis* if we maintain current speed of eight knots, which is all we can maintain."

"So you're requesting breaking radio silence to request a rendezvous," Halsey asked.

"Sir, it's not my place to advise," Stubbs replied.

It was their only hope, Halsey realized, otherwise they would have to abandon all the destroyers, and even then he doubted they would get within five hundred miles of the West Coast. One destroyer was being detailed off to take the most critically wounded back to Pearl. Running the potential gauntlet of submarines was worth the risk compared to their chances if they did not get intensive care immediately. Once transfer of the wounded was complete and the destroyer on its way, it could relay the signal.

He took it in and looked to his petty officer.

"The destroyer with the wounded aboard — signal them to contact Pearl once well clear of us and request a rendezvous of an oiler with our group. Are Pearl Harbor communications back up?"

"We've been monitoring them again. Still that Hungarian code, sir, for voice."

"Send it Morse, latest code. We need an oiler rendezvous. They can reply with coordinates. Signal traffic to an absolute minimum."

"Sir, maybe the message should be hand carried by the destroyer rather than sent by radio?"

A good suggestion. He thought about it but finally decided against. If the destroyer got nailed by a sub, the message would be lost and they might never know it. Also, it'd take at least a day for the destroyer to get in, and in that time an oiler might steam a couple of hundred miles in the wrong direction for a rendezvous. He'd have to go with the risk.

"Have them send the signal."

"Yes, sir."

"Come on, Stubbs, let's walk," Halsey

said, and stretching he left the bridge, rubbing his face, realizing he needed a shave, a long hot shower . . . maybe only a shave with cold water, but the second, that wouldn't happen until they were stateside.

He went down the flights of stairs and out onto the deck. It felt so lonely in a way, completely devoid of any activity other than a fire crew cleaning its equipment, gunners around one of the five-inch turrets, barrel depressed, swabbing the bore out, farther forward a work crew, laboring to lay temporary planking over the gaping hole that had been the forward elevator.

Stubbs walked by his side.

"Good job, Stubbs, about time you get a promotion."

"No, thanks, sir. That means leaving her."

He looked at him and smiled.

"It could be weeks, months before we're back in it again."

"I'll have most of her repaired before we make San Diego, sir," Stubbs replied. "I want to stay with this beauty when we come back out here and give it back to those bastards again."

Halsey grinned.

"Fine then, no promotion, if that's what you want, Stubbs. You saved her, she's yours."

"Thank you, sir."

A nod indicated that he wished now to be alone, and Stubbs stepped back as Admiral Halsey walked forward, pausing for a moment to watch the crew laboring to string temporary supports across where the forward elevator had been. Apparently Stubbs had given up on the idea of repairing it while at sea, but wanted an active deck ready regardless. The sailors, filthy, most with shirts off, were precariously balanced as crews down below were setting up twelve-by-twelve oak beams, locking them into place, already laying out the first cross-deck stringer, men heaving and cursing. Most likely, it would not be able to support the weight of a fully loaded Devastator, but a Wildcat on rollout for liftoff could most likely safely pass over it.

Some of the men noticed who was watching, called out that the admiral was present, but he gestured for them to stay at ease, continue with their work, and walked on.

Farther forward more men were working, tearing out torn pieces of deck planking, bolting in replacement planks, gun crews for the forty-millimeter mounts polishing down their pieces. Several had red suns painted on the barrels, claiming their kills.

He reached the bow. Two sailors, taking a

smoke break, both of them filthy with oil stains and smoke, saw him approach and started to step back. He motioned for them to stand easy.

"Where you boys from?" he asked.

"Seaman First Class Hurt," the first announced. "I'm from Black Mountain, North Carolina, sir."

"Seaman First Class Minneci, sir, Newark, New Jersey," the other said proudly, his Jersey accent clearly evident.

"Your battle stations?"

The two proudly pointed to the forty-millimeter gun perched forward, below the bow.

"We got one of the bastards yesterday, sir," Minneci said. "Bang, head-on shot, he never dropped his torpedo!"

"Good work, son."

There was an awkward moment, for after all the gulf between admirals and seamen first class was a broad one.

"Sir?"

It was Minneci.

"Think we'll make it all the way, sir?"

"Make it?" and there was a touch of a sharp tone in his reply.

"No, sir, I don't mean back to the States. We all figured you would pull that off."

He relaxed, and nodded a thanks as Hurt

offered him a cigarette, which he took, bowing his head over as Hurt lit it off the stub of his own.

"I mean back into the fight, sir. We want back in."

He looked at the two, begrimed, hollow eyed with exhaustion. Below their feet, he could see where their neighboring forty-millimeter mount had been destroyed, nothing but black twisted wreckage. Fate had decreed, by not much more than a few feet, a fraction of a second in time, that their neighboring comrades had all died, but they were still alive and now asking him this question.

"Back in the fight?"

"Yes, sir."

"Hell, on the day we sail into Tokyo Bay, you two boys personally look me up and I'll shake your hands. Of course we're going to be in the fight.

"To the end."

Hickam Army Air Force Base
12:45 hrs local time

James stood up, rubbing his eyes. Radio traffic had quieted down and word had just been passed that naval personnel were to report back to Pearl, where signals were being rebuilt in an administrative office near the old CinCPac building. Headquarters were to be reestablished there.

He walked out of the hangar, Collingwood by his side, watching as the lone surviving B-17 on the island came in on final approach, shot up even more, it seemed, landing gear not down, all holding their breath as Gloria Ann pancaked in, props of the four engines either shearing off or bending back. The plane slid to a stop in the middle of the runway, fire trucks rolling alongside it. Fortunately, there was no fire as it was hosed down with foam, crew staggering out.

She had made a final run over the Japanese fleet, dropped a bomb load, without effect, but had radioed in the crucial report. They were steaming west, leaving the oil slick of what was believed to be *Akagi,* thirty miles astern of their position.

There had been one final air skirmish, a second Japanese strike launched against *Lexington*'s escorts. The escorts were pulling away at flank speed to the northeast, having inflicted one last blow, crippling, perhaps sinking a Japanese cruiser that had attempted to engage. The air strike had managed to sink but one destroyer in return.

Over thirty of *Lexington*'s "orphans" had made it in, some landing at Wheeler, others here, a dozen others reportedly ditching near the tramp steamer off Kauai, or near the sub, which had finally given up the stern chase as the Japanese fleet pulled away. It meant the island had at least some strike capability again, but it also meant that far more than half of *Lexington*'s planes had been lost in the morning battle.

All within the radio hangar knew the battle was winding down, though the rest of the island was still on high alert, with rumors of invasion rampant, and other rumors reaching the base of more than one incident of backlash, of two lynchings, several shootings, and just random senseless destruction of homes and businesses. General Short, at noon, had allowed a civilian station to go back on the air, the first announcement being that martial law was still in effect, and that any acts of violence or rioting would be met with deadly force.

He was worried about Margaret and his mother-in-law. He just wanted to go home, but didn't quite know how to pull away yet, until Collingwood finally suggested that their work was done for now and they both needed some rest.

They slowly walked to Collingwood's car, as if both were half hoping to be called back. For two days their lives had been totally absorbed by this moment, and by walking away, they knew they were stepping away from it, that it was now in the past, something of history, rather than the pressing reality of the moment.

"How many do you think we really got?" James asked, as they got in Collingwood's DeSoto and started back to the naval base.

He shook his head.

"Hell, you know as much as I do."

"I'm guessing two," James replied. "One for *Enterprise,* one for *Lexington.*"

"Only one confirmed, and that was *Akagi,*" Collingwood replied. "Remember, guessing is our business, but when it comes to counting carriers sunk, I'll play conservative."

Akagi. He remembered his old friend Fuchida. Fuchida had talked about the first of Japan's carriers, his love for it. His guess was that it had indeed served as the flagship and that Yamamoto himself was most likely on board, a hunch that Collingwood agreed with and had passed up the chain, for what it was worth. If true, there was a chance that Yamamoto might be dead . . . and his old friend as well.

"And we lost *Lexington,* and *Enterprise* is a cripple," James said wearily.

It startled all of them when a destroyer briefly broke radio silence, using a prewar code, requesting an oiler rendezvous, if possible tomorrow, five hundred miles to the southeast of Oahu, with Pearl to broadcast the coordinates, and then gone off the air. One could read a lot into that message. The subtext was clear. The destroyer had been escorting *Enterprise.* It had made the broadcast rather than run in with the message because the situation was desperate. *Enterprise* was most likely severely damaged to the point that it needed a dry dock, and it was slowly limping back to the West Coast, desperately short on fuel.

The worry now was that the Japanese had picked up the signal as well, perhaps had already cracked the prewar code, and surmised the same, that *Enterprise* was still alive, crippled, and desperately short of fuel . . . and would send a reception committee of subs to whatever coordinate was broadcast.

After several backups, a long snarl in traffic moving between Hickam and Pearl, they finally reached the parking lot where James had left his car . . . to confront a gaping crater fifty feet across and half as deep.

"God damn, it makes you think it's personal," James sighed, realizing his old reliable Plymouth had taken a direct hit from a fourteen-inch shell.

As they backed up and drove off, he

remembered a clause in his auto insurance policy. "Void if damaged or destroyed by acts of war."

He hoped Margaret wouldn't insist upon selling his plane now, to pay for a new car. But then again, was his old beloved Aeronca Chief still intact? Or had it been shot up as well? If so, even more than the loss of the car, that would really piss him off.

They finally turned onto Pali Highway, and Collingwood drove him home before turning back around to head to his apartment near Waikiki. Still the same: roadblock, East Coast evacuated, the Japs might invade.

Neither said a word as they produced their IDs and were finally waved through.

"A guy on the next floor of my apartment keeps a Studebaker here on the island. Good guy, Josh Morris, he usually winters here from L.A., some Hollywood agent type. I got the keys to his car, turn it over for him every few weeks or so. I'll bring it over tomorrow; you can use it until he shows up, if ever."

"Thanks." He was still brooding on the loss of his car, wondering if maybe since it was lost in the line of duty, the Navy might help pick up the bill. Hell, a year ago I was retired. I sacrificed a third of my pay when I was called back up.

But then again, he almost felt guilty thinking of it as they passed a block of houses, half of them burned out, a crater marking where someone's life or lives had been randomly cut short — like millions of other lives in this insane world of 1941. And he thought of Joe, who had so eagerly donated his entire business in order to get their communications up and running again. Chances were he'd never get a dime back for his efforts, and he didn't seem to care. He was proud of what he had done for his country.

They turned onto the street where Margaret's cousin lived. And as always, he wondered if she had some sort of secret telescope to know when he was coming home. She was already out the door.

"I'll pick you up tomorrow, we'll get that other car," Collingwood said, as James started to get out.

"OK."

"James."

"Sir?"

"You did good, damn good."

He sighed.

"But not good enough. None of us did good enough."

Collingwood touched his left shoulder and James winced. Though the infection seemed arrested for the moment, it still hurt like hell.

"That was two days ago. I'm talking about now, about tomorrow. I'll see you in the morning."

He smiled and got out, Margaret helping him.

"You OK?" he asked, sensing something.

"Sure," she said forcing a smile.

He was surprised to see Dianne standing by the door, his beloved mother-in-law by her side, the old woman with her arm around Dianne. Dianne's features had a look of exhaustion. He noticed the pistol in her hand.

Something had happened, he didn't know what, whether it boded well or ill.

"I'll tell you about it later," Margaret said. "Thank God you're home safe."

Epilogue

Kaga
540 miles west of Oahu
December 10, 1941
23:55 hrs local time

The summons from Tokyo had come as he expected it would. It was ordered that the Commander in Chief, Naval Forces Pacific, was to report immediately to Tokyo for consultations with the government, the Naval Board, and the Emperor. By midday, a four-engine seaplane would meet the fleet to take him back.

A full squadron of Zeroes would provide escort as they flew the thousand-mile gap between Wake Island and Midway, still held by the Americans, finally to be handed off to Zeroes that would provide cover to the Marshalls. Once refueled, the plane would start the long two-day journey back to Tokyo.

He smiled at his two subordinates, sensing that they were still fuming with rage over the summons received last night.

"It is but of the moment," he said with a smile. "Those back home wanted a war, but never truly understood the price of war, and they must be educated to it and its risks if we are to win."

Genda started to say something but then lowered his head.

"Go on, Genda, I trust your judgment."

"Sir, they will try to hang the loss of *Akagi, Hiei,* a cruiser, and a hundred and forty aircraft on you."

He held up his hand, motioning for him to relax.

"And in rcturn we can confirm the annihilation of their battleship line, the destruction of their main Pacific naval base, the decimation of their aircraft, and the sinking of one of their precious carriers, perhaps two, even three."

"I would claim at least two," Fuchida interjected.

"I thought the same until we intercepted that signal from their destroyer. Why send an urgent demand for oil with a meeting hundreds of miles southeast of Oahu? Surely we did not destroy all of their reserves on Pearl Harbor. Also, your brave attack destroyed the only dry dock that could repair a ship as big as their *Enterprise.* Therefore, I believe it is still afloat, crippled, and heading to their West Coast. Your gallant attack has therefore left us the chance to still finish their carrier off."

Fuchida did not say anything.

"If it had been *Akagi*'s pilots who led that strike, with Fuchida as commander," Genda replied forcefully, "that ship would be confirmed sunk."

"Are you casting aspersions on the bravery or accuracy of reports of the pilots from *Soryu* and *Hiryu?*"

Genda, embarrassed, shook his head.

"And can our gallant Fuchida be everywhere at once?"

Fuchida reddened and lowered his head.

"I thank the gods he was with us yesterday. His sharp vision alone perhaps saved *Kaga* from the same fate as *Akagi.*"

The admiral sighed and looked out the window.

"No, I am not worried about the whining of petty politicians and bureaucrats. As I said, they need to be educated. They wanted a war, they have one now, and it will come with a price.

"If we had turned aside after our two strikes, even the three strikes on Pearl Harbor and the other land bases, then we would be haunted with the knowledge that two, perhaps three or more of their carriers were still afloat, ready to strike back. We can confirm only one."

He hesitated.

"And, yes, for argument's sake for now, I'll claim another, though I doubt it. To claim it subtly but lay the prospect before them is a gambit of the moment. Though with the foolish breaking of their radio silence and our dispatching of three submarines in pursuit, maybe there will be an additional American carrier in the bag, as they say."

He smiled.

"It has only started. There will be more risks, more damage to be absorbed, but unless we unhinge the Americans now, drive them back with ferocity and continually defeat what they throw at us, in the long run, it will wear us down. We can not give them breathing room, time to rearm, to build anew. We must force them to continue the fight now. Hopefully our blows will be so hard that the political will that their president has so far marshaled will crumble into bitter political wrangling and casting of blame. If that happens and we continue to defeat them, perhaps with their will weakened by internal squabbling, they will agree to negotiate after all."

Later this day, as the fleet passed south of Midway, a strike would be launched against that American base by the four carriers still serviceable, even while an attack from land-based aircraft again pounded Wake Island.

His plans were already forming: once his carriers were refueled, resupplied, and fresh squadrons loaded on board, to turn back around, and seize those two islands . . . and from there to enforce a stranglehold blockade on the Hawaiian Islands. They had no carriers in the Pacific, unless, as he suspected in his heart, at least one of their *Saratoga*-class ships had evaded him completely undamaged. If that were so, then he must sink that next.

Though he knew Japan did not now have the strength to invade Oahu — anyone who thought otherwise was a fool — he could still blockade it, perhaps even seize one of the smaller islands as a forward base, and thus lure their remaining carriers to transfer from the Atlantic to the Pacific, out for a climatic battle, another Tsushima.

He thought of the report just handed to him before the summons arrived from Tokyo. Land-based planes had located the British battleship *Prince of Wales* and the battle cruiser *Repulse* and were preparing to engage come dawn. If that strike was successful, not only would it offset even the loss of *Hiei,* it would shatter British ocean power in the Pacific as thoroughly as he was destroying American power.

Perhaps then reason might prevail, concessions be made. Japan would hold the British, Dutch, and French possessions in the Pacific. American will might disintegrate, or they might fall into their traditional bickering amongst themselves and accept the inevitable. The American politicians, weary of the struggle and given a chance to unhinge the power held by their President Roosevelt, would urge compromise. They would see the gesture of returning the Philippines to them as compensation for signing a peace agreement that left Japan with its new empire intact. The subtext would be that those arrayed against Roosevelt could finally break his political power as well. A strange country, so powerful when aroused, but some within ready to turn upon the best interests of their own country if they saw political gain.

It was a long shot, as the Americans say, but then again, he had always been a gambler, and had won on more than one "long shot."

December 11, 1941
10:00 hrs Washington time
15:00 hrs London time

"I think it is time we told the President the bad news," Winston Churchill commented to his senior naval aide as he picked up the telephone. "Please get me the President," he asked his special secure operator.

Ten minutes later the connection on the secure, highly secret, and primitively scrambled Atlantic cable was completed, and the White House operator could be heard on the other end.

"Winston," the enthusiastic patrician voice came pouring across the Atlantic. "It is always good to hear from you even in these difficult days," FDR charmingly began the conversation.

"Mr. President, I am afraid I have to add to your burdens," Churchill responded in a somber, quieter than usual voice. "We have learned that the Japanese apparently caught the *Prince of Wales* and *Repulse* without air cover, and we have suffered a catastrophic defeat."

The President could not speak for a moment. Only four months ago he had been on the deck of *Prince of Wales,* off the coast of Newfoundland, for a secret meeting with Winston. He remembered the ship fondly, and well. All those young men, the choir who had sang at the church service, the bright faces filled with pride to be hosting such a meeting. And now? Were any of them still alive?

He took a brief moment. "Into Thy hands Lord . . ." he whispered softly, and then braced himself.

"No number of defeats and catastrophes will weaken the will of the American people." The President's voice began gathering energy and determination. "We are furious that the Japanese surprised us at Pearl Harbor and in the Philippines. This massacre will make us even angrier. Your losses are our losses. Your defeats are our defeats. We will go forward together and we will crush those who have violated the laws of civilization."

"Thank you, Mr. President," Churchill replied. "As you know, we are stretched very thin with the German threat here in Europe and now the Japanese attack in the Pacific. We could not cope with both without your magnificent help. The loss of our lone capital ships on the Asian coast leaves us open clear to India, perhaps even to the coast of Africa. You know, my friend, the full implications of that."

"The guttersnipe," Franklin said after a

long pause. "He will take advantage of that as well. Any news?"

Both had been waiting all day for a "Führer announcement" that Berlin Radio had started to trumpet shortly after noon London time. It might be their first public acknowledgment of the setback in the battle before Moscow, but both sensed what it would be . . . that Germany would declare war on America.

Compounded with the sharp defeats of the last few days, the President knew it would hit America hard, but aroused as the public was, he knew they would rally even more to the fight ahead.

"We are going to be distracted by the scale of the Pearl Harbor disaster, which I will brief you on when you visit Washington," the President replied, not willing to speculate on events in Berlin at this moment. His focus had to be on the here and now. "The defense of the Hawaiian Islands and the Philippines will require us to spend more energy and resources in the Pacific than we had envisioned last August," Roosevelt added.

"However, we will continue to emphasize the Atlantic battle with submarines and the resources needed to contain and then defeat Germany in Europe. It will be harder because the anger of the American people is so overwhelmingly focused on the Japanese, but you and I are in total agreement that Hitler is the more dangerous enemy, and we will act accordingly," the President continued, reassuring Churchill about his greatest fear.

"For the near future, however, I have to shift some aircraft carriers and other ships into the Pacific to slow down the Japanese onslaught. We are moving ships from the Atlantic to the Pacific to ensure that their empire cannot get to Australia or cut off our supply lines across the South Pacific."

"For our part," Churchill responded, "we will continue to reinforce Malaya and Singapore in the expectation that we can stop the Japanese offensive on land and rebuild our air power as a first step back toward defeating them decisively."

"As soon as my military commanders have assessed our resources, I will get back to you about what we can do in the next few weeks," FDR promised.

He did not add that a major shakeup was already in the works. Commander in Chief Pacific (CinCPac) would go to Admiral Nimitz, and for the time being would be based out of San Diego. He had requested, as well, that some key personnel from Pearl be flown back Stateside immediately to confer with Nimitz, and then if need be forwarded on to Washington. He wanted a firsthand report, as quickly as possible, as to what had gone wrong prior to the battles of December 7 through 9.

Earlier in the day he had been handed a report by Admiral Stark that had gradually worked its way up the chain of command, dated the day before the attack, from an intelligence officer named Watson, warning that Pearl itself might be the target, his assessment based on analysis of signal traffic. He had called for the man's file and already had plans for what he might be doing next, to make sure more such surprises did not land on their doorstep.

"I want you to know, Mr. President," the Prime Minister said, interrupting his thoughts, "that even though we have taken some hard hits in the last few days, I am very confident that we will win through to victory. No dictatorship can withstand the combined fury of the British and American people."

"That's the spirit, my old friend. Eleanor and I look forward to your visit at Christmas. Together we will plot our revenge and our ultimate victory."

"Until then, Mr. President," Churchill

replied as he hung up.

President Roosevelt sat back in his wheelchair, lit a cigarette, and closed his eyes.

The speech by Hitler would start any minute now, and he knew what it would be, it would be like that guttersnipe to leap on what he assumed was a fallen prey. The Japanese had dealt a deadly blow, far worse than he had first thought after the initial attacks of December 7. More such defeats would undoubtedly follow in the months, perhaps even year to come.

But the fight had just started, and together with his friend on the other side of the Atlantic, as long as their will was not shaken, surely they would win through to inevitable victory.

FREEDOM ALLIANCE

Scholarship Fund — *Supporting the Children of America's Military Heroes*

The Freedom Alliance Scholarship Fund honors the bravery and dedication of Americans in our armed forces who have sacrificed life or limb by providing college scholarships to their children. Through the generosity of the American public, the Scholarship Fund has awarded more than $1 million to the sons and daughters of American heroes.

Many of freedom's brave defenders, who have lost their lives fighting terrorism, have left behind young children. We believe it is our duty to help their children meet the rising costs of a college education, but more importantly to remind them that their parents' sacrifice will never be forgotten by a grateful nation.

SUPPORT OUR TROOPS — *Honoring America's Armed Forces*

The Freedom Alliance Support Our Troops program honors and supports our servicemen and women and their families — especially those that are serving on the front lines, or who have been wounded and are recuperating at our military hospitals.

Freedom Alliance provides financial assistance and gift packages to these troops. The program also includes events such as Military Appreciation Dinners and special holiday activities. Freedom Alliance sponsors these activities to say "thank you" to our service members and their families.

Freedom Alliance, which was founded in 1990 by Lieutenant Colonel Oliver North, USMC (Ret.), is a nonprofit 501(c)(3) charitable and educational organization dedicated to advancing the American heritage of freedom by honoring and encouraging military service, defending the sovereignty of the United States, and promoting a strong national defense.

For more information or to donate,
contact:
FREEDOM ALLIANCE
22570 Markey Court, Suite 240
Dulles, Virginia 20166-6919
1(800)475-6620
www.freedomalliance.org
"LEST WE FORGET"

ABOUT THE AUTHORS

Newt Gingrich, former Speaker of the House, is the author of several bestselling books, including *Gettysburg* and *Grant Comes East.* He is a member of the Defense Policy Board, cochair of the UN Task Force, and is the longest-serving teacher of the Joint War Fighting course for Major Generals. Gingrich served in Congress for twenty years and was *Time* magazine's 1995 "Man of the Year." He is the founder of the Center for Health Transformation, the chairman of American Solutions, and a commentator for the Fox News Channel. He resides in Virginia with his wife, Callista. The Gingrich family includes two daughters, two sons-in-law, and two grandchildren.

William R. Forstchen, is a Faculty Fellow at Montreat College in Montreat, North Carolina. He received his doctorate from Purdue University and specialized in the

American Civil War. He is the author of more than forty books, including the award-winning *We Look Like Men of War,* a young-adult novel about an African-American regiment that fought at the Battle of the Crater, which is based upon his doctoral dissertation. William is a pilot and currently flies an L-3, an original WWII recon plane. He resides near Asheville, North Carolina, with his daughter, Meghan.